WITCHES of BROOKLYN
S'MORE MAGIC

Also by Sophie Escabasse

Witches of Brooklyn
Witches of Brooklyn: What the Hex?!

Sophie Escabasse

Witches of BROOKLYN

S'MORE MAGIC

RH
GRAPHIC

NEW YORK

WITCHES OF BROOKLYN: S'MORE MAGIC was drawn with pencil, and then all the pages were scanned. Inking and coloring were done with Procreate and Photoshop.

Text, cover art, and interior illustrations copyright © 2022 by Sophie Escabasse
Case art used under license from Shutterstock.com

All rights reserved. Published in the United States by RH Graphic, an imprint of Random House Children's Books, a division of Penguin Random House LLC, New York.

RH Graphic with the book design is a trademark of Penguin Random House LLC.

Visit us on the Web! RHKidsGraphic.com • @RHKidsGraphic

Educators and librarians, for a variety of teaching tools, visit us at RHTeachersLibrarians.com

Library of Congress Cataloging-in-Publication Data is available upon request.
ISBN 978-0-593-12552-6 (hardcover) — ISBN 978-0-593-11933-4 (paperback)
ISBN 978-0-593-11935-8 (ebook)

Designed by Patrick Crotty

MANUFACTURED IN CHINA
10 9 8 7 6 5 4 3 2 1
First Edition

A comic on every bookshelf.

To my mom and dad—
the witch and the plant whisperer

Chapter 1

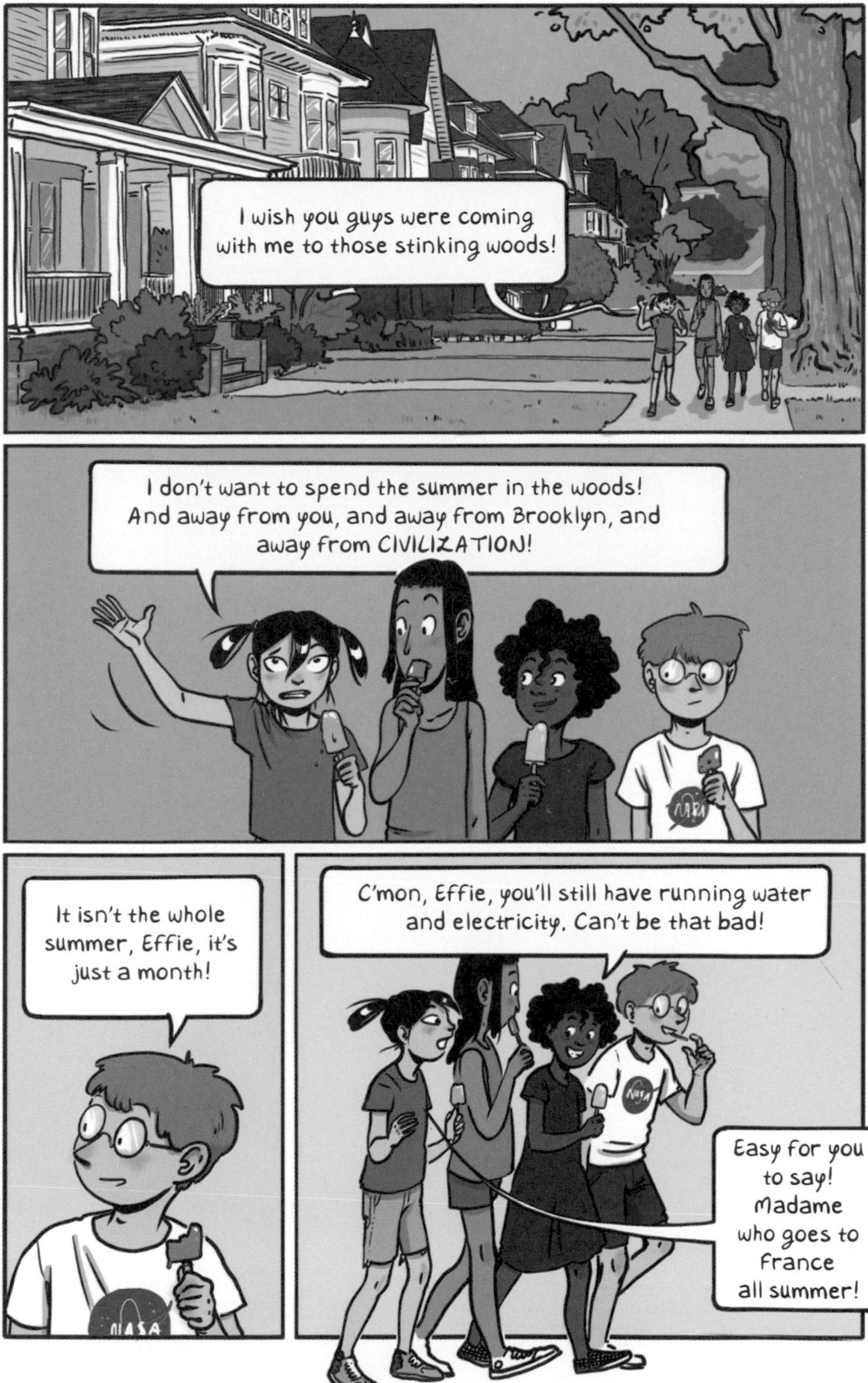
I wish you guys were coming with me to those stinking woods!
I don't want to spend the summer in the woods! And away from you, and away from Brooklyn, and away from CIVILIZATION!
It isn't the whole summer, Effie, it's just a month!
C'mon, Effie, you'll still have running water and electricity. Can't be that bad!
Easy for you to say! Madame who goes to France all summer!

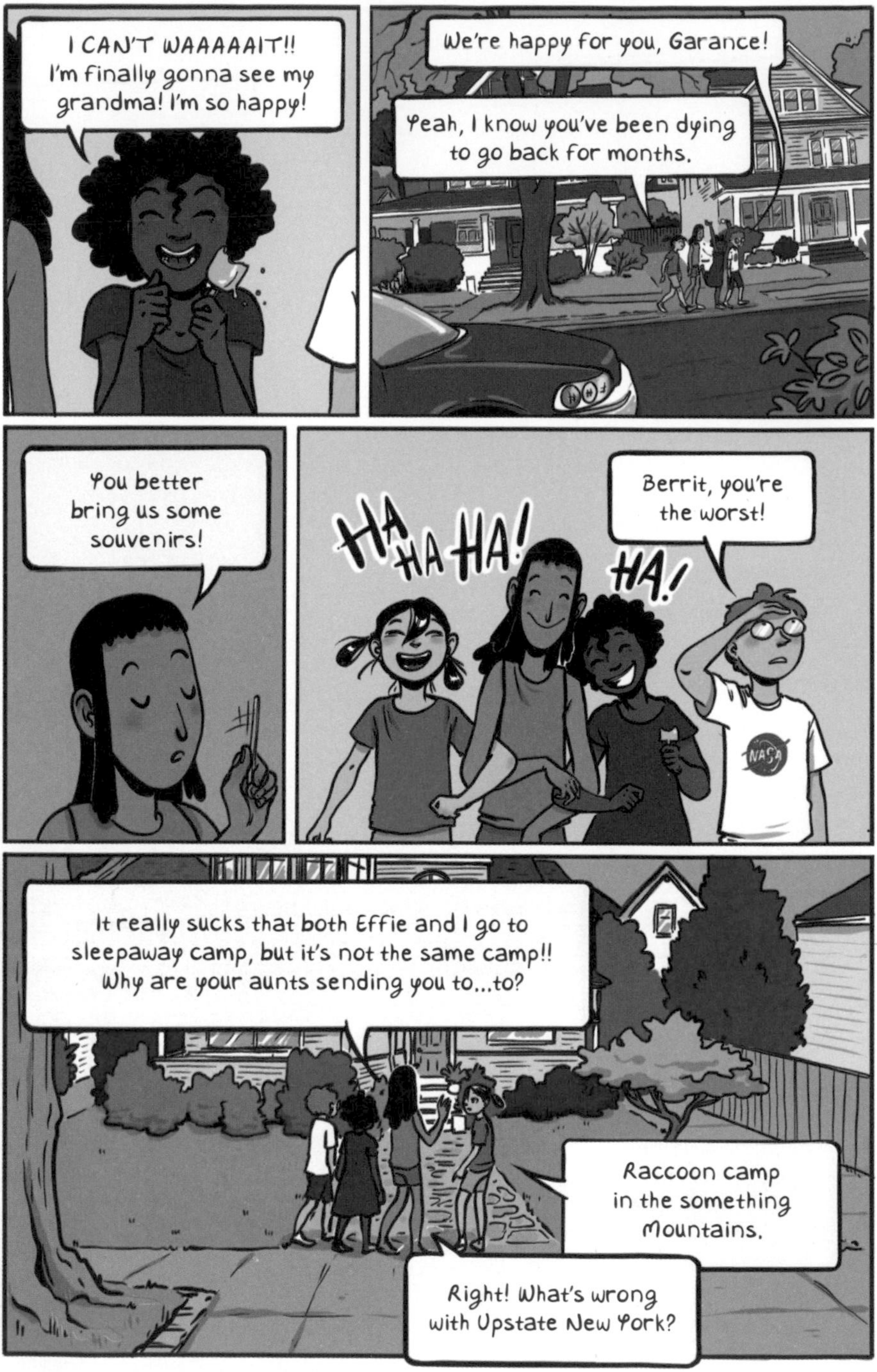
I CAN'T WAAAAAIT!! I'm finally gonna see my grandma! I'm so happy!
We're happy for you, Garance!
Yeah, I know you've been dying to go back for months.
You better bring us some souvenirs!
HA HA HA!
HA!
Berrit, you're the worst!
It really sucks that both Effie and I go to sleepaway camp, but it's not the same camp!! Why are your aunts sending you to...to?
Raccoon camp in the something Mountains.
Right! What's wrong with Upstate New York?

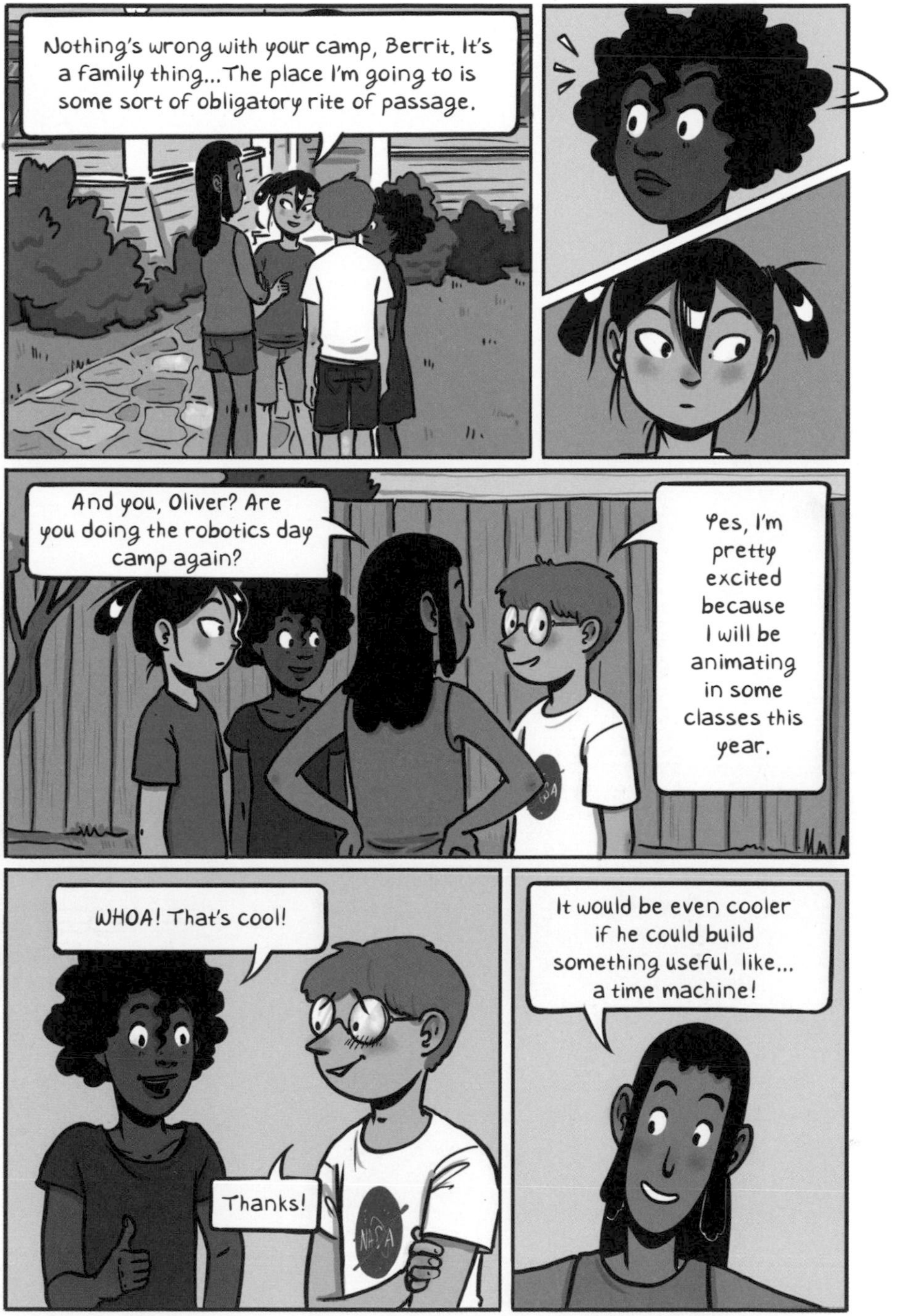
Nothing's wrong with your camp, Berrit. It's a family thing...The place I'm going to is some sort of obligatory rite of passage.
And you, Oliver? Are you doing the robotics day camp again?
Yes, I'm pretty excited because I will be animating in some classes this year.
WHOA! That's cool!
Thanks!
It would be even cooler if he could build something useful, like... a time machine!

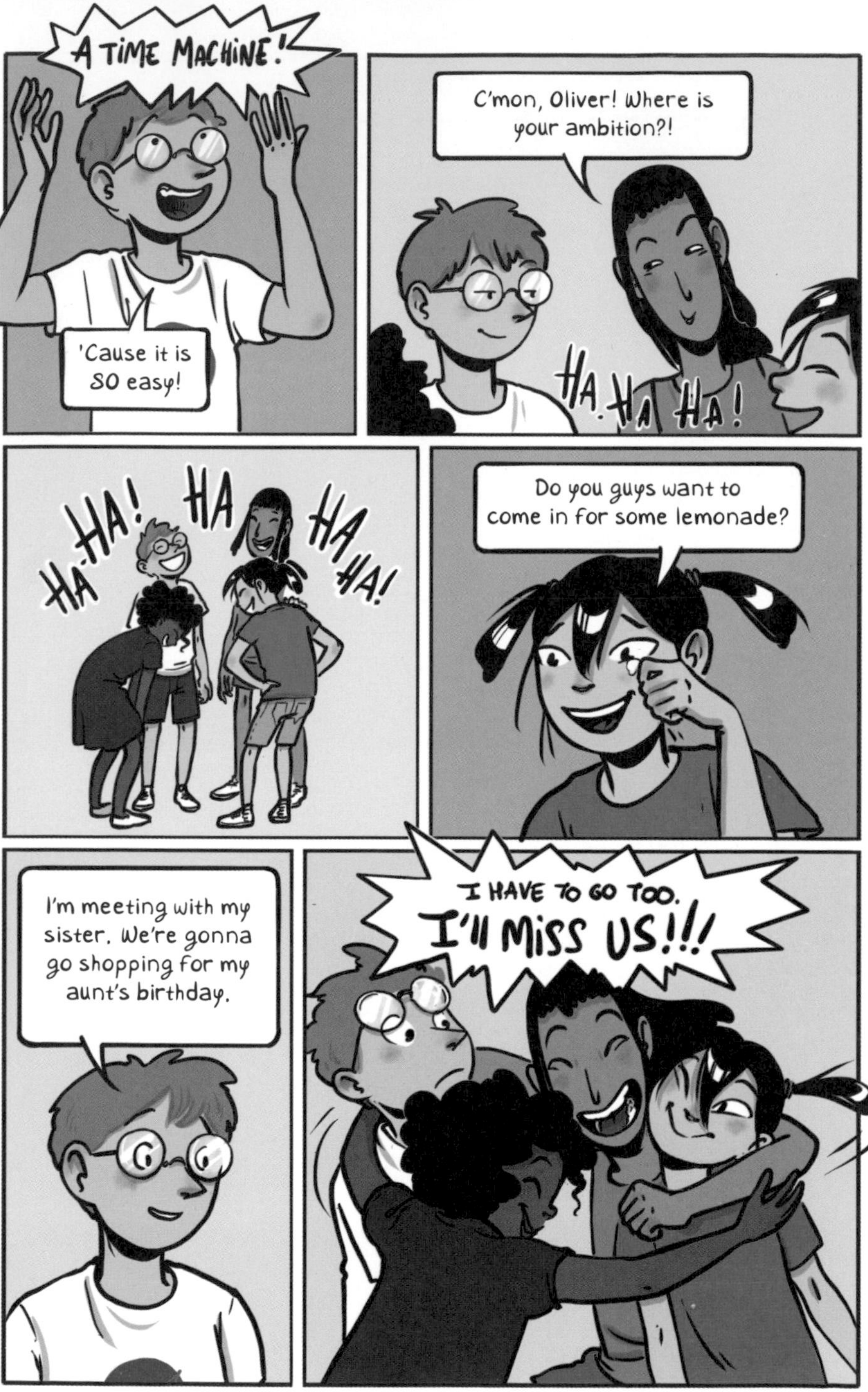
A TIME MACHINE!
'Cause it is SO easy!
C'mon, Oliver! Where is your ambition?!
HA. HA HA!
HA-HA! HA HA HA HA!
Do you guys want to come in for some lemonade?
I'm meeting with my sister. We're gonna go shopping for my aunt's birthday.
I HAVE TO GO TOO.
I'LL MISS US!!!

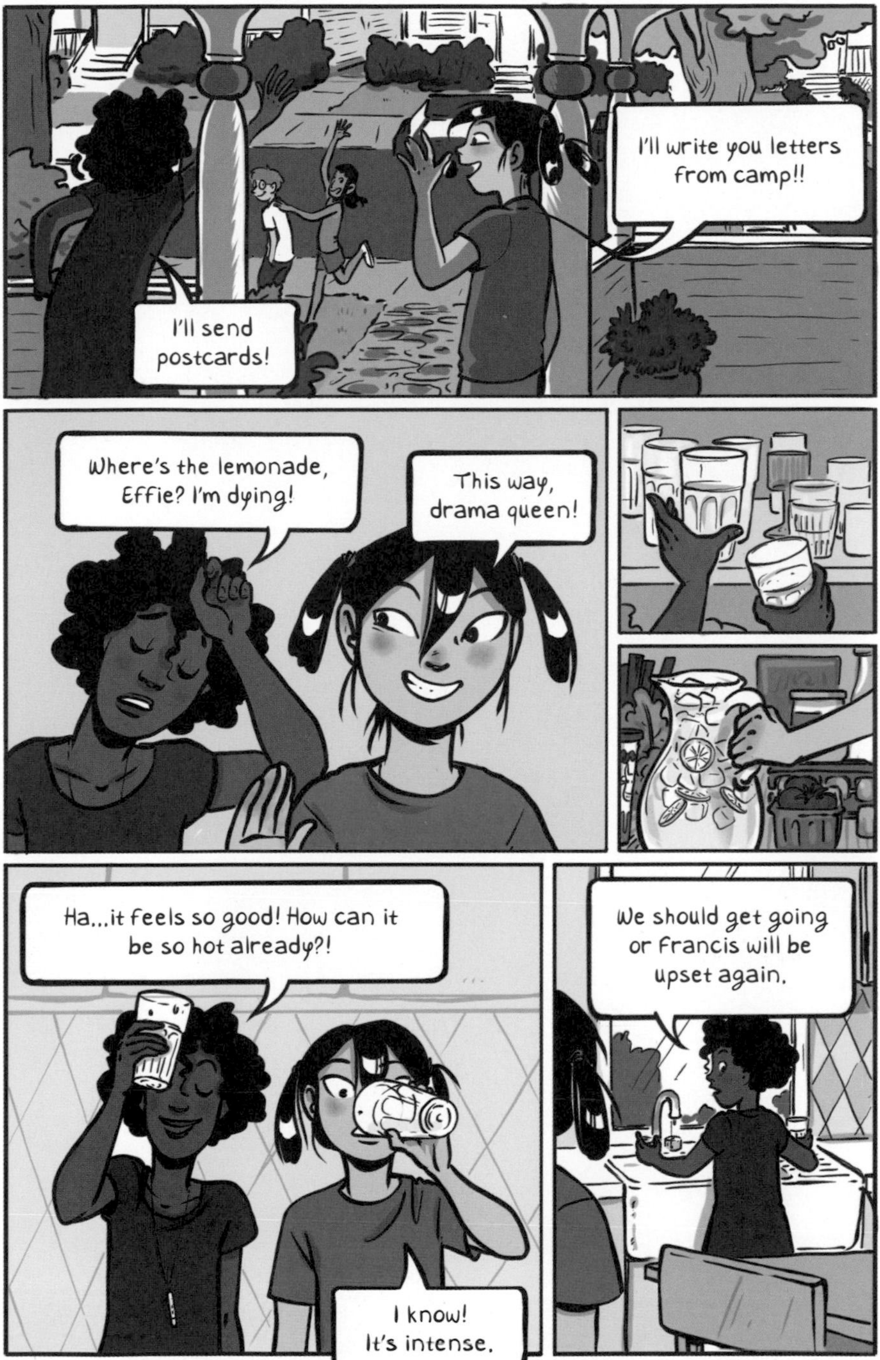
I'll write you letters from camp!!
I'll send postcards!
Where's the lemonade, Effie? I'm dying!
This way, drama queen!
Ha...it feels so good! How can it be so hot already?!
I know! It's intense.
We should get going or Francis will be upset again.

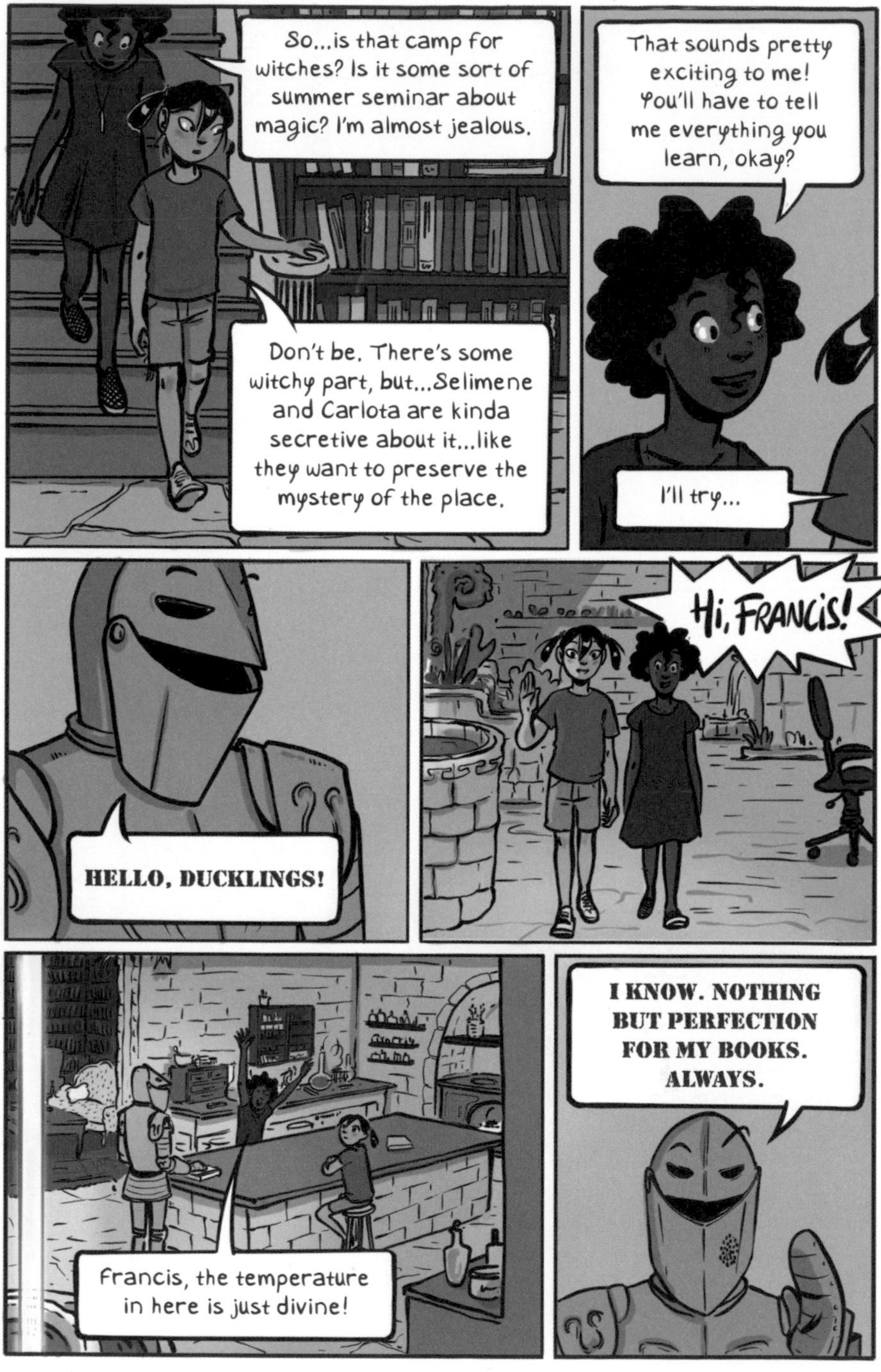
So...is that camp for witches? Is it some sort of summer seminar about magic? I'm almost jealous.
Don't be. There's some witchy part, but...Selimene and Carlota are kinda secretive about it...like they want to preserve the mystery of the place.
That sounds pretty exciting to me! You'll have to tell me everything you learn, okay?
I'll try...
HELLO, DUCKLINGS!
Hi, FRANCIS!
Francis, the temperature in here is just divine!
I KNOW. NOTHING BUT PERFECTION FOR MY BOOKS. ALWAYS.

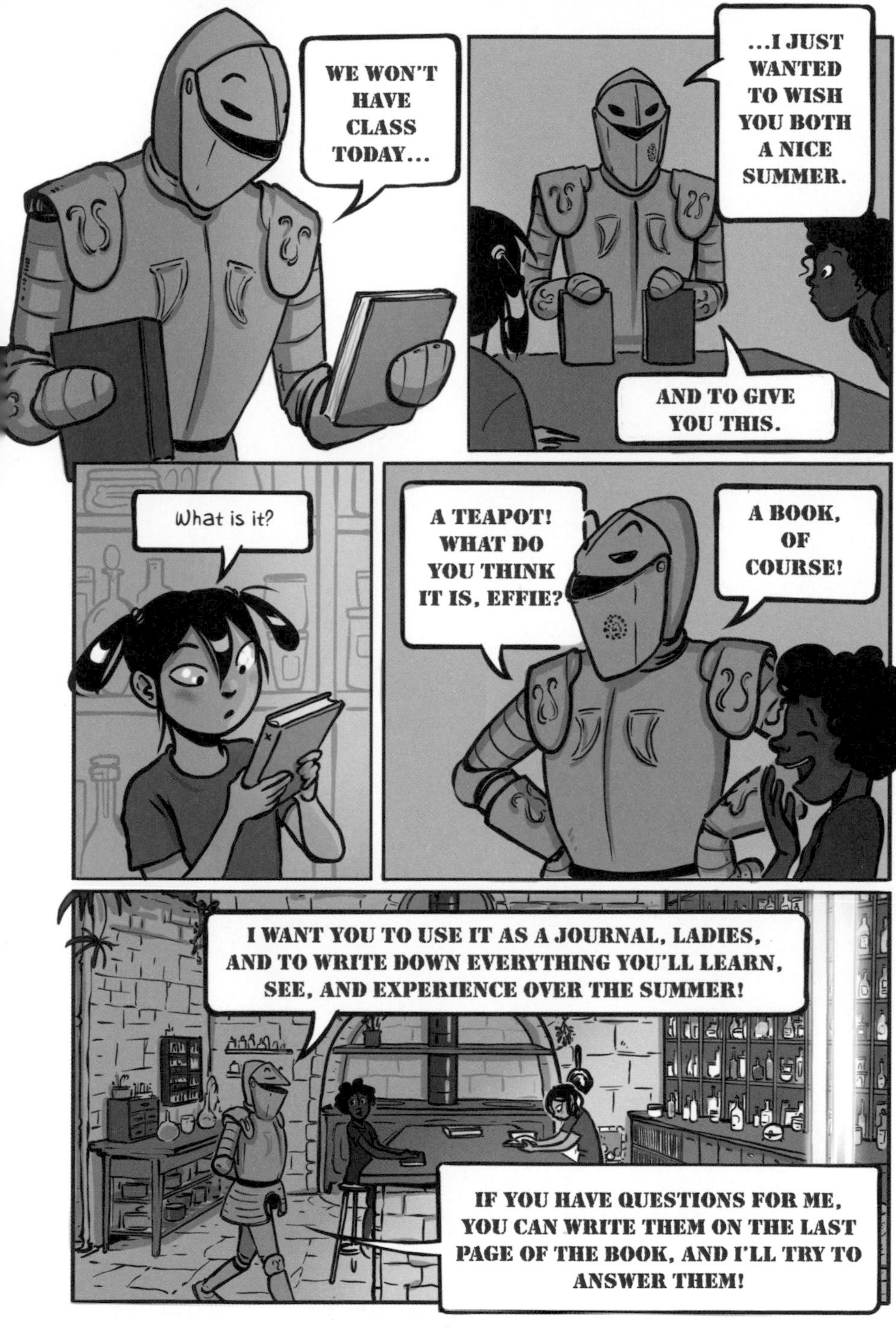
WE WON'T HAVE CLASS TODAY...
...I JUST WANTED TO WISH YOU BOTH A NICE SUMMER.
AND TO GIVE YOU THIS.
What is it?
A TEAPOT! WHAT DO YOU THINK IT IS, EFFIE?
A BOOK, OF COURSE!
I WANT YOU TO USE IT AS A JOURNAL, LADIES, AND TO WRITE DOWN EVERYTHING YOU'LL LEARN, SEE, AND EXPERIENCE OVER THE SUMMER!
IF YOU HAVE QUESTIONS FOR ME, YOU CAN WRITE THEM ON THE LAST PAGE OF THE BOOK, AND I'LL TRY TO ANSWER THEM!

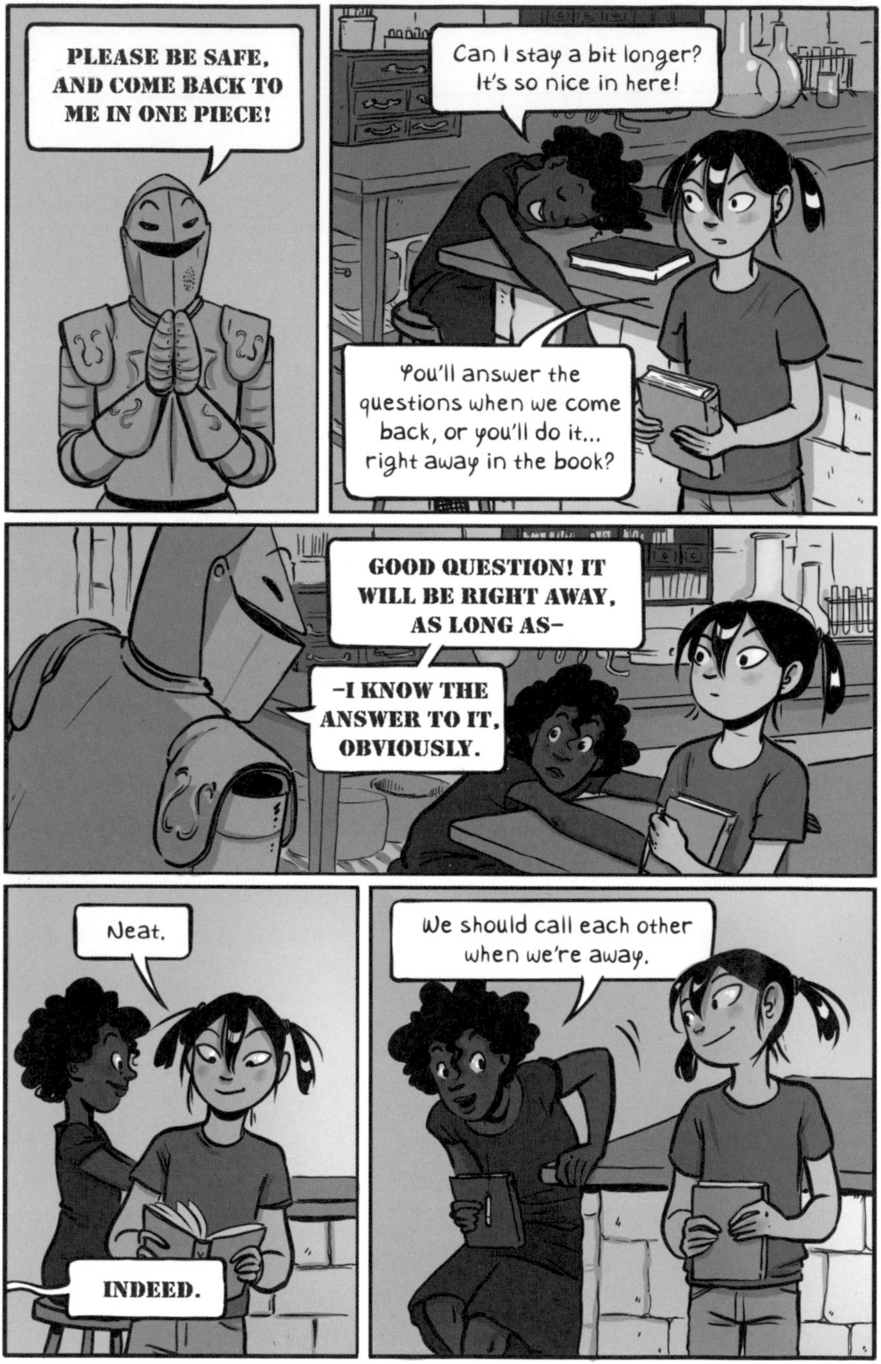
PLEASE BE SAFE, AND COME BACK TO ME IN ONE PIECE!
Can I stay a bit longer? It's so nice in here!
You'll answer the questions when we come back, or you'll do it... right away in the book?
GOOD QUESTION! IT WILL BE RIGHT AWAY, AS LONG AS–
–I KNOW THE ANSWER TO IT, OBVIOUSLY.
Neat.
INDEED.
We should call each other when we're away.

Sissi made my necklace into a Jewelunis last week so that we'll be able to stay in touch for my classes.

Boy, I hope she'll remember the time difference...

She'll definitely wake you up a bunch of times. Get used to the idea!

I know.

I've never called anyone but Selimene and Carlota with my necklace, though. How would I reach you?

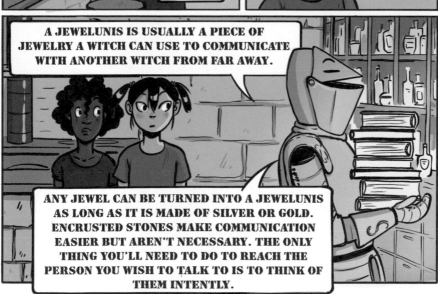

A JEWELUNIS IS USUALLY A PIECE OF JEWELRY A WITCH CAN USE TO COMMUNICATE WITH ANOTHER WITCH FROM FAR AWAY.

ANY JEWEL CAN BE TURNED INTO A JEWELUNIS AS LONG AS IT IS MADE OF SILVER OR GOLD. ENCRUSTED STONES MAKE COMMUNICATION EASIER BUT AREN'T NECESSARY. THE ONLY THING YOU'LL NEED TO DO TO REACH THE PERSON YOU WISH TO TALK TO IS TO THINK OF THEM INTENTLY.

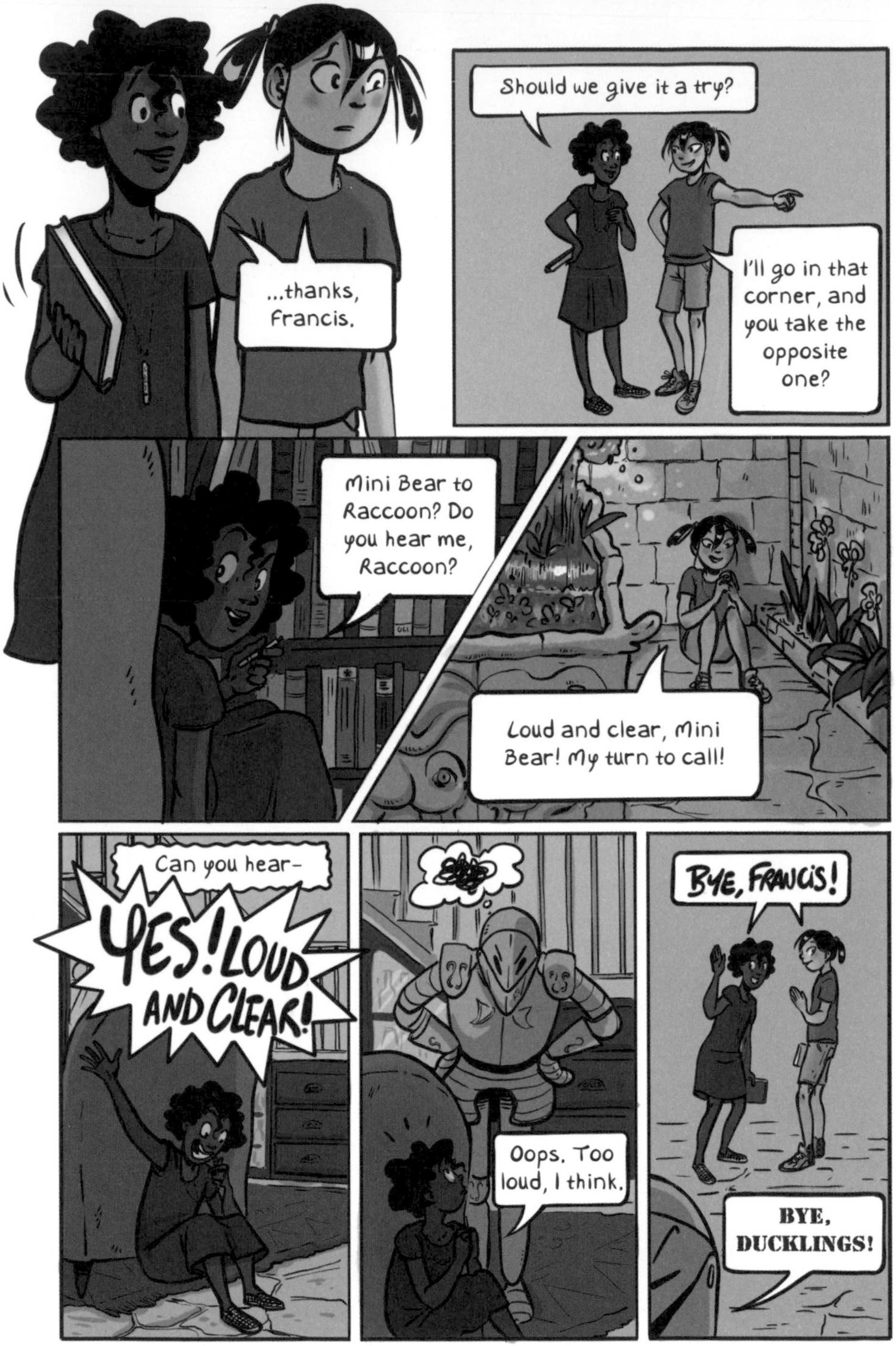

...thanks, Francis.
Should we give it a try?
I'll go in that corner, and you take the opposite one?
Mini Bear to Raccoon? Do you hear me, Raccoon?
Loud and clear, Mini Bear! My turn to call!
Can you hear-
YES! LOUD AND CLEAR!
Oops. Too loud, I think.
BYE, FRANCIS!
BYE, DUCKLINGS!

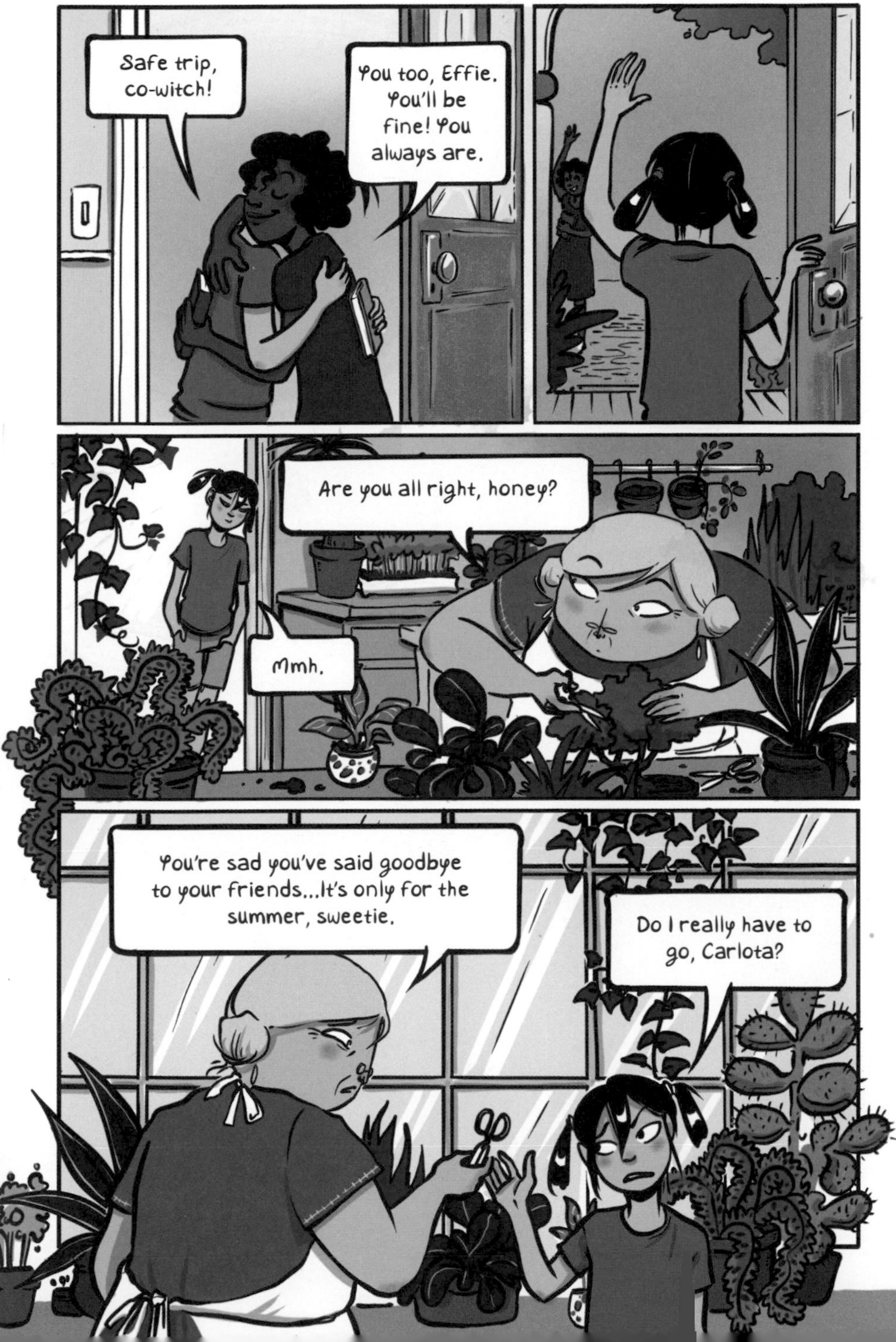
Safe trip, co-witch!
You too, Effie. You'll be fine! You always are.
Are you all right, honey?
Mmh.
You're sad you've said goodbye to your friends...It's only for the summer, sweetie.
Do I really have to go, Carlota?

Oh yes, and I assure you that you'll be much happier and comfortable in the woods than here.

Aaaah!

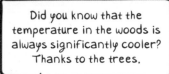

Did you know that the temperature in the woods is always significantly cooler? Thanks to the trees.

Mmh.

Aren't you curious to see if you have a green thumb? A wood immersion can trigger it!

I thought I was doing well with plants...?

OF COURSE!

You're fantastic with plants! I'm talking about the real green thumb!

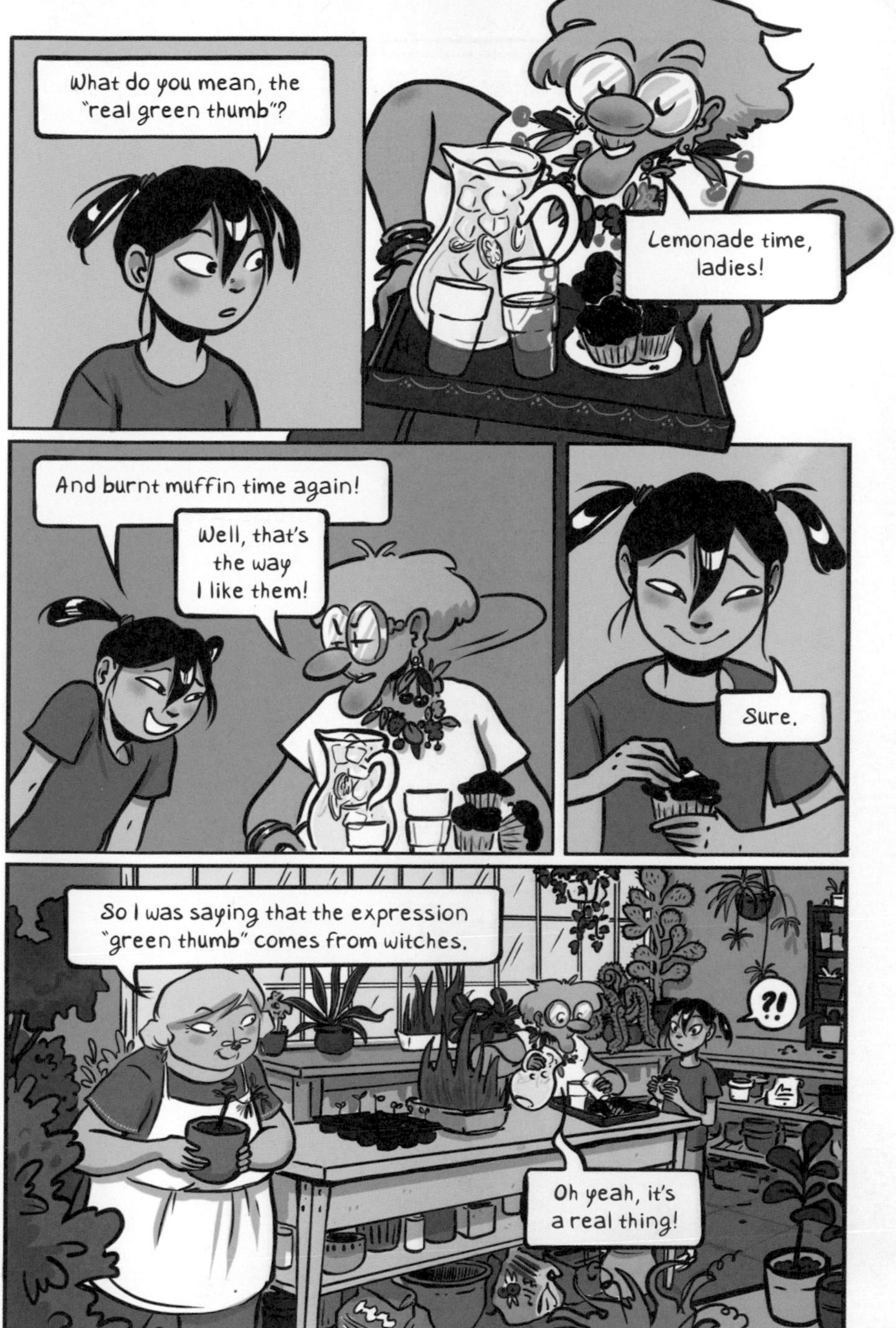
What do you mean, the "real green thumb"?
Lemonade time, ladies!
And burnt muffin time again!
Well, that's the way I like them!
Sure.
So I was saying that the expression "green thumb" comes from witches.
?!
Oh yeah, it's a real thing!

Are you making fun of me right now?

Absolutely not, honey!

But not all witches have it, of course!

Do you have it? Your thumbs aren't green.

They don't stay green forever, pumpkin!

And yes, both Selimene and I experienced a plant bonding.

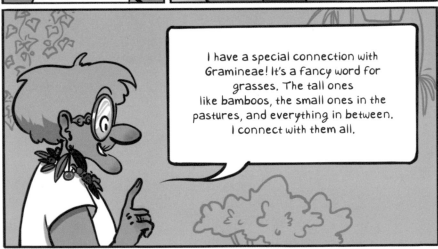

I have a special connection with Gramineae! It's a fancy word for grasses. The tall ones like bamboos, the small ones in the pastures, and everything in between. I connect with them all.

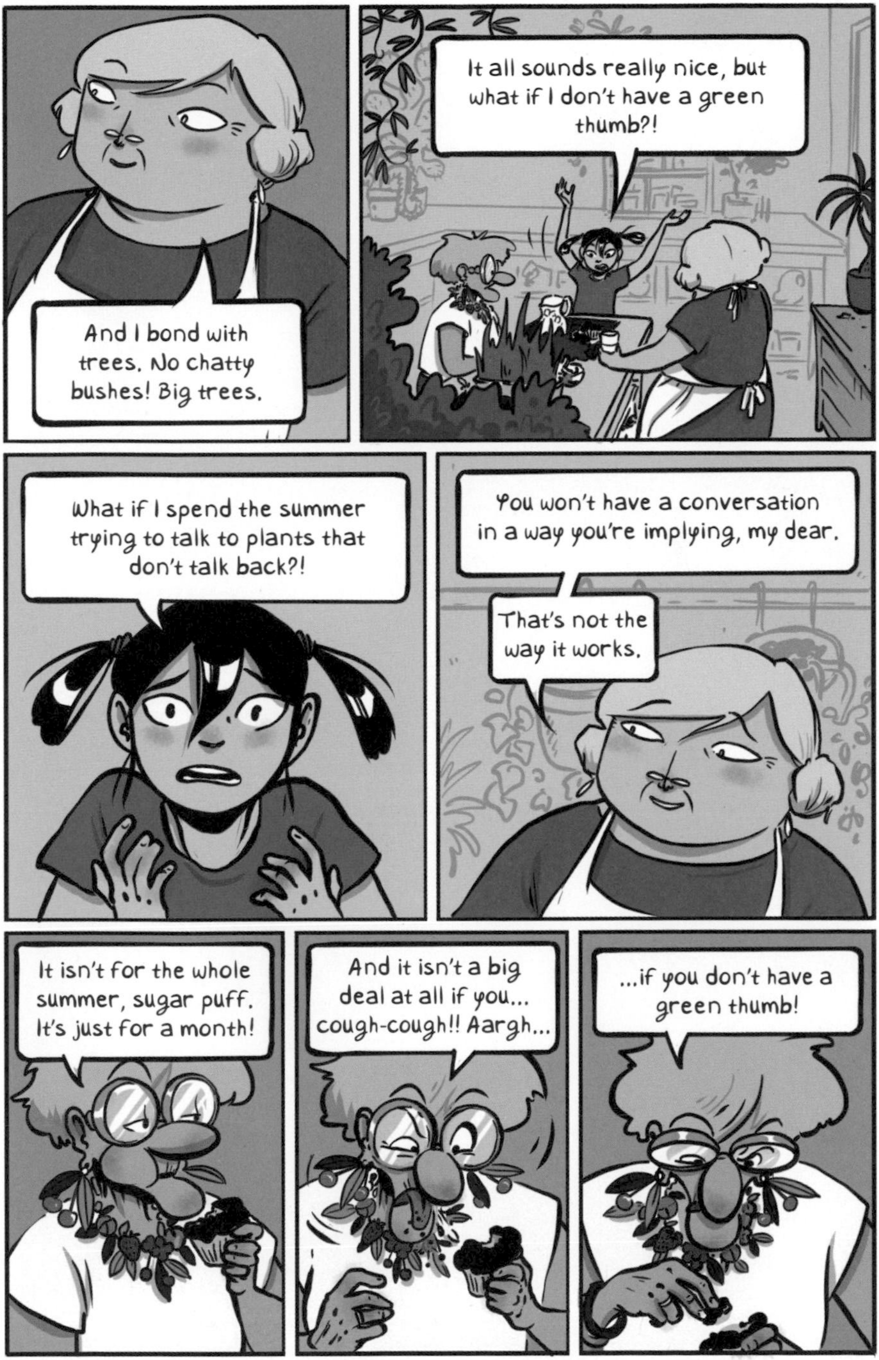
And I bond with trees. No chatty bushes! Big trees.
It all sounds really nice, but what if I don't have a green thumb?!
What if I spend the summer trying to talk to plants that don't talk back?!
You won't have a conversation in a way you're implying, my dear.
That's not the way it works.
It isn't for the whole summer, sugar puff. It's just for a month!
And it isn't a big deal at all if you... cough-cough!! Aargh...
...if you don't have a green thumb!

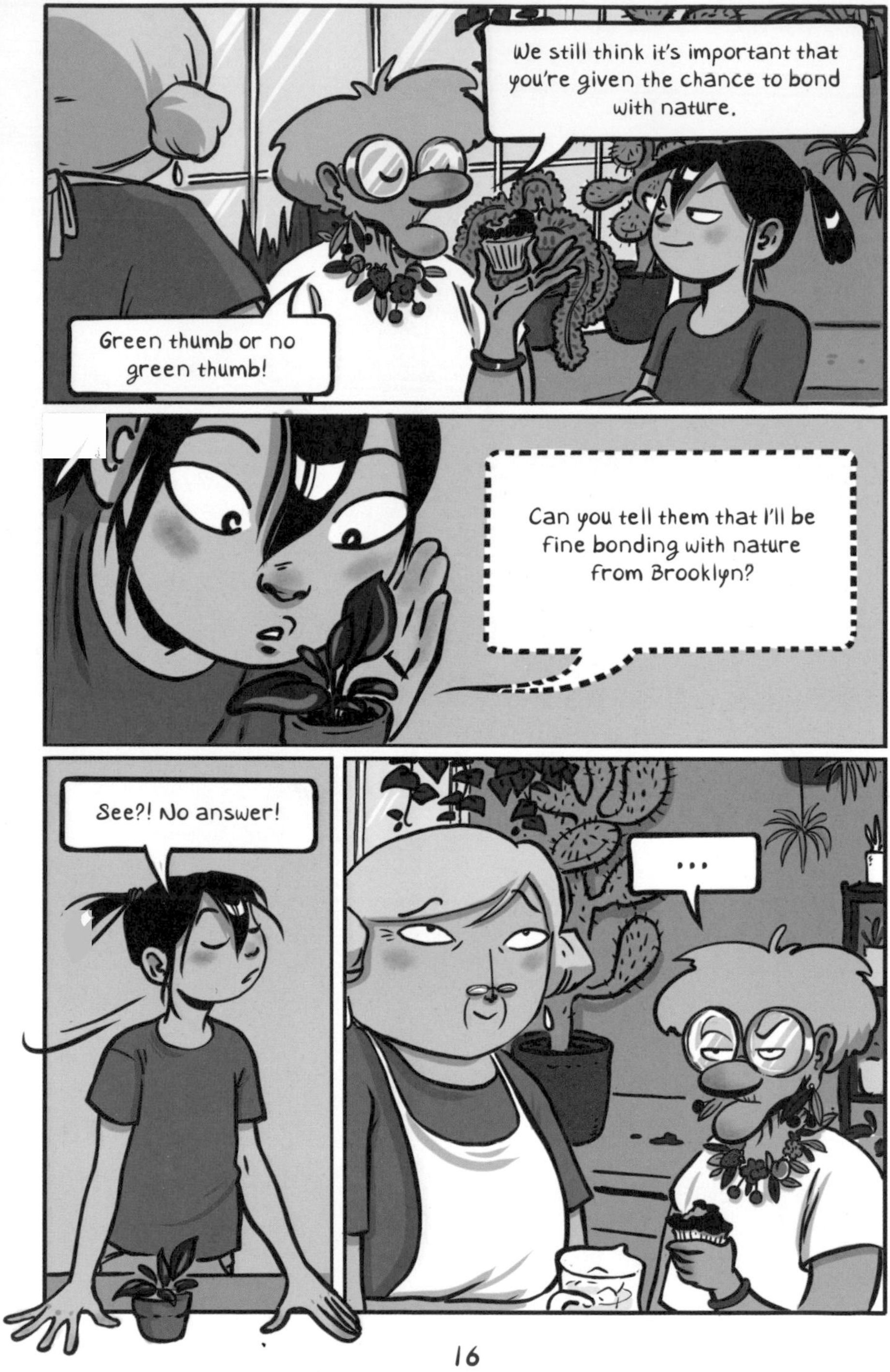

We still think it's important that you're given the chance to bond with nature.
Green thumb or no green thumb!
Can you tell them that I'll be fine bonding with nature from Brooklyn?
See?! No answer!
...

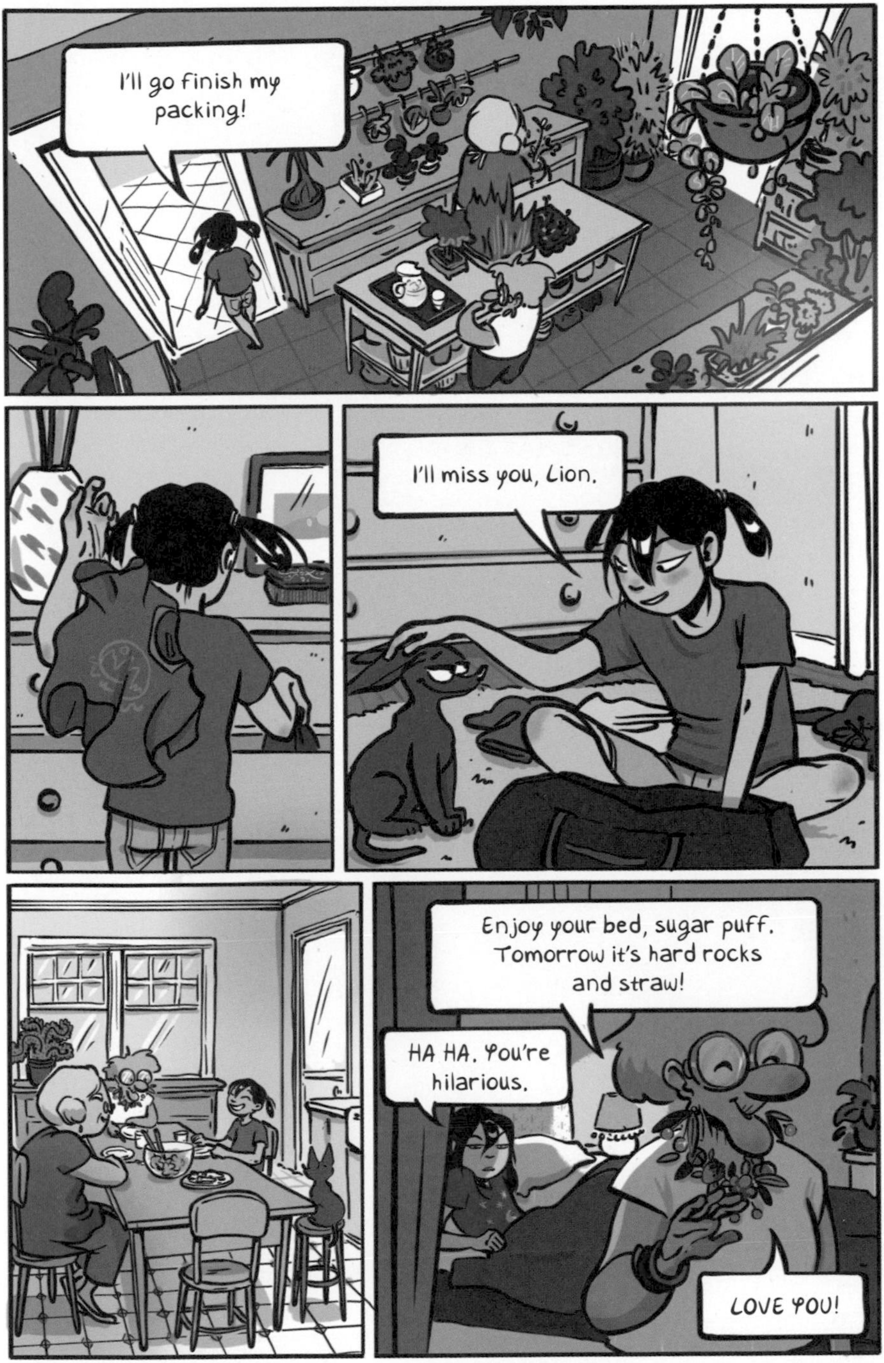

I'll go finish my packing!
I'll miss you, Lion.
Enjoy your bed, sugar puff. Tomorrow it's hard rocks and straw!
HA HA. You're hilarious.
LOVE YOU!

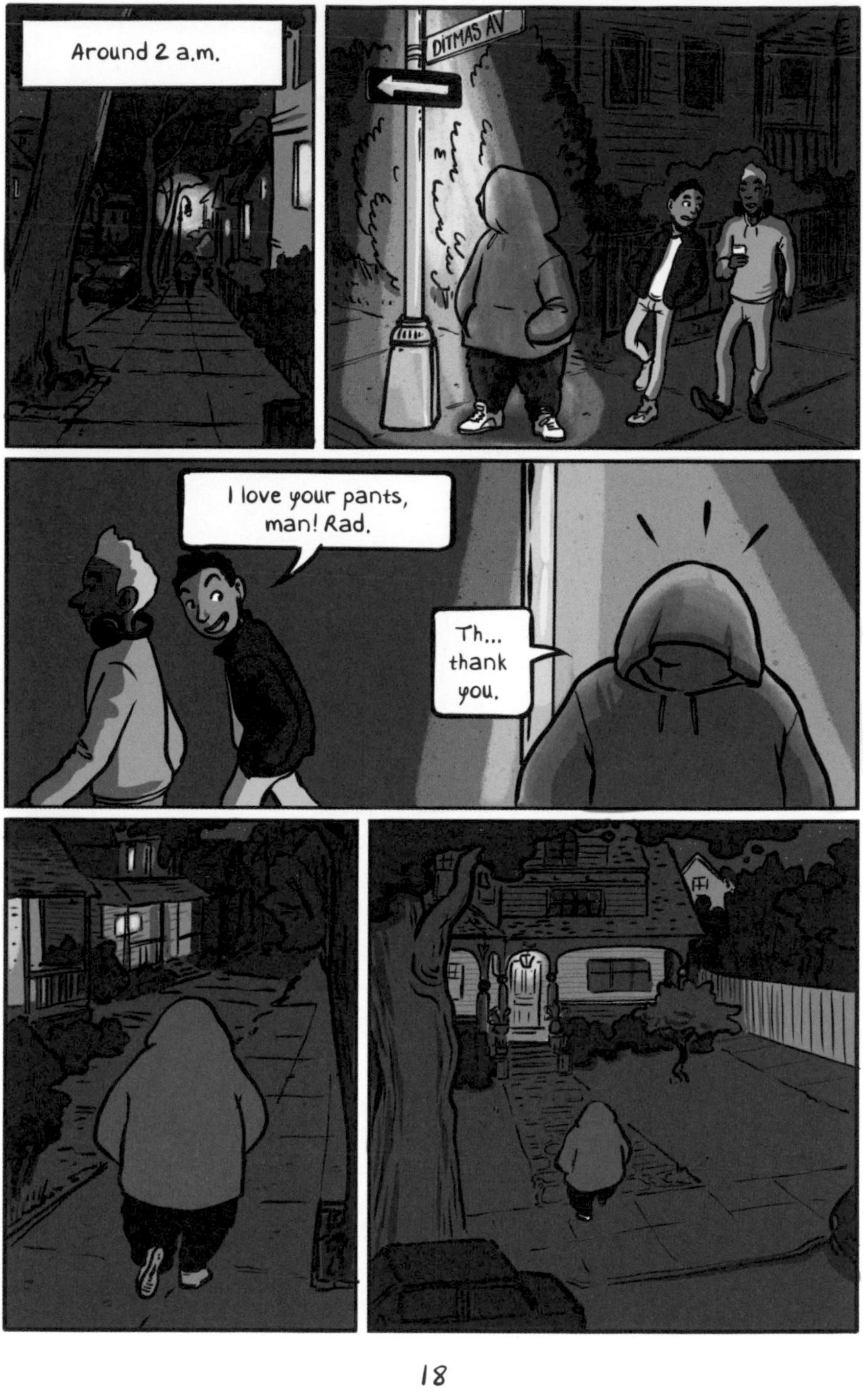
Around 2 a.m.
DITMAS AV
I love your pants, man! Rad.
Th... thank you.

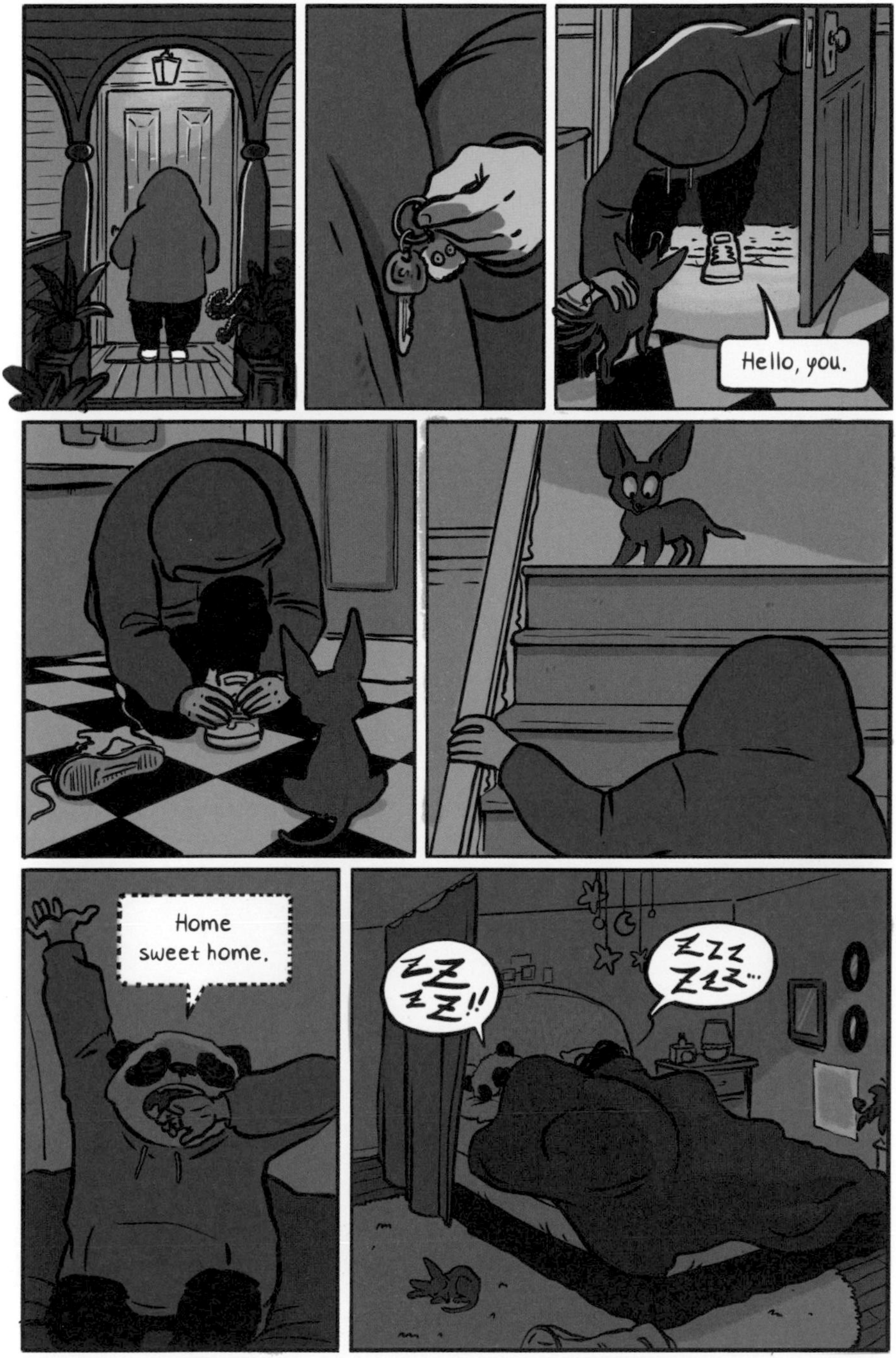
Hello, you.
Home sweet home.
ZZ ZZ!!
ZZZ ZZZ...

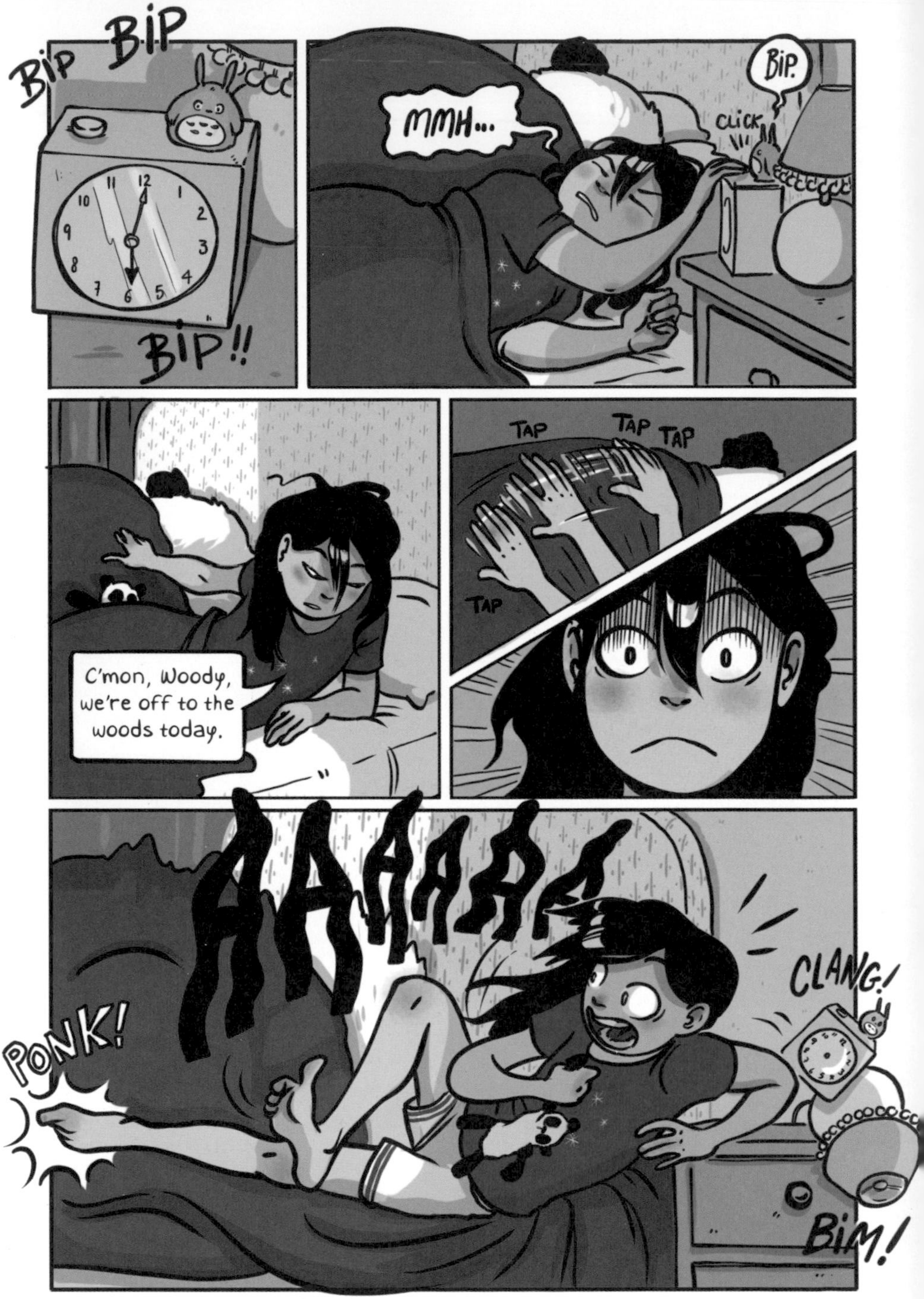
BIP BIP
BIP!!
MMH...
BIP.
CLICK
C'mon, Woody, we're off to the woods today.
TAP TAP TAP
TAP
AAAAAA
CLANG!
PONK!
BIM!

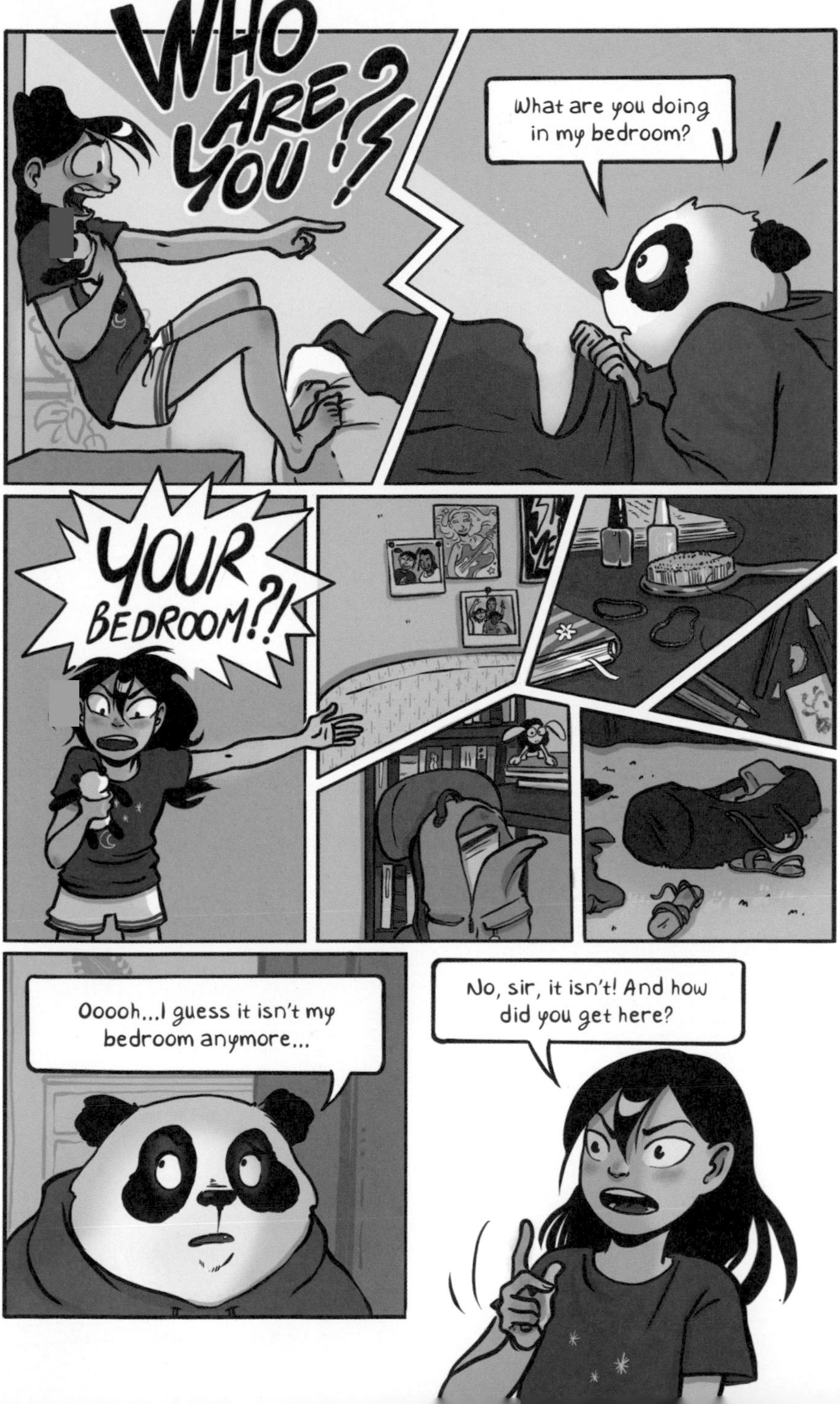
WHO ARE YOU ?!
What are you doing in my bedroom?
YOUR BEDROOM?!
Ooooh...I guess it isn't my bedroom anymore...
No, sir, it isn't! And how did you get here?

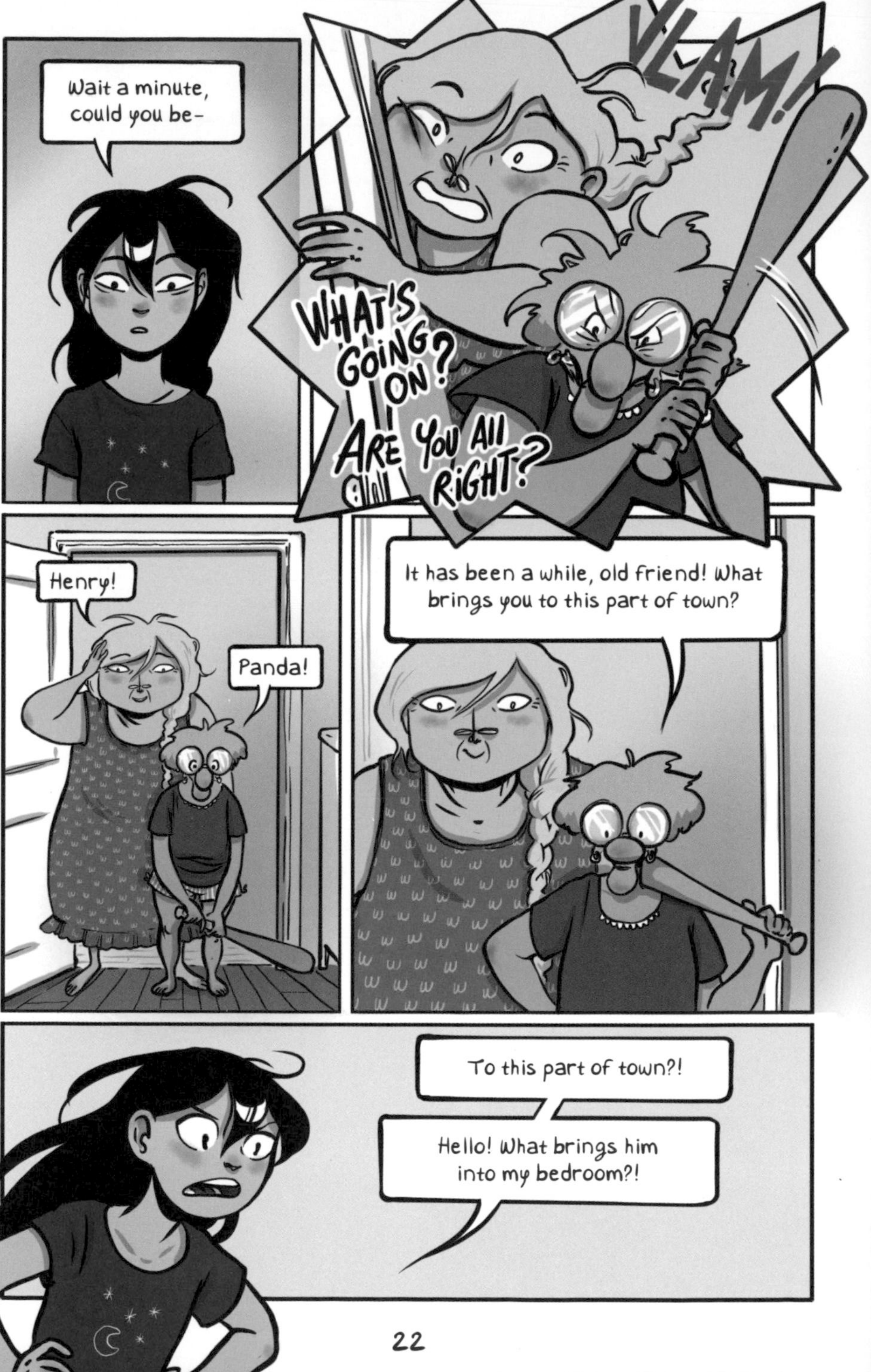
Wait a minute, could you be-
VLAM!
WHAT'S GOING ON? ARE YOU ALL RIGHT?
Henry!
Panda!
It has been a while, old friend! What brings you to this part of town?
To this part of town?!
Hello! What brings him into my bedroom?!

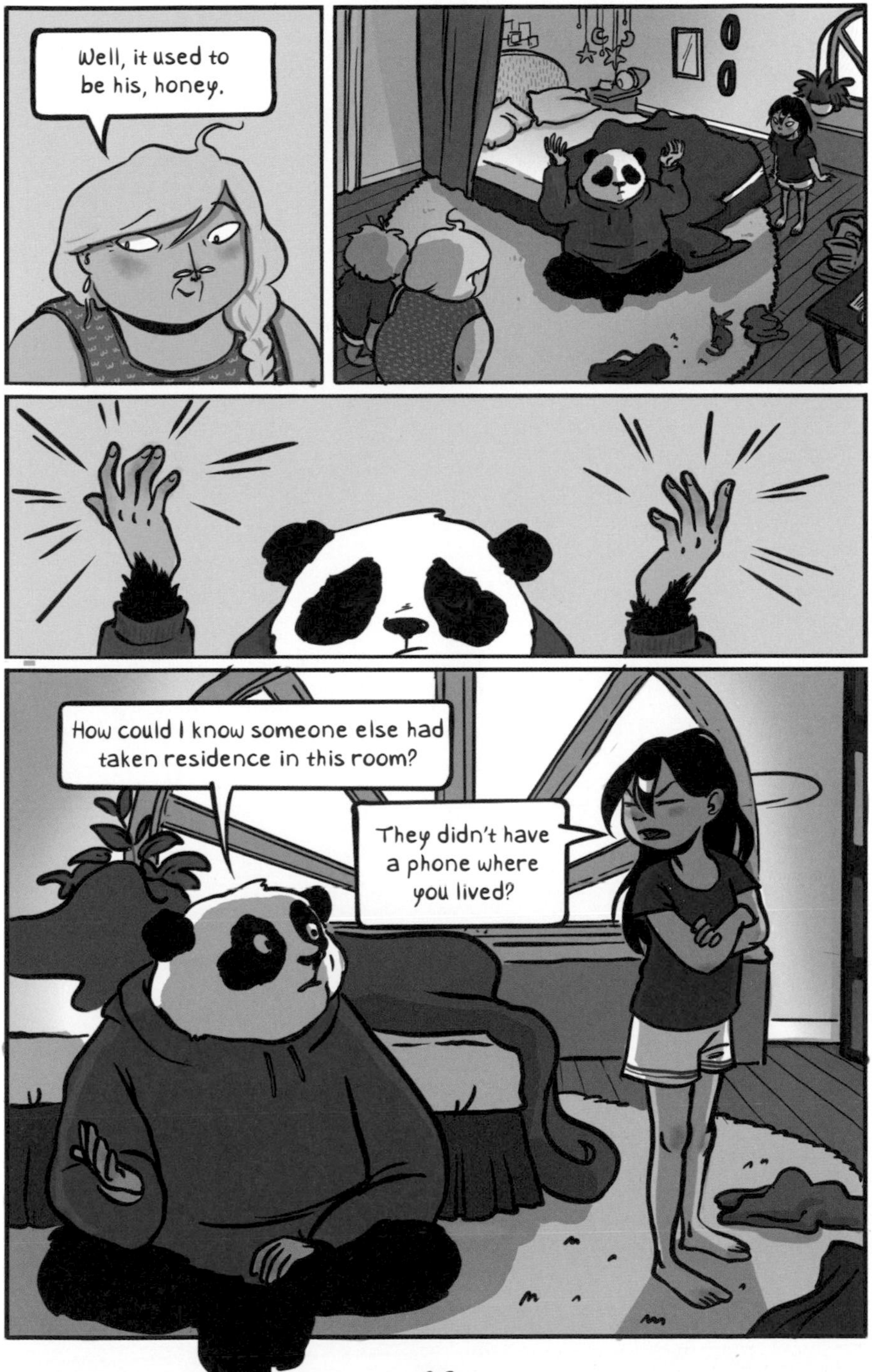
Well, it used to be his, honey.
How could I know someone else had taken residence in this room?
They didn't have a phone where you lived?

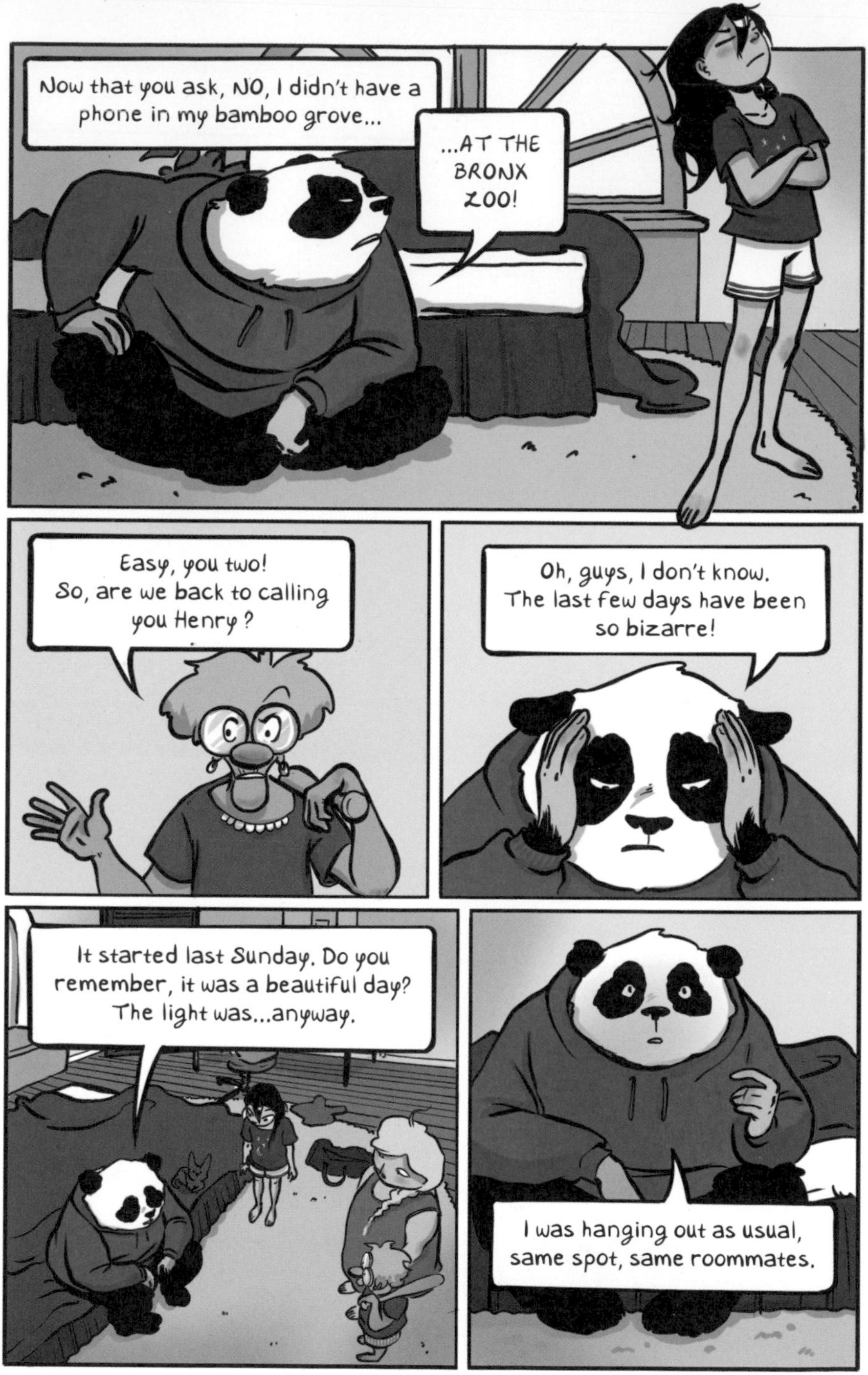
Now that you ask, NO, I didn't have a phone in my bamboo grove...
...AT THE BRONX ZOO!
Easy, you two! So, are we back to calling you Henry?
Oh, guys, I don't know. The last few days have been so bizarre!
It started last Sunday. Do you remember, it was a beautiful day? The light was...anyway.
I was hanging out as usual, same spot, same roommates.

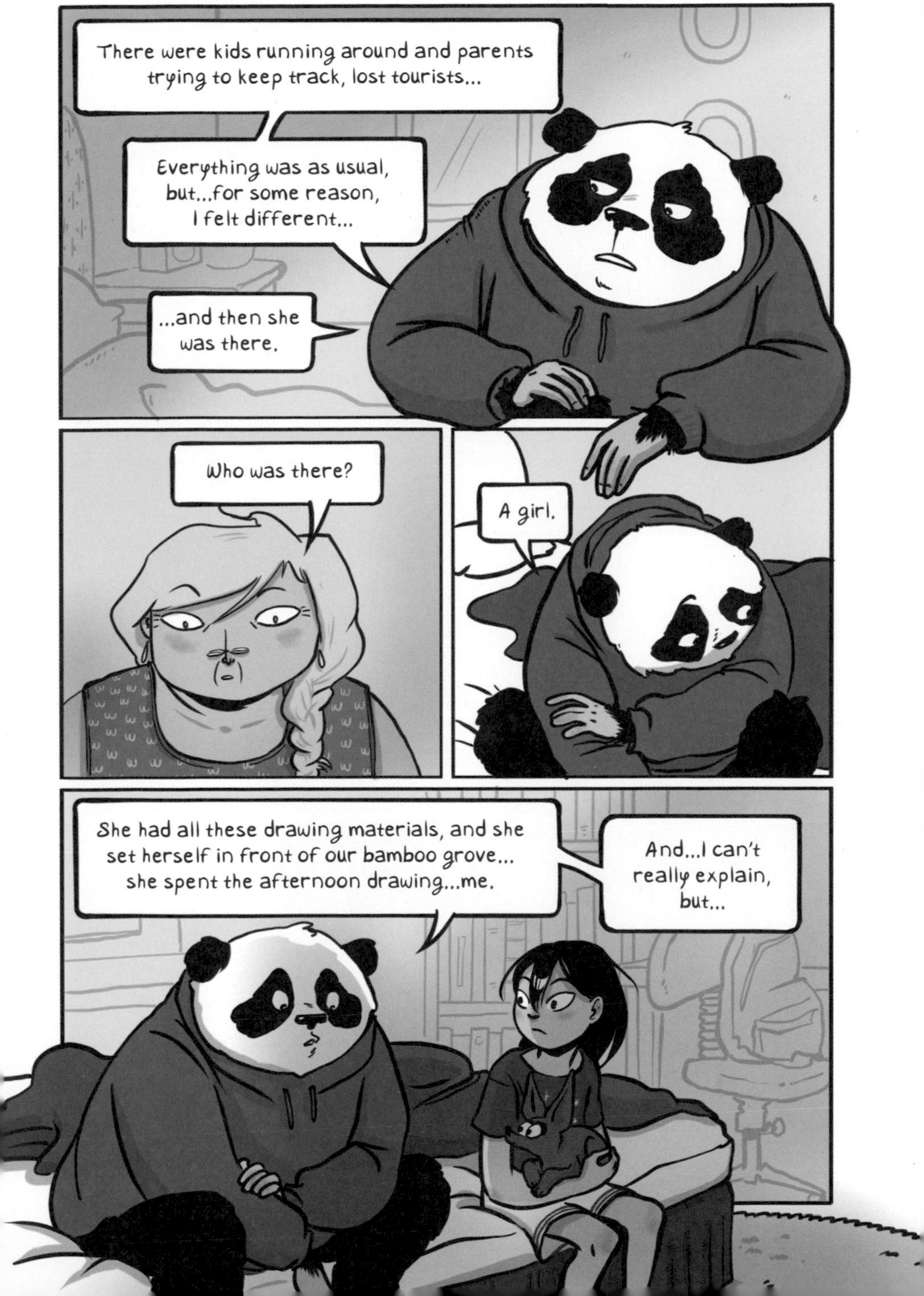

There were kids running around and parents trying to keep track, lost tourists...
Everything was as usual, but...for some reason, I felt different...
...and then she was there.
Who was there?
A girl.
She had all these drawing materials, and she set herself in front of our bamboo grove... she spent the afternoon drawing...me.
And...I can't really explain, but...

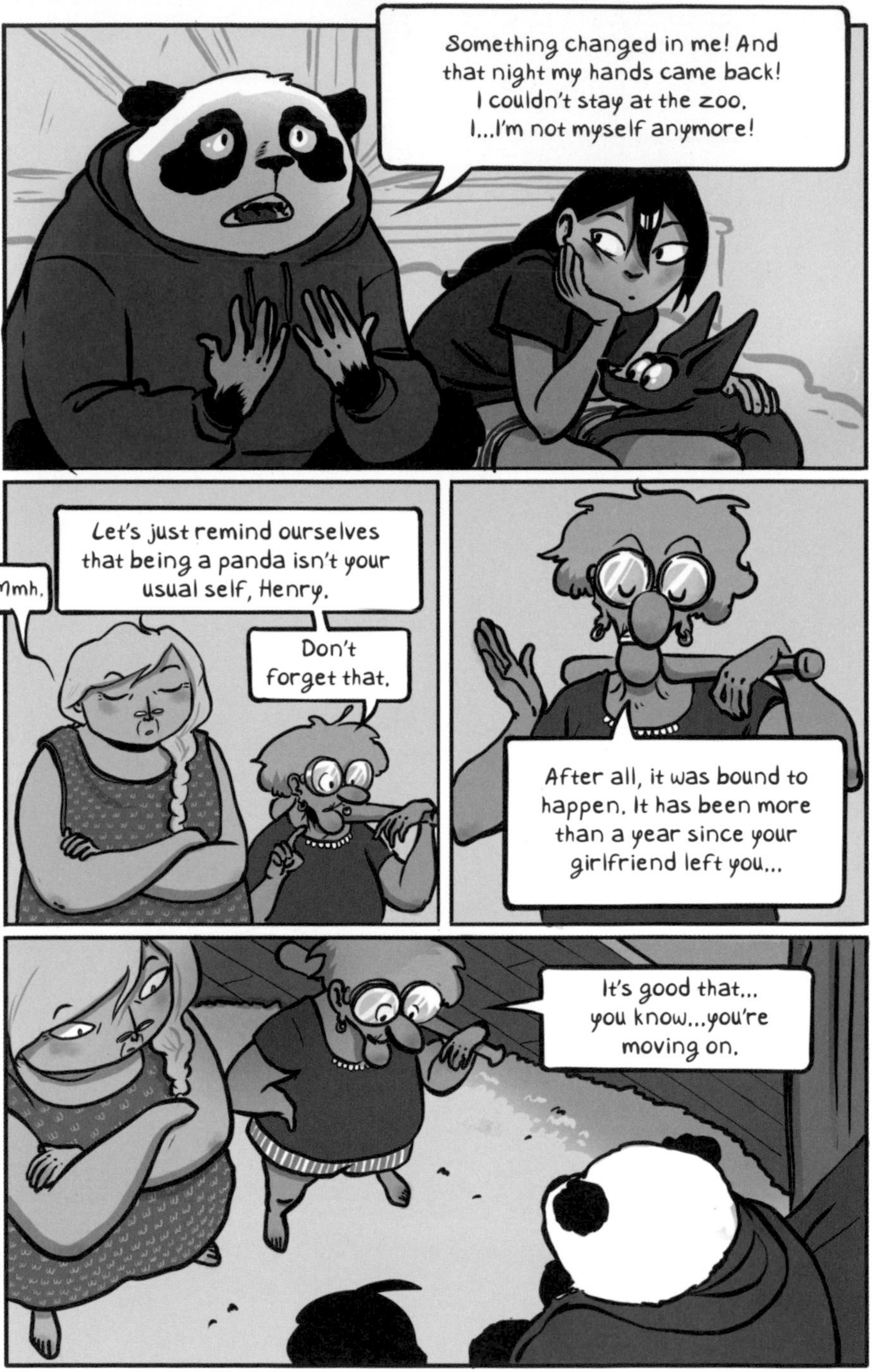
Something changed in me! And that night my hands came back! I couldn't stay at the zoo. I...I'm not myself anymore!
Let's just remind ourselves that being a panda isn't your usual self, Henry.
Mmh.
Don't forget that.
After all, it was bound to happen. It has been more than a year since your girlfriend left you...
It's good that... you know...you're moving on.

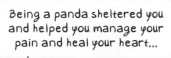
Being a panda sheltered you and helped you manage your pain and heal your heart...

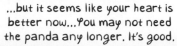
...but it seems like your heart is better now...You may not need the panda any longer. It's good.

Do you think that's what's happening? Do you think I'm gonna be a man again?

I've been stuck for so long...I don't even know if I'll remember how...

Oh, don't worry, most men are beasts anyway!

HA HA HA HA HA

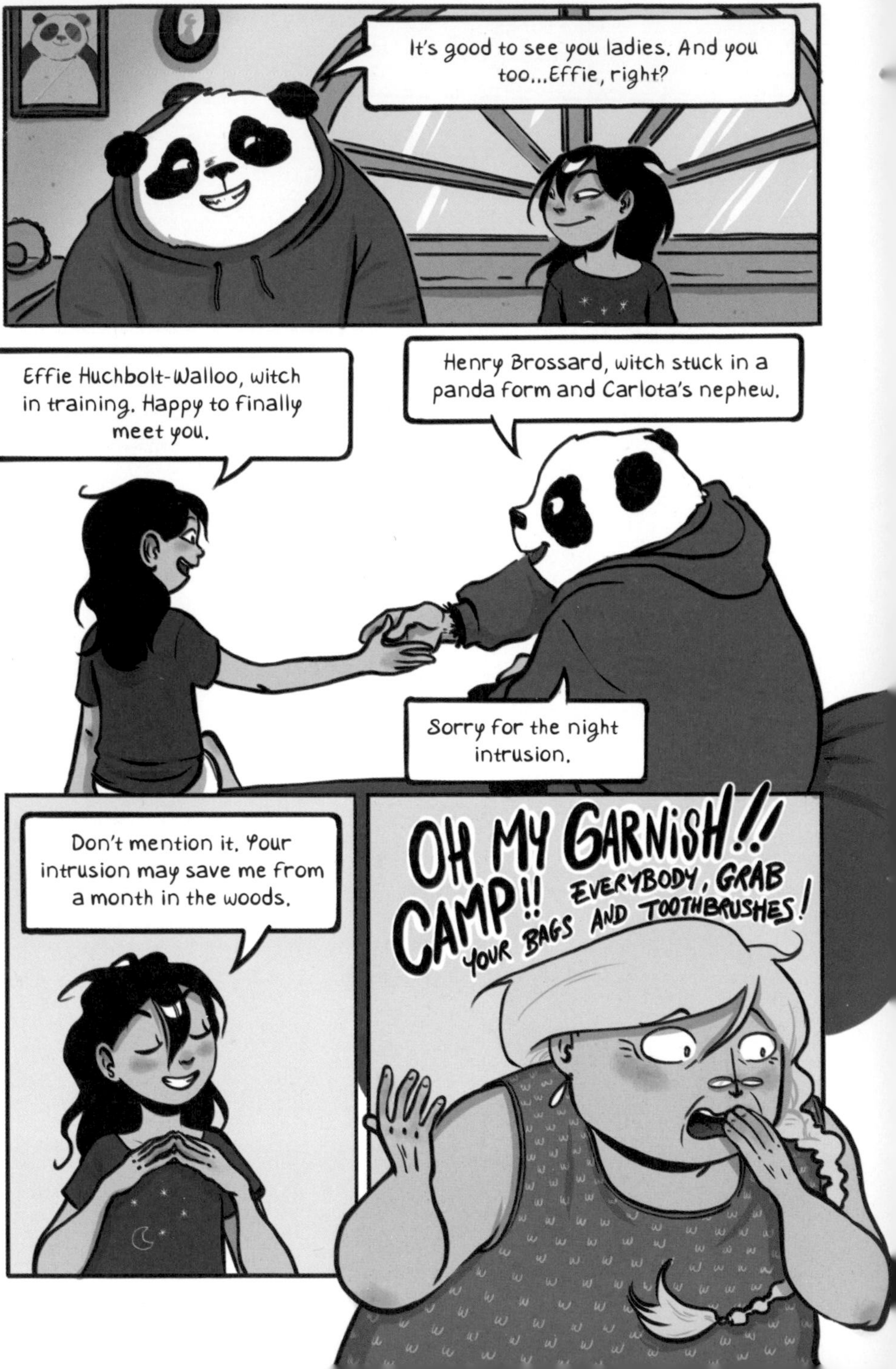

It's good to see you ladies. And you too...Effie, right?
Effie Huchbolt-Walloo, witch in training. Happy to finally meet you.
Henry Brossard, witch stuck in a panda form and Carlota's nephew.
Sorry for the night intrusion.
Don't mention it. Your intrusion may save me from a month in the woods.
OH MY GARNISH!! CAMP!!
EVERYBODY, GRAB YOUR BAGS AND TOOTHBRUSHES!

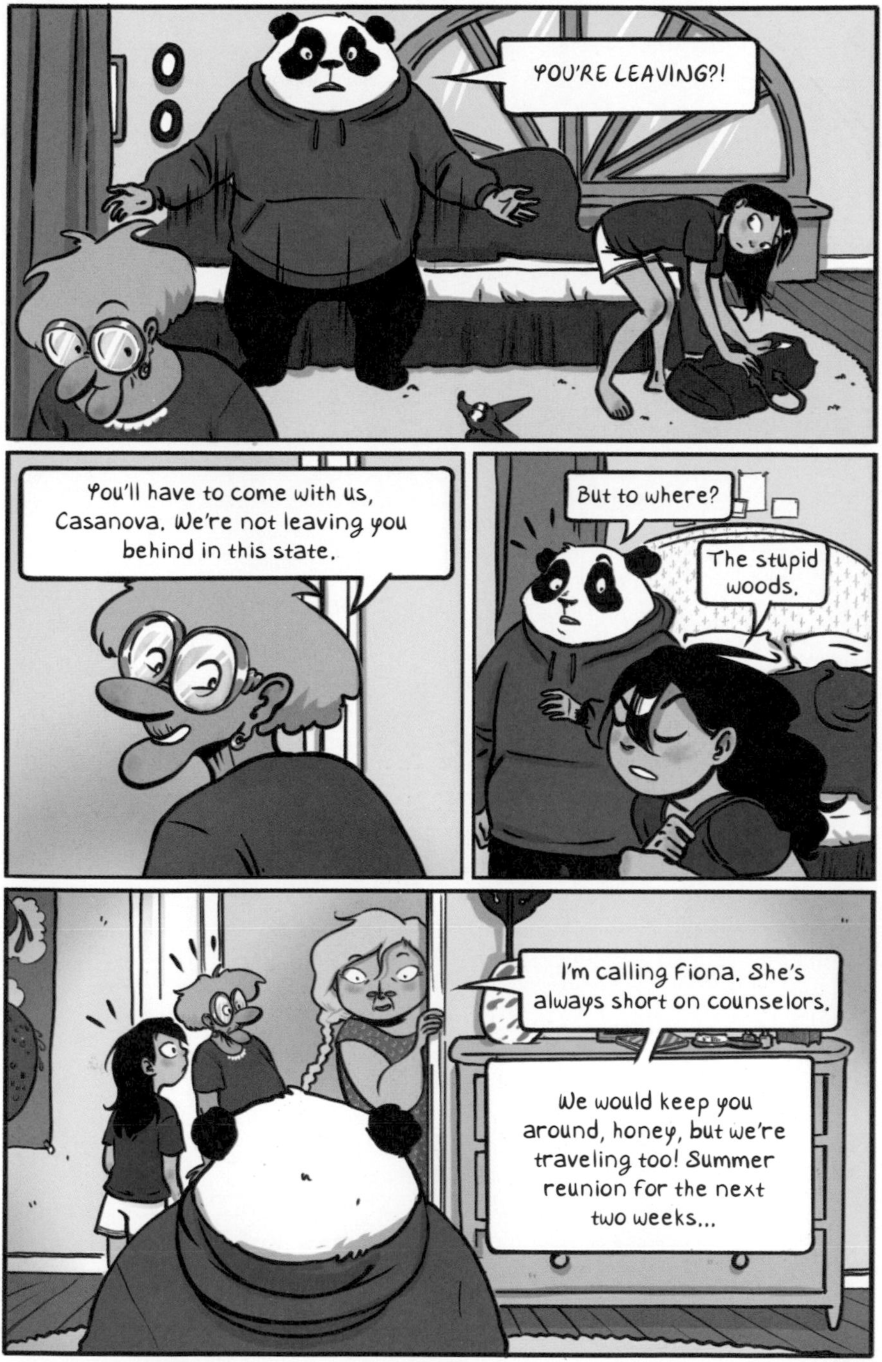
YOU'RE LEAVING?!
You'll have to come with us, Casanova. We're not leaving you behind in this state.
But to where?
The stupid woods.
I'm calling Fiona. She's always short on counselors.
We would keep you around, honey, but we're traveling too! Summer reunion for the next two weeks...

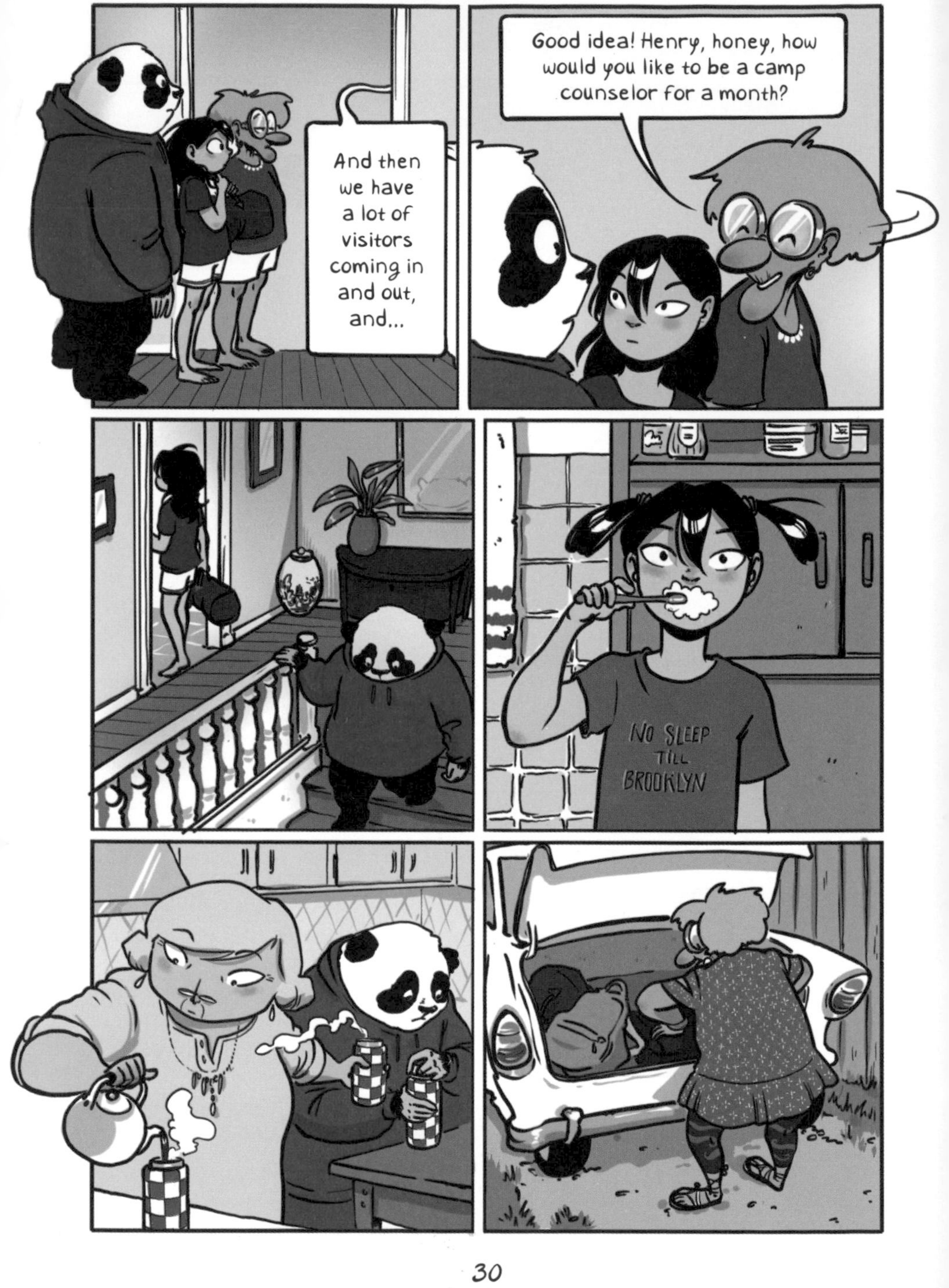

And then we have a lot of visitors coming in and out, and...
Good idea! Henry, honey, how would you like to be a camp counselor for a month?
NO SLEEP TILL BROOKLYN

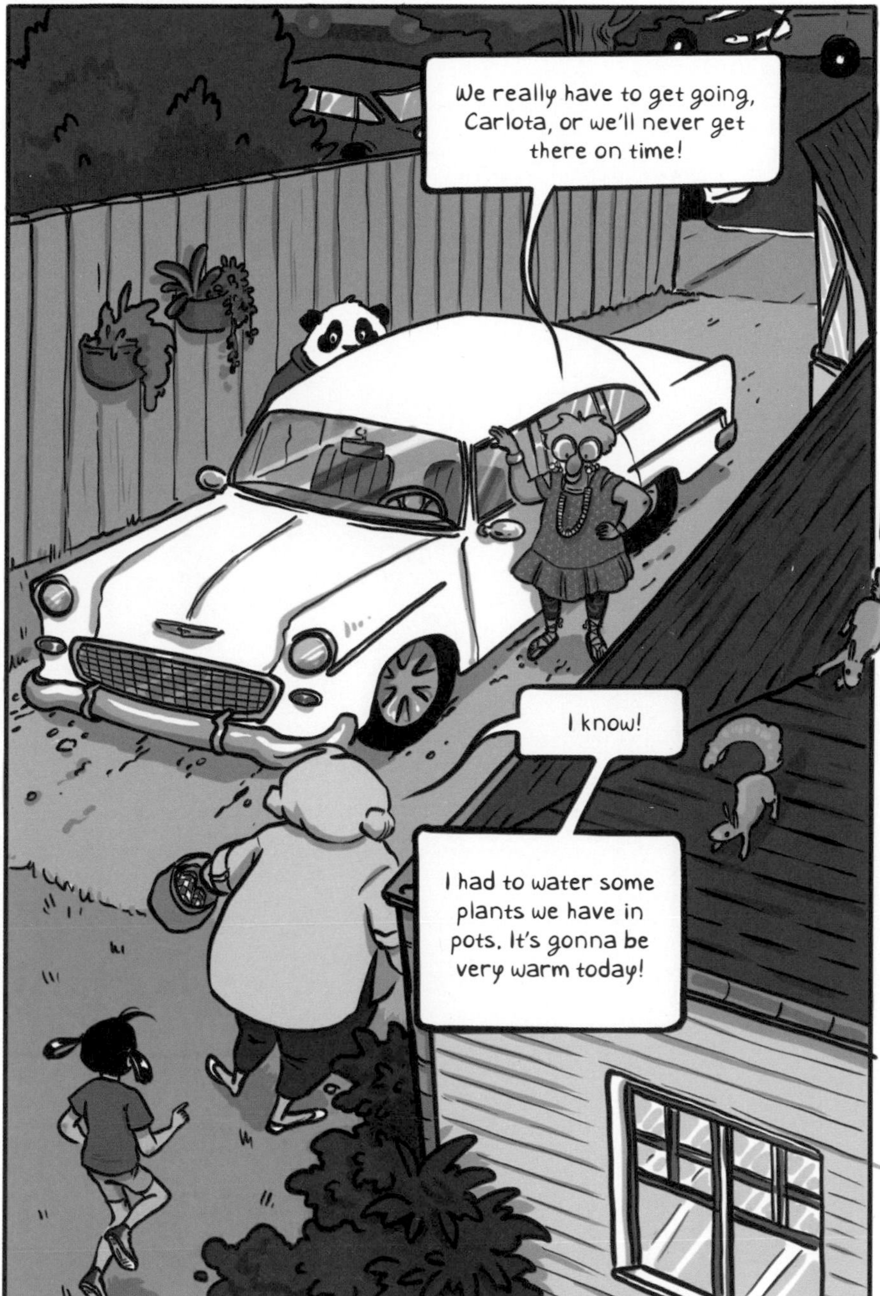
We really have to get going, Carlota, or we'll never get there on time!
I know!
I had to water some plants we have in pots. It's gonna be very warm today!

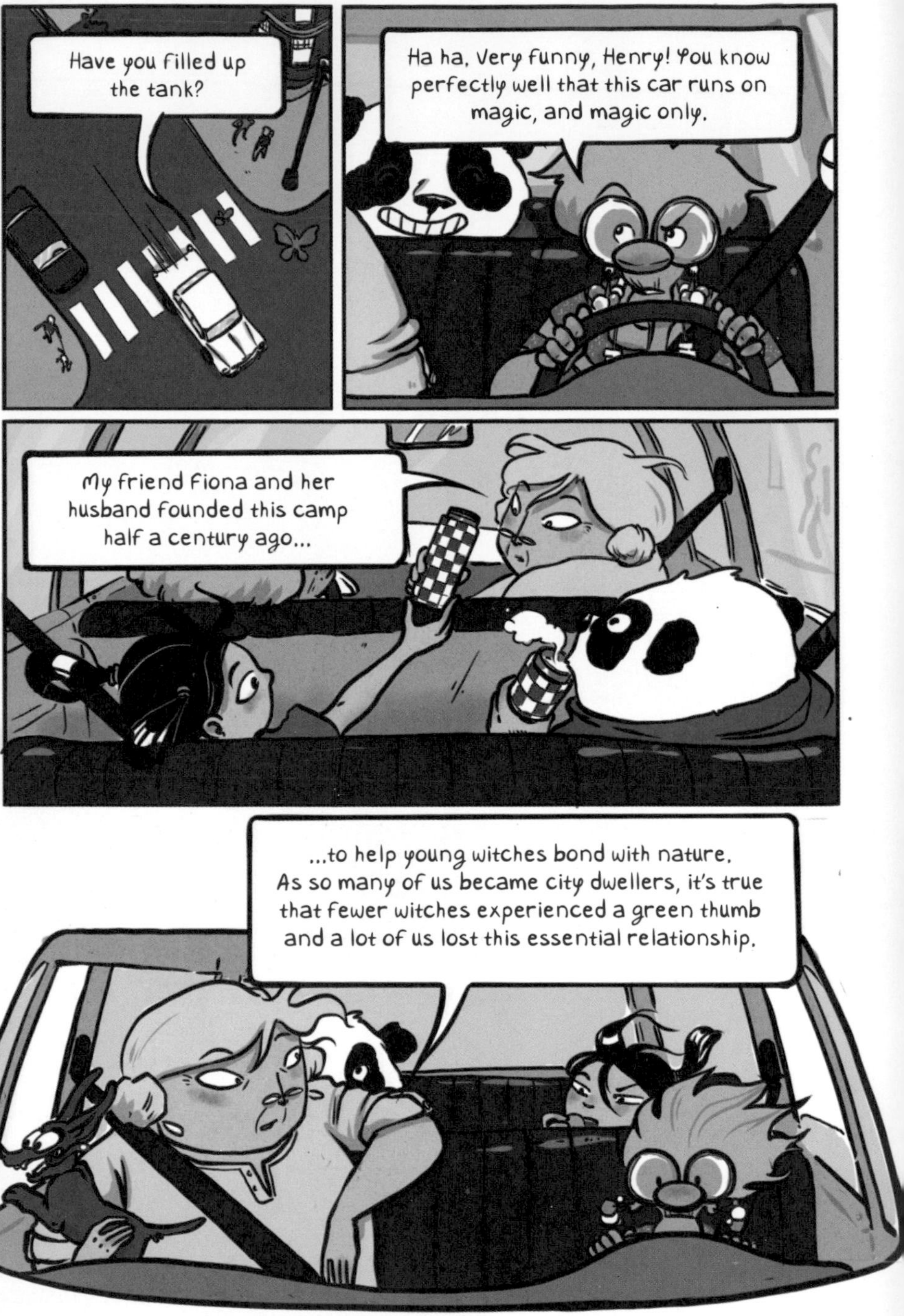
Have you filled up the tank?
Ha ha, Very funny, Henry! You know perfectly well that this car runs on magic, and magic only.
My friend Fiona and her husband founded this camp half a century ago...
...to help young witches bond with nature. As so many of us became city dwellers, it's true that fewer witches experienced a green thumb and a lot of us lost this essential relationship.

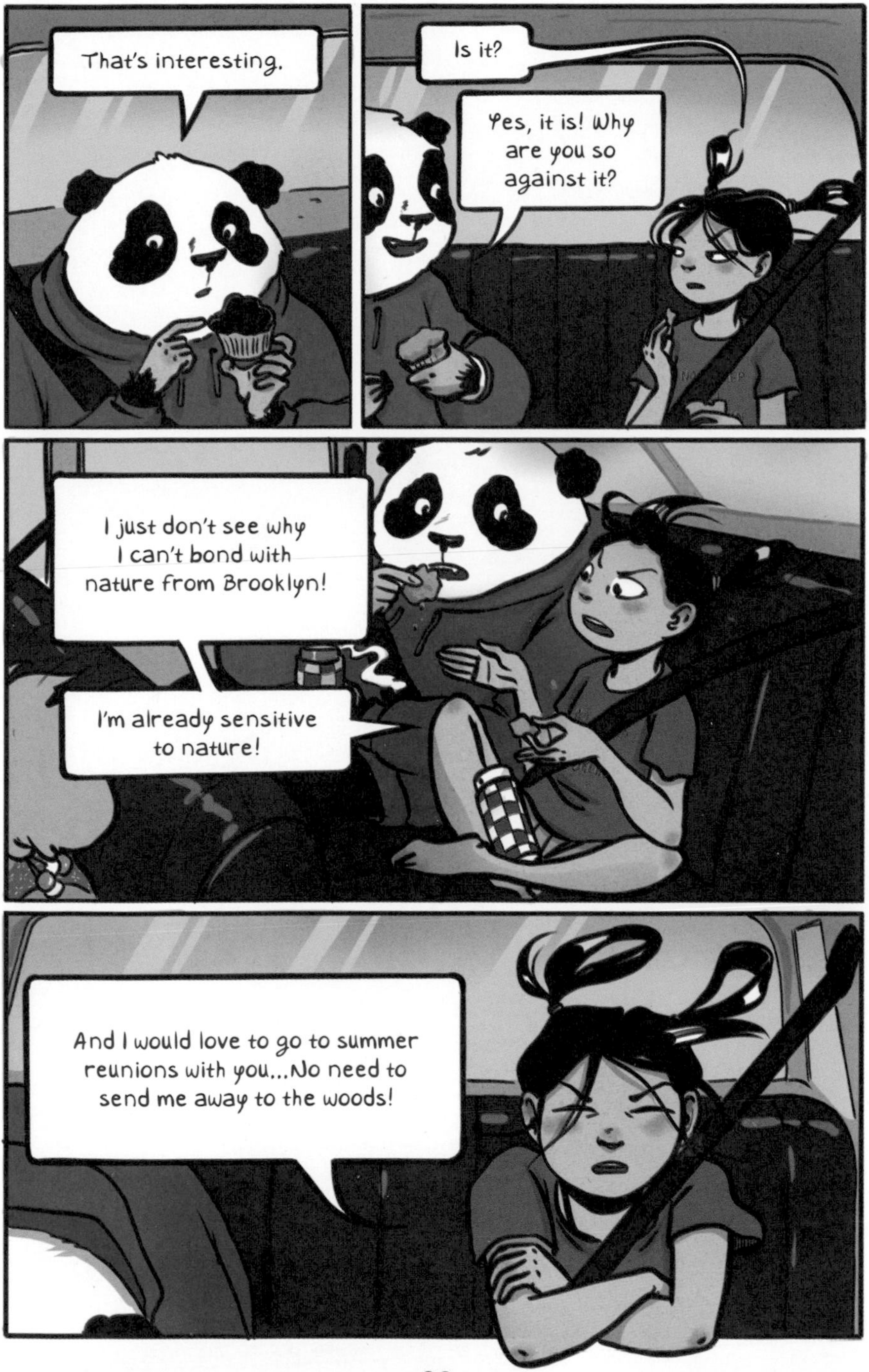
That's interesting.
Is it?
Yes, it is! Why are you so against it?
I just don't see why I can't bond with nature from Brooklyn!
I'm already sensitive to nature!
And I would love to go to summer reunions with you...No need to send me away to the woods!

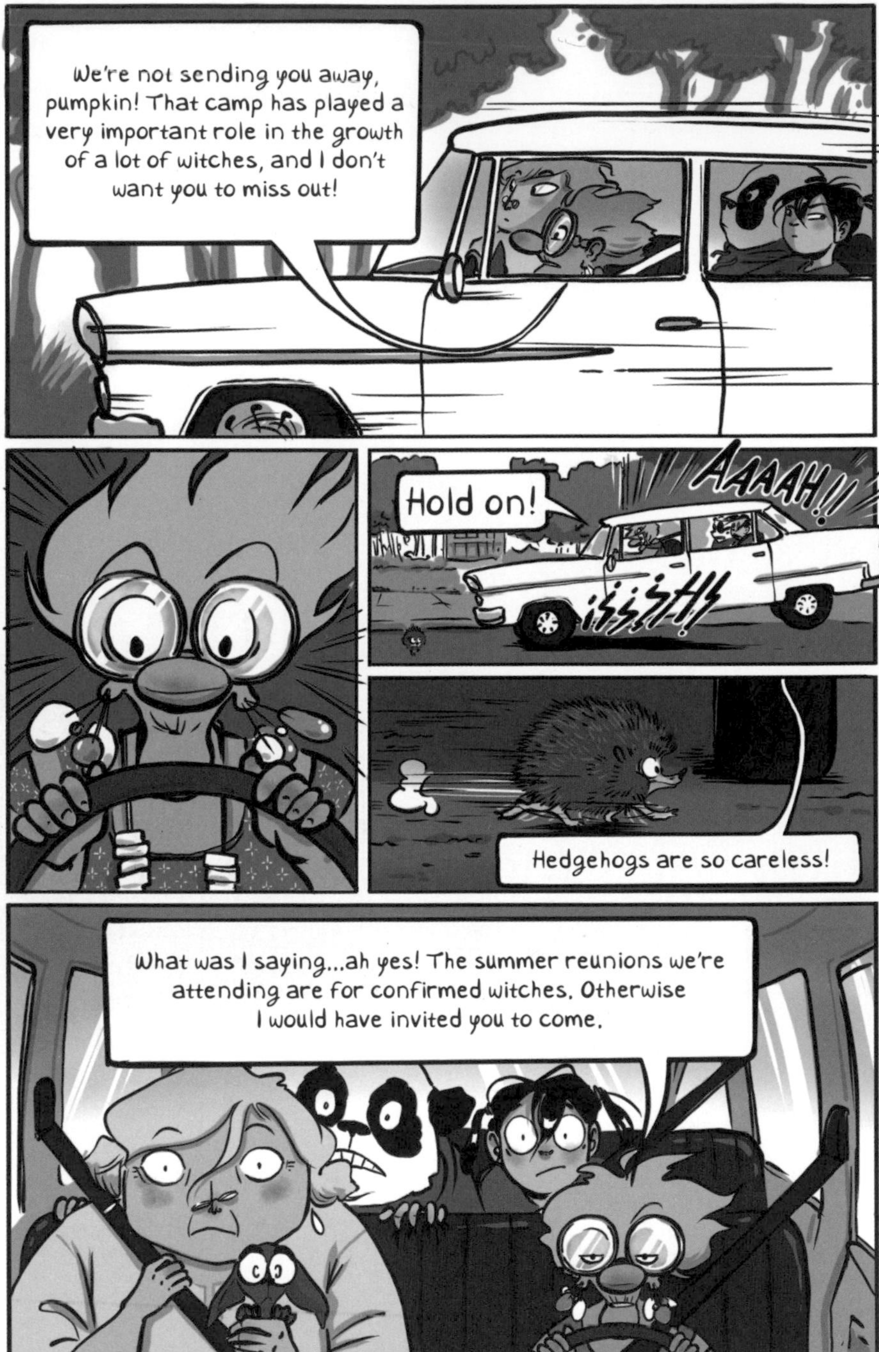
We're not sending you away, pumpkin! That camp has played a very important role in the growth of a lot of witches, and I don't want you to miss out!
Hold on!
AAAAH!!
iSSSH!!
Hedgehogs are so careless!
What was I saying...ah yes! The summer reunions we're attending are for confirmed witches. Otherwise I would have invited you to come.

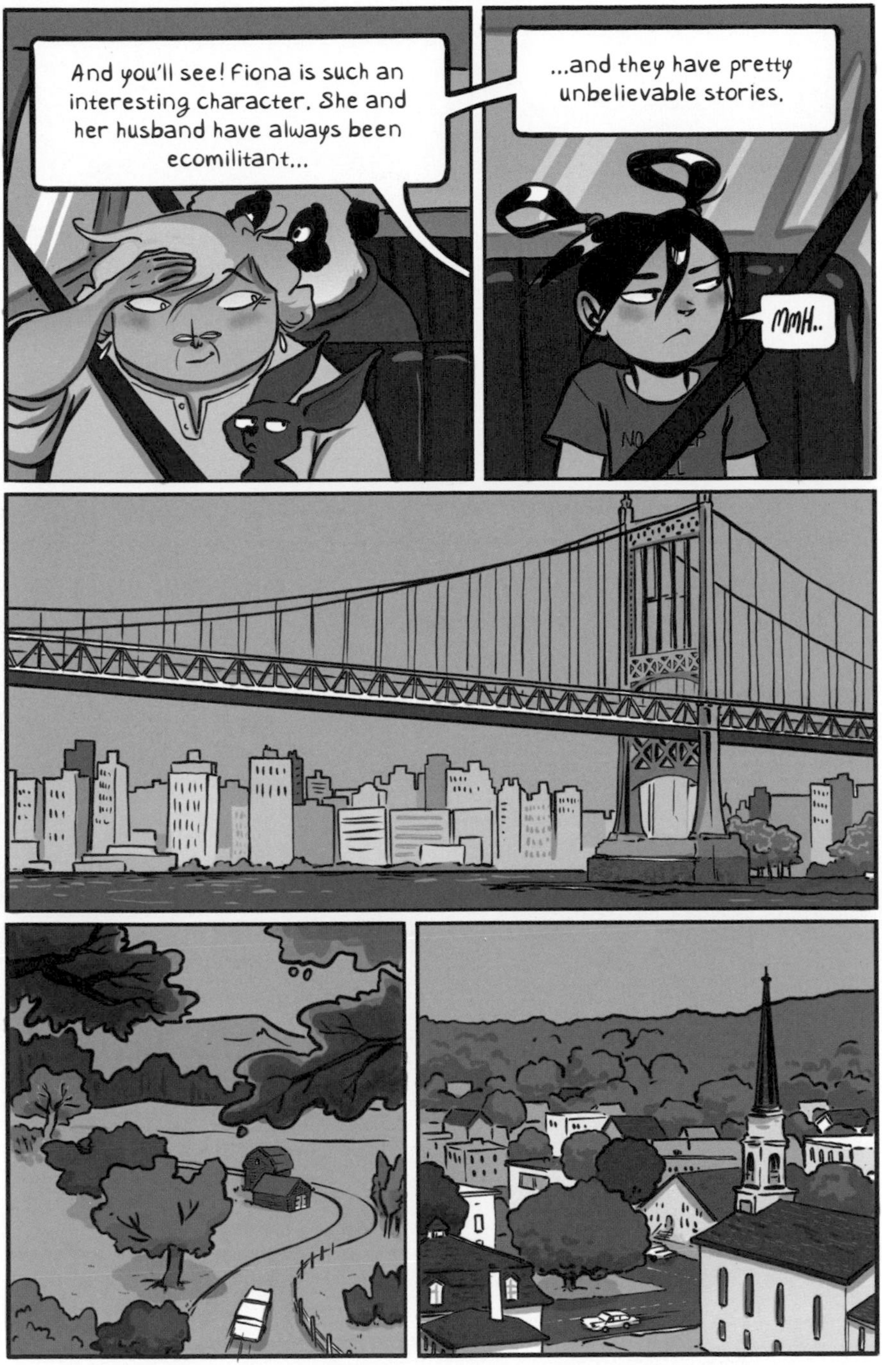
And you'll see! Fiona is such an interesting character. She and her husband have always been ecomilitant...
...and they have pretty unbelievable stories.
MMH..

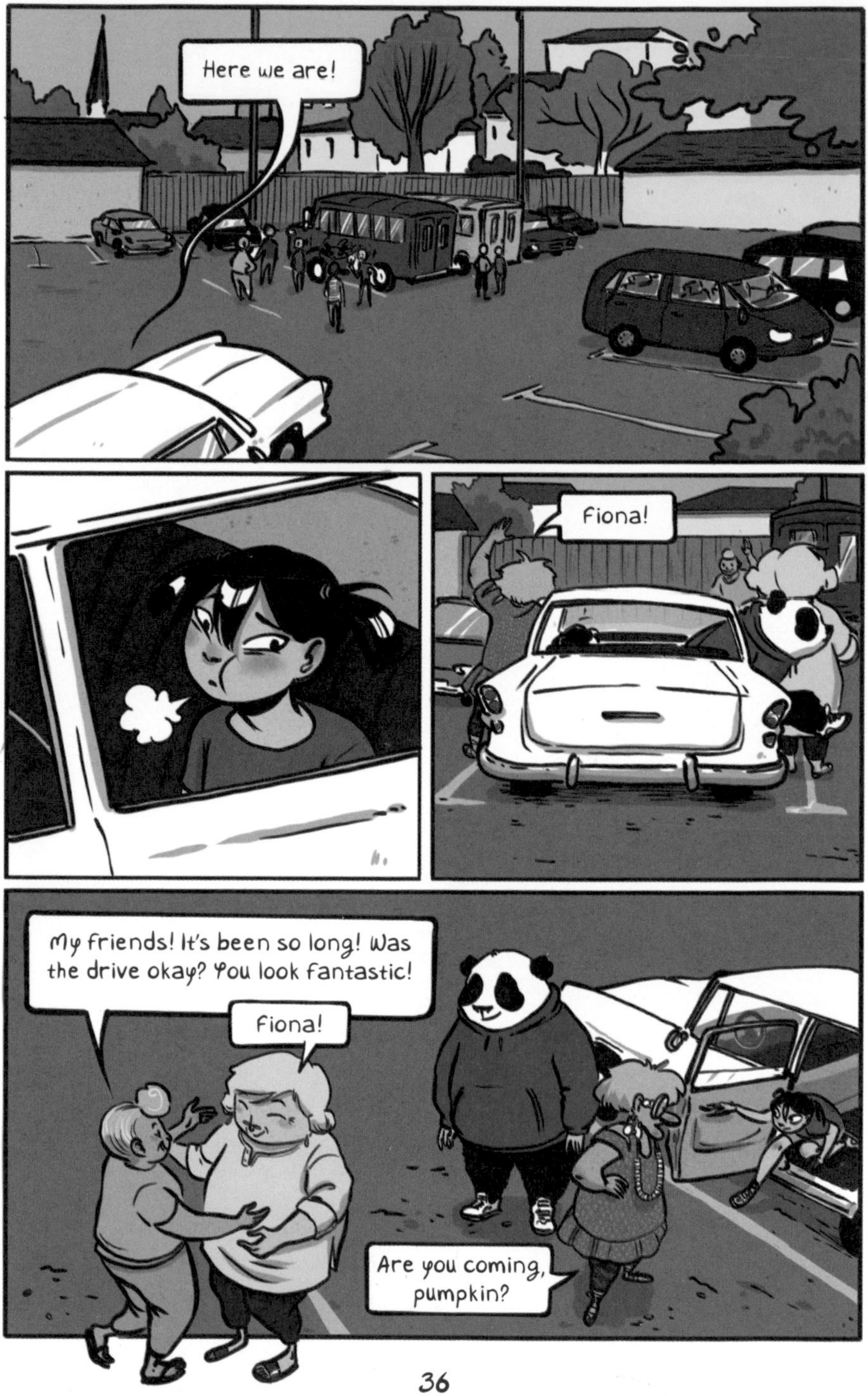
Here we are!
Fiona!
My friends! It's been so long! Was the drive okay? You look fantastic!
Fiona!
Are you coming, pumpkin?

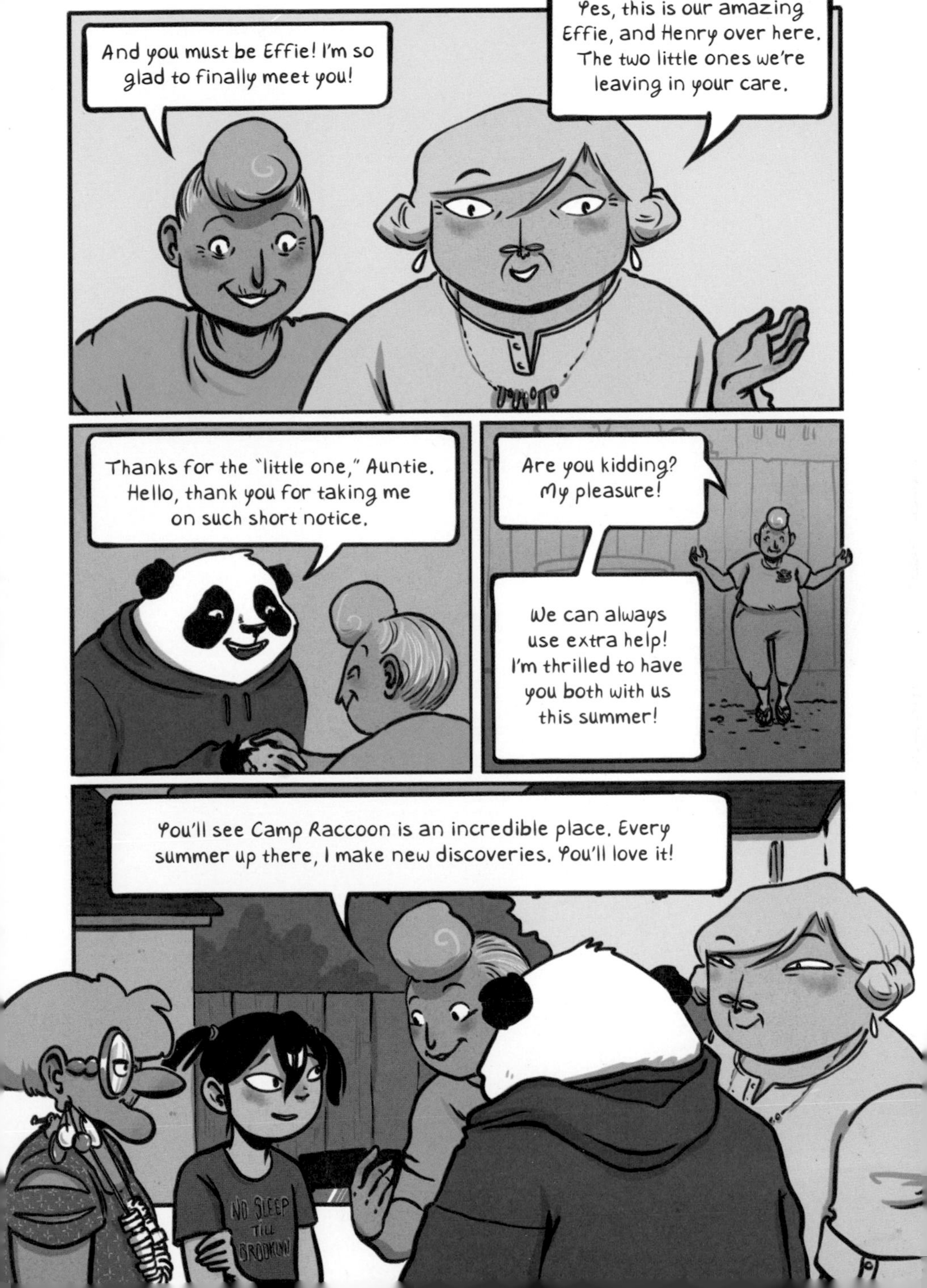
And you must be Effie! I'm so glad to finally meet you!
Yes, this is our amazing Effie, and Henry over here. The two little ones we're leaving in your care.
Thanks for the "little one," Auntie. Hello, thank you for taking me on such short notice.
Are you kidding? My pleasure!
We can always use extra help! I'm thrilled to have you both with us this summer!
You'll see Camp Raccoon is an incredible place. Every summer up there, I make new discoveries. You'll love it!
NO SLEEP TILL BROOKLYN

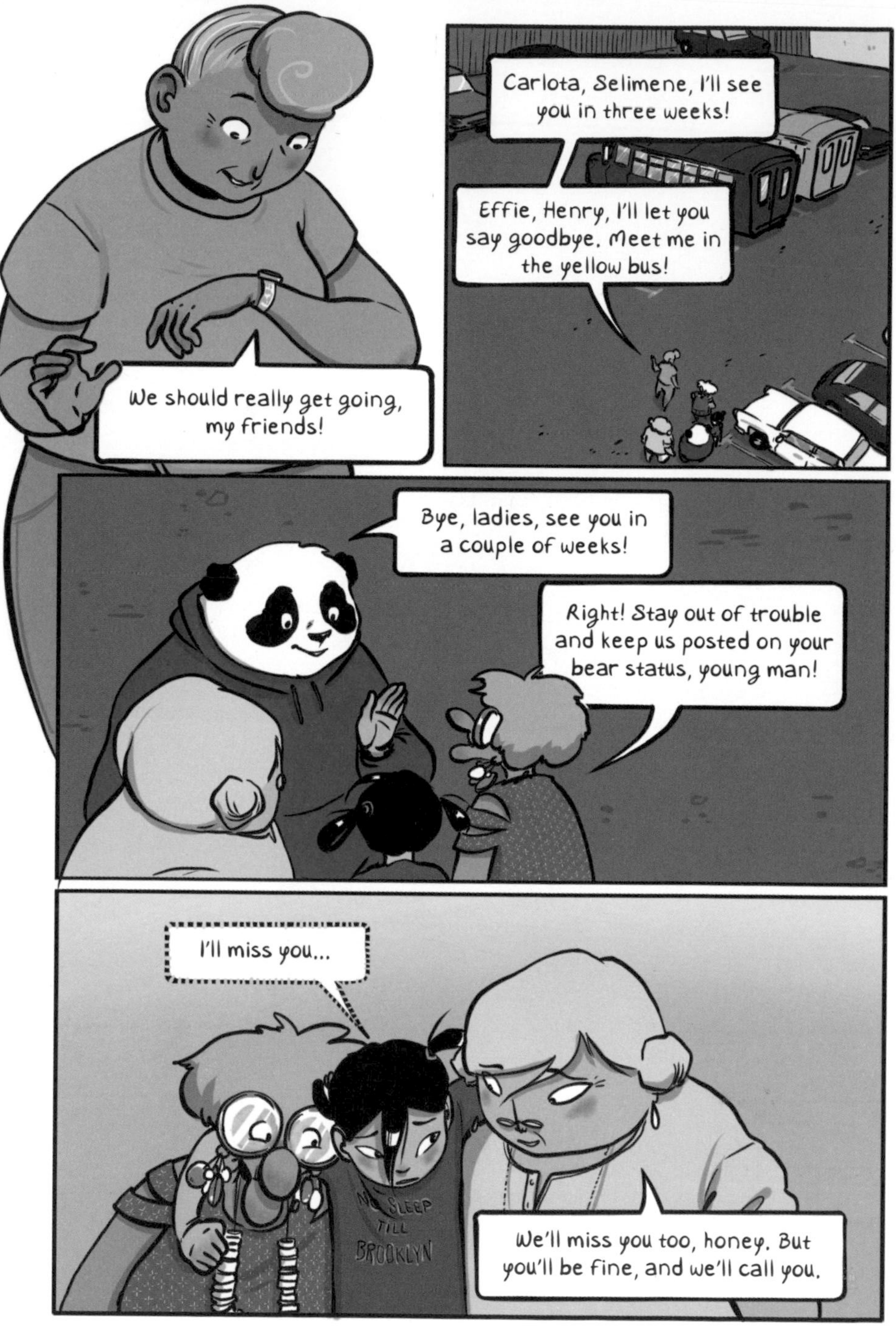
We should really get going, my friends!
Carlota, Selimene, I'll see you in three weeks!
Effie, Henry, I'll let you say goodbye. Meet me in the yellow bus!
Bye, ladies, see you in a couple of weeks!
Right! Stay out of trouble and keep us posted on your bear status, young man!
I'll miss you...
NO SLEEP TILL BROOKLYN
We'll miss you too, honey. But you'll be fine, and we'll call you.

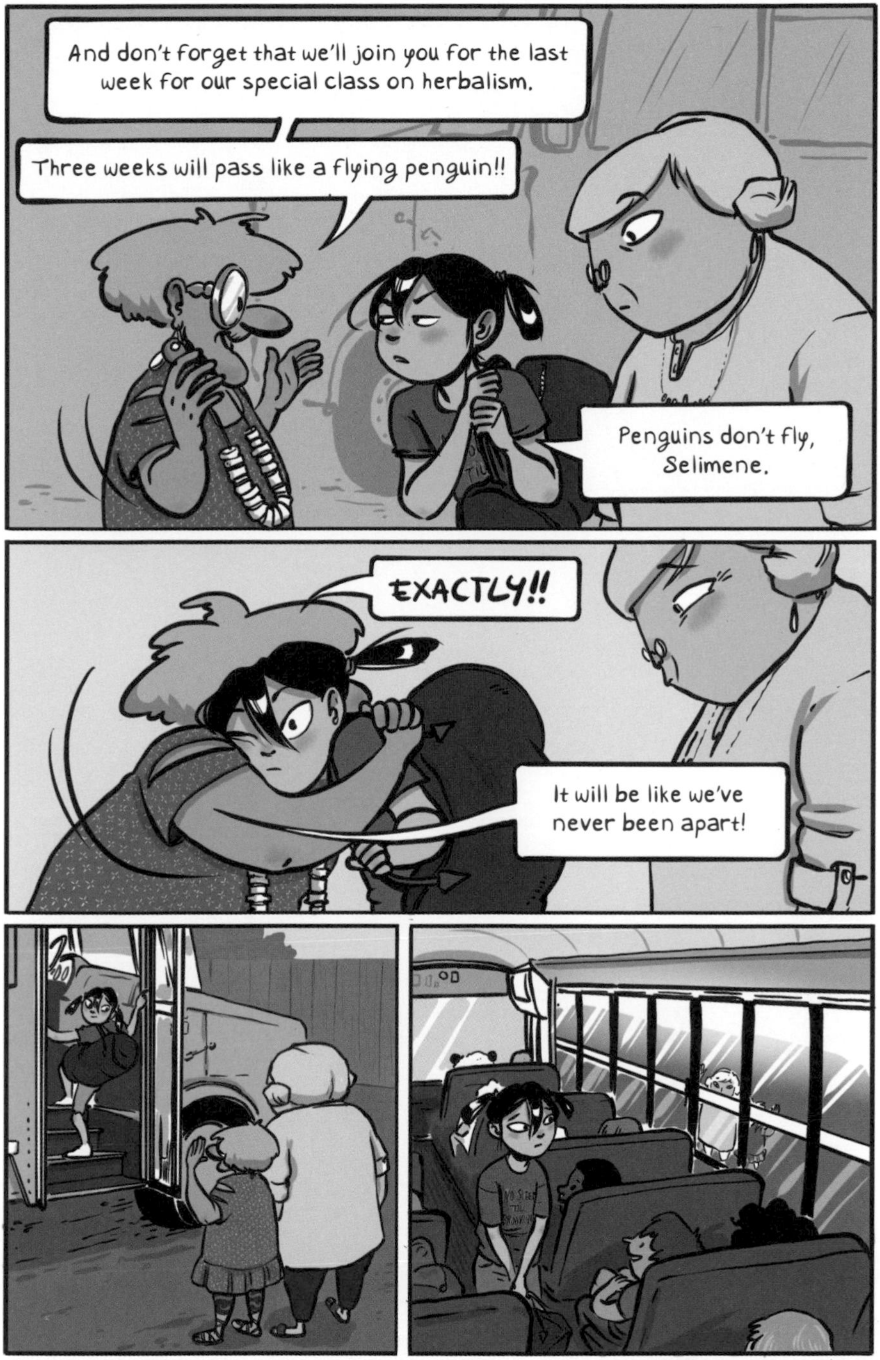
And don't forget that we'll join you for the last week for our special class on herbalism.
Three weeks will pass like a flying penguin!!
Penguins don't fly, Selimene.
EXACTLY!!
It will be like we've never been apart!

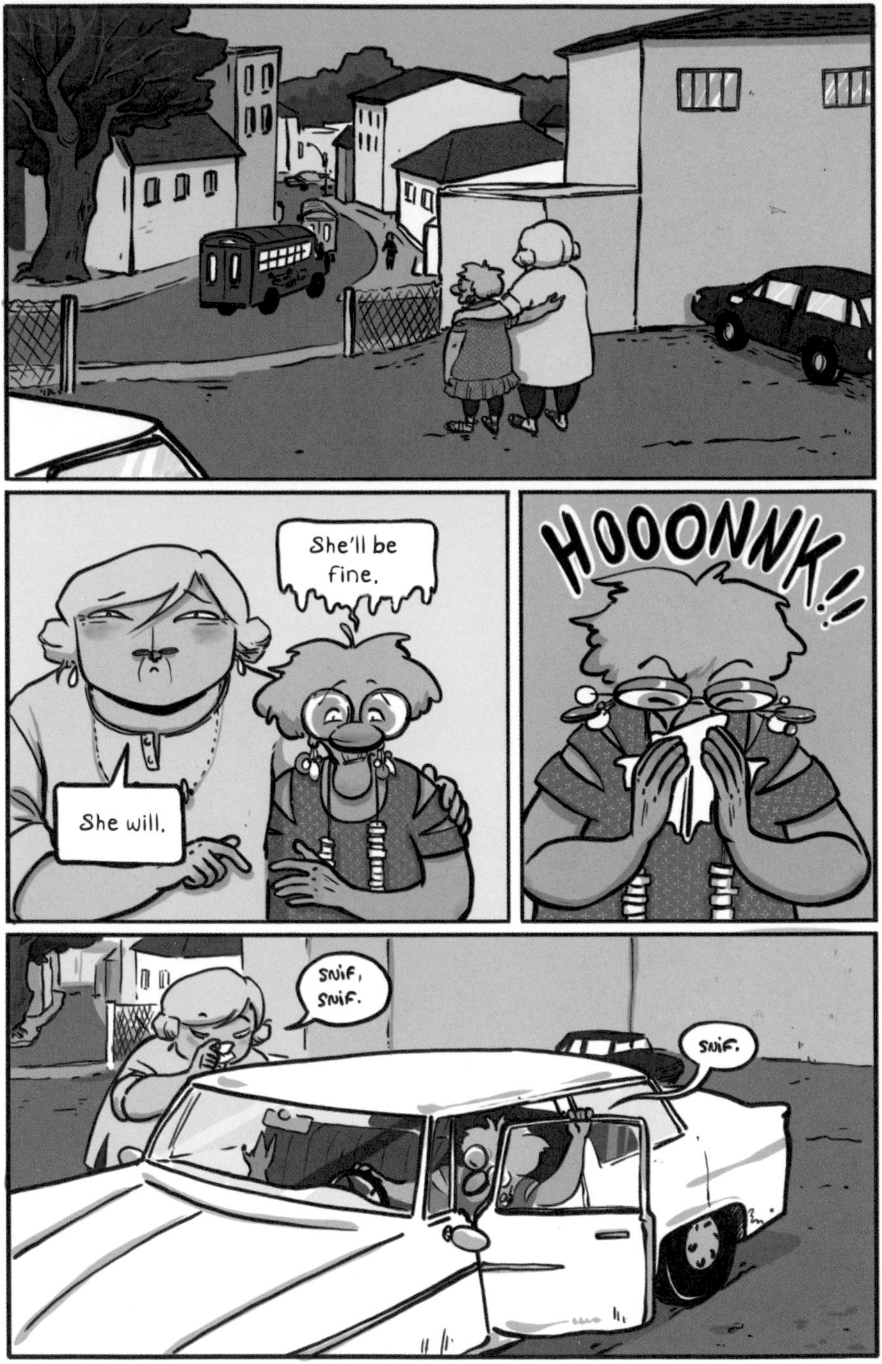
She'll be fine.
She will.
HOOONNK!!
SNIF, SNIF.
SNIF.

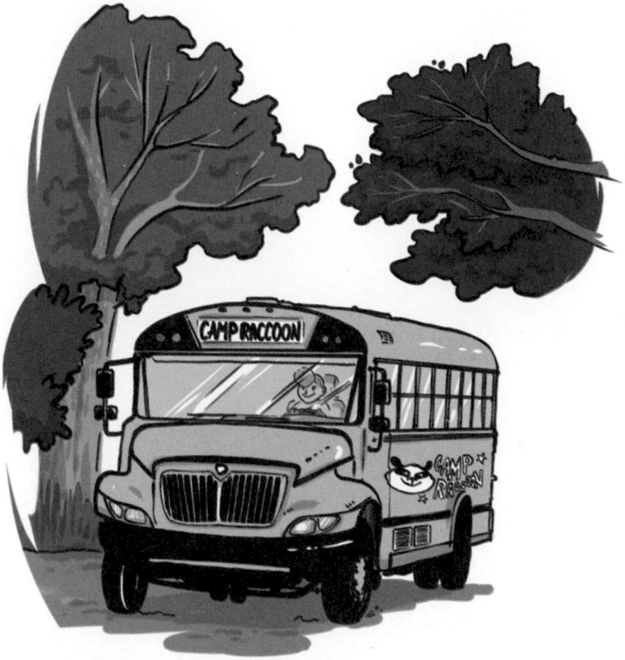
CAMP RACCOON
CAMP RACCOON

Chapter 2

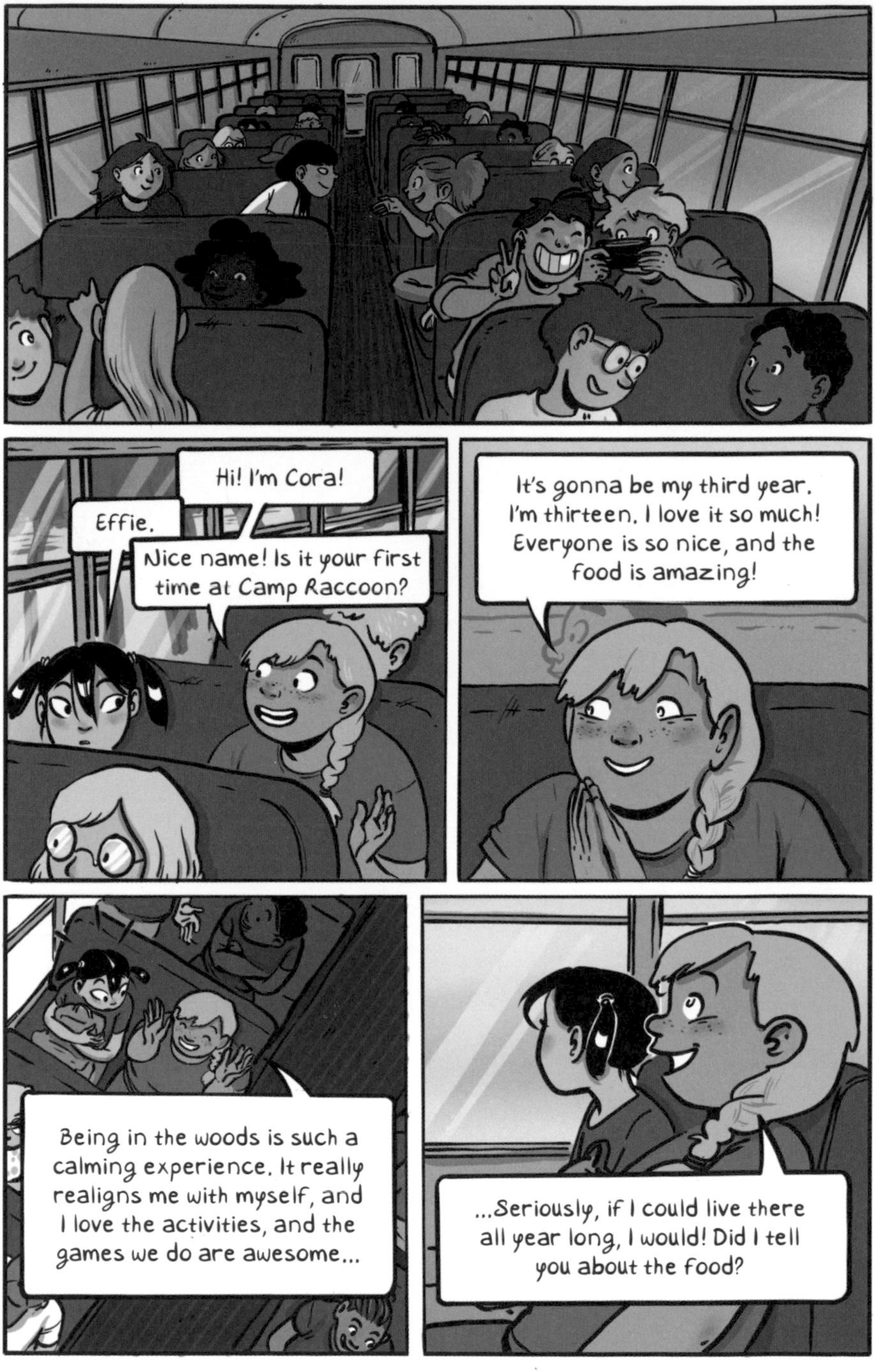
Hi! I'm Cora!
Effie.
Nice name! Is it your first time at Camp Raccoon?
It's gonna be my third year. I'm thirteen. I love it so much! Everyone is so nice, and the food is amazing!
Being in the woods is such a calming experience. It really realigns me with myself, and I love the activities, and the games we do are awesome...
...Seriously, if I could live there all year long, I would! Did I tell you about the food?

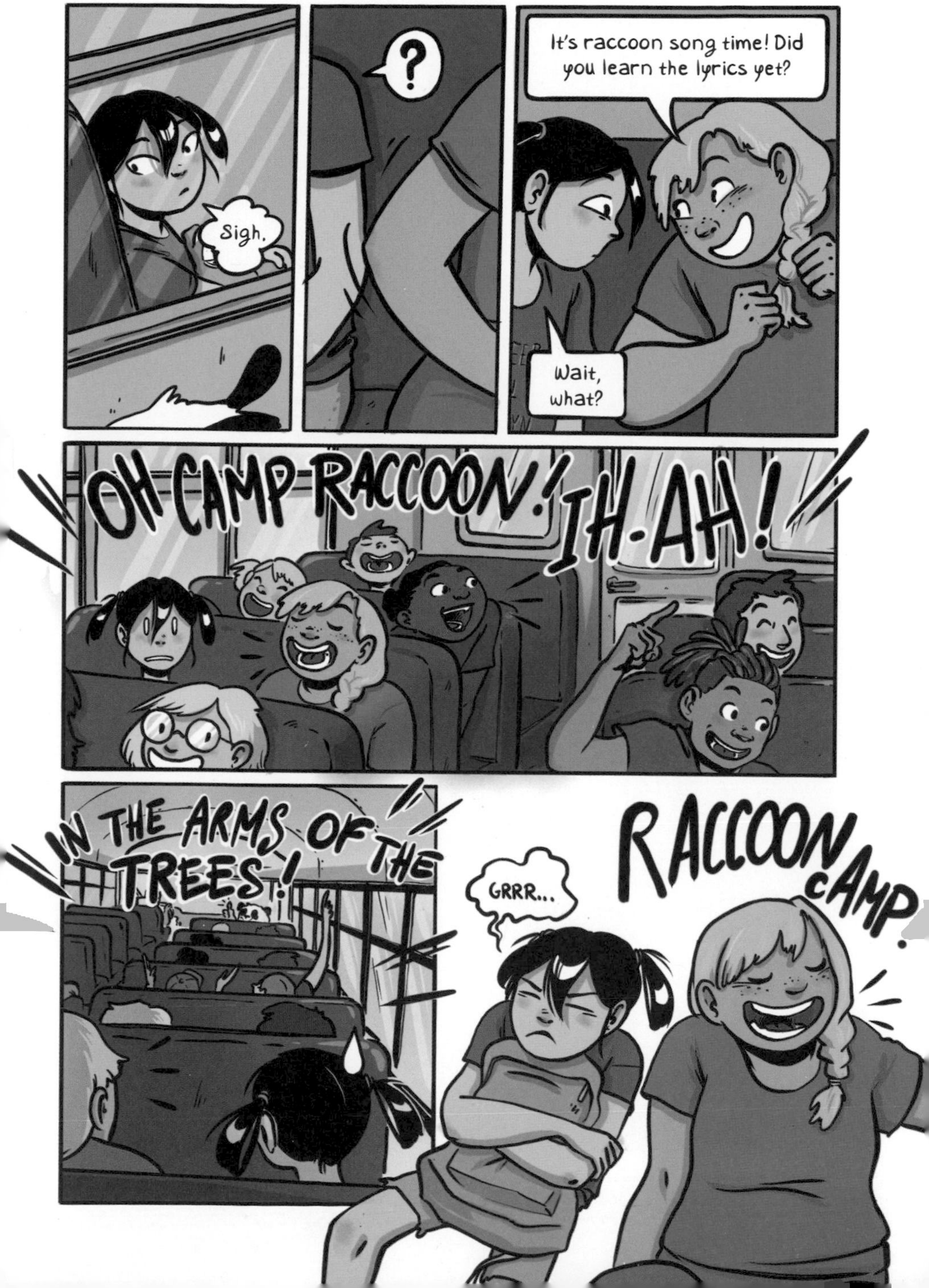

Sigh.
?
It's raccoon song time! Did you learn the lyrics yet?
Wait, what?
OH CAMP RACCOON!
IH-AH!
IN THE ARMS OF THE TREES!
GRRR...
RACCOON CAMP!

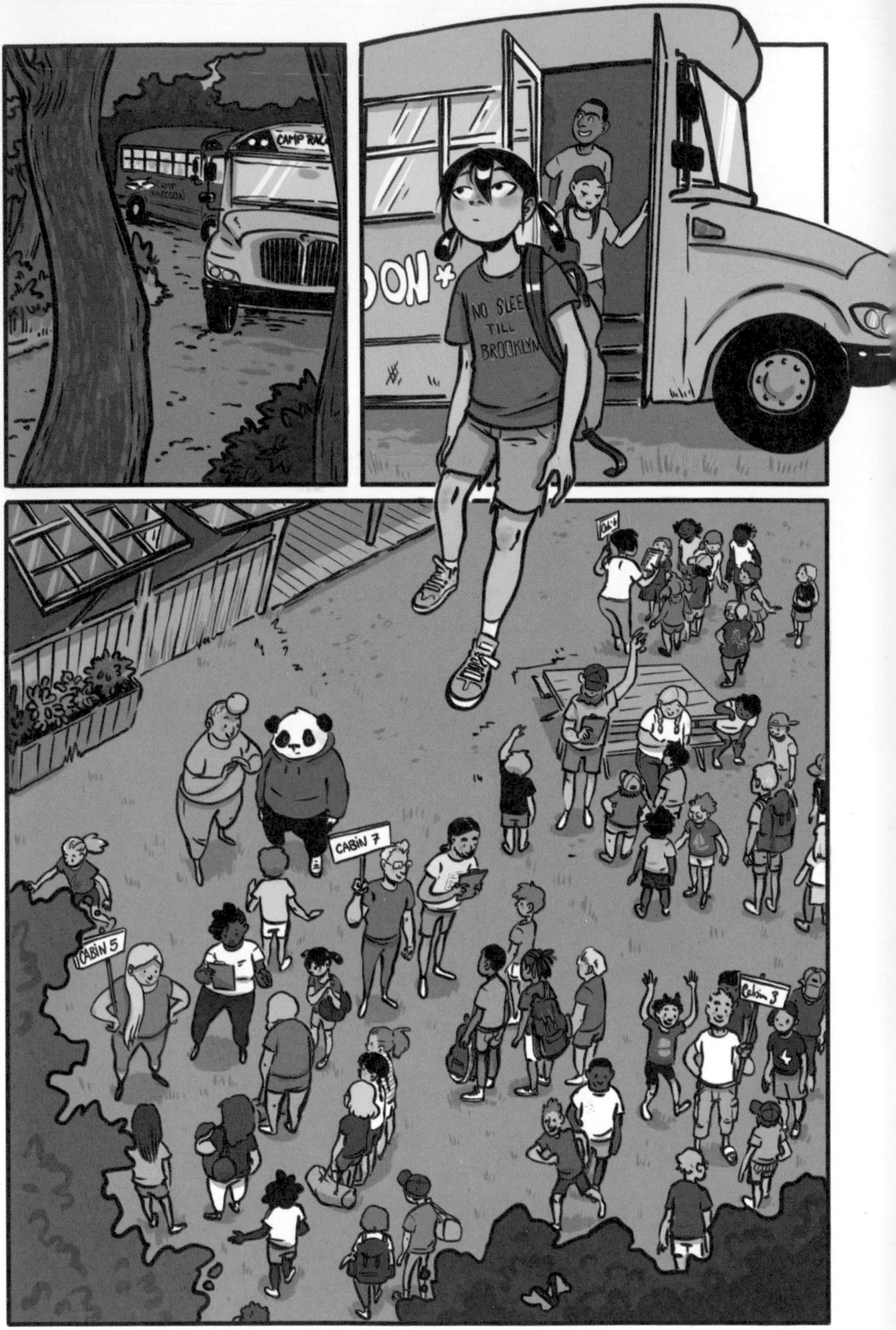
CAMP RACCOON
NO SLEE
TILL
BROOKLYN
CABIN 7
CABIN 5
Cabin 3

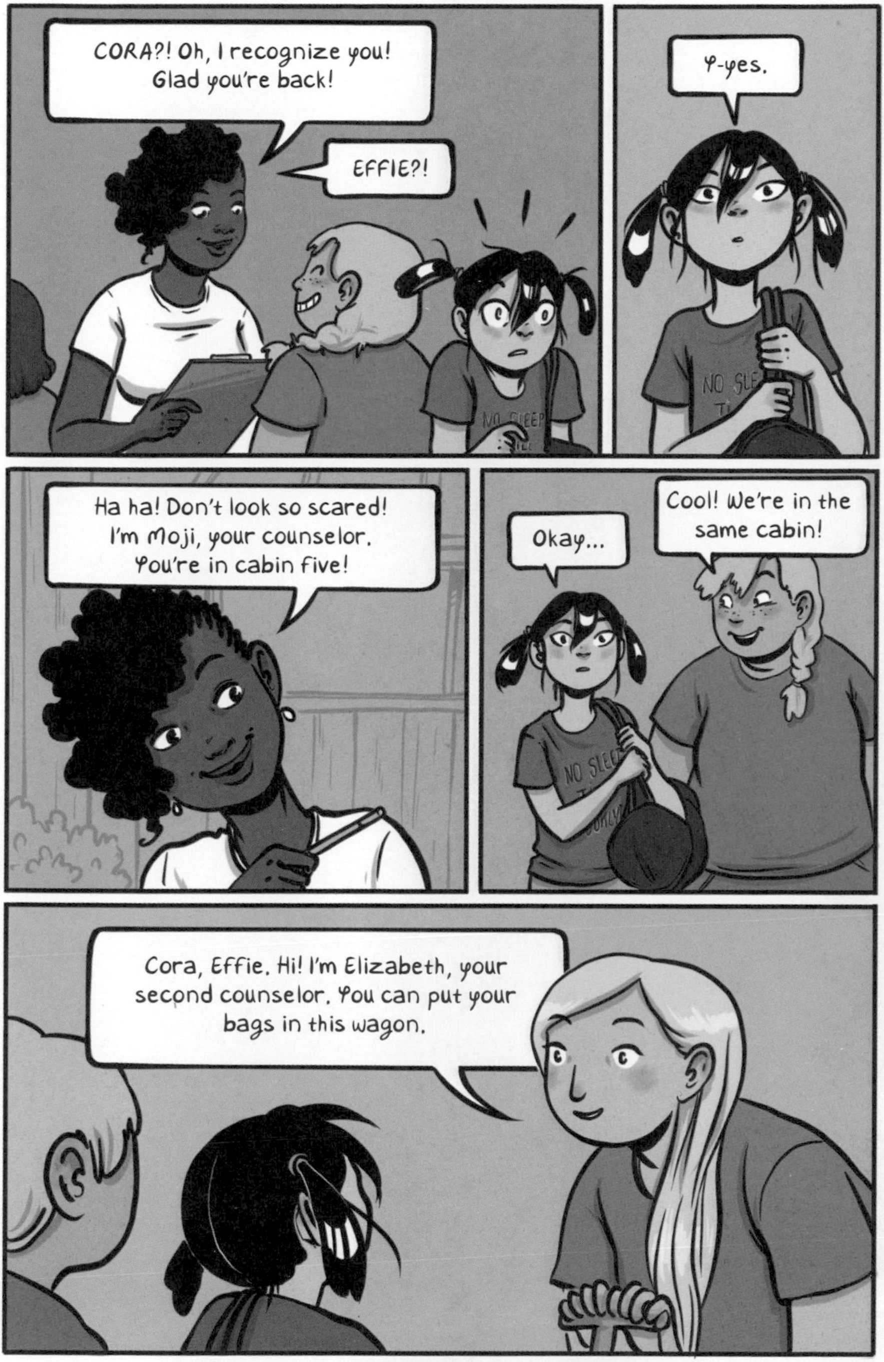
CORA?! Oh, I recognize you! Glad you're back!
EFFIE?!
Y-yes.
Ha ha! Don't look so scared! I'm Moji, your counselor. You're in cabin five!
Okay...
Cool! We're in the same cabin!
Cora, Effie. Hi! I'm Elizabeth, your second counselor. You can put your bags in this wagon.

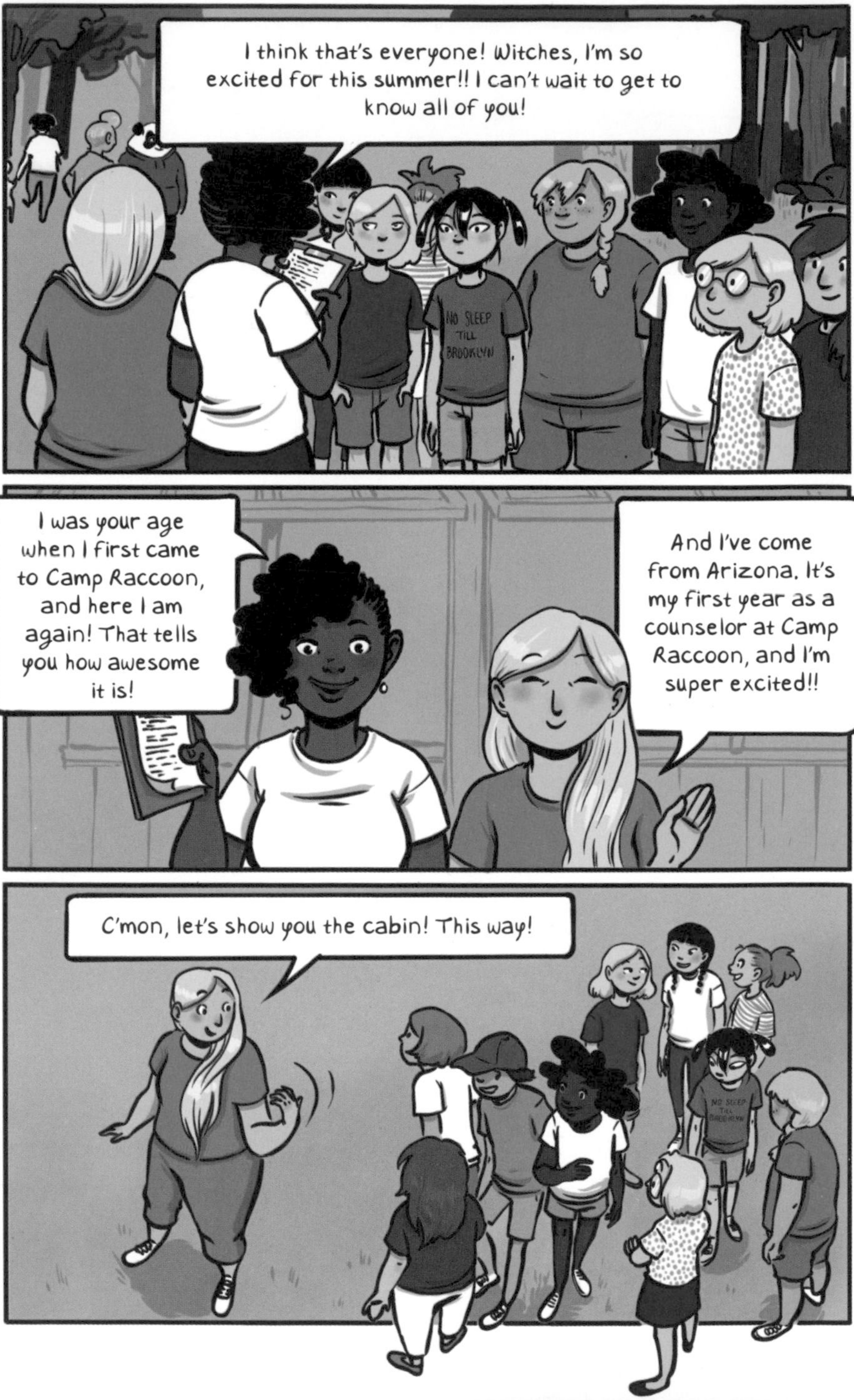
I think that's everyone! Witches, I'm so excited for this summer!! I can't wait to get to know all of you!
NO SLEEP TILL BROOKLYN
I was your age when I first came to Camp Raccoon, and here I am again! That tells you how awesome it is!
And I've come from Arizona. It's my first year as a counselor at Camp Raccoon, and I'm super excited!!
C'mon, let's show you the cabin! This way!

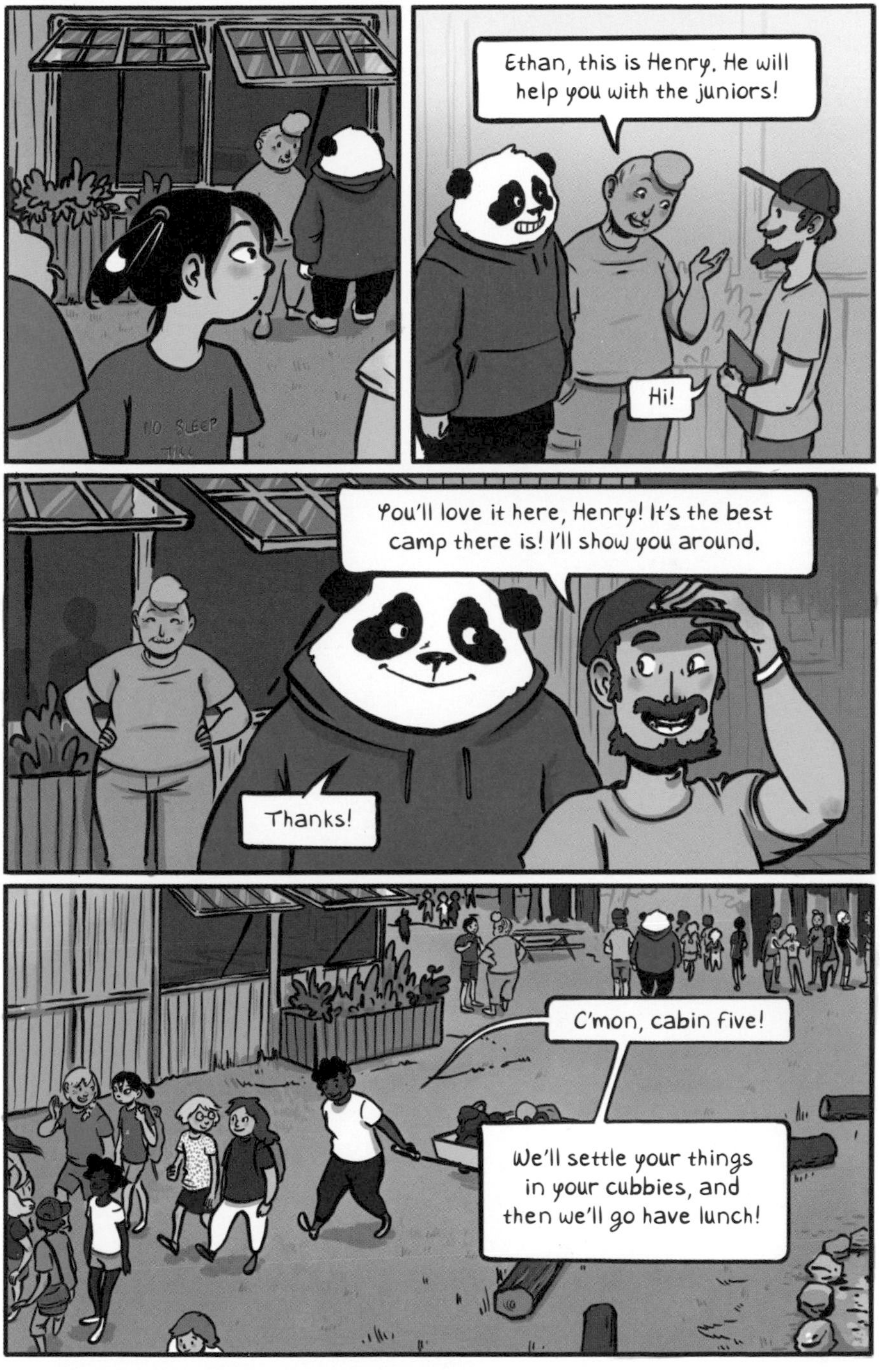

NO SLEEP TILL
Ethan, this is Henry. He will help you with the juniors!
Hi!
You'll love it here, Henry! It's the best camp there is! I'll show you around.
Thanks!
C'mon, cabin five!
We'll settle your things in your cubbies, and then we'll go have lunch!

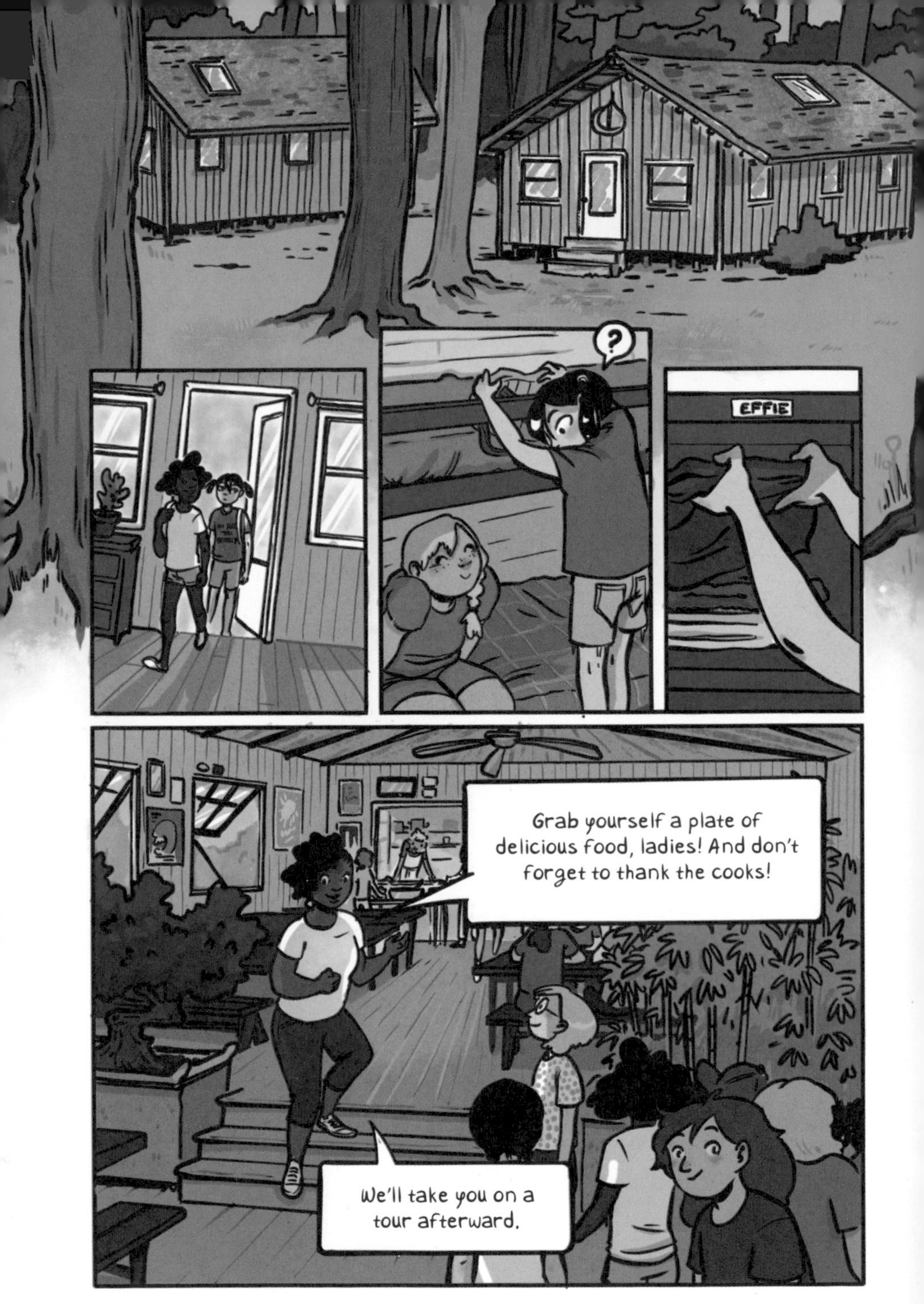
?
EFFIE
Grab yourself a plate of delicious food, ladies! And don't forget to thank the cooks!
We'll take you on a tour afterward.

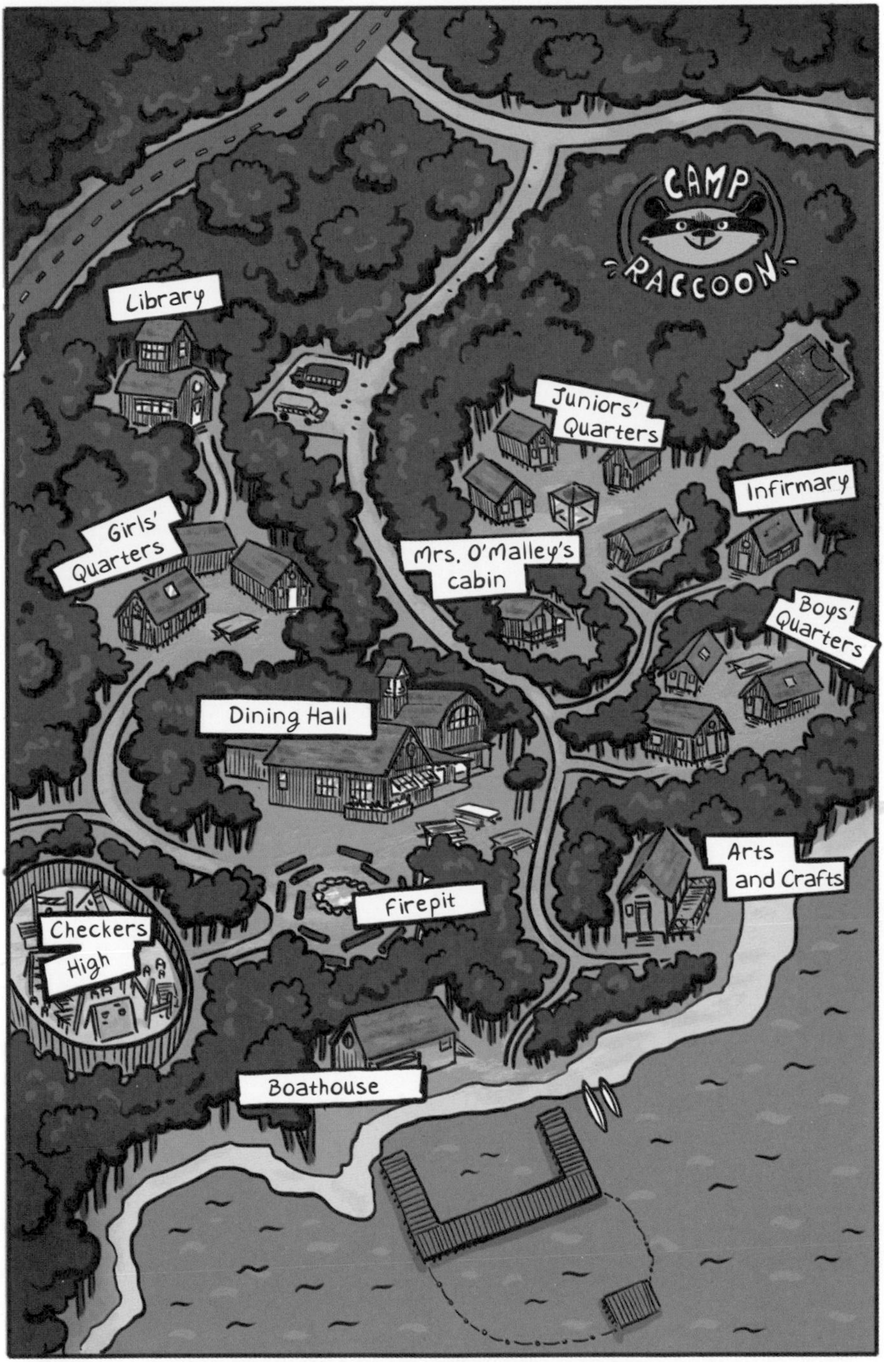
CAMP RACCOON
Library
Juniors' Quarters
Infirmary
Girls' Quarters
Mrs. O'Malley's cabin
Boys' Quarters
Dining Hall
Arts and Crafts
Firepit
Checkers High
Boathouse

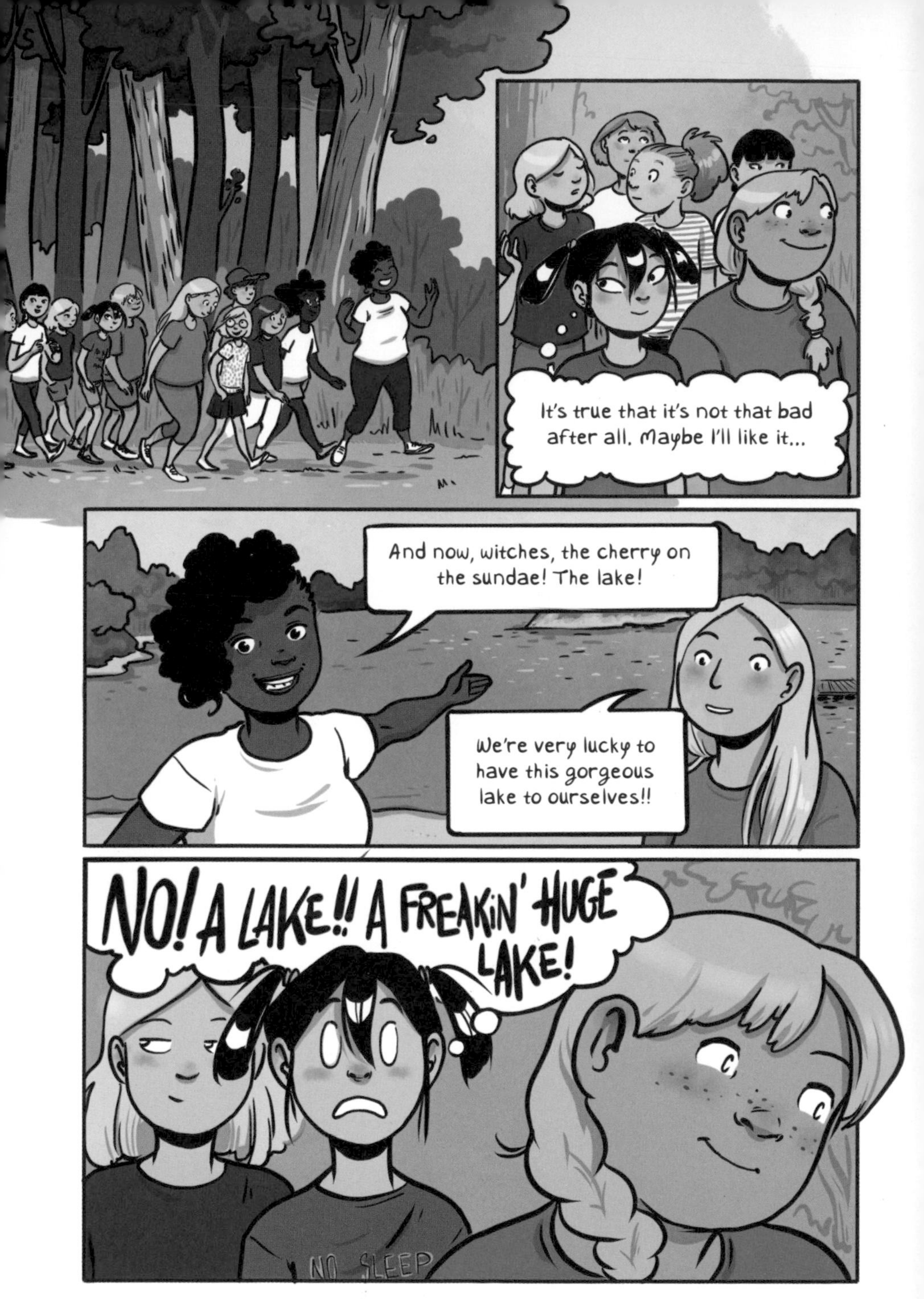

It's true that it's not that bad after all. Maybe I'll like it...
And now, witches, the cherry on the sundae! The lake!
We're very lucky to have this gorgeous lake to ourselves!!
NO! A LAKE!! A FREAKIN' HUGE LAKE!
NO SLEEP

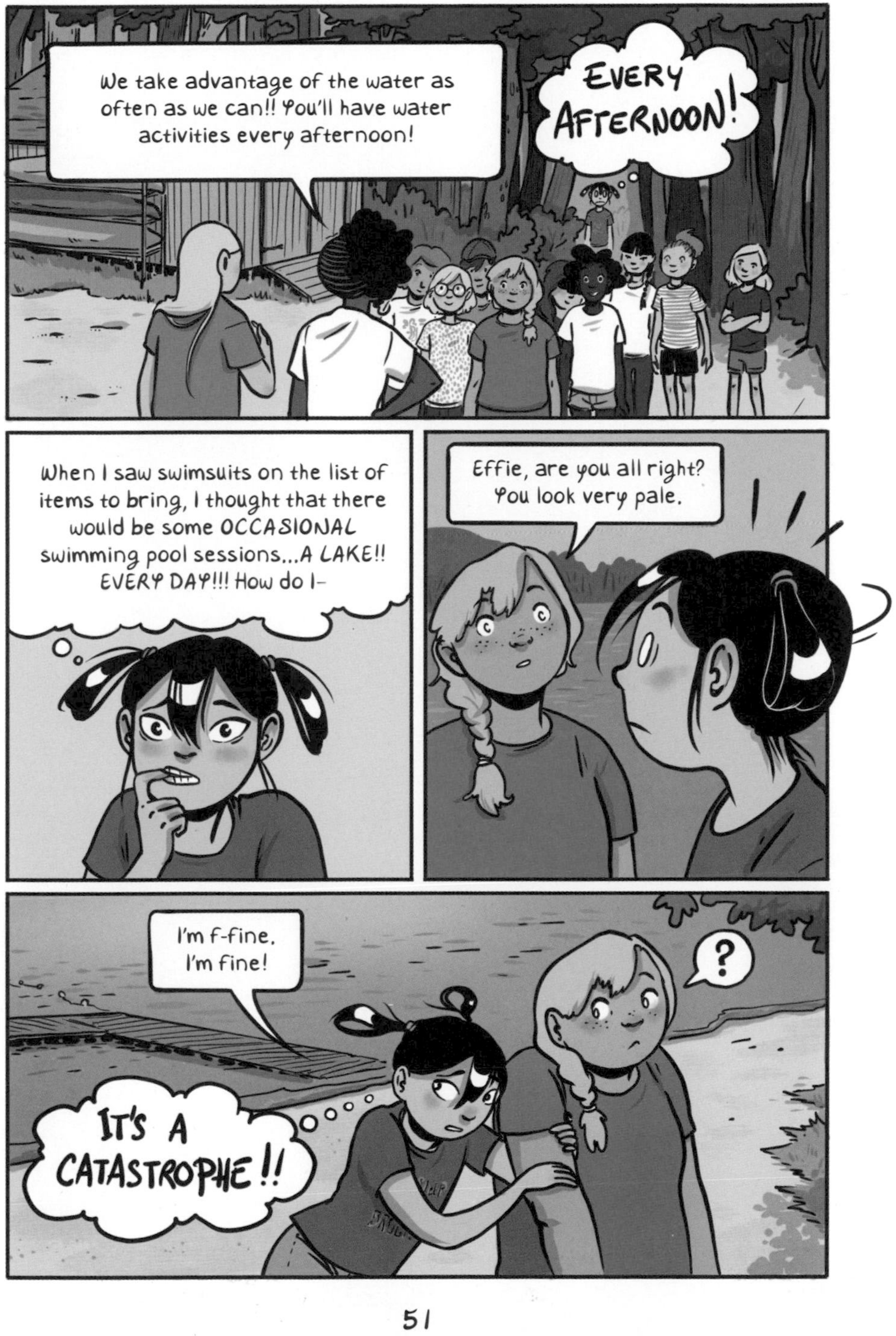
We take advantage of the water as often as we can!! You'll have water activities every afternoon!
EVERY AFTERNOON!
When I saw swimsuits on the list of items to bring, I thought that there would be some OCCASIONAL swimming pool sessions...A LAKE!! EVERY DAY!!! How do I-
Effie, are you all right? You look very pale.
I'm f-fine. I'm fine!
?
IT'S A CATASTROPHE!!

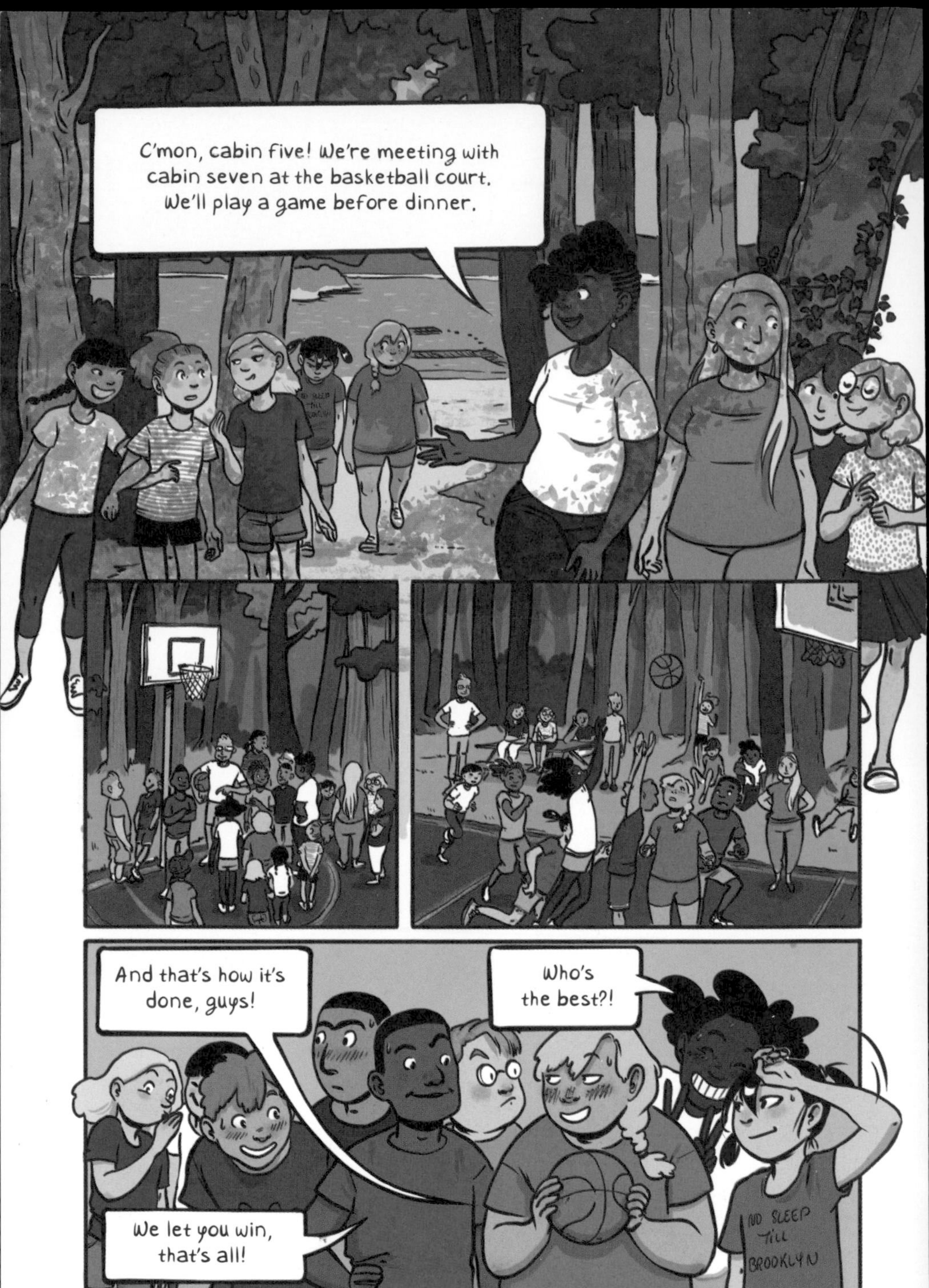
C'mon, cabin five! We're meeting with cabin seven at the basketball court. We'll play a game before dinner.
NO SLEEP TILL BROOKLYN
And that's how it's done, guys!
Who's the best?!
We let you win, that's all!
NO SLEEP TILL BROOKLYN

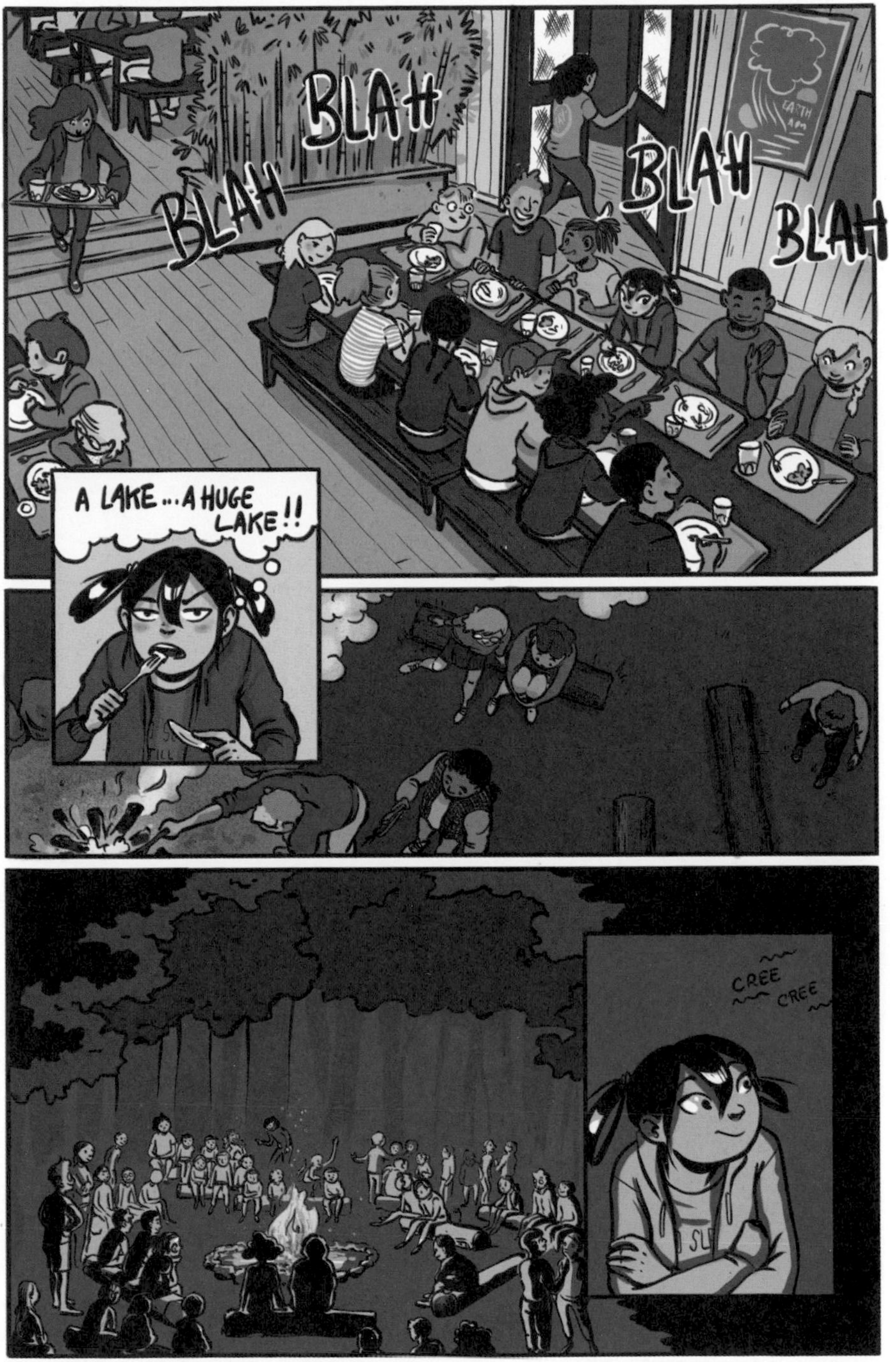
BLAH
BLAH
BLAH
BLAH
A LAKE... A HUGE LAKE!!
CREE CREE

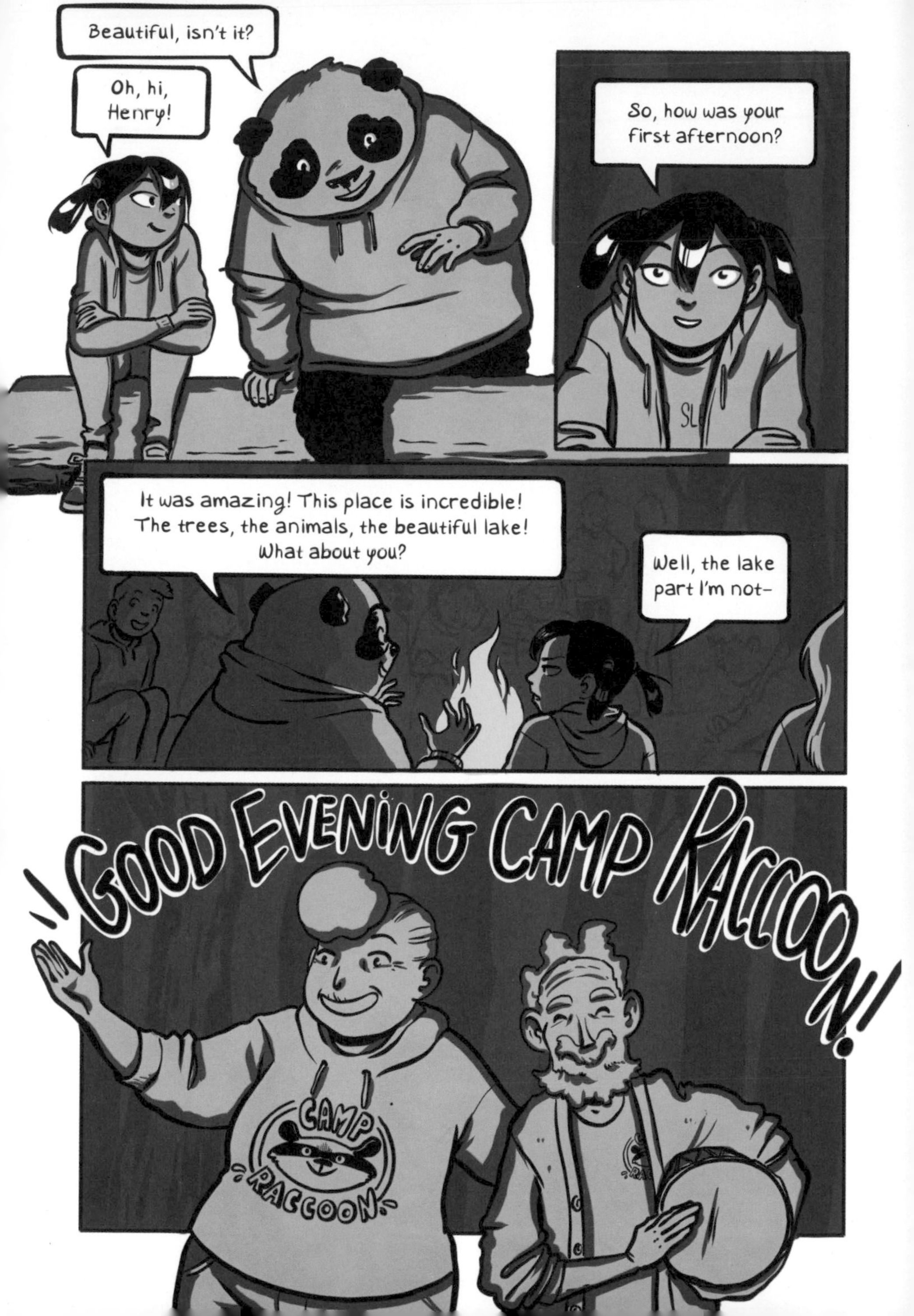
Beautiful, isn't it?
Oh, hi, Henry!
So, how was your first afternoon?
It was amazing! This place is incredible! The trees, the animals, the beautiful lake! What about you?
Well, the lake part I'm not-
GOOD EVENING CAMP RACCOON!
CAMP RACCOON

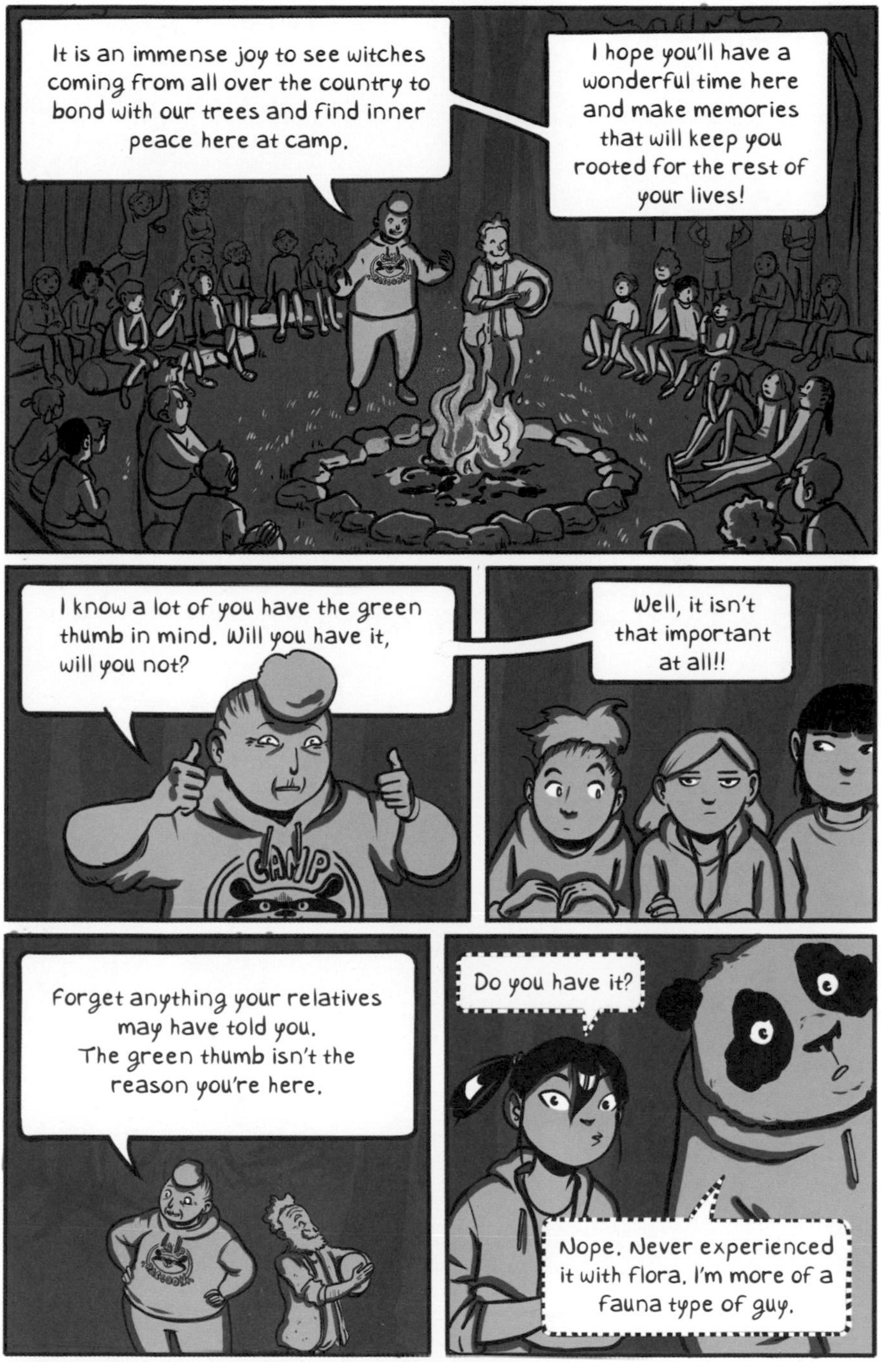
It is an immense joy to see witches coming from all over the country to bond with our trees and find inner peace here at camp.
I hope you'll have a wonderful time here and make memories that will keep you rooted for the rest of your lives!
I know a lot of you have the green thumb in mind. Will you have it, will you not?
Well, it isn't that important at all!!
CAMP
Forget anything your relatives may have told you. The green thumb isn't the reason you're here.
Do you have it?
Nope. Never experienced it with flora. I'm more of a fauna type of guy.

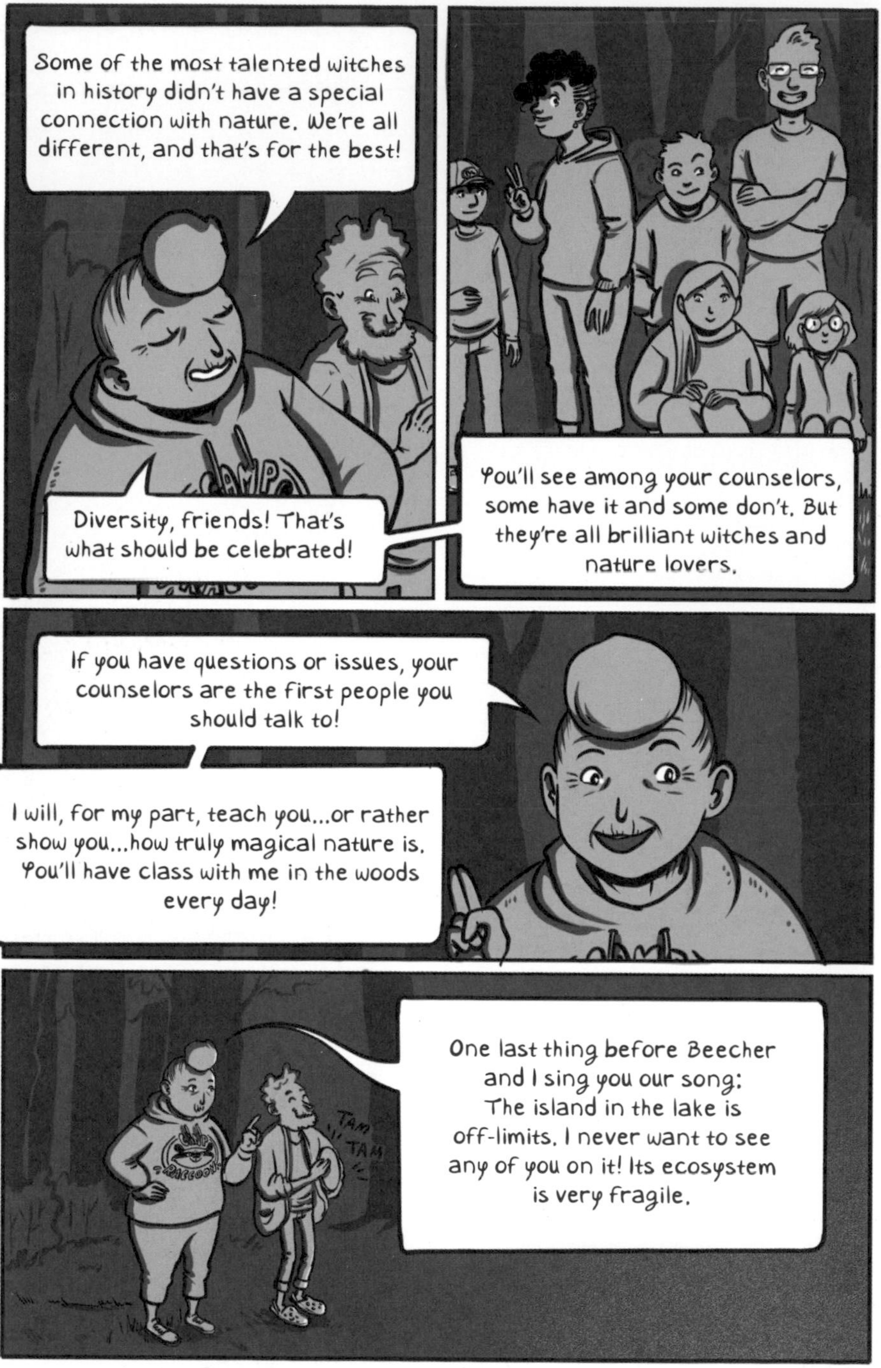

Some of the most talented witches in history didn't have a special connection with nature. We're all different, and that's for the best!
Diversity, friends! That's what should be celebrated!
You'll see among your counselors, some have it and some don't. But they're all brilliant witches and nature lovers.
If you have questions or issues, your counselors are the first people you should talk to!
I will, for my part, teach you...or rather show you...how truly magical nature is. You'll have class with me in the woods every day!
One last thing before Beecher and I sing you our song: The island in the lake is off-limits. I never want to see any of you on it! Its ecosystem is very fragile.
TAM TAM

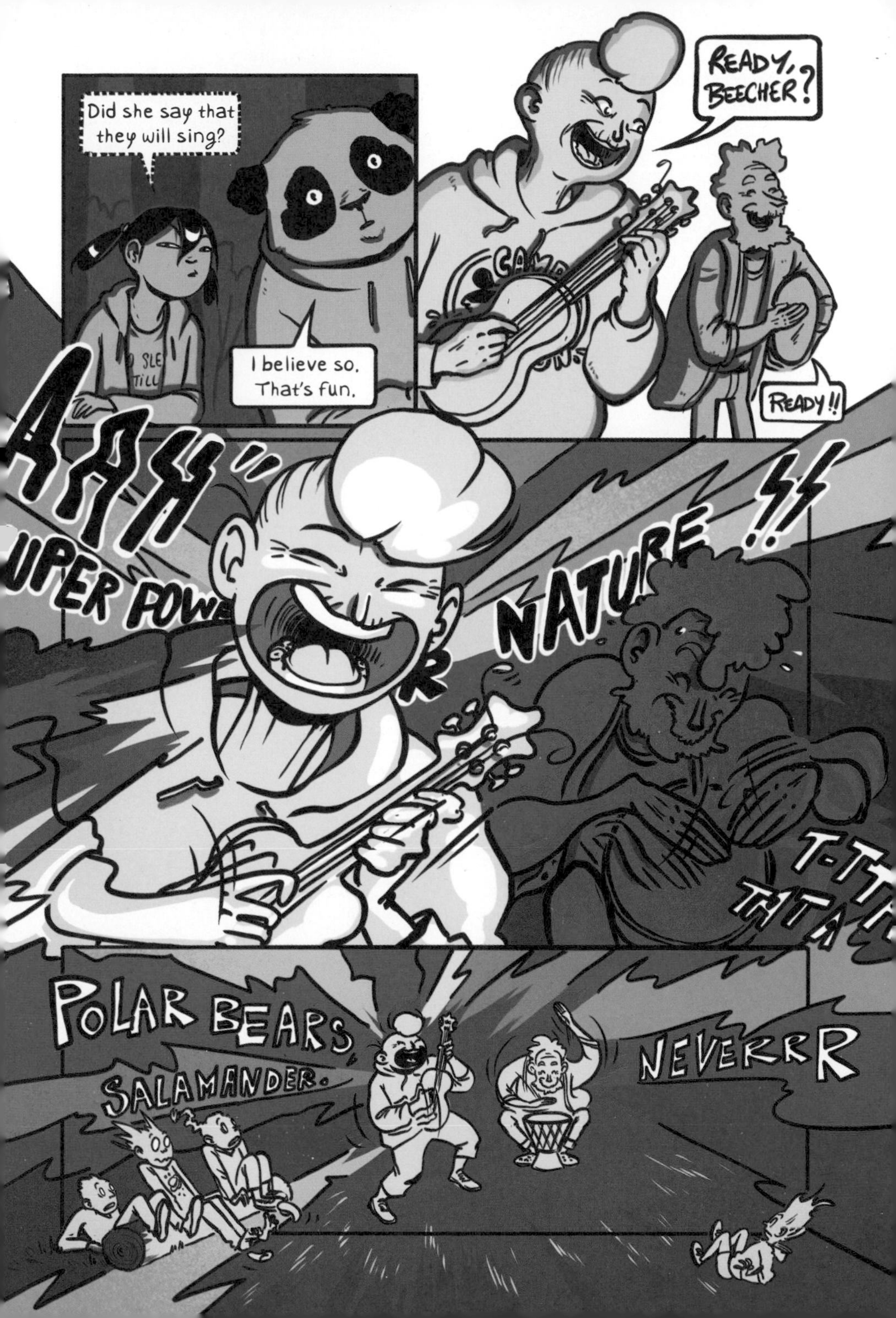
Did she say that they will sing?
I believe so. That's fun.
READY, BEECHER?
READY!!
AAAH"
UPER POWE
R
NATURE!!
T-TT
TATA
POLAR BEARS,
SALAMANDER.
NEVERRR

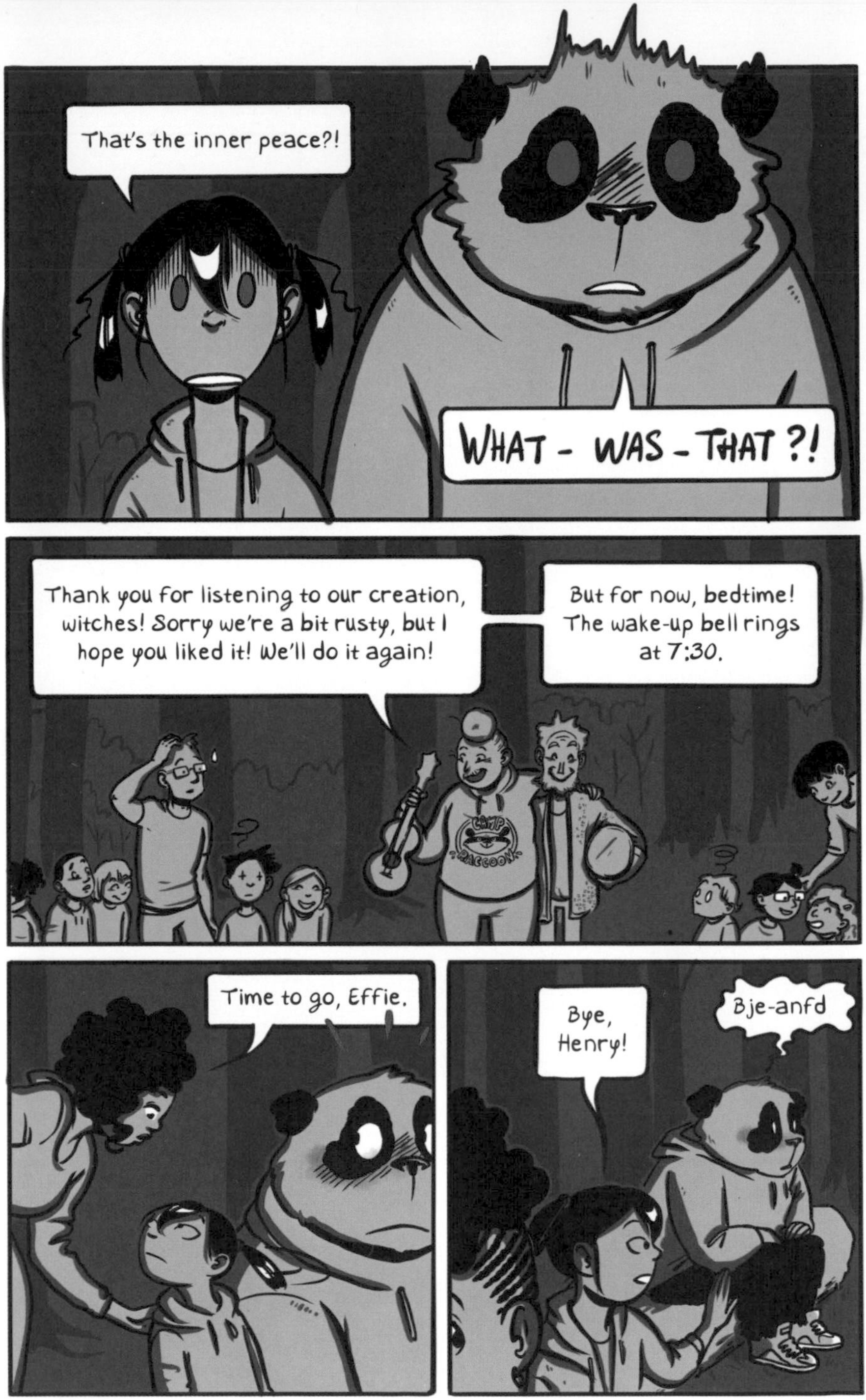
That's the inner peace?!
WHAT - WAS - THAT ?!
Thank you for listening to our creation, witches! Sorry we're a bit rusty, but I hope you liked it! We'll do it again!
But for now, bedtime! The wake-up bell rings at 7:30.
CAMP RACCOON
Time to go, Effie.
Bye, Henry!
Bje-anfd

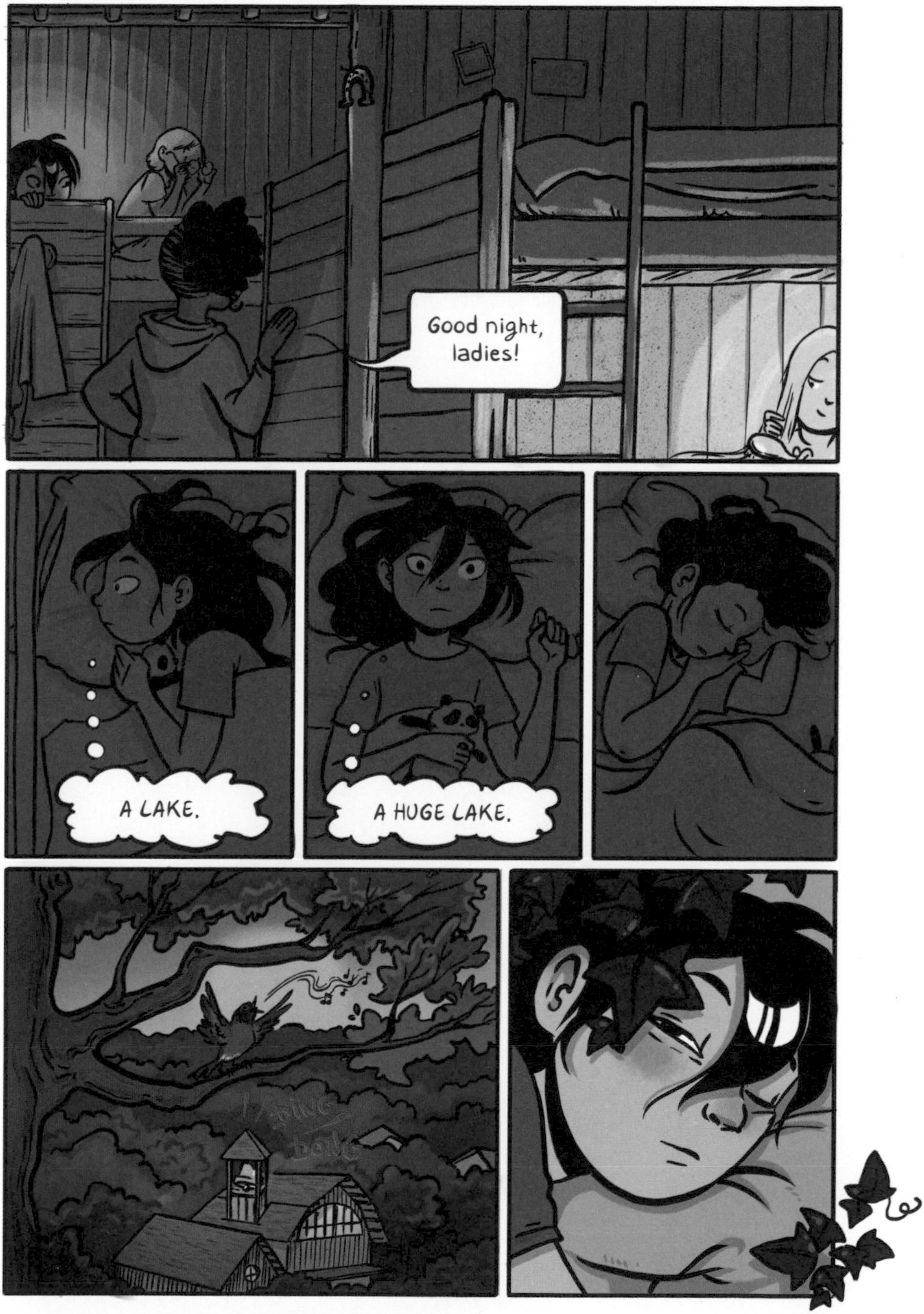

Good night, ladies!
A LAKE.
A HUGE LAKE.
DING
DONG

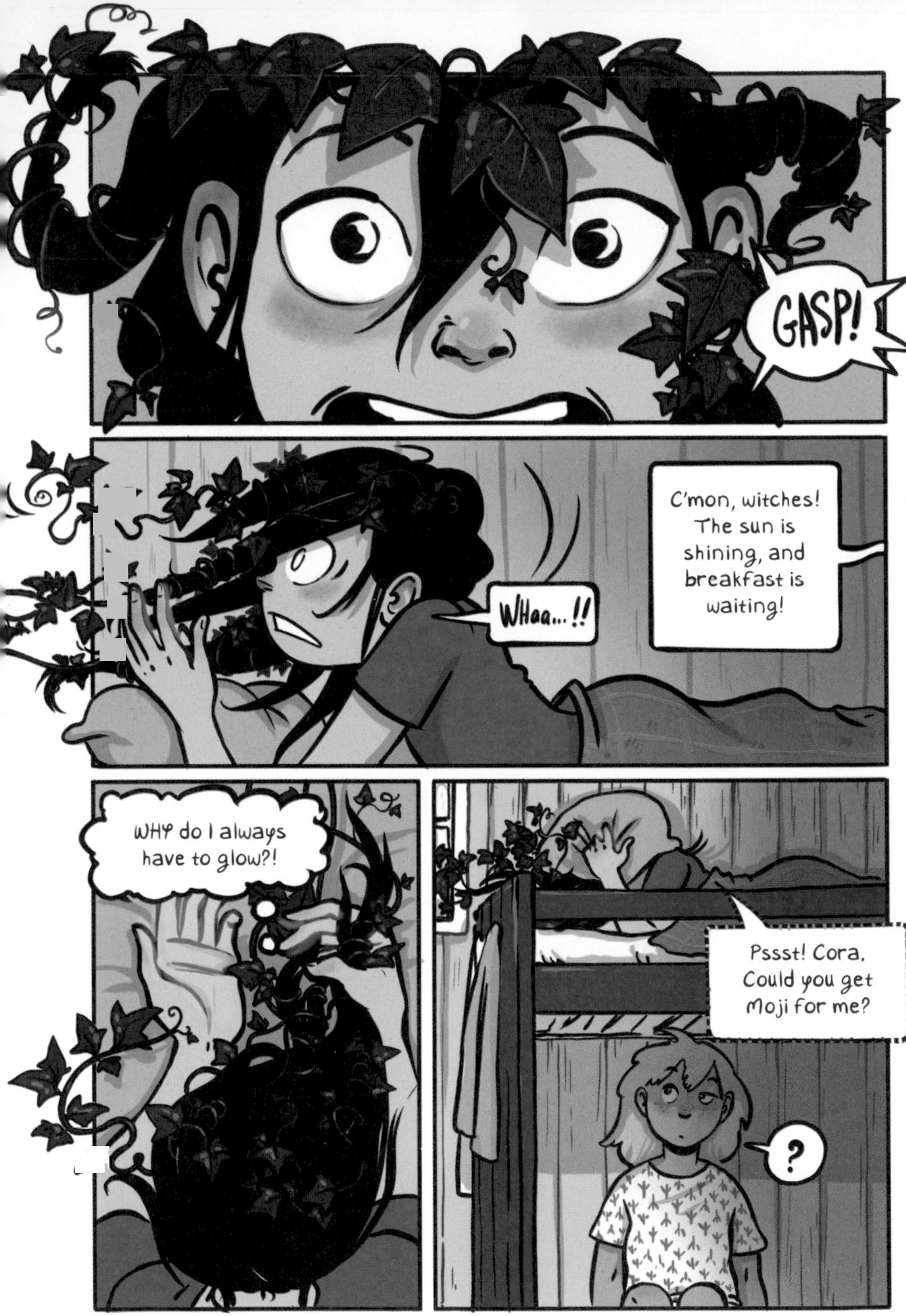
GASP!
WHaa...!!
C'mon, witches! The sun is shining, and breakfast is waiting!
WHY do I always have to glow?!
Pssst! Cora. Could you get Moji for me?
?

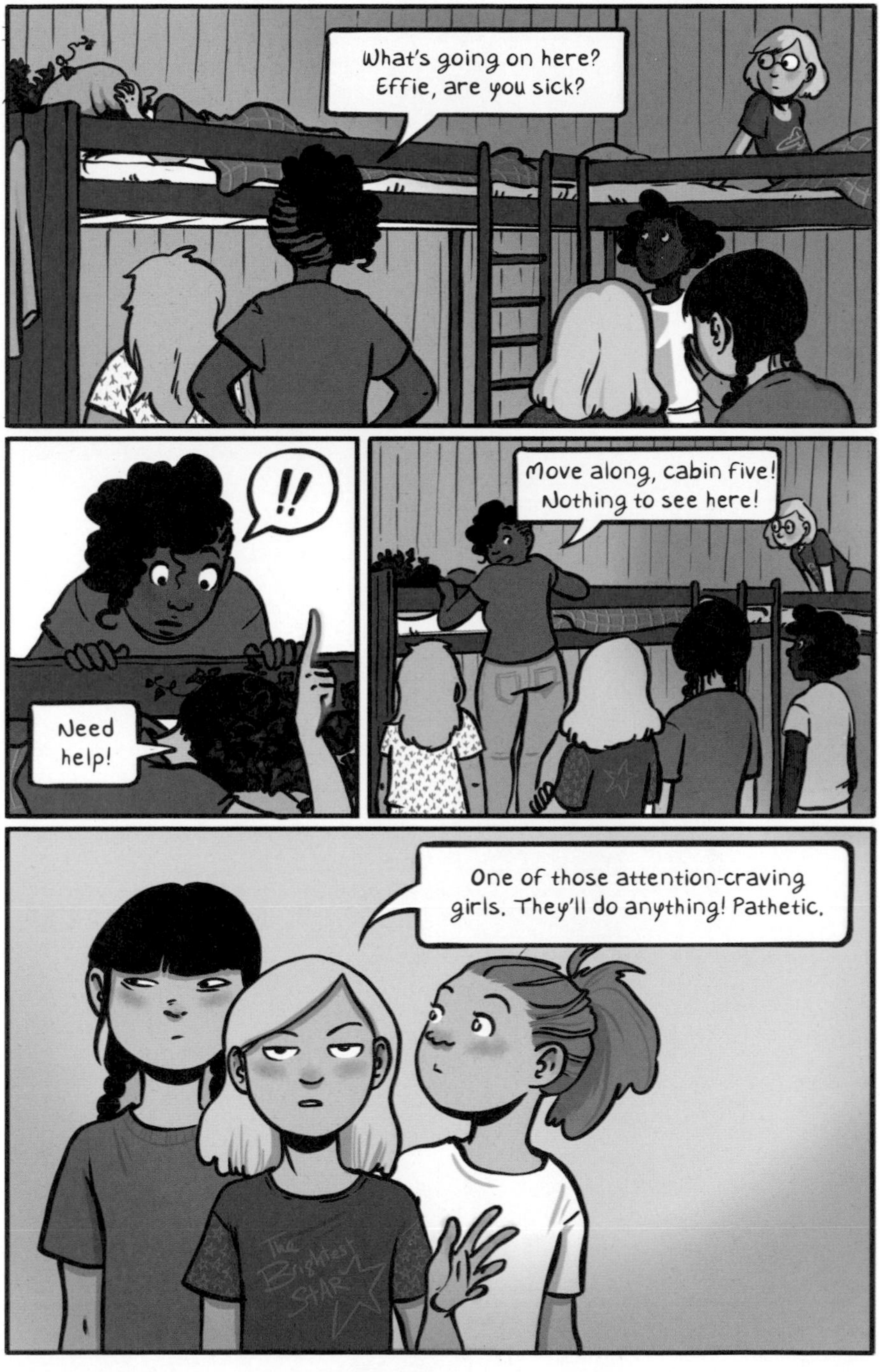
What's going on here? Effie, are you sick?
!!
Need help!
Move along, cabin five! Nothing to see here!
One of those attention-craving girls. They'll do anything! Pathetic.
The Brightest Star

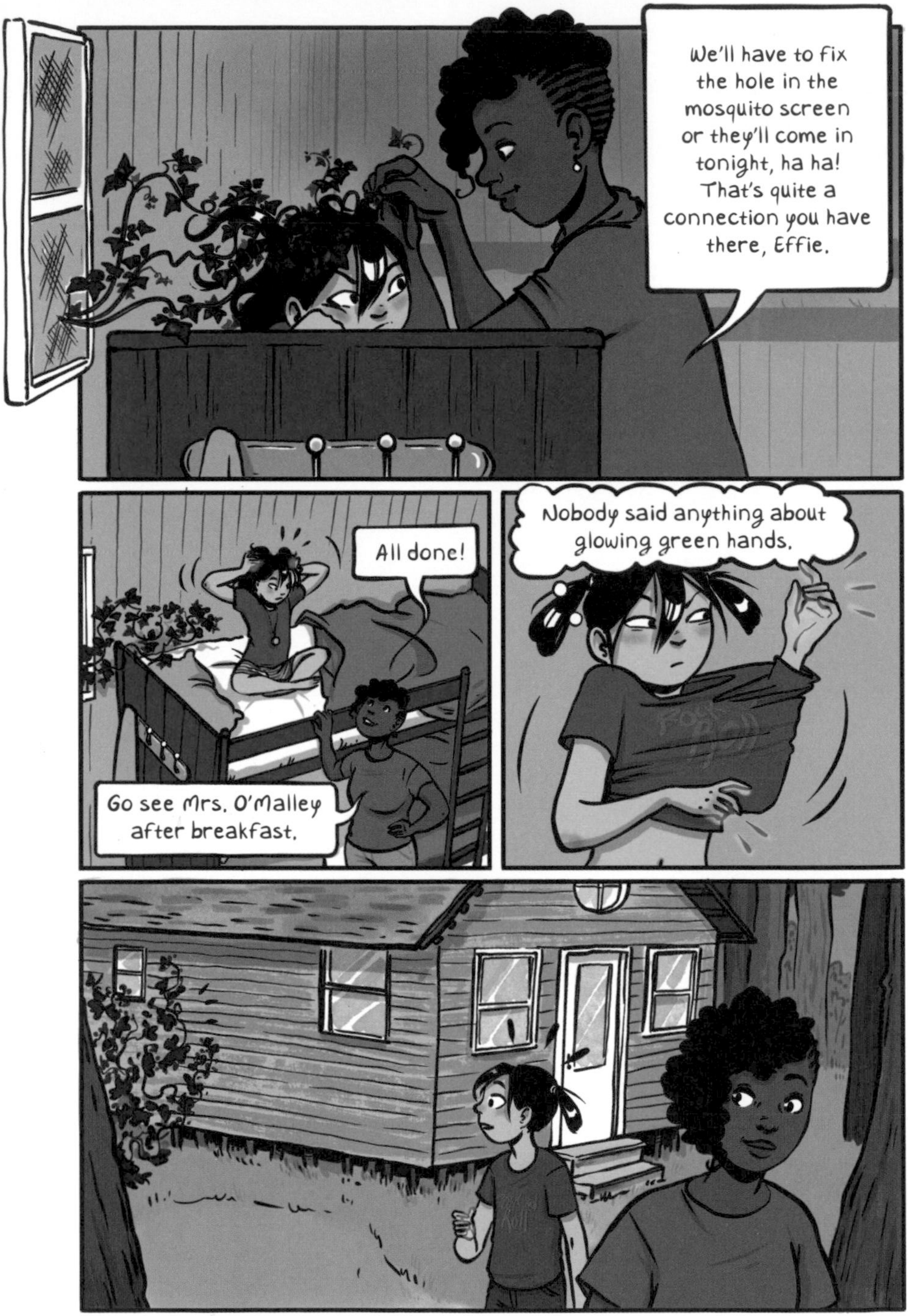

We'll have to fix the hole in the mosquito screen or they'll come in tonight, ha ha! That's quite a connection you have there, Effie.
All done!
Go see Mrs. O'Malley after breakfast.
Nobody said anything about glowing green hands.

Effie!!

SCOOT

Thank you.

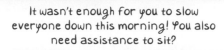

It wasn't enough for you to slow everyone down this morning! You also need assistance to sit?

!

Nice to meet you too!

Ooooh!! So pretty.

Your hands look incredible!! Mine looked nothing like that when I discovered my green thumb.

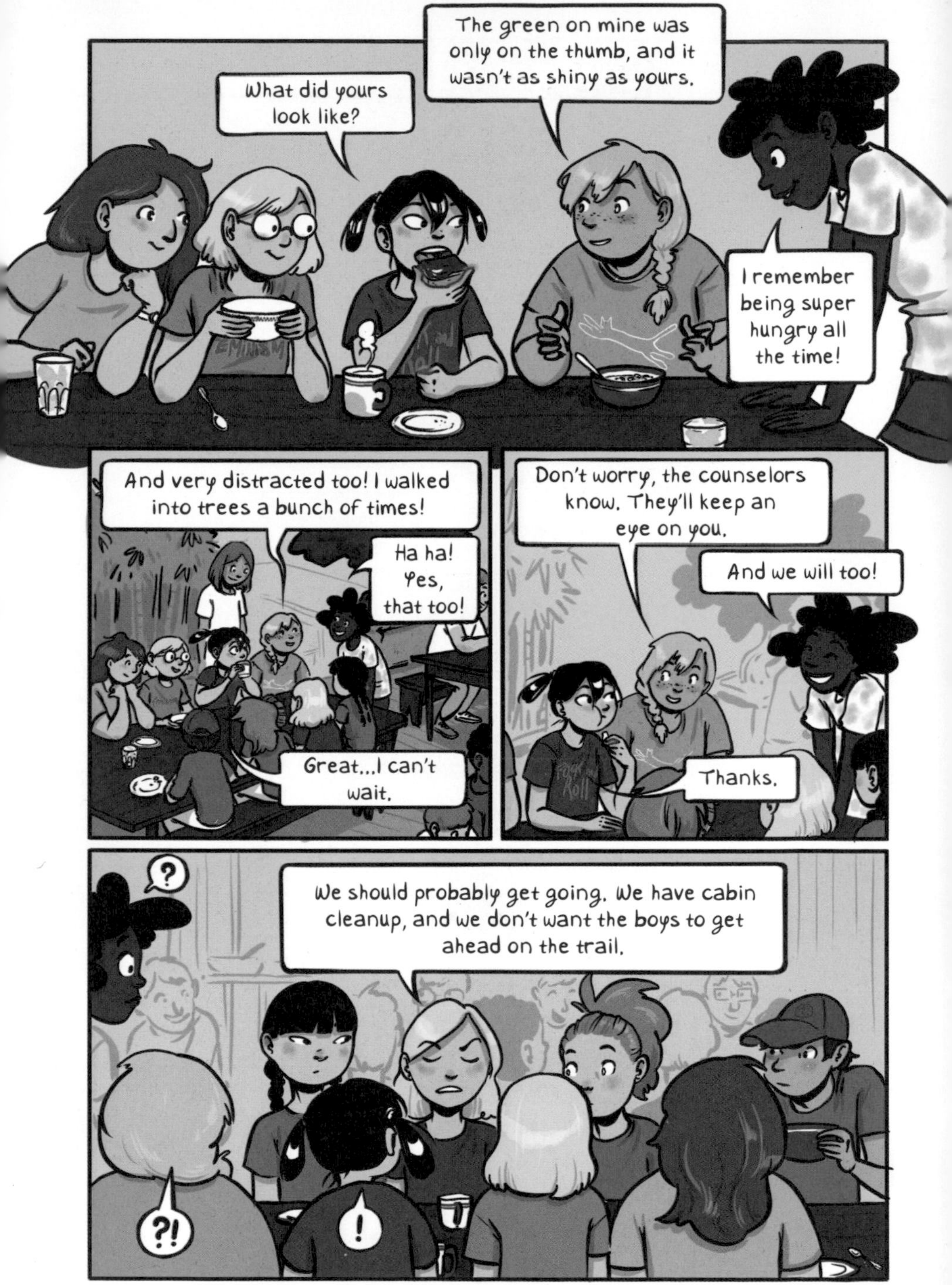
What did yours look like?
The green on mine was only on the thumb, and it wasn't as shiny as yours.
I remember being super hungry all the time!
And very distracted too! I walked into trees a bunch of times!
Ha ha! Yes, that too!
Great...I can't wait.
Don't worry, the counselors know. They'll keep an eye on you.
And we will too!
Thanks.
?
We should probably get going. We have cabin cleanup, and we don't want the boys to get ahead on the trail.
?!
!

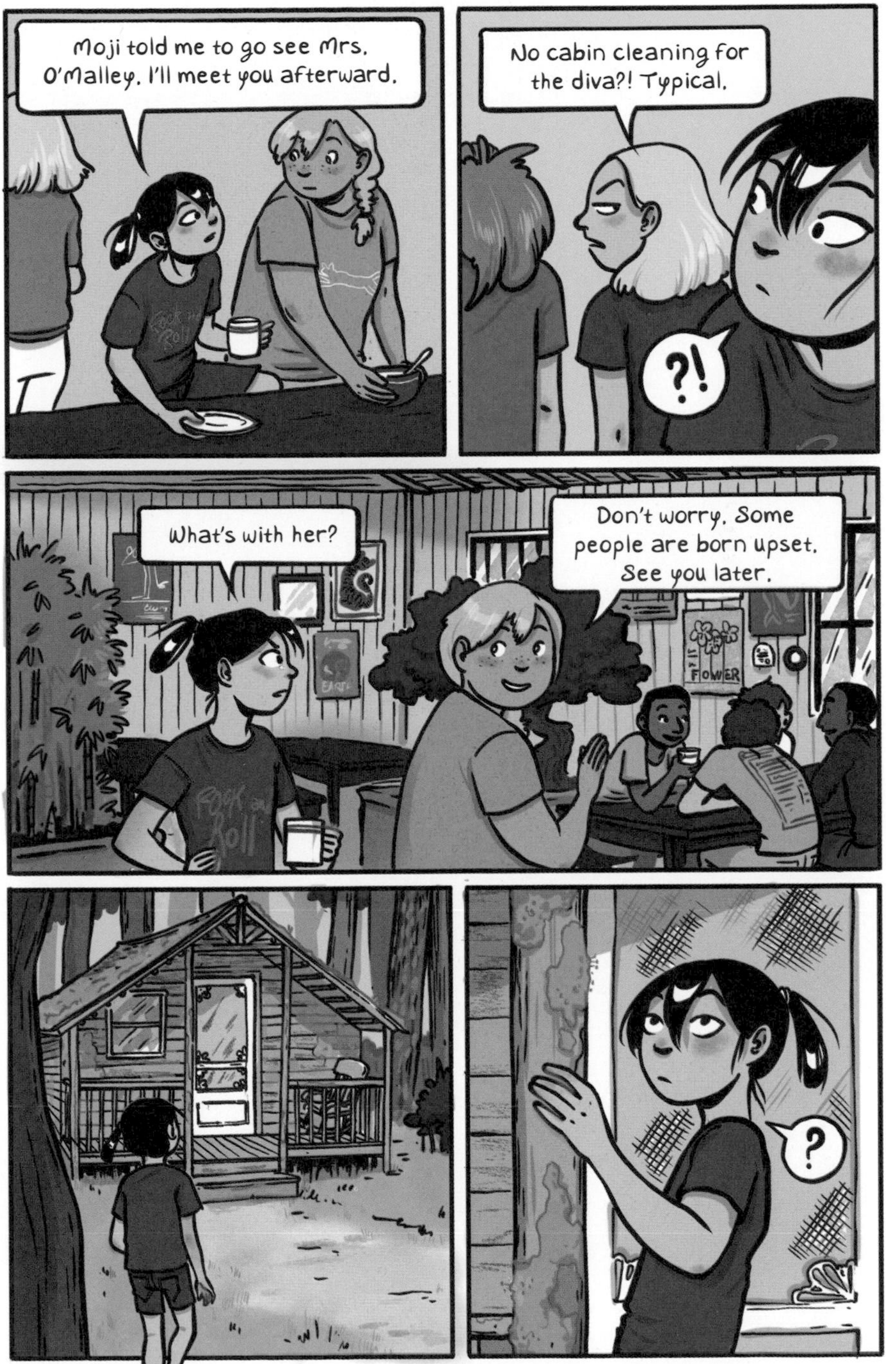
Moji told me to go see Mrs. O'Malley. I'll meet you afterward.
No cabin cleaning for the diva?! Typical.
?!
What's with her?
Don't worry. Some people are born upset. See you later.
FLOWER
?

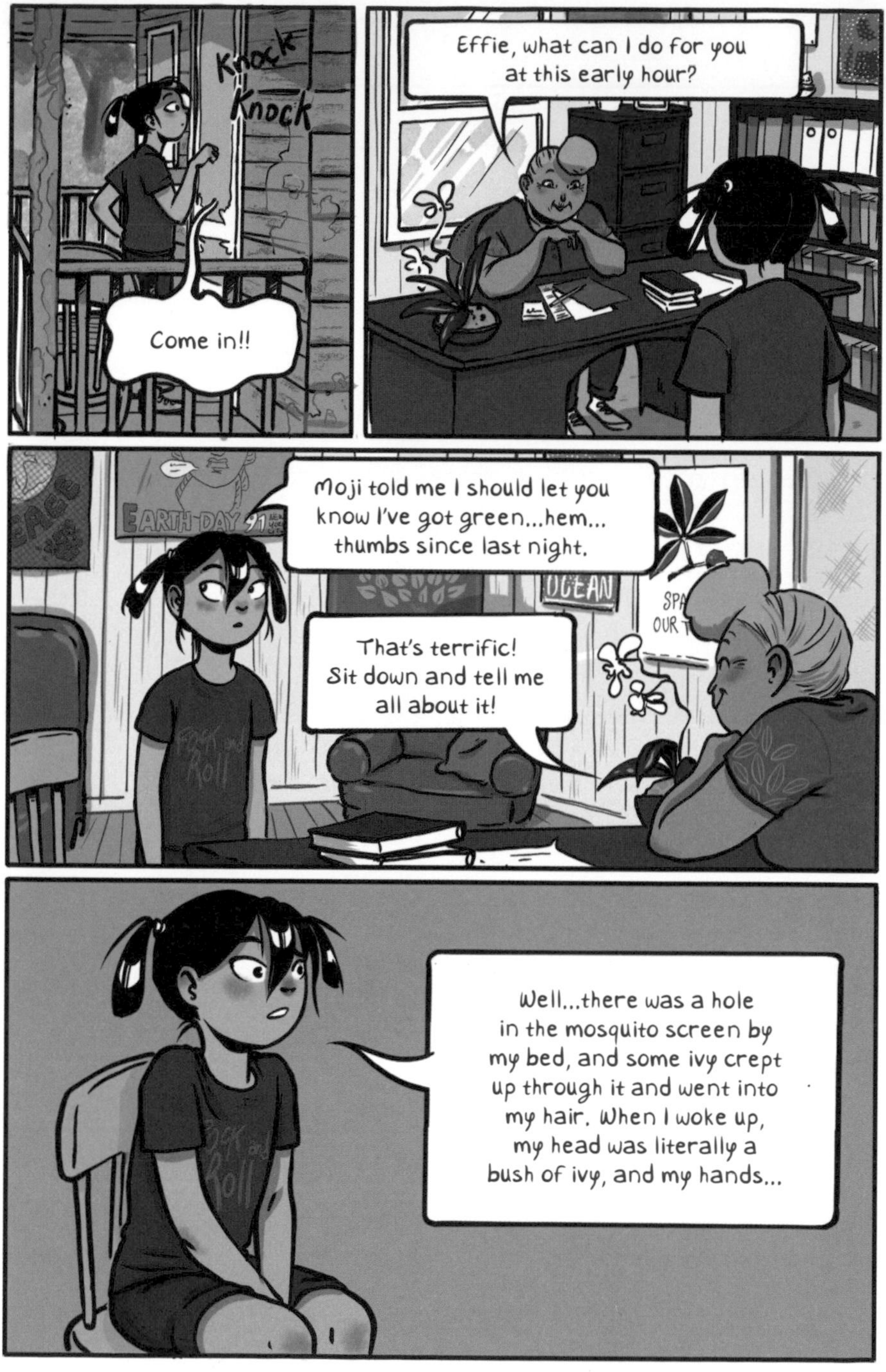
Knock
Knock
Come in!!
Effie, what can I do for you at this early hour?
EARTH DAY 91
OCEAN
Moji told me I should let you know I've got green...hem... thumbs since last night.
That's terrific! Sit down and tell me all about it!
Rock and Roll
Well...there was a hole in the mosquito screen by my bed, and some ivy crept up through it and went into my hair. When I woke up, my head was literally a bush of ivy, and my hands...

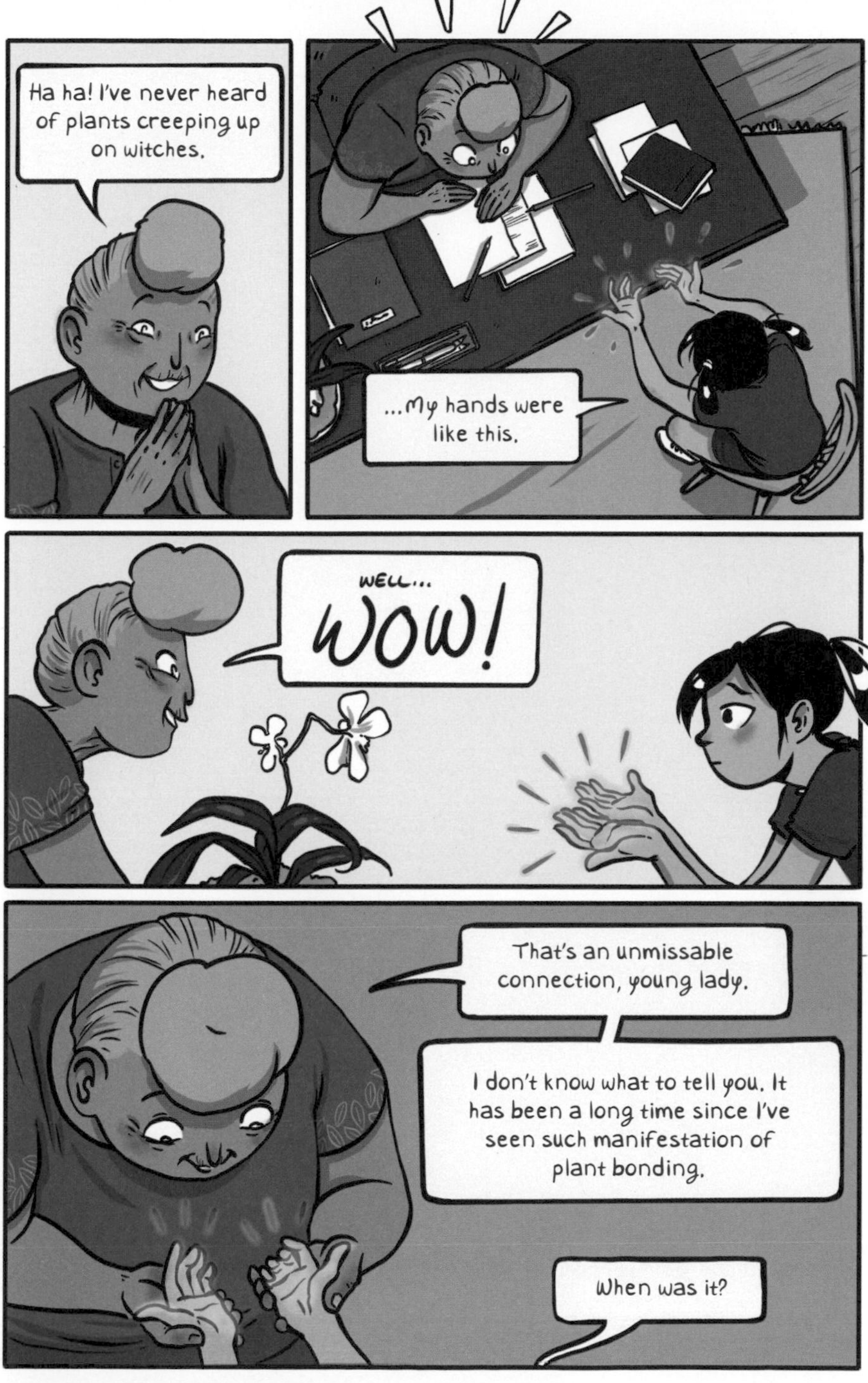
Ha ha! I've never heard of plants creeping up on witches.
...My hands were like this.
WELL...
WOW!
That's an unmissable connection, young lady.
I don't know what to tell you. It has been a long time since I've seen such manifestation of plant bonding.
When was it?

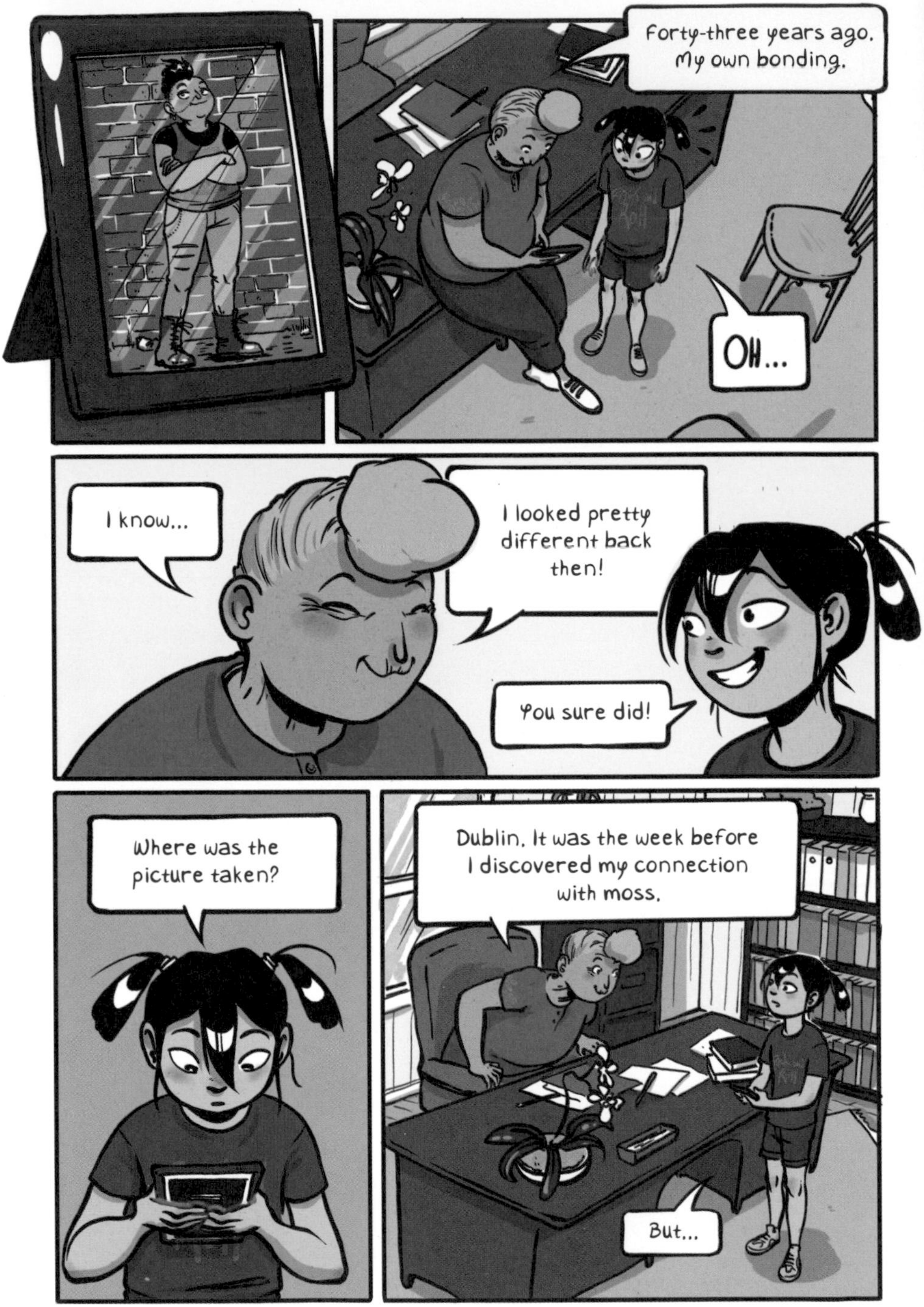
Forty-three years ago. My own bonding.
OH...
I know...
I looked pretty different back then!
You sure did!
Where was the picture taken?
Dublin. It was the week before I discovered my connection with moss.
But...

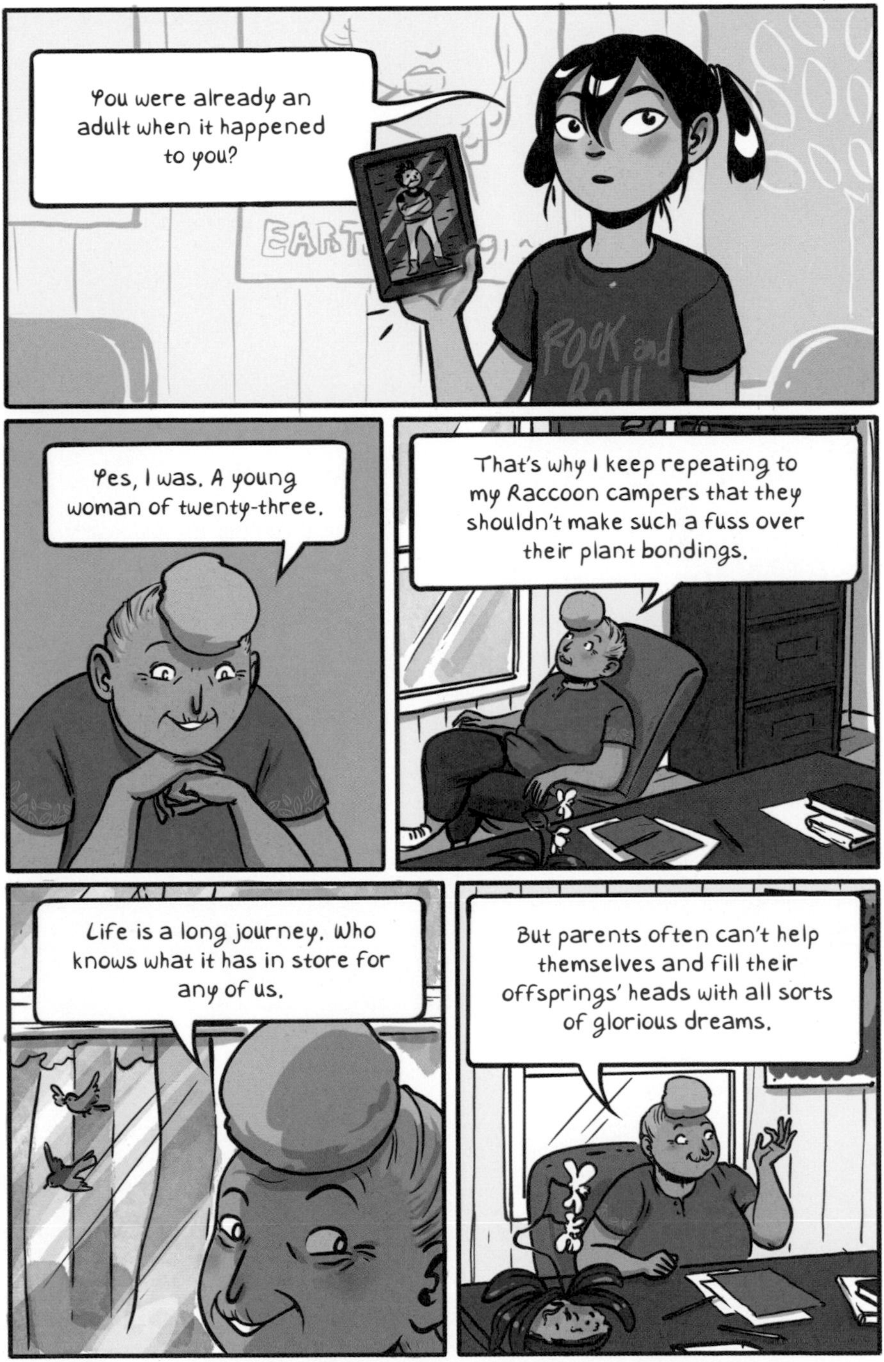
You were already an adult when it happened to you?
EARTH
ROCK and Roll
Yes, I was. A young woman of twenty-three.
That's why I keep repeating to my Raccoon campers that they shouldn't make such a fuss over their plant bondings.
Life is a long journey. Who knows what it has in store for any of us.
But parents often can't help themselves and fill their offsprings' heads with all sorts of glorious dreams.

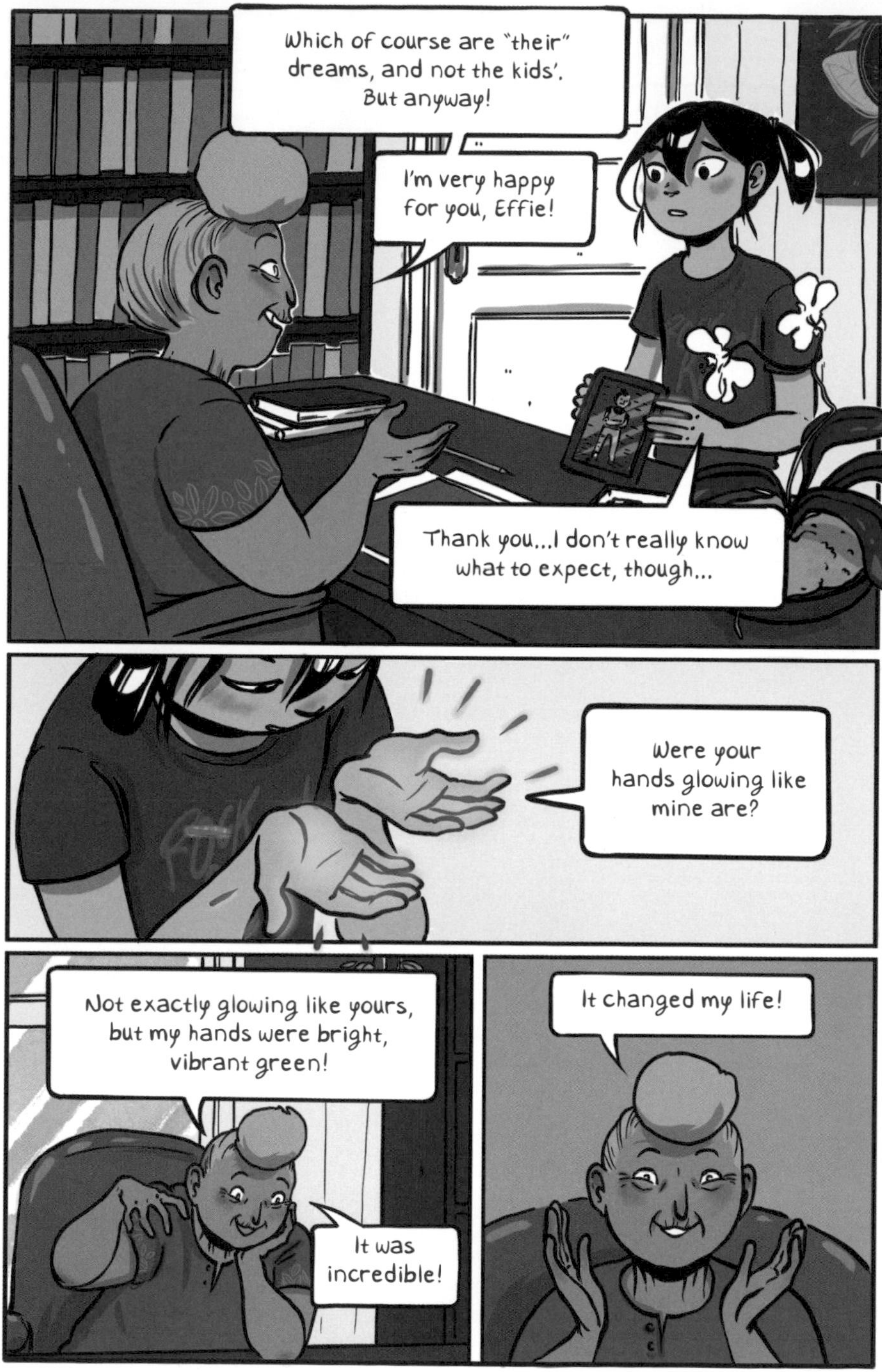
Which of course are "their" dreams, and not the kids'. But anyway!
I'm very happy for you, Effie!
Thank you...I don't really know what to expect, though...
Were your hands glowing like mine are?
Not exactly glowing like yours, but my hands were bright, vibrant green!
It was incredible!
It changed my life!

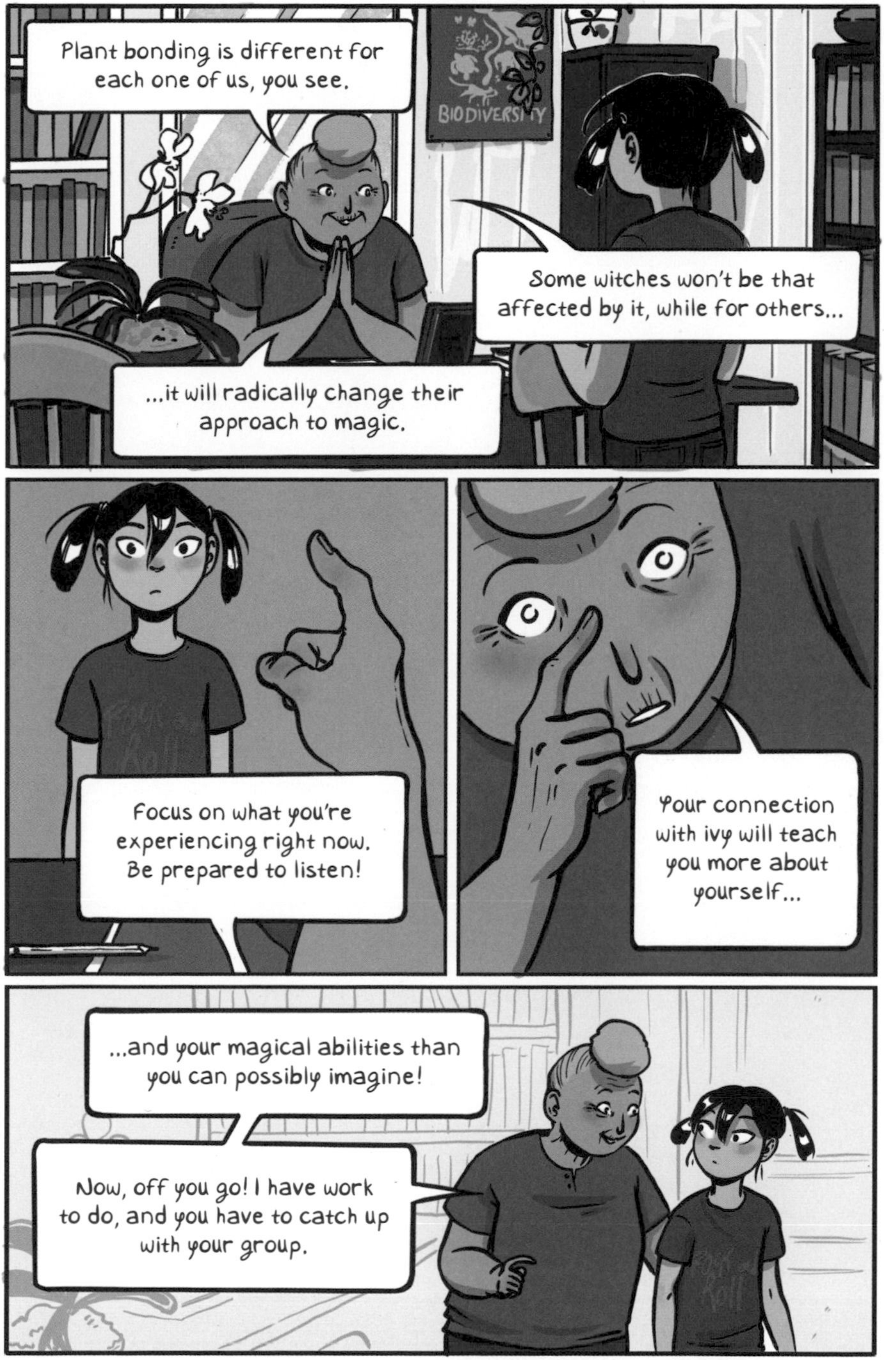
Plant bonding is different for each one of us, you see.
BIODIVERSITY
Some witches won't be that affected by it, while for others...
...it will radically change their approach to magic.
Focus on what you're experiencing right now. Be prepared to listen!
Your connection with ivy will teach you more about yourself...
...and your magical abilities than you can possibly imagine!
Now, off you go! I have work to do, and you have to catch up with your group.

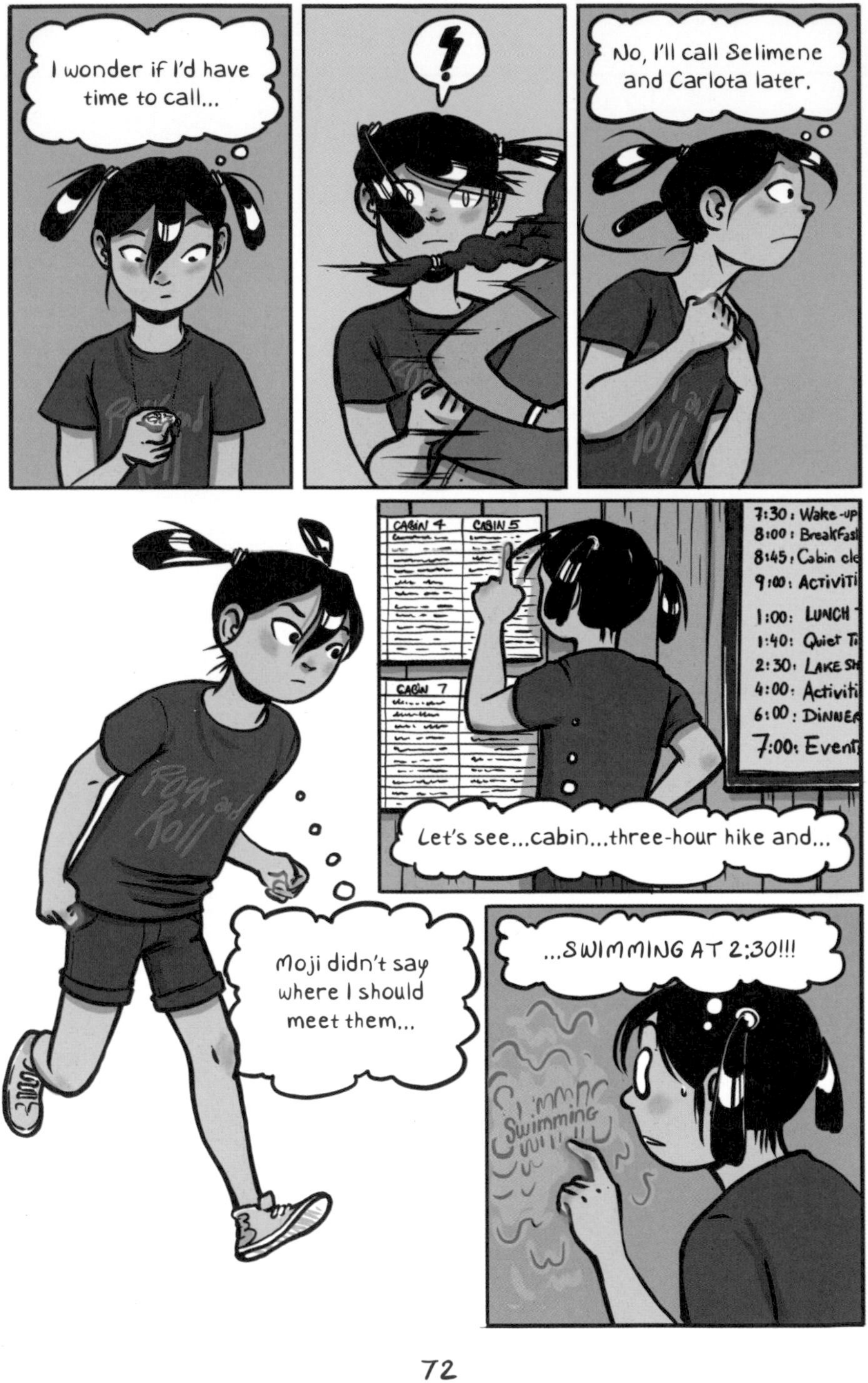
I wonder if I'd have time to call...
!
No, I'll call Selimene and Carlota later.
CABIN 4
CABIN 5
CABIN 7
7:30: Wake-up
8:00: Breakfast
8:45: Cabin cle
9:00: ACTIVITI
1:00: LUNCH
1:40: Quiet Ti
2:30: LAKE SH
4:00: Activiti
6:00: DINNER
7:00: Event
Let's see...cabin...three-hour hike and...
Moji didn't say where I should meet them...
...SWIMMING AT 2:30!!!
Swimming

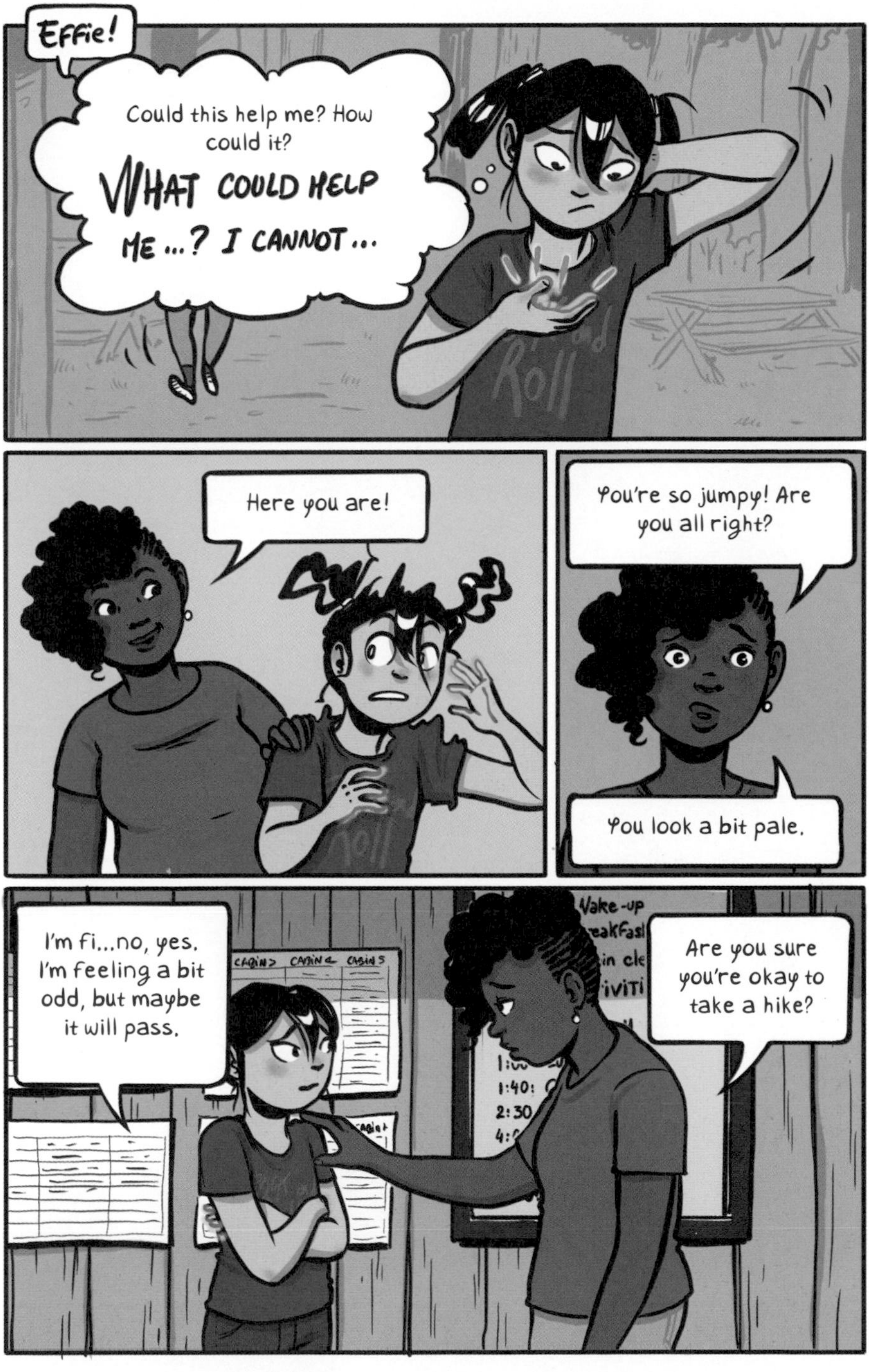
Effie!
Could this help me? How could it?
WHAT COULD HELP ME...? I CANNOT...
Here you are!
You're so jumpy! Are you all right?
You look a bit pale.
I'm fi...no, yes. I'm feeling a bit odd, but maybe it will pass.
Are you sure you're okay to take a hike?

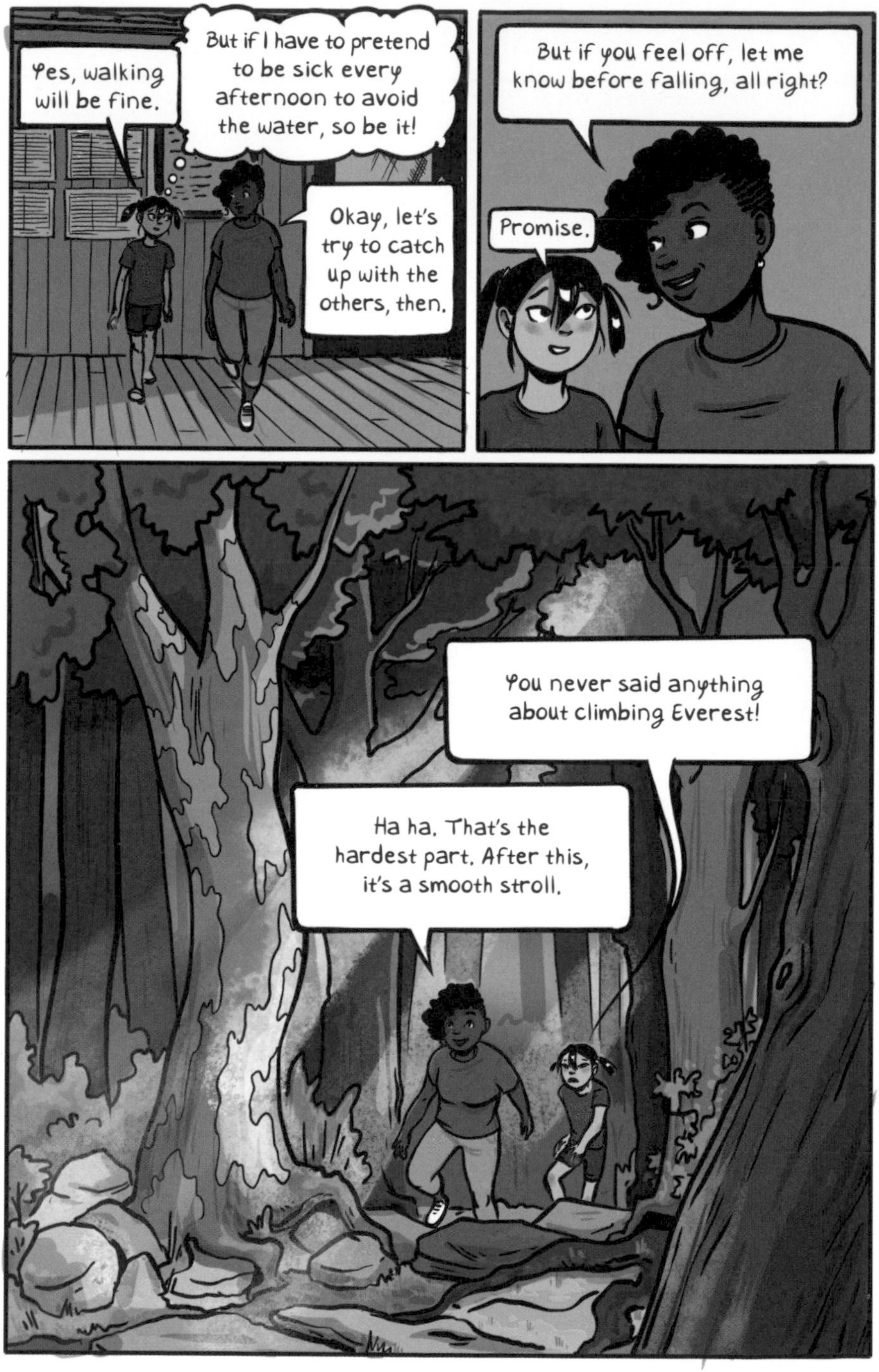
Yes, walking will be fine.
But if I have to pretend to be sick every afternoon to avoid the water, so be it!
Okay, let's try to catch up with the others, then.
But if you feel off, let me know before falling, all right?
Promise.
You never said anything about climbing Everest!
Ha ha. That's the hardest part. After this, it's a smooth stroll.

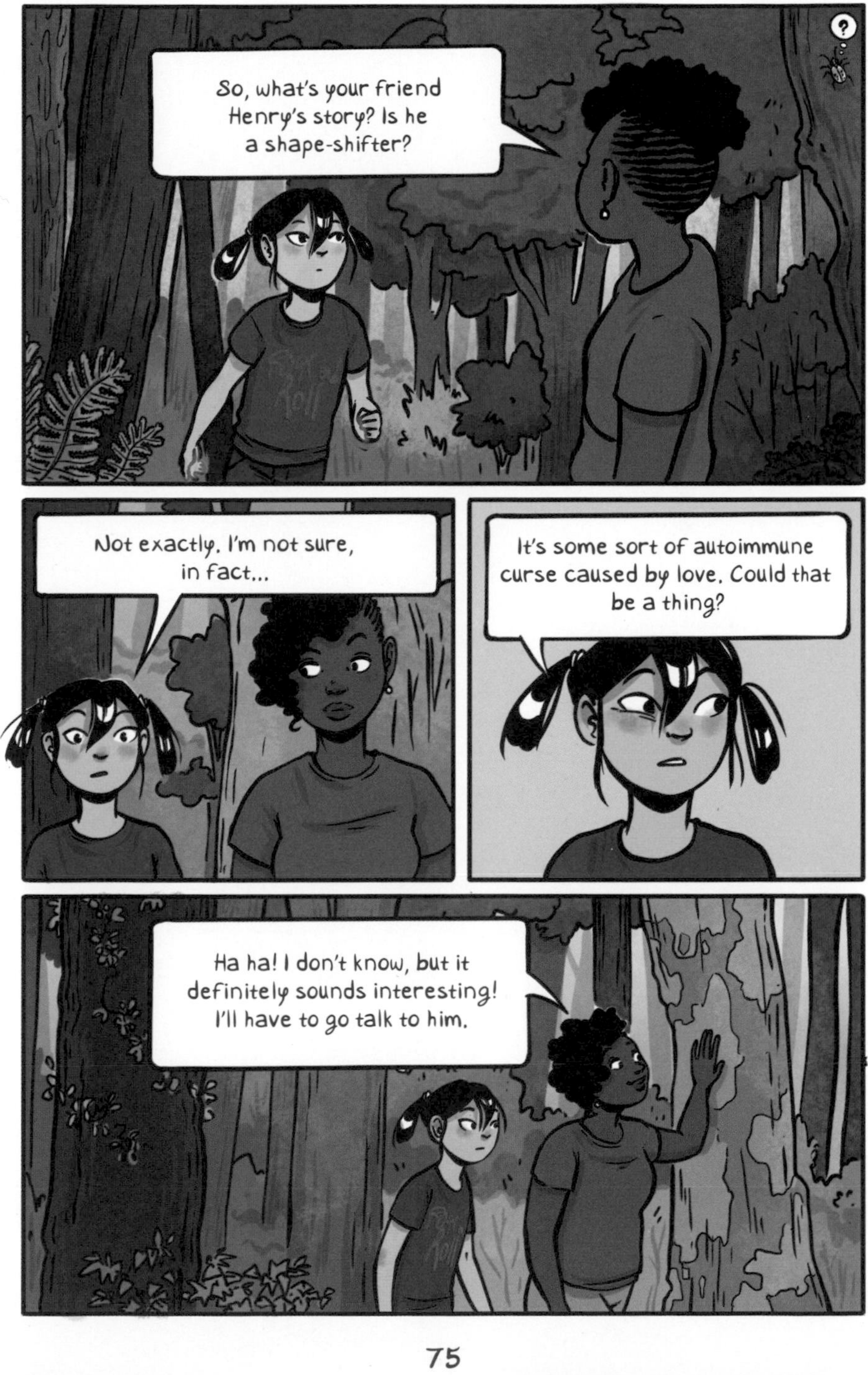
?
So, what's your friend Henry's story? Is he a shape-shifter?
Not exactly. I'm not sure, in fact...
It's some sort of autoimmune curse caused by love. Could that be a thing?
Ha ha! I don't know, but it definitely sounds interesting! I'll have to go talk to him.

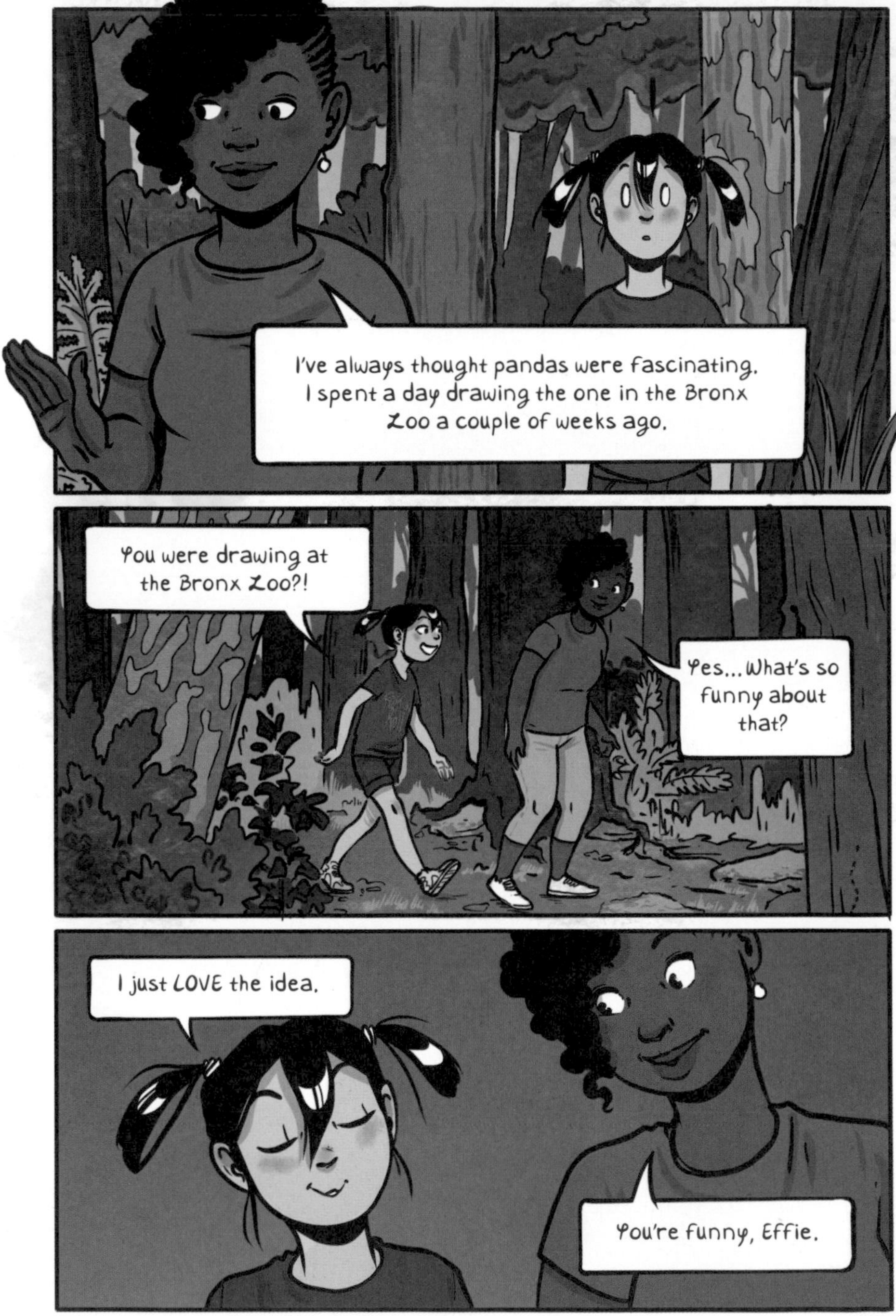
I've always thought pandas were fascinating. I spent a day drawing the one in the Bronx Zoo a couple of weeks ago.
You were drawing at the Bronx Zoo?!
Yes... What's so funny about that?
I just LOVE the idea.
You're funny, Effie.

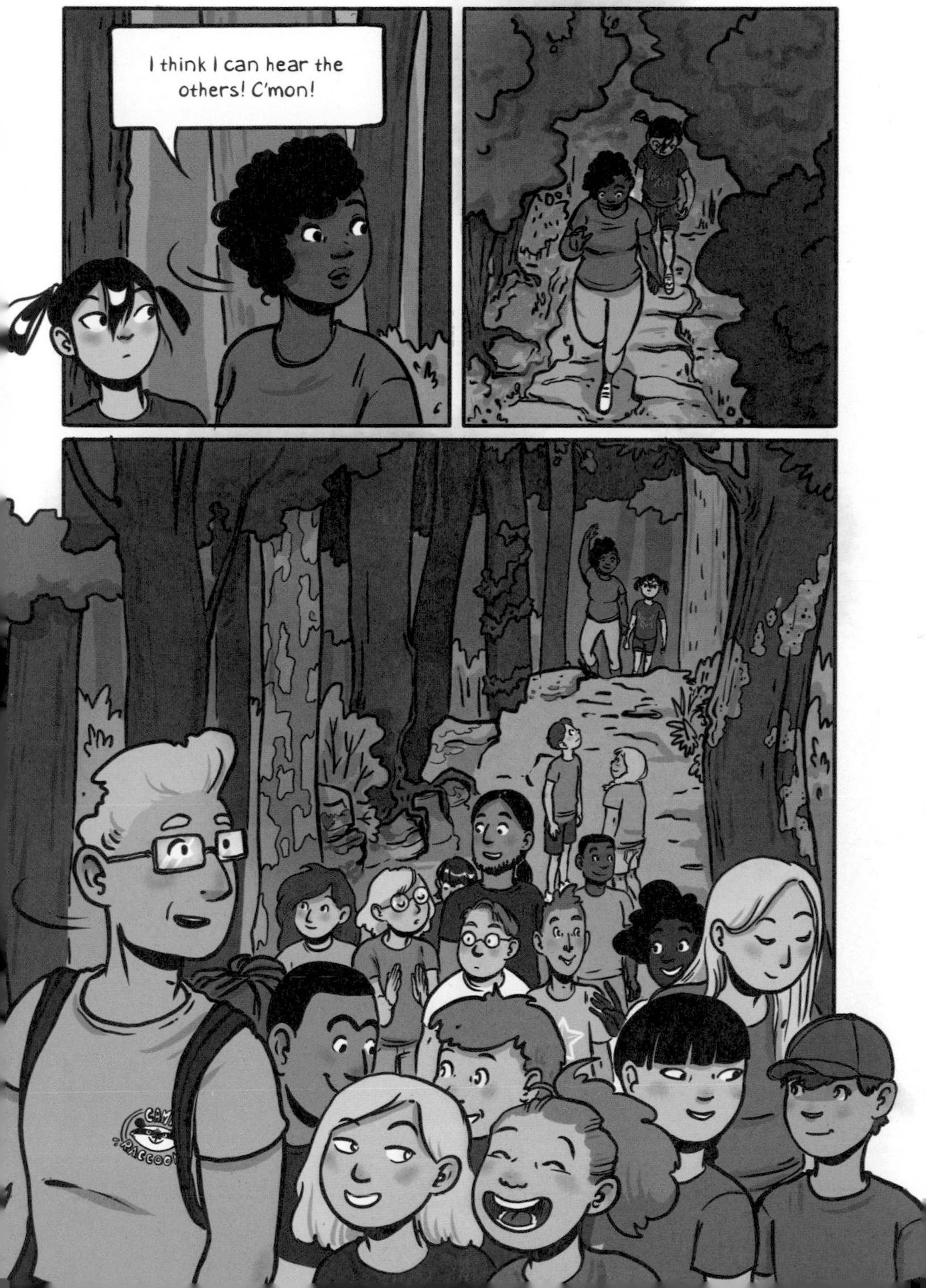
I think I can hear the others! C'mon!

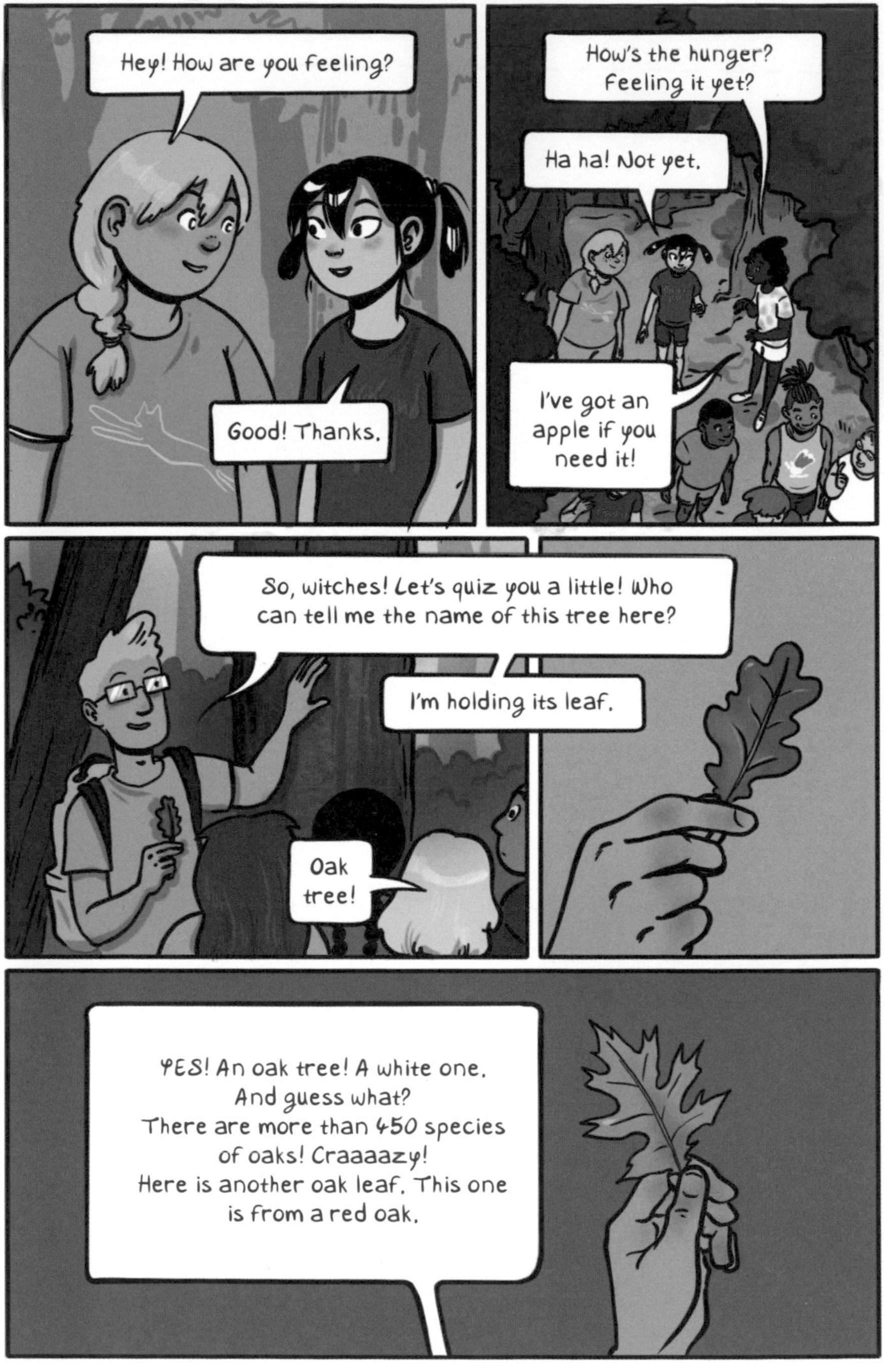
Hey! How are you feeling?
Good! Thanks.
How's the hunger? Feeling it yet?
Ha ha! Not yet.
I've got an apple if you need it!
So, witches! Let's quiz you a little! Who can tell me the name of this tree here?
I'm holding its leaf.
Oak tree!
YES! An oak tree! A white one. And guess what? There are more than 450 species of oaks! Craaaazy! Here is another oak leaf. This one is from a red oak.

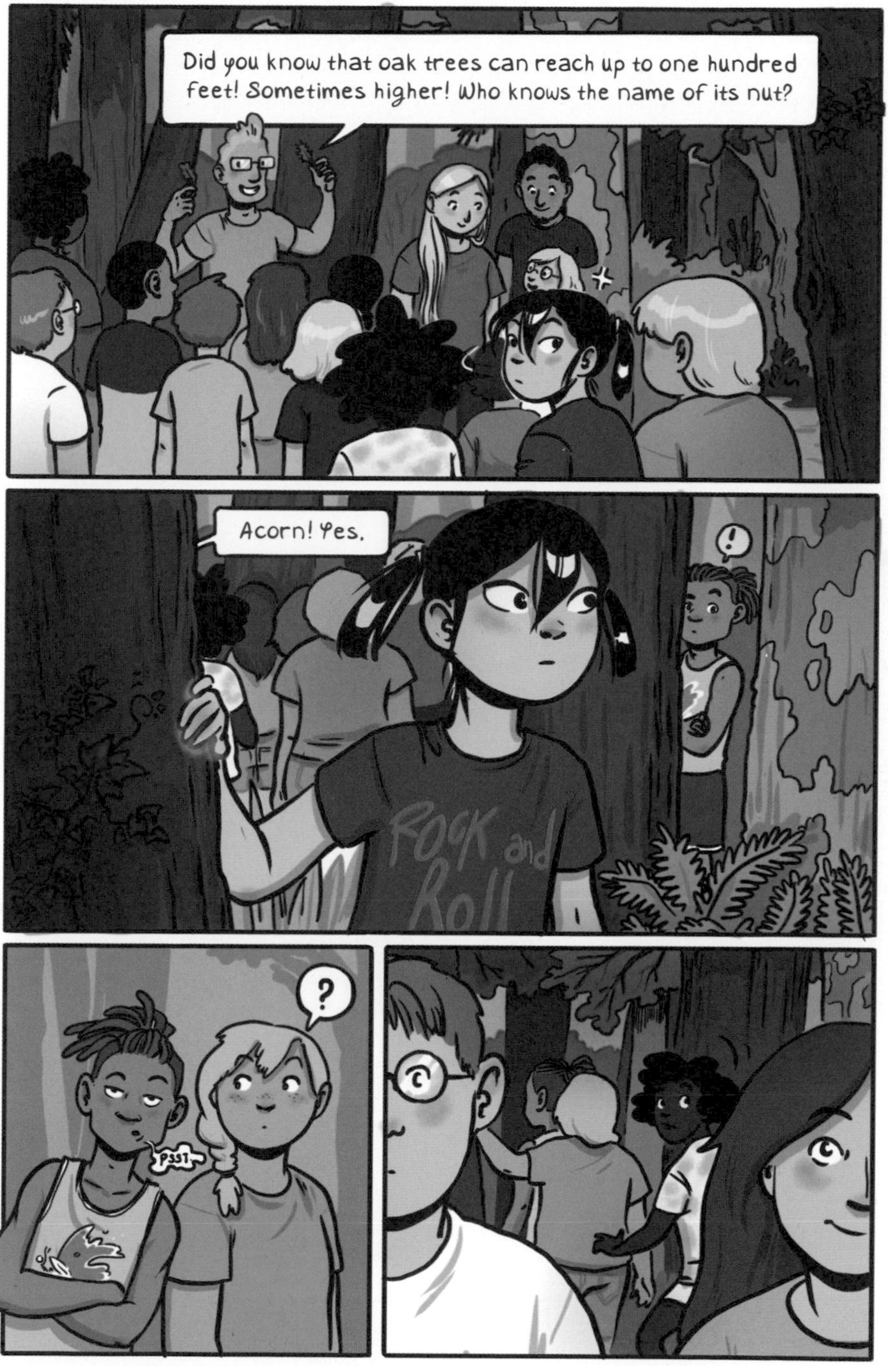
Did you know that oak trees can reach up to one hundred feet! Sometimes higher! Who knows the name of its nut?
Acorn! Yes.
!
?
PSST

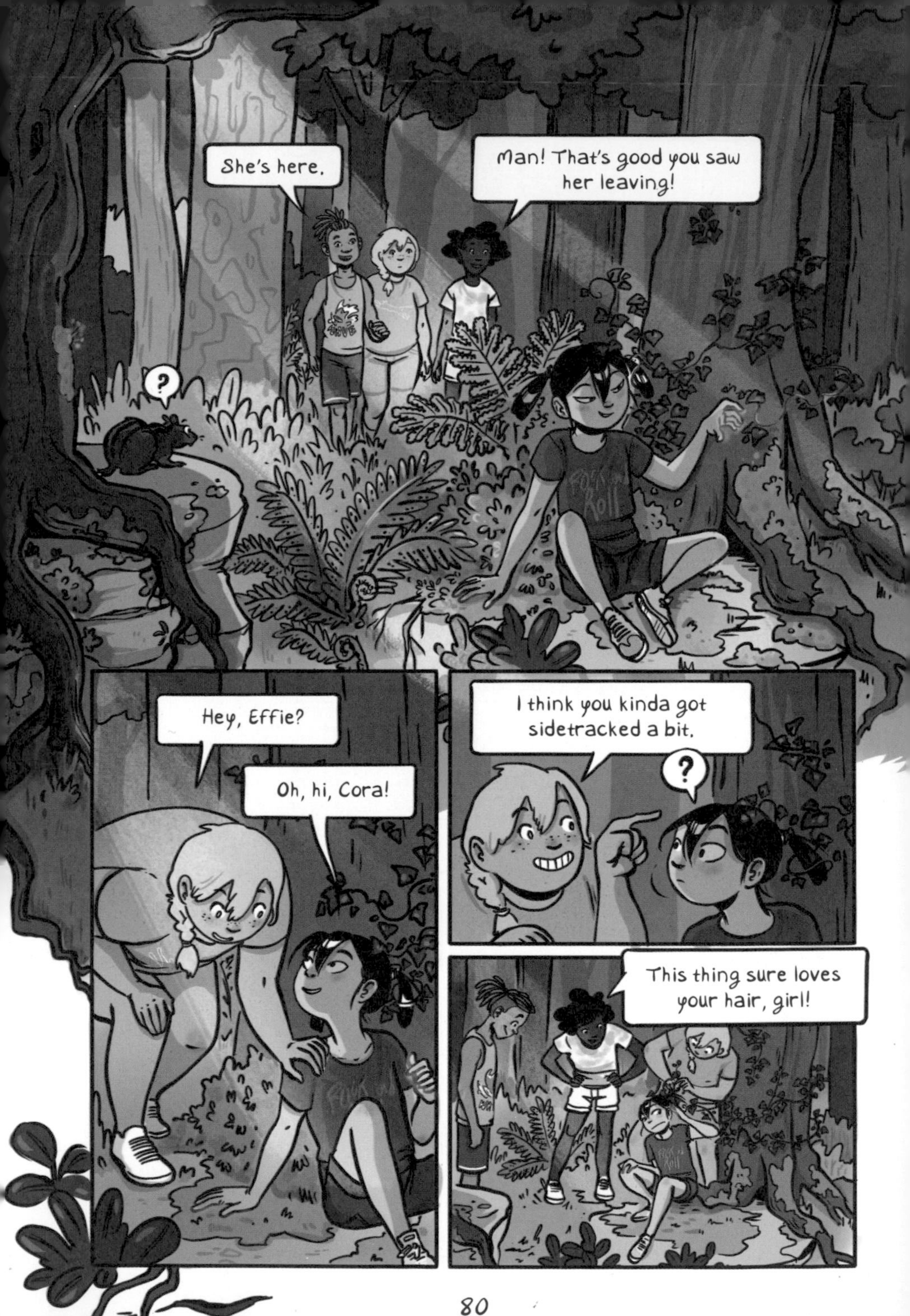
She's here.
Man! That's good you saw her leaving!
?
Hey, Effie?
Oh, hi, Cora!
I think you kinda got sidetracked a bit.
?
This thing sure loves your hair, girl!

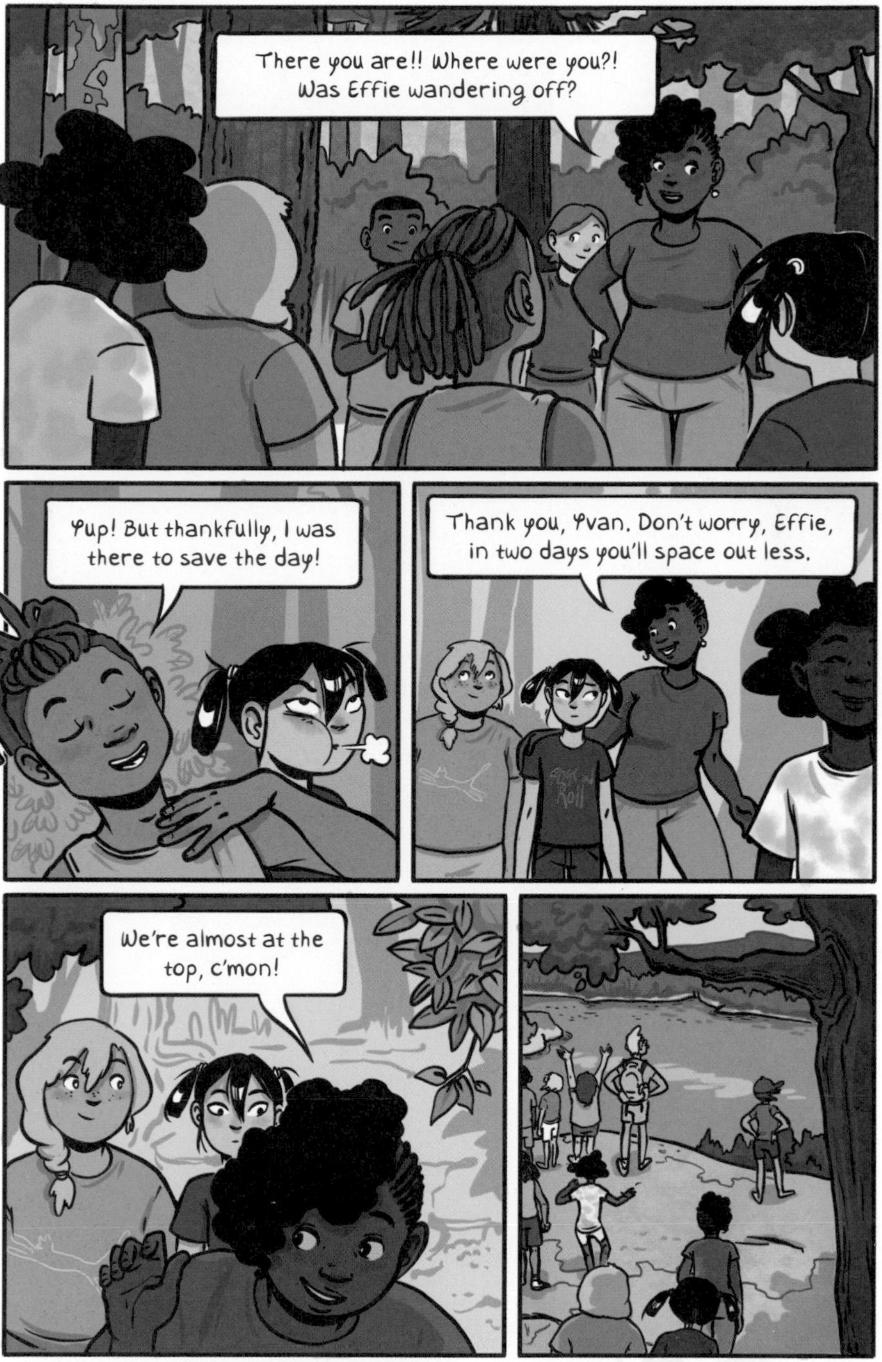
There you are!! Where were you?! Was Effie wandering off?
Yup! But thankfully, I was there to save the day!
Thank you, Yvan. Don't worry, Effie, in two days you'll space out less.
We're almost at the top, c'mon!

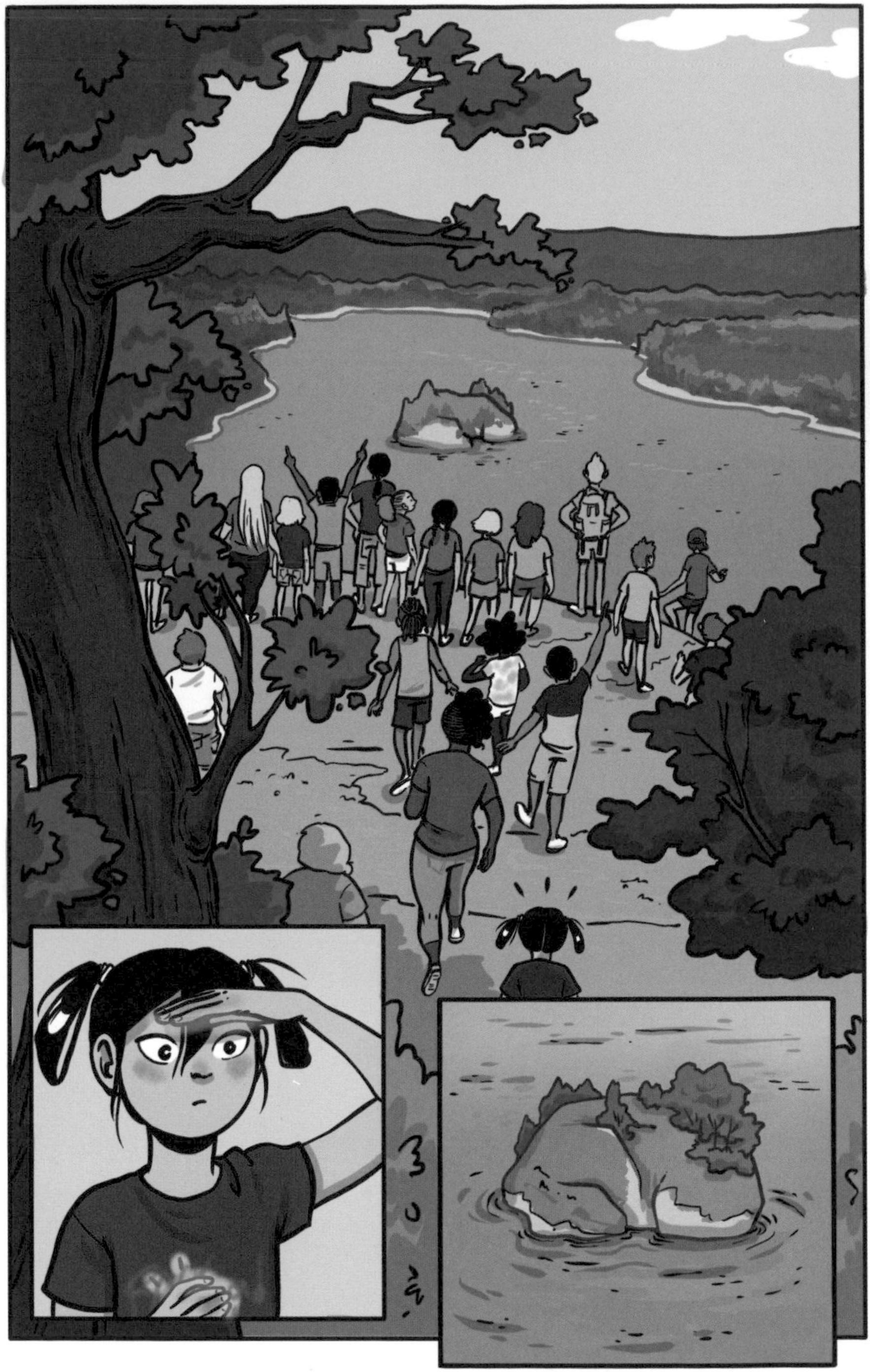

Chapter 3

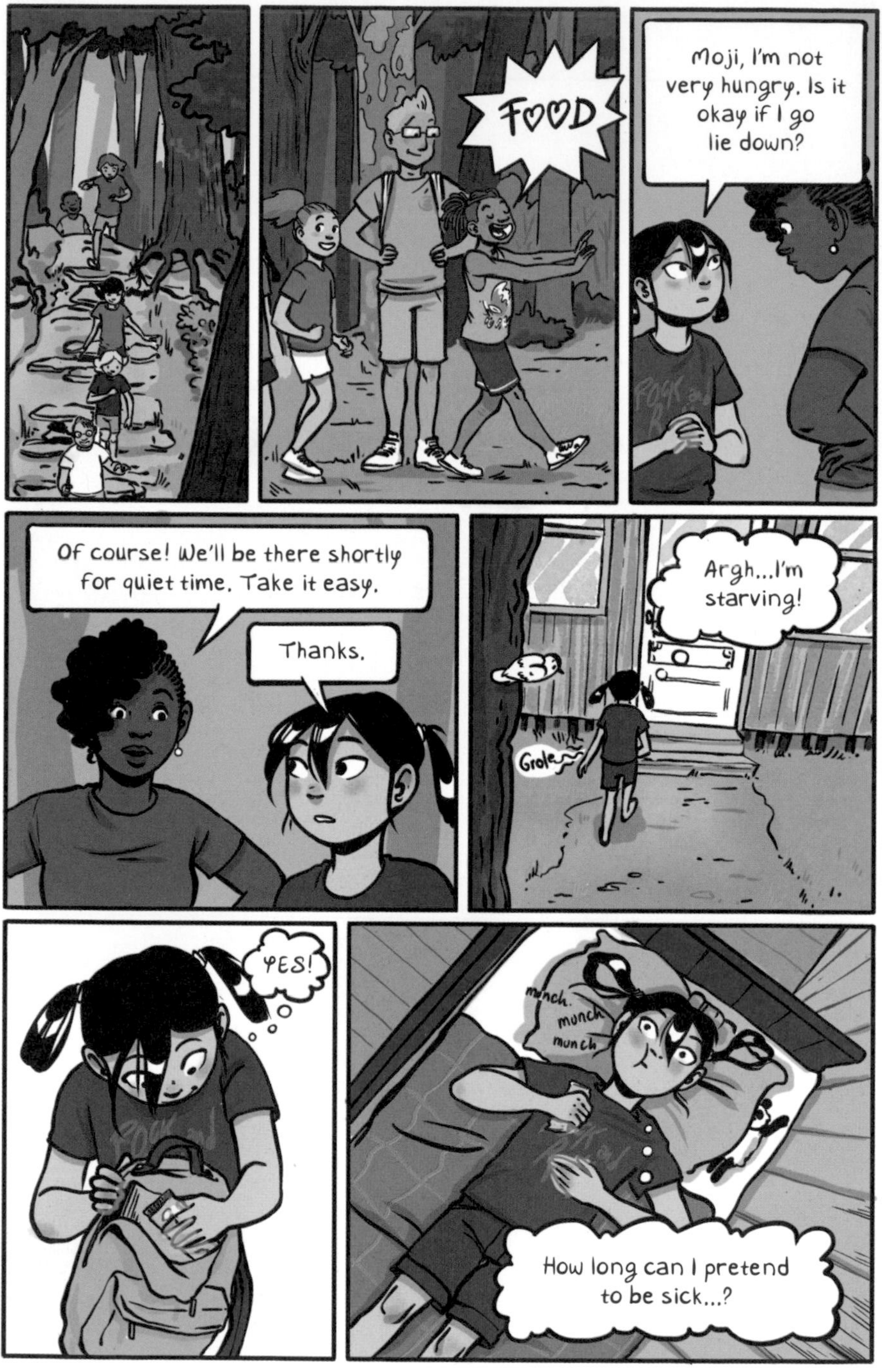
FOOD
Moji, I'm not very hungry. Is it okay if I go lie down?
Of course! We'll be there shortly for quiet time. Take it easy.
Thanks.
Argh...I'm starving!
Grole
YES!
munch
munch
munch
How long can I pretend to be sick...?

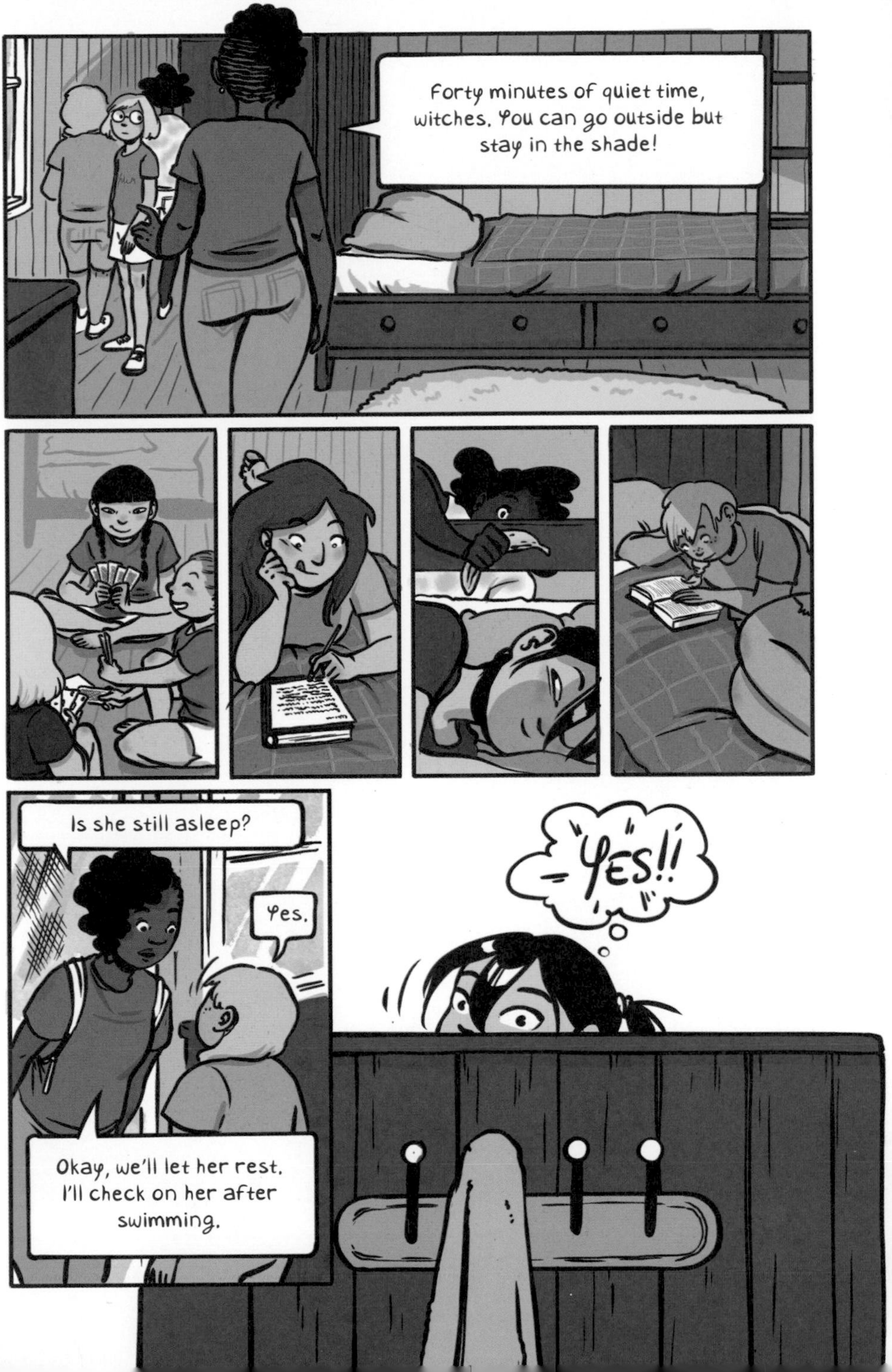

Forty minutes of quiet time, witches. You can go outside but stay in the shade!
Is she still asleep?
Yes.
Okay, we'll let her rest. I'll check on her after swimming.
YES!!

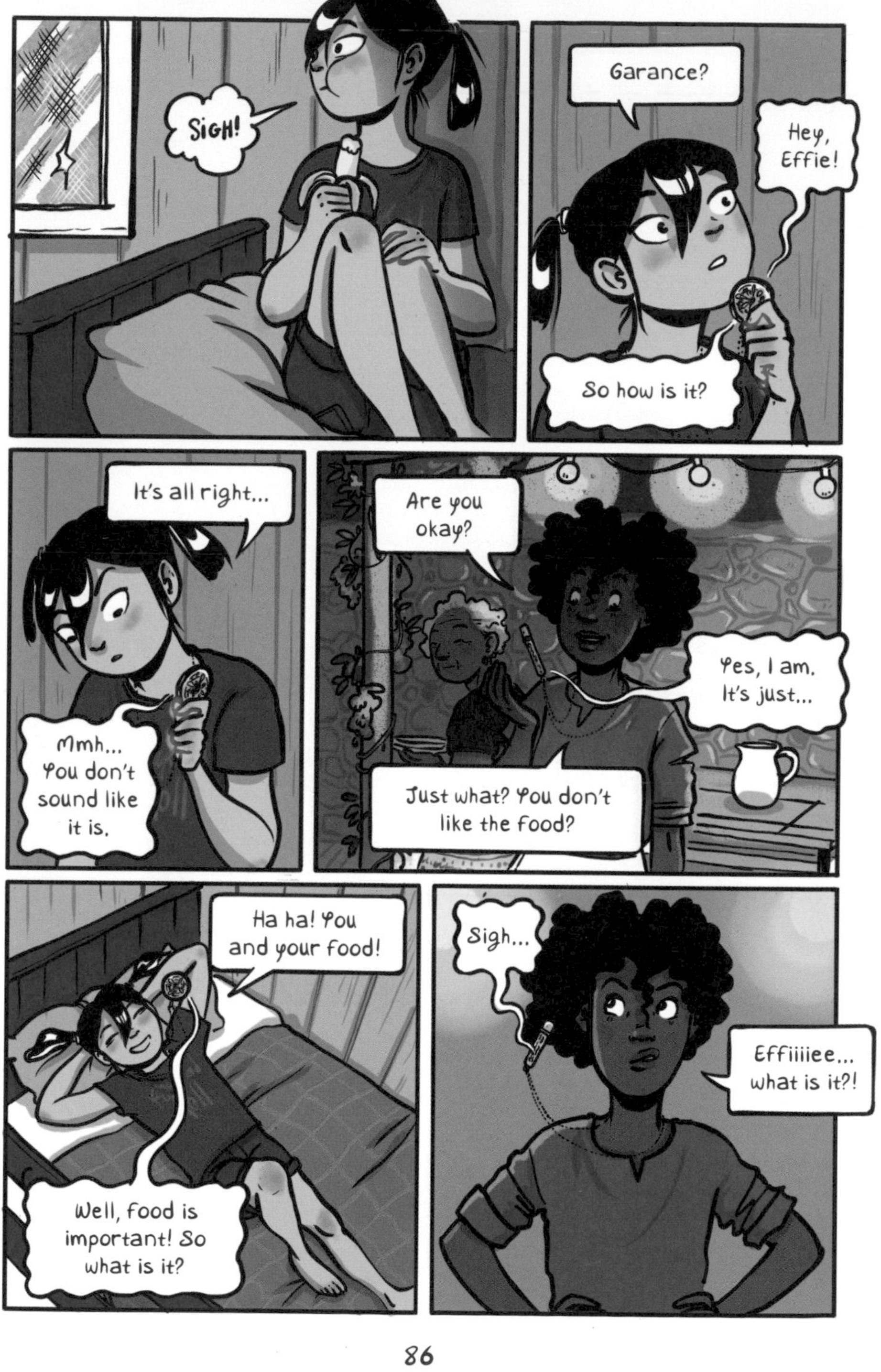
SIGH!
Garance?
Hey, Effie!
So how is it?
It's all right...
Mmh... You don't sound like it is.
Are you okay?
Yes, I am. It's just...
Just what? You don't like the food?
Ha ha! You and your food!
Well, food is important! So what is it?
Sigh...
Effiiiiee... what is it?!

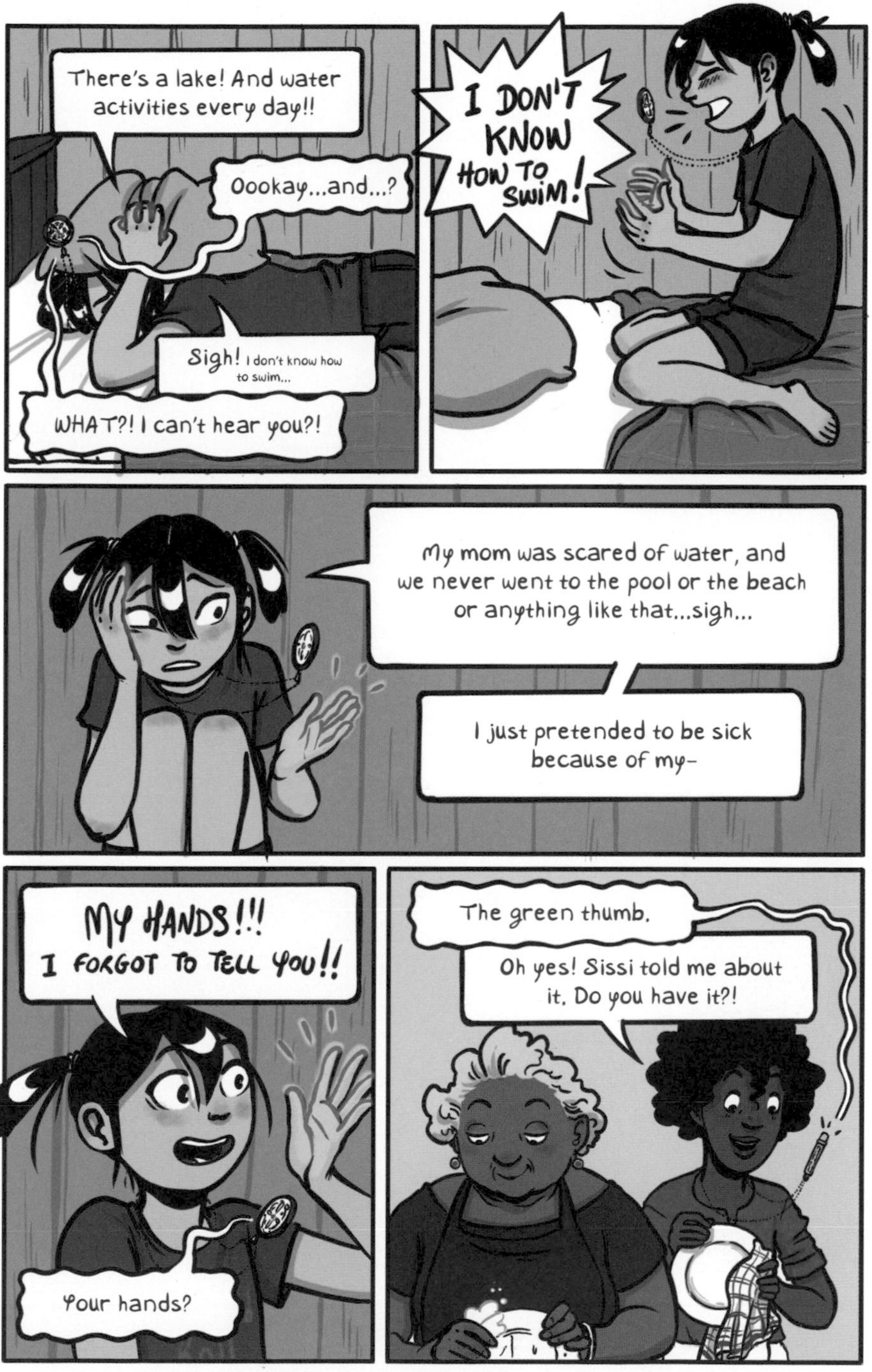
There's a lake! And water activities every day!!
Oookay...and...?
Sigh! I don't know how to swim...
WHAT?! I can't hear you?!
I DON'T KNOW HOW TO SWIM!
My mom was scared of water, and we never went to the pool or the beach or anything like that...sigh...
I just pretended to be sick because of my-
MY HANDS!!! I FORGOT TO TELL YOU!!
Your hands?
The green thumb.
Oh yes! Sissi told me about it. Do you have it?!

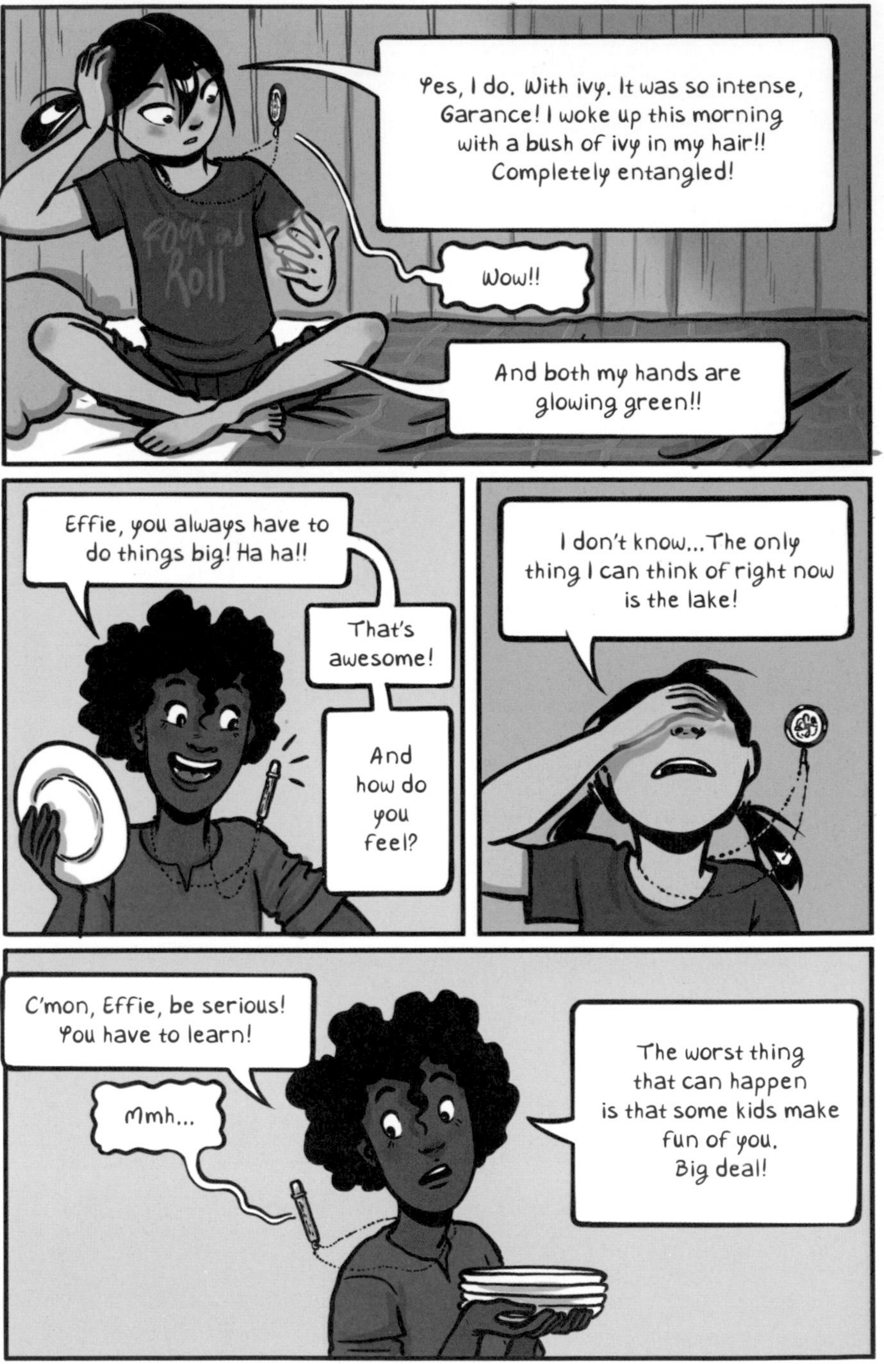
Yes, I do. With ivy. It was so intense, Garance! I woke up this morning with a bush of ivy in my hair!! Completely entangled!
Wow!!
And both my hands are glowing green!!
Effie, you always have to do things big! Ha ha!!
That's awesome!
And how do you feel?
I don't know... The only thing I can think of right now is the lake!
C'mon, Effie, be serious! You have to learn!
Mmh...
The worst thing that can happen is that some kids make fun of you. Big deal!

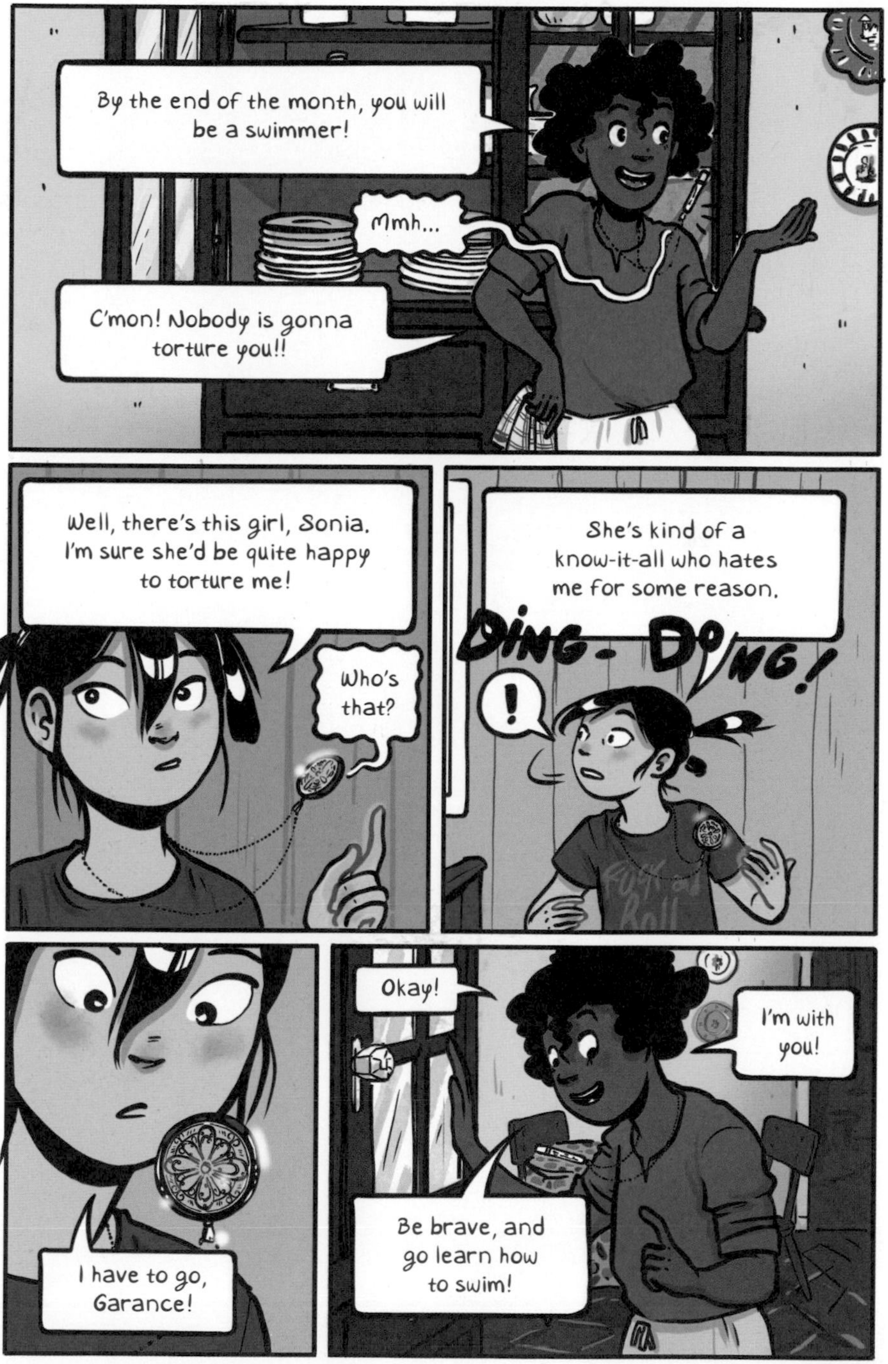
By the end of the month, you will be a swimmer!
Mmh...
C'mon! Nobody is gonna torture you!!
Well, there's this girl, Sonia. I'm sure she'd be quite happy to torture me!
Who's that?
She's kind of a know-it-all who hates me for some reason.
DING-DONG!
!
I have to go, Garance!
Okay!
I'm with you!
Be brave, and go learn how to swim!

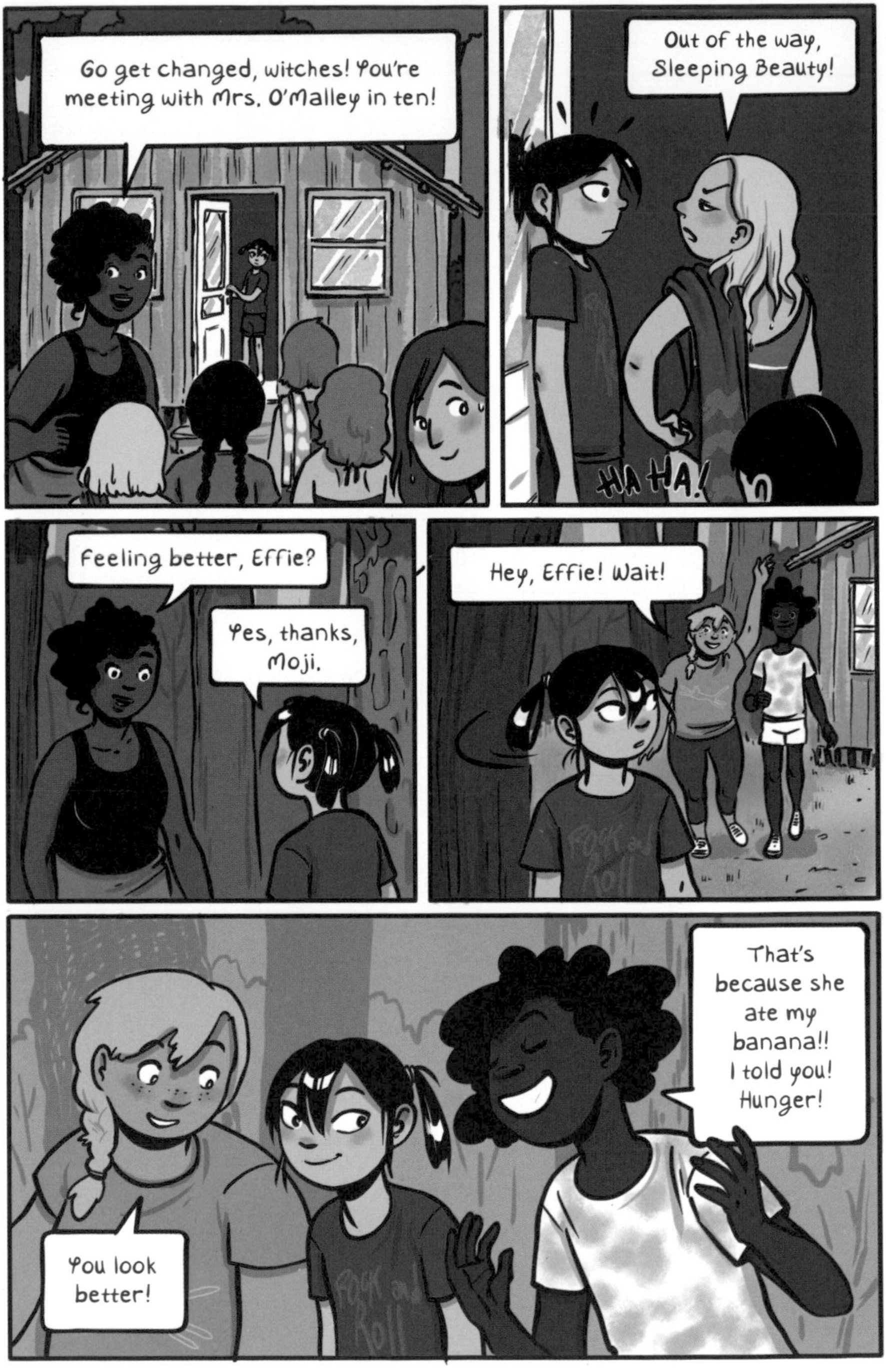
Go get changed, witches! You're meeting with Mrs. O'Malley in ten!
Out of the way, Sleeping Beauty!
HA HA!
Feeling better, Effie?
Yes, thanks, Moji.
Hey, Effie! Wait!
That's because she ate my banana!! I told you! Hunger!
You look better!

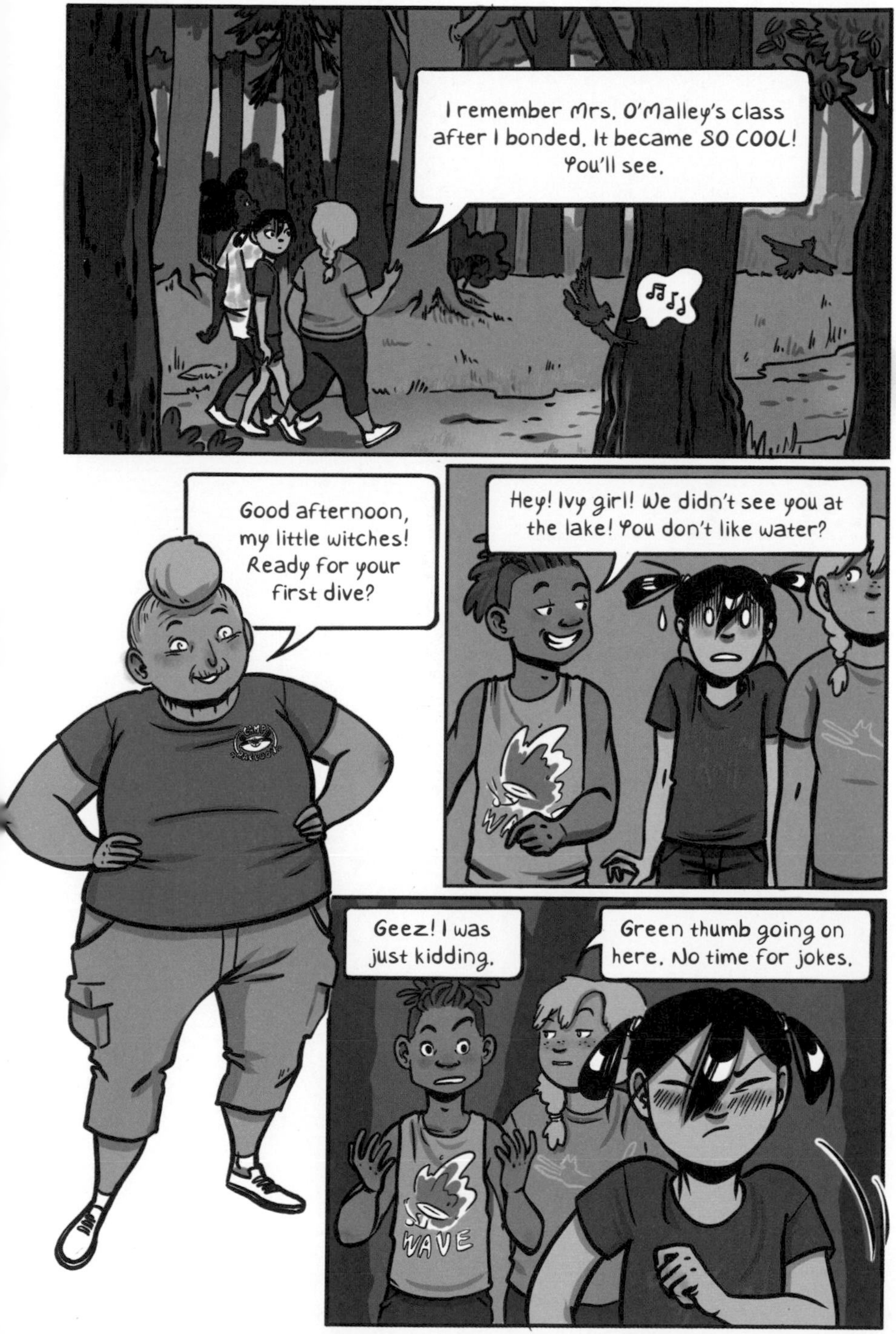
I remember Mrs. O'Malley's class after I bonded. It became SO COOL! You'll see.
♫♪♪
Good afternoon, my little witches! Ready for your first dive?
Hey! Ivy girl! We didn't see you at the lake! You don't like water?
Geez! I was just kidding.
Green thumb going on here. No time for jokes.
WAVE

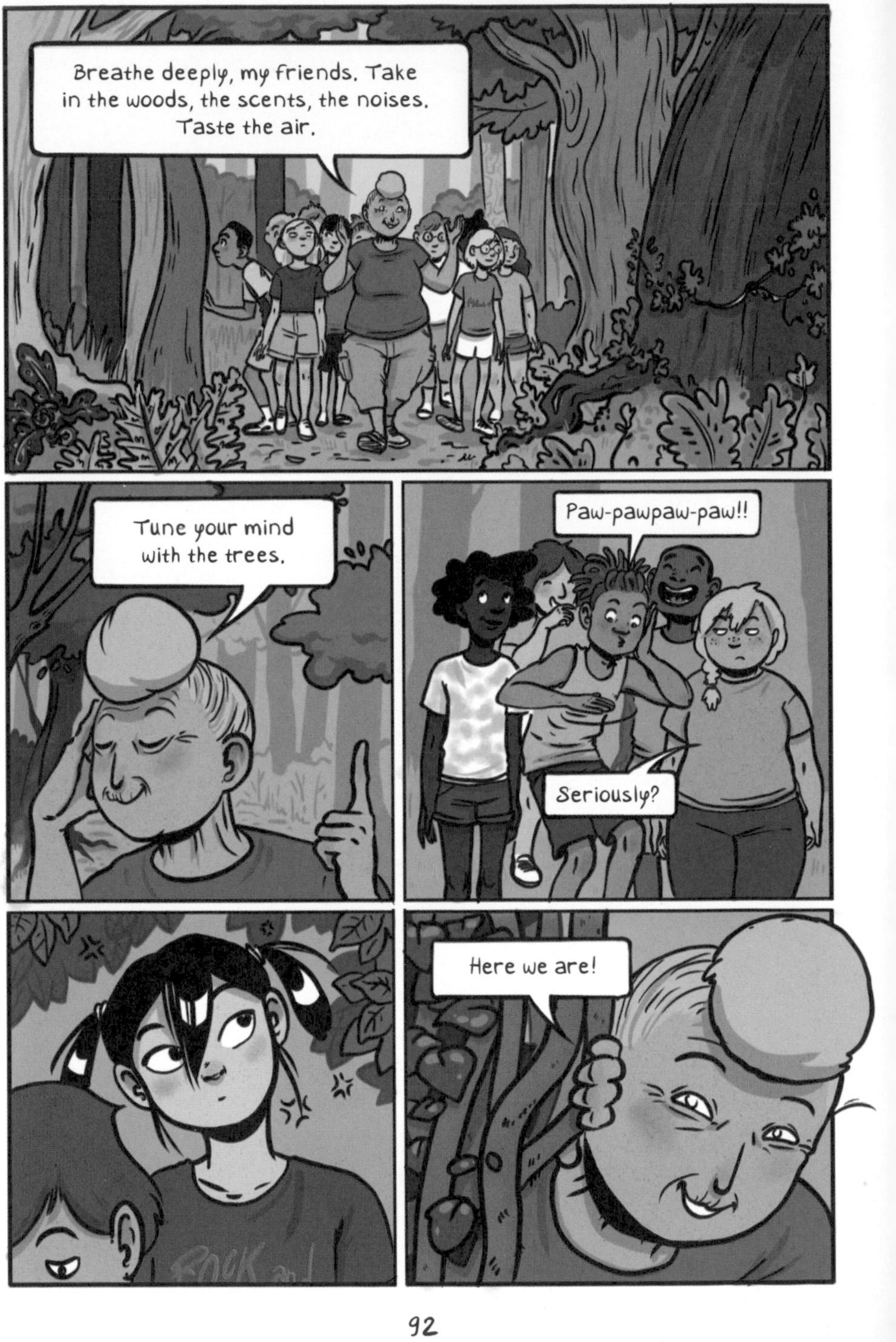
Breathe deeply, my friends. Take in the woods, the scents, the noises. Taste the air.
Tune your mind with the trees.
Paw-pawpaw-paw!!
Seriously?
Here we are!

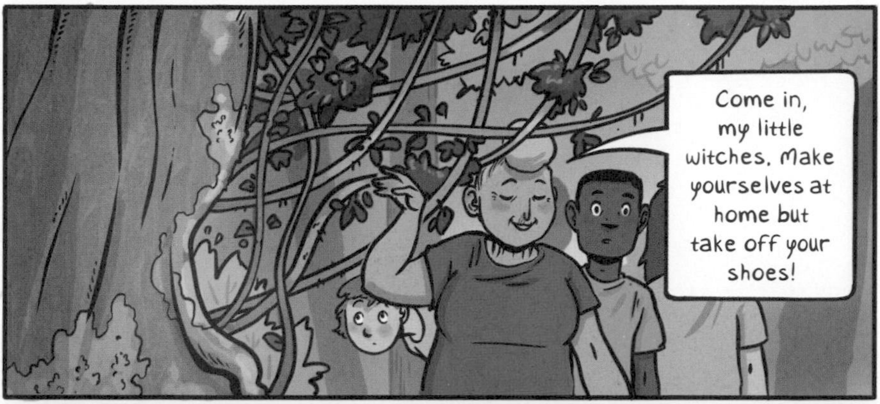
Come in, my little witches. Make yourselves at home but take off your shoes!

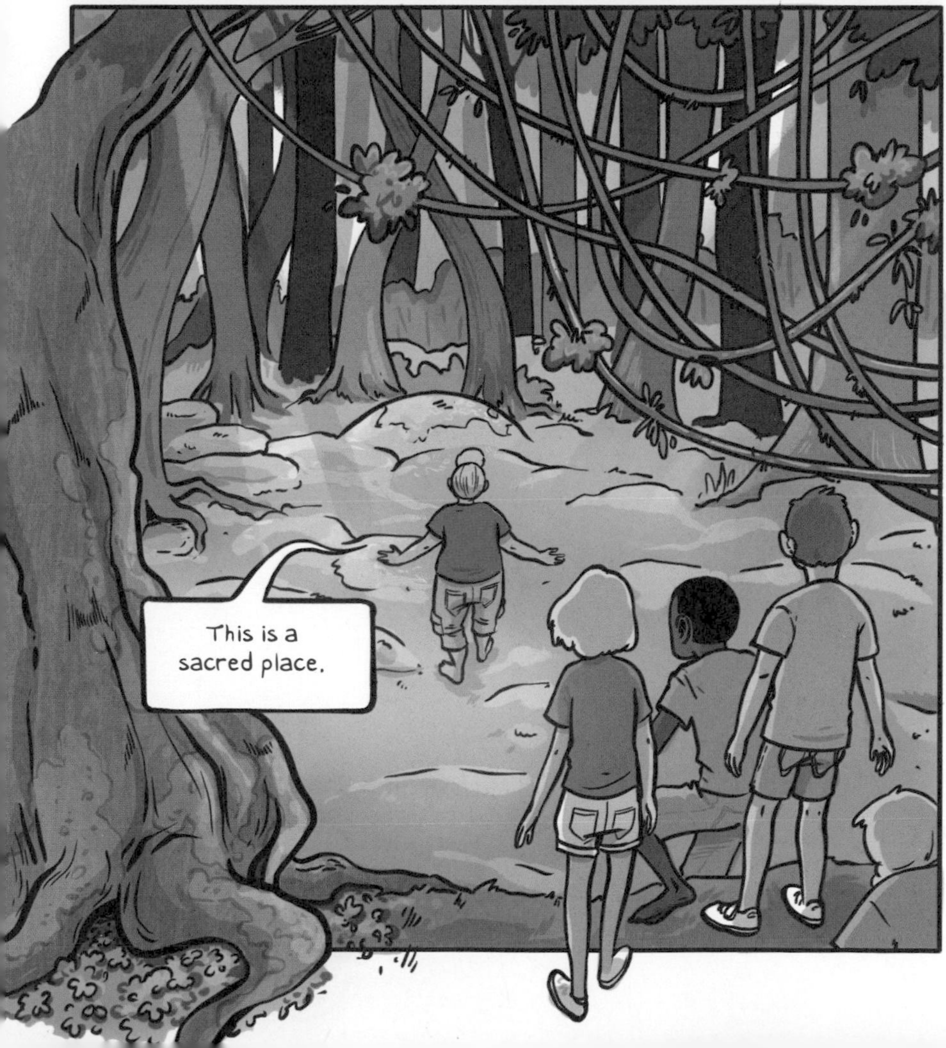
This is a sacred place.

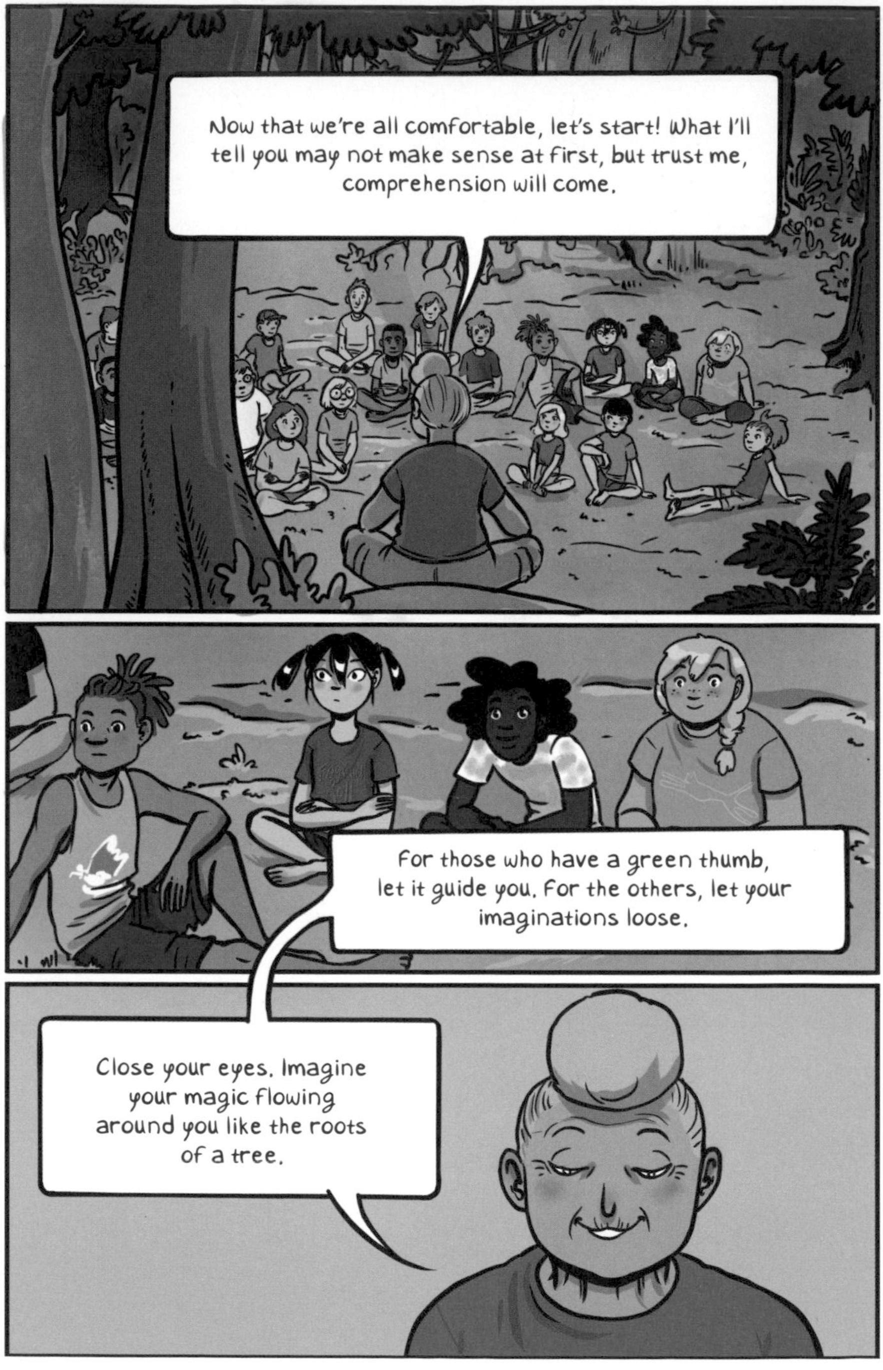
Now that we're all comfortable, let's start! What I'll tell you may not make sense at first, but trust me, comprehension will come.
For those who have a green thumb, let it guide you. For the others, let your imaginations loose.
Close your eyes. Imagine your magic flowing around you like the roots of a tree.

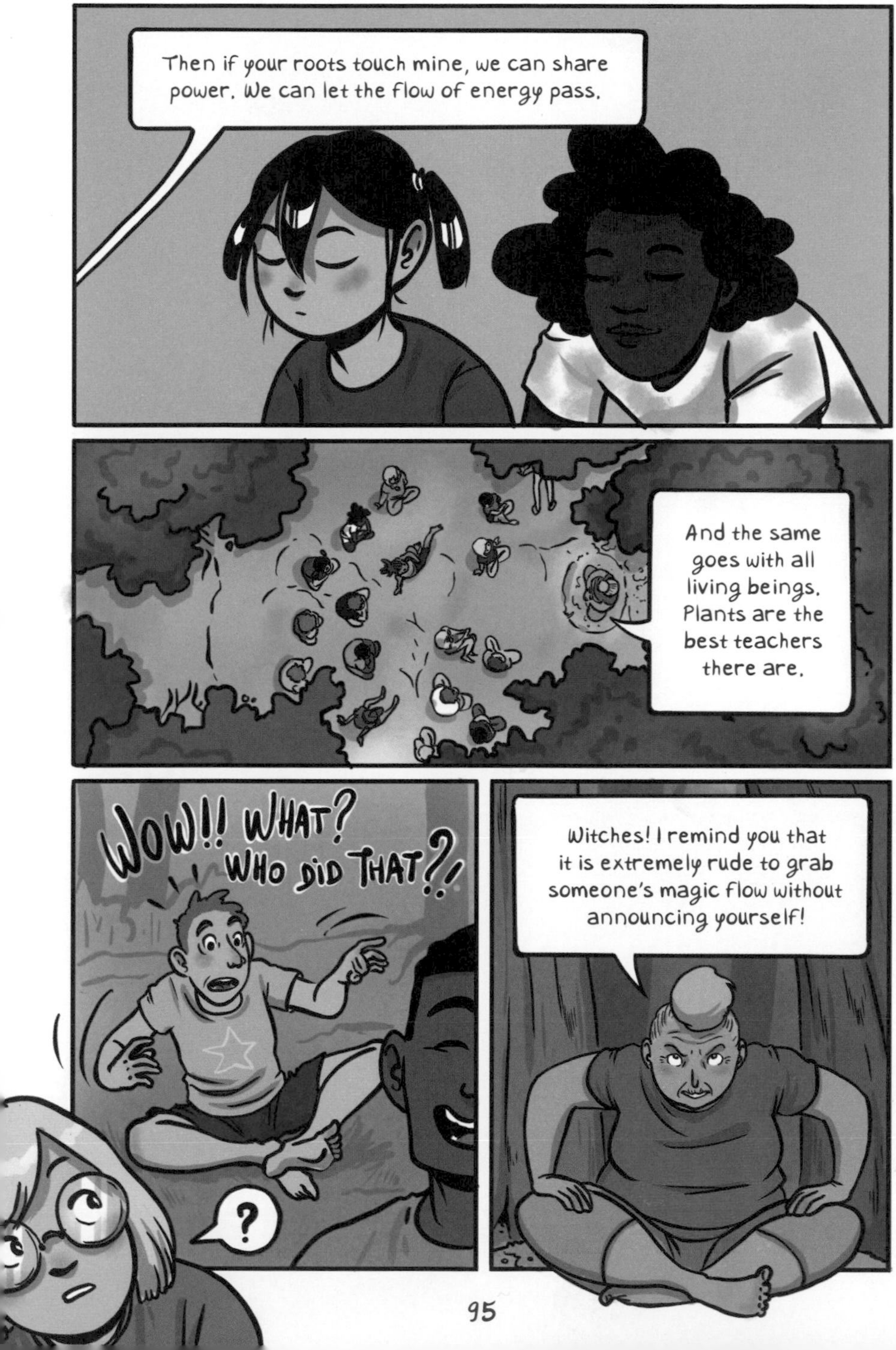
Then if your roots touch mine, we can share power. We can let the flow of energy pass.
And the same goes with all living beings. Plants are the best teachers there are.
WOW!! WHAT? WHO DID THAT?!
?
Witches! I remind you that it is extremely rude to grab someone's magic flow without announcing yourself!

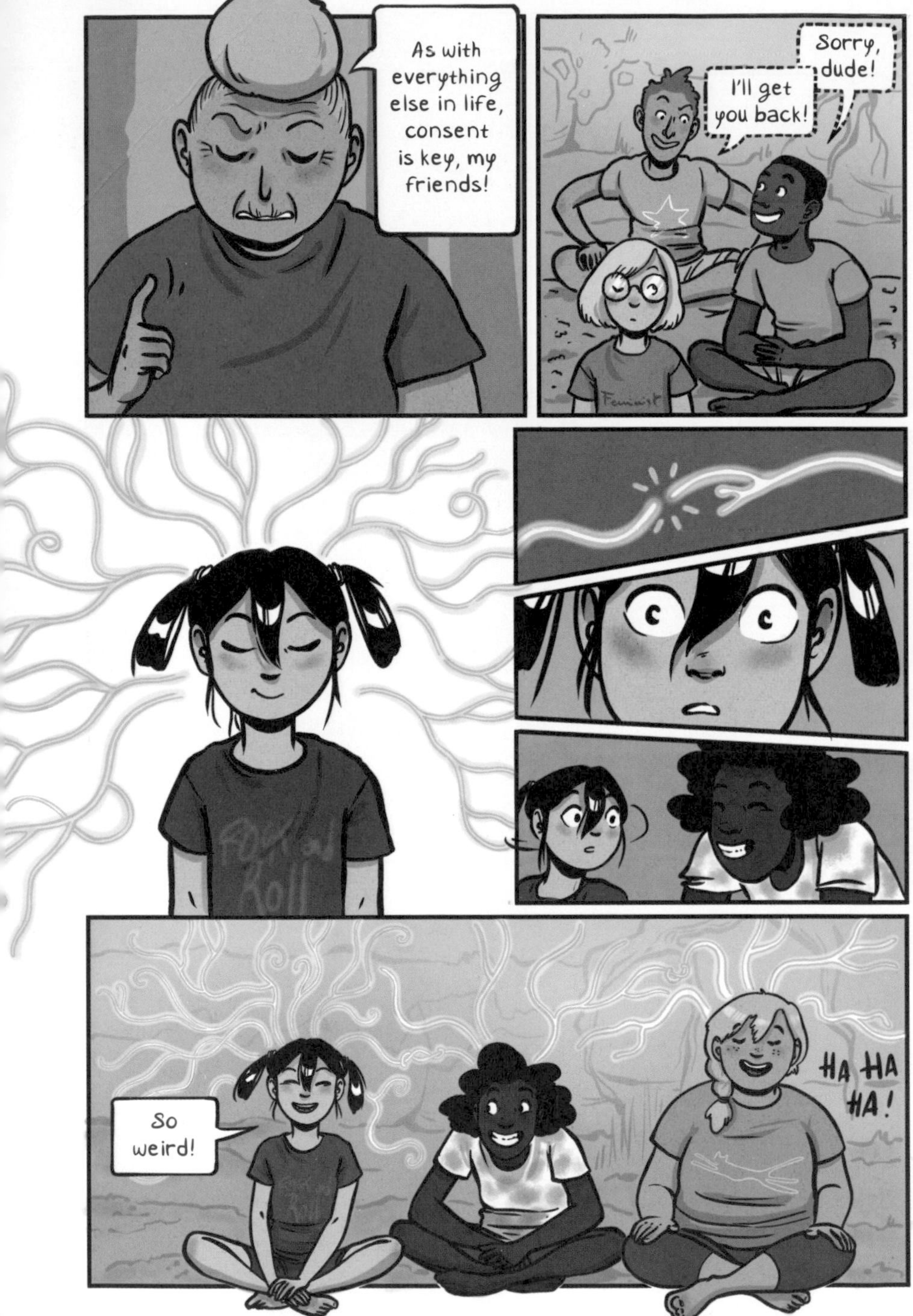

As with everything else in life, consent is key, my friends!
I'll get you back!
Sorry, dude!
Feminist
So weird!
HA HA HA!

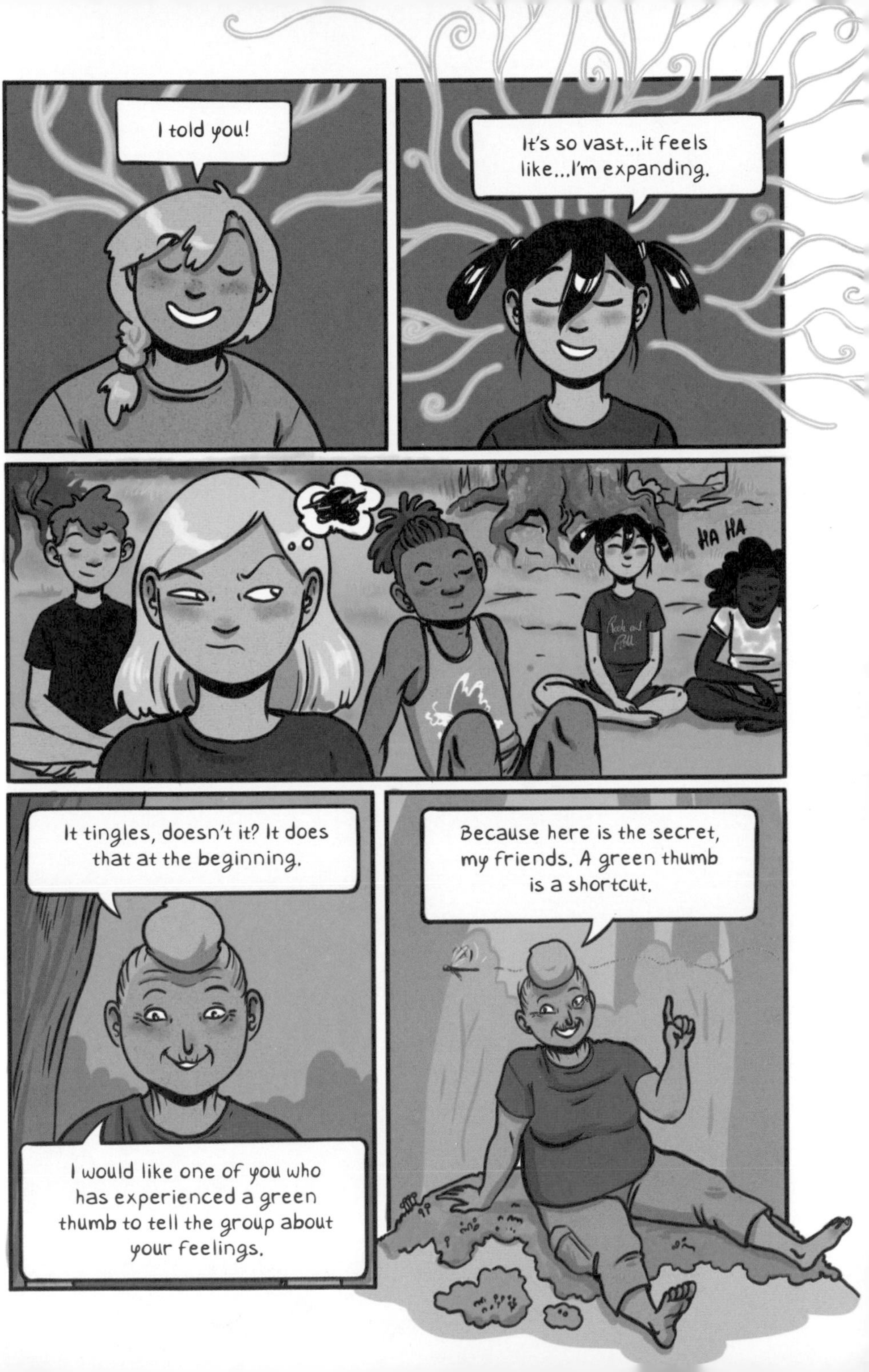
I told you!
It's so vast...it feels like...I'm expanding.
HA HA
It tingles, doesn't it? It does that at the beginning.
I would like one of you who has experienced a green thumb to tell the group about your feelings.
Because here is the secret, my friends. A green thumb is a shortcut.

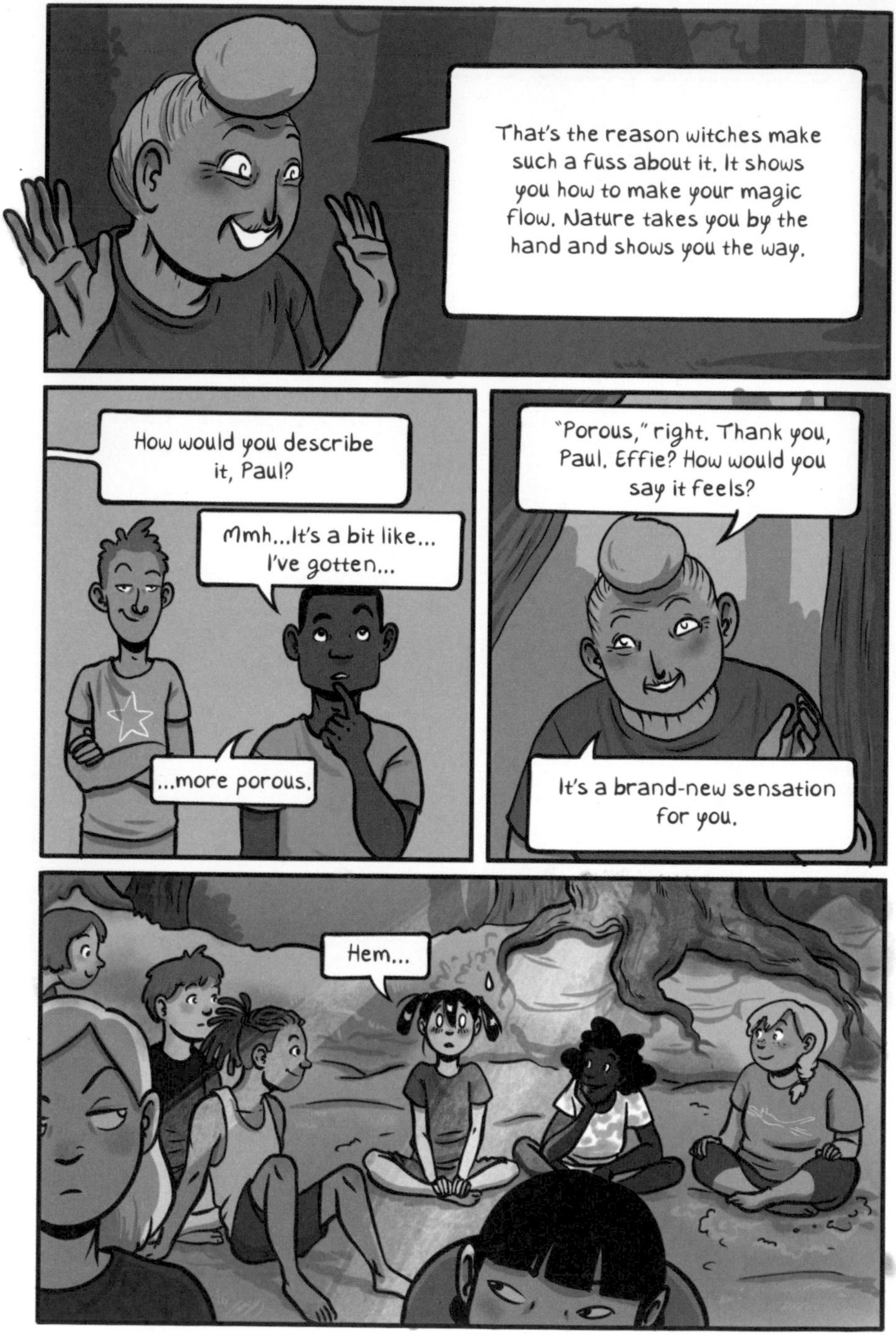
That's the reason witches make such a fuss about it. It shows you how to make your magic flow. Nature takes you by the hand and shows you the way.
How would you describe it, Paul?
Mmh...It's a bit like... I've gotten...
...more porous.
"Porous," right. Thank you, Paul. Effie? How would you say it feels?
It's a brand-new sensation for you.
Hem...

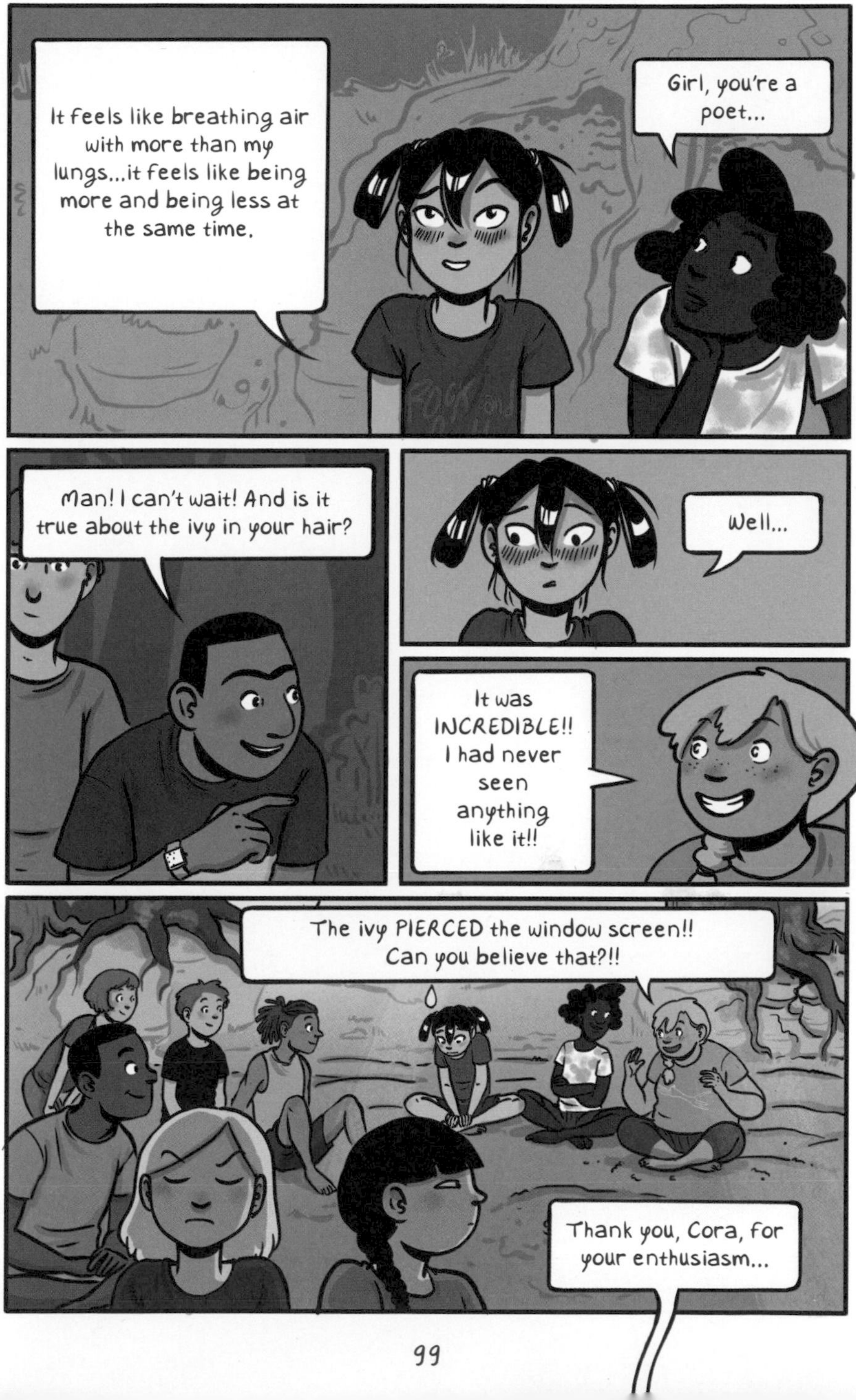
It feels like breathing air with more than my lungs...it feels like being more and being less at the same time.
Girl, you're a poet...
Man! I can't wait! And is it true about the ivy in your hair?
Well...
It was INCREDIBLE!! I had never seen anything like it!!
The ivy PIERCED the window screen!! Can you believe that?!!
Thank you, Cora, for your enthusiasm...

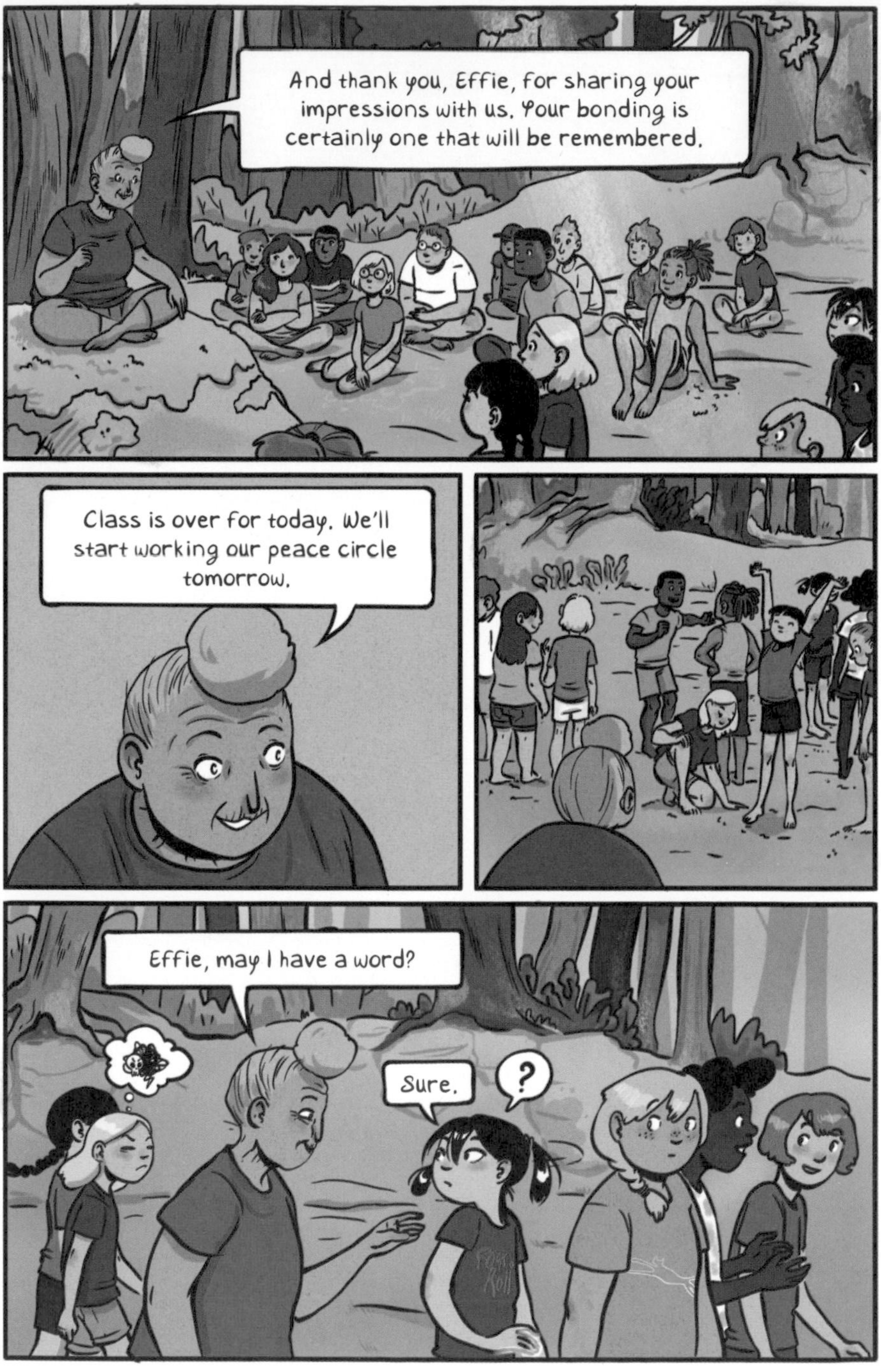
And thank you, Effie, for sharing your impressions with us. Your bonding is certainly one that will be remembered.
Class is over for today. We'll start working our peace circle tomorrow.
Effie, may I have a word?
Sure.
?

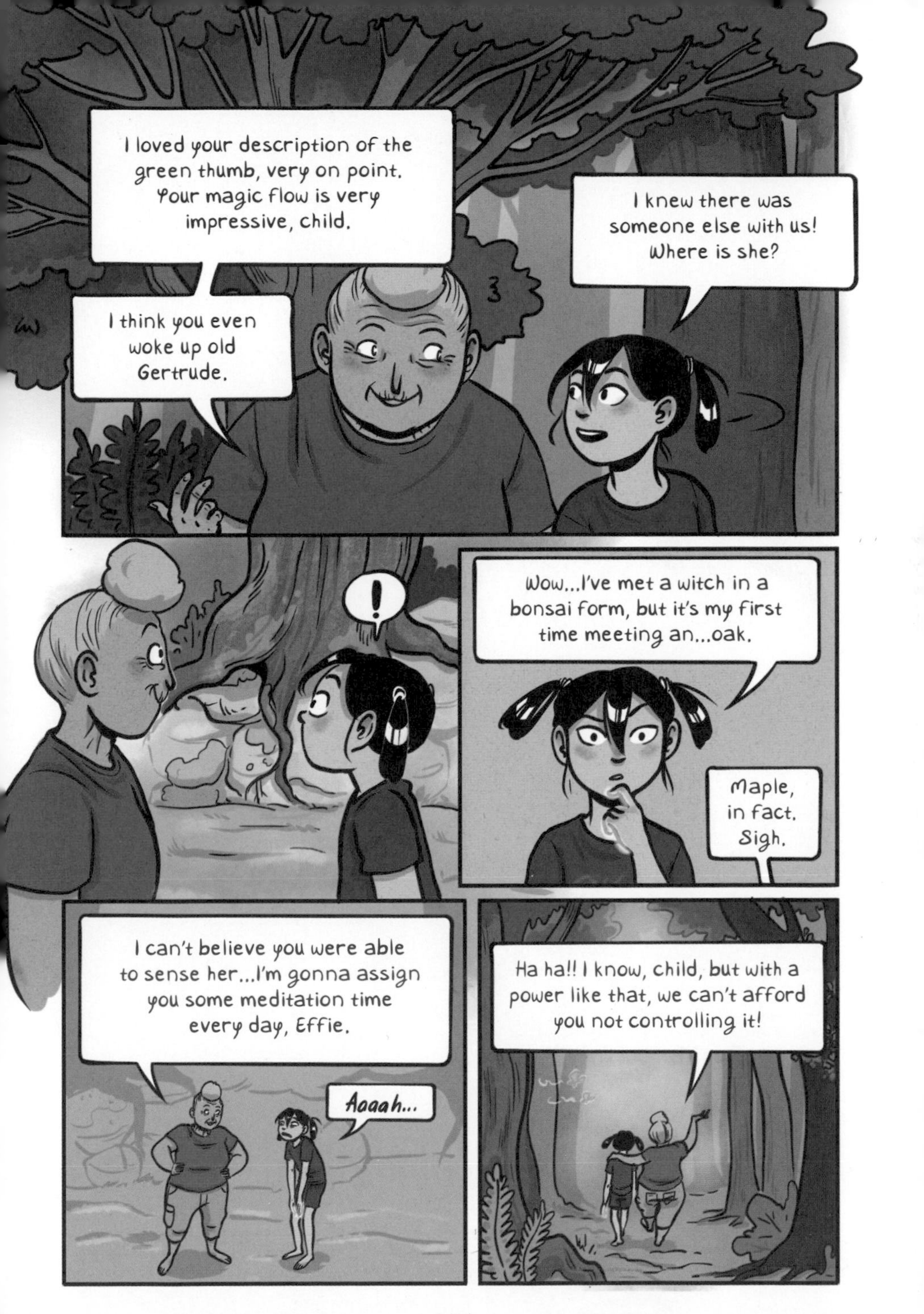
I loved your description of the green thumb, very on point. Your magic flow is very impressive, child.
I think you even woke up old Gertrude.
I knew there was someone else with us! Where is she?
!
Wow...I've met a witch in a bonsai form, but it's my first time meeting an...oak.
Maple, in fact. Sigh.
I can't believe you were able to sense her...I'm gonna assign you some meditation time every day, Effie.
Aaaah...
Ha ha!! I know, child, but with a power like that, we can't afford you not controlling it!

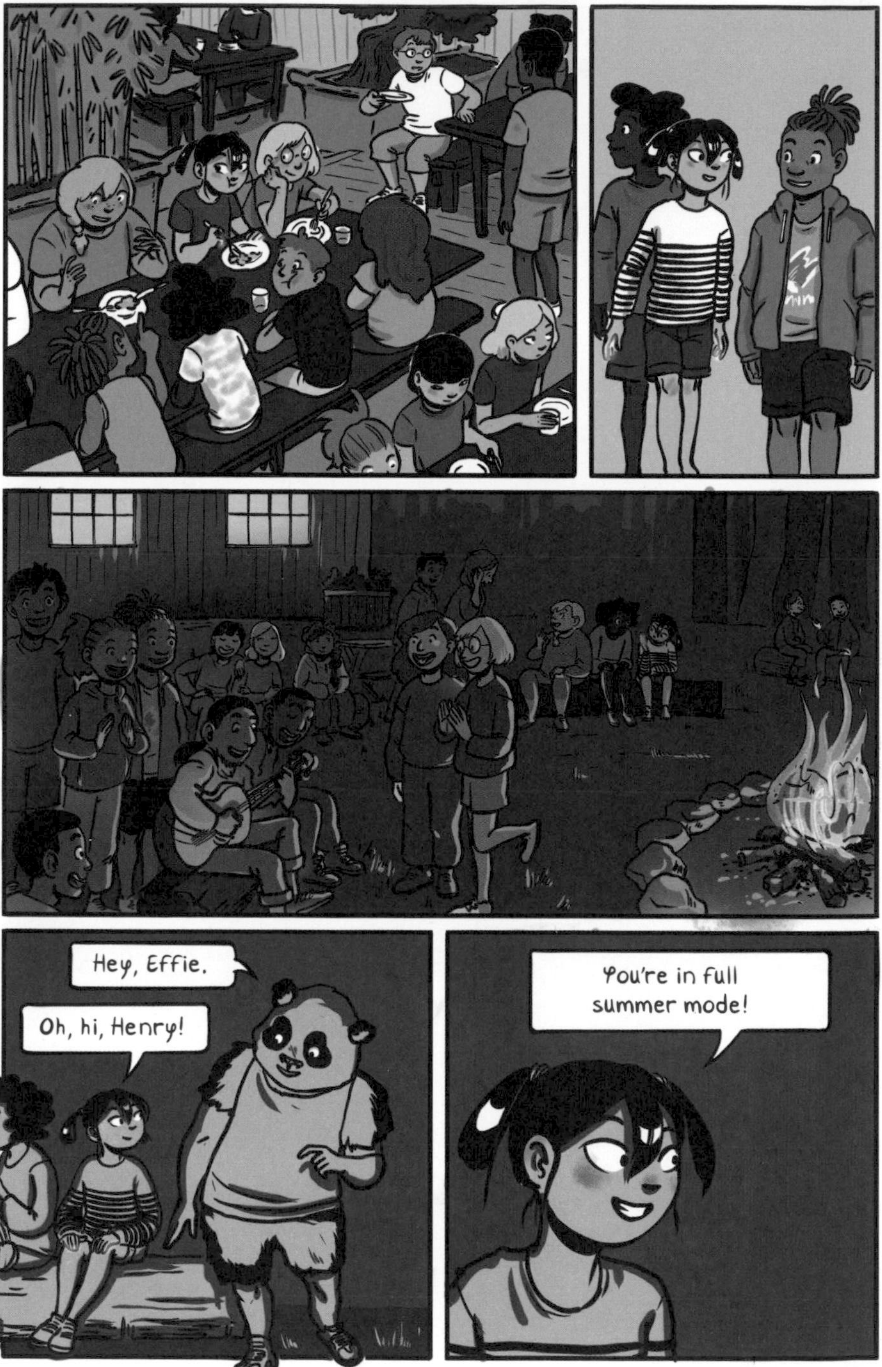
Hey, Effie.
Oh, hi, Henry!
You're in full summer mode!

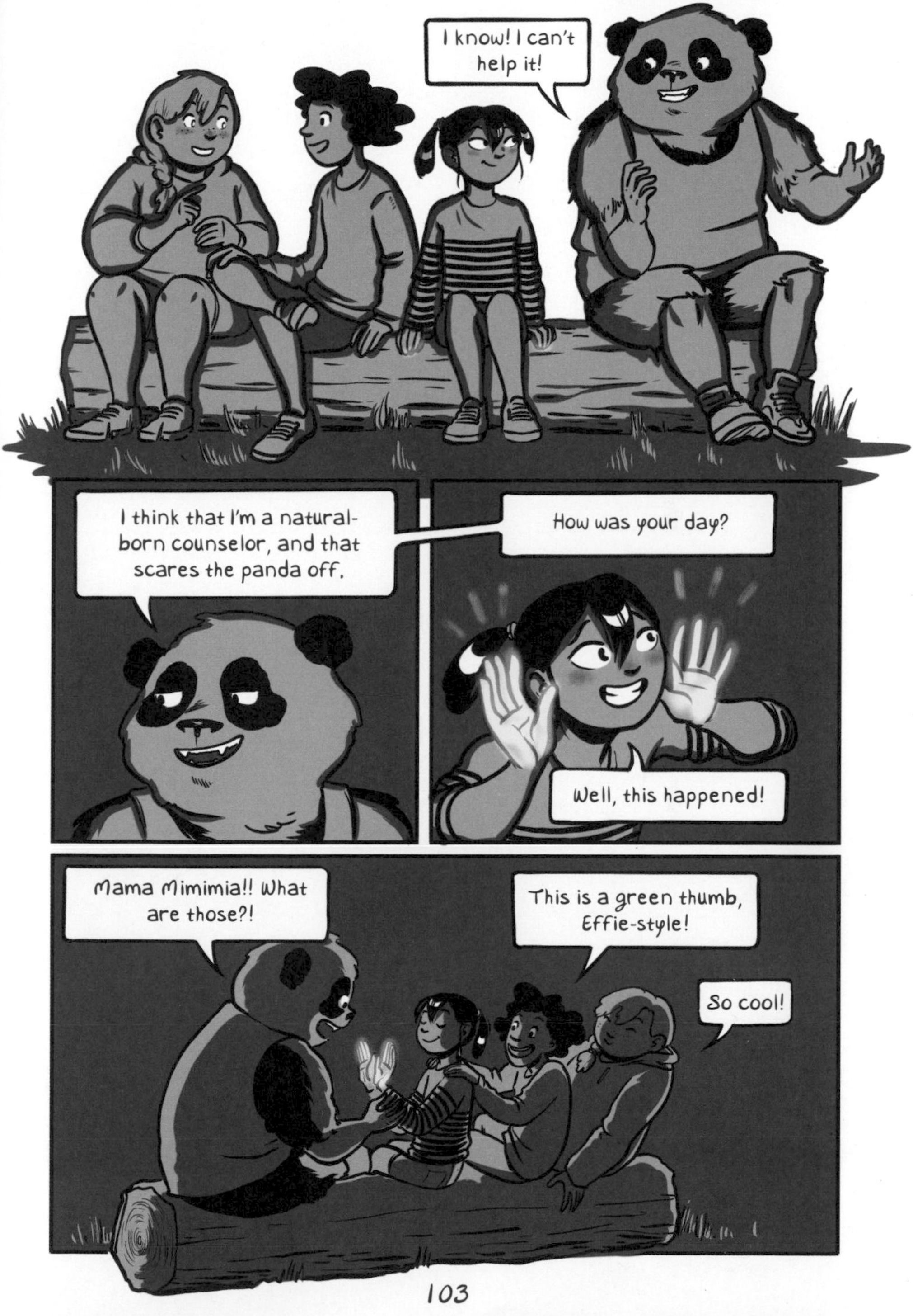
I know! I can't help it!
I think that I'm a natural-born counselor, and that scares the panda off.
How was your day?
Well, this happened!
Mama Mimimia!! What are those?!
This is a green thumb, Effie-style!
So cool!

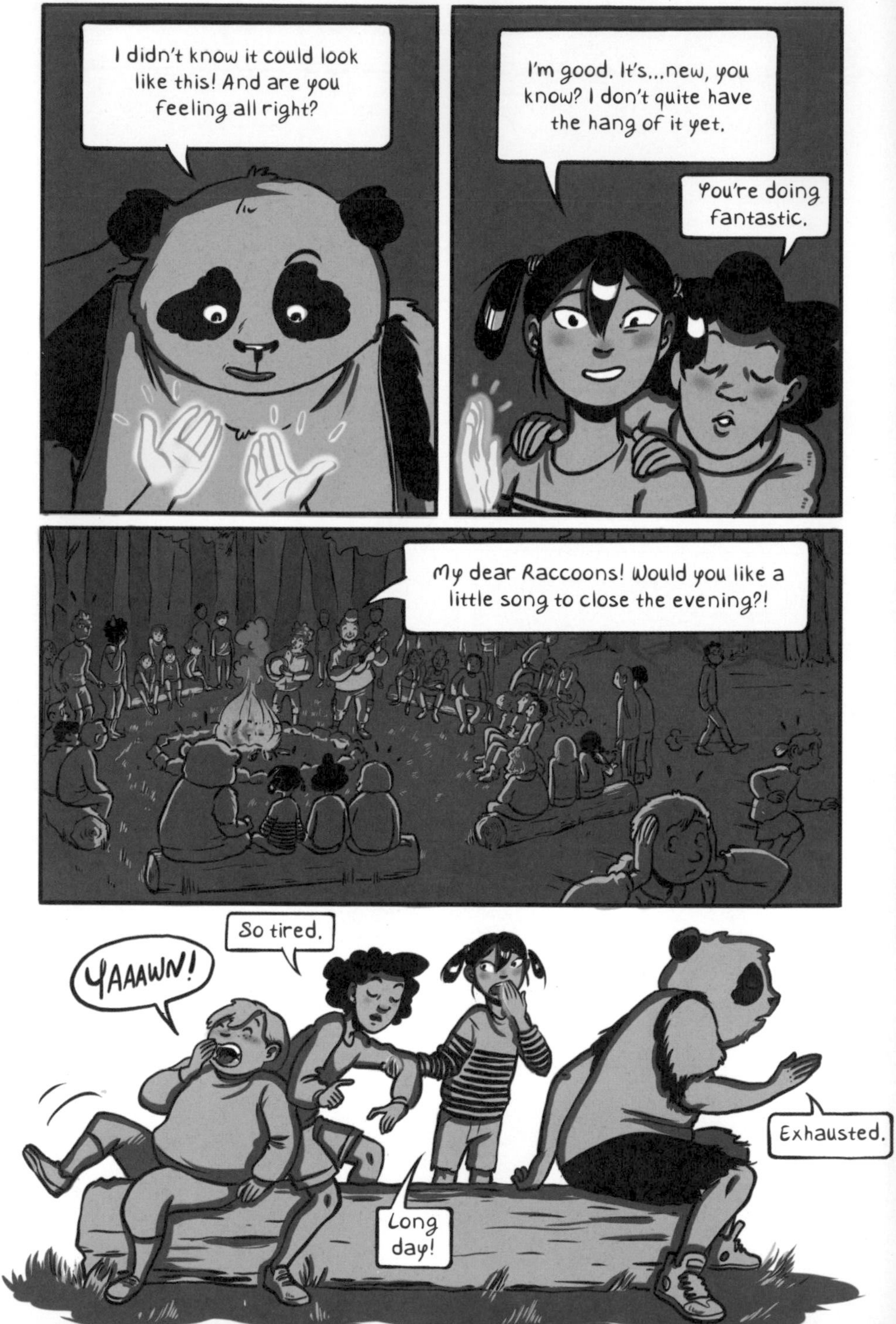
I didn't know it could look like this! And are you feeling all right?
I'm good. It's...new, you know? I don't quite have the hang of it yet.
You're doing fantastic.
My dear Raccoons! Would you like a little song to close the evening?!
YAAAWN!
So tired.
Long day!
Exhausted.

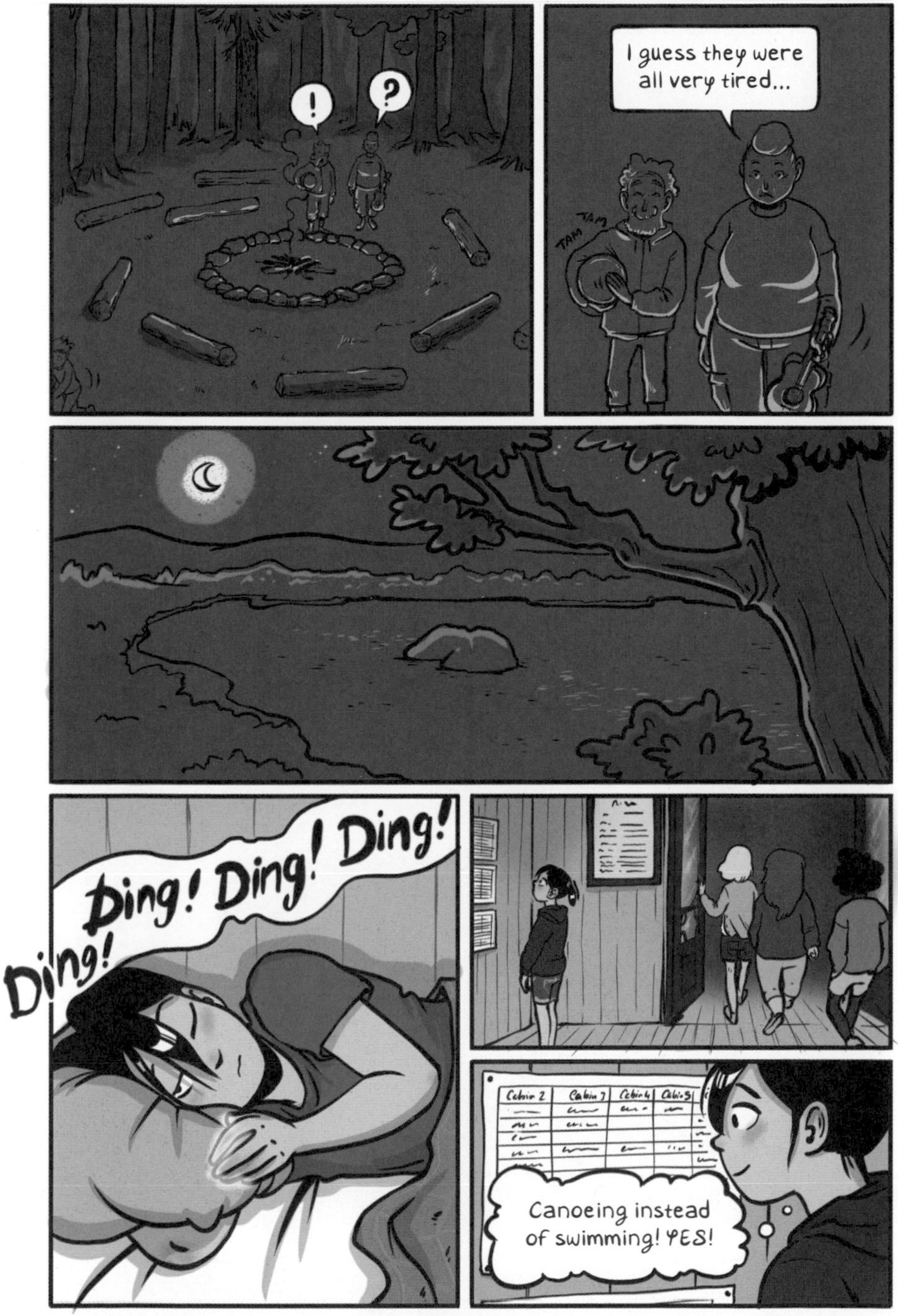

!
?
I guess they were all very tired...
TAM TAM
Ding! Ding! Ding! Ding!
Canoeing instead of swimming! YES!

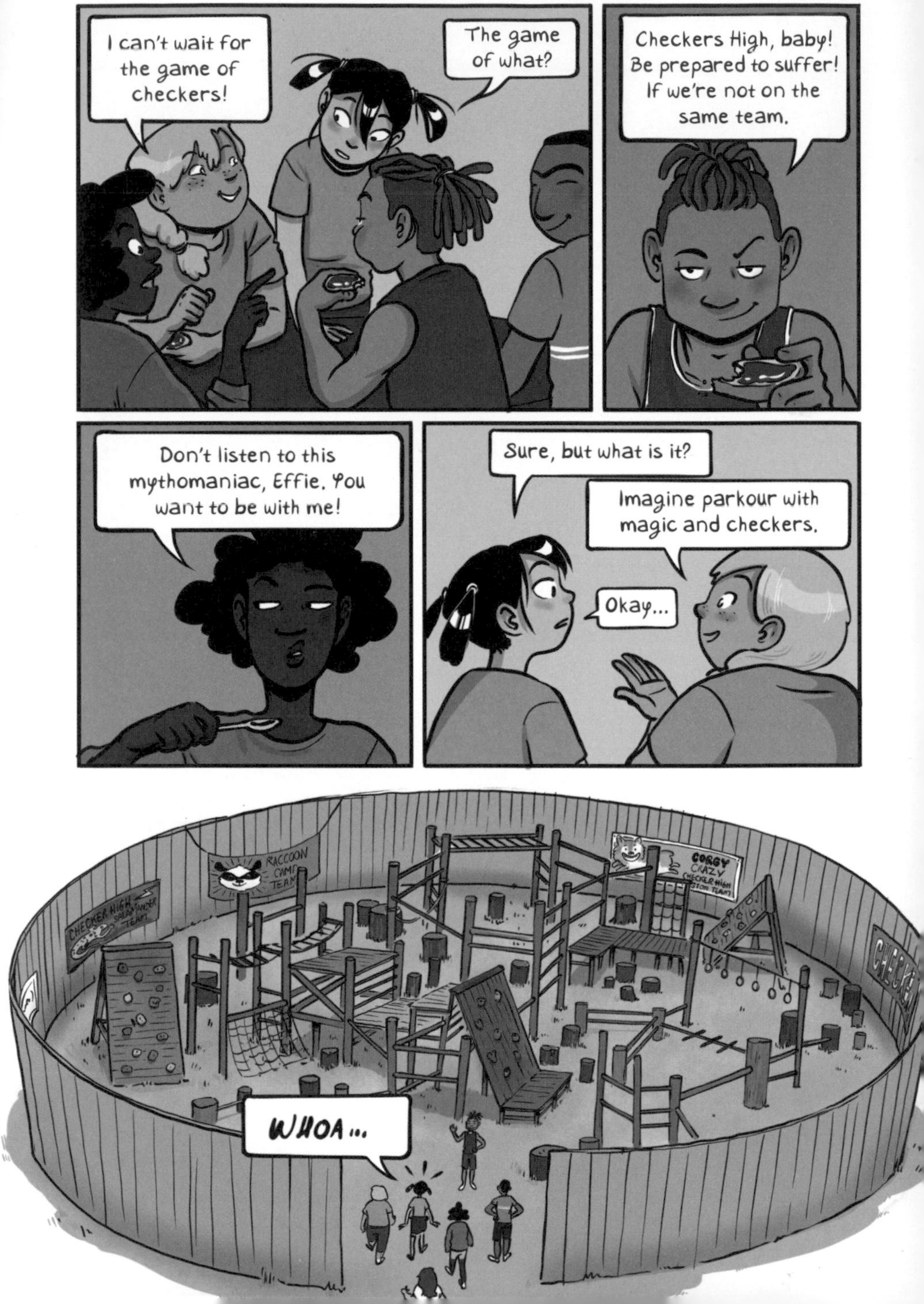
I can't wait for the game of checkers!
The game of what?
Checkers High, baby! Be prepared to suffer! If we're not on the same team.
Don't listen to this mythomaniac, Effie. You want to be with me!
Sure, but what is it?
Imagine parkour with magic and checkers.
Okay...
RACCOON CAMP TEAM
CHECKER HIGH SALAMANDER TEAM
CORGY CRAZY
WHOA...

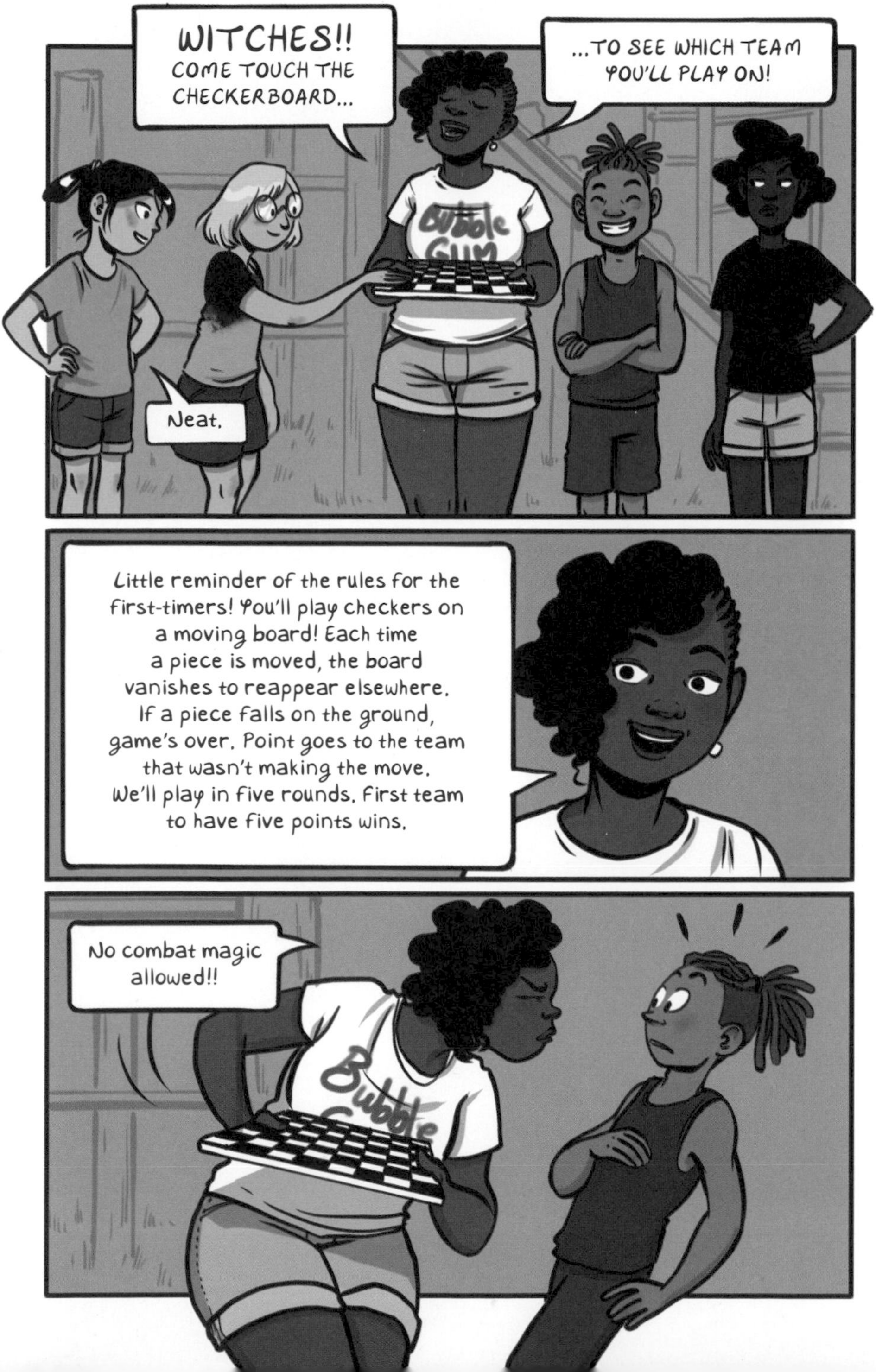
WITCHES!! COME TOUCH THE CHECKERBOARD...
...TO SEE WHICH TEAM YOU'LL PLAY ON!
Neat.
Little reminder of the rules for the first-timers! You'll play checkers on a moving board! Each time a piece is moved, the board vanishes to reappear elsewhere. If a piece falls on the ground, game's over. Point goes to the team that wasn't making the move. We'll play in five rounds. First team to have five points wins.
No combat magic allowed!!

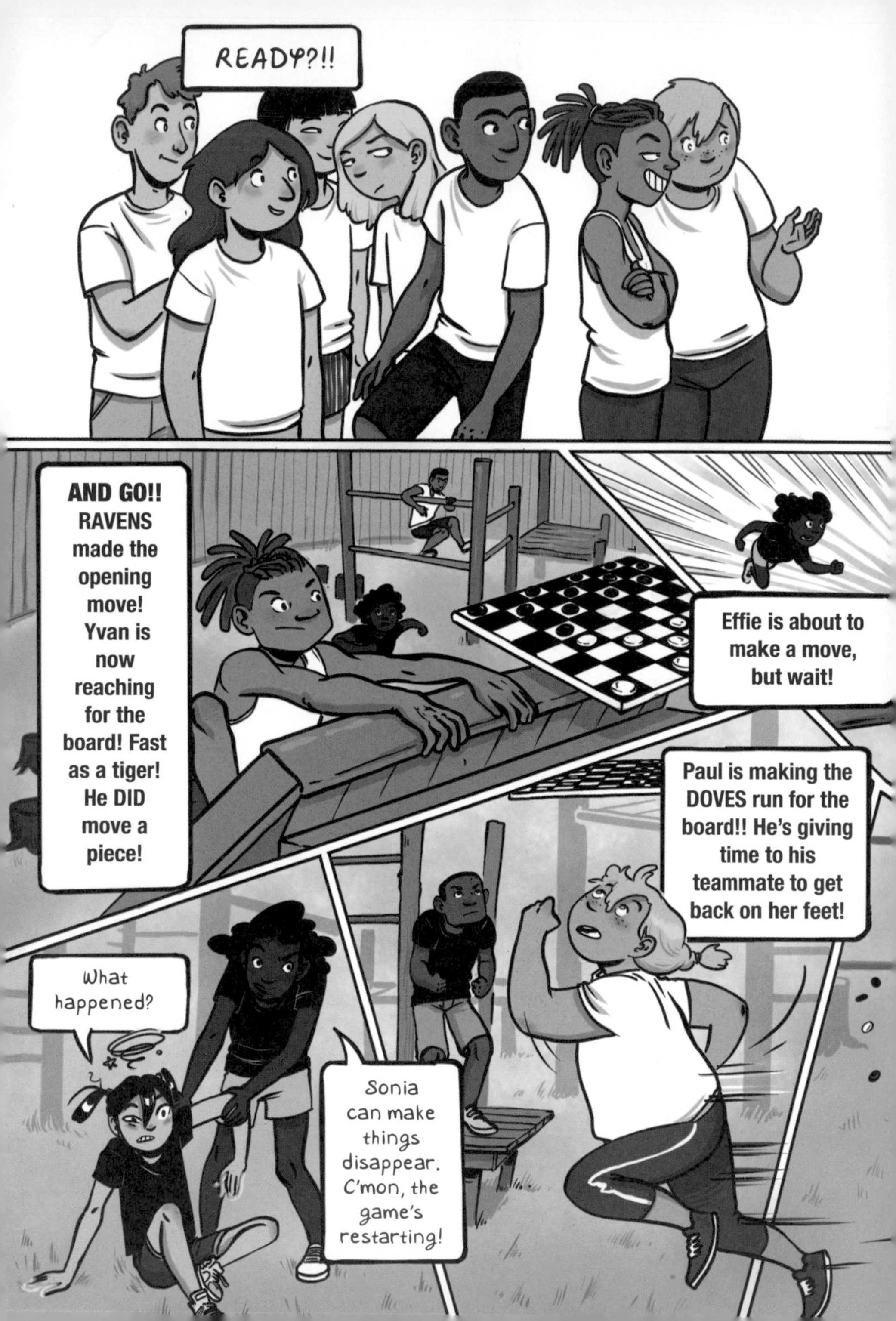
READY?!!
AND GO!! RAVENS made the opening move! Yvan is now reaching for the board! Fast as a tiger! He DID move a piece!
Effie is about to make a move, but wait!
Paul is making the DOVES run for the board!! He's giving time to his teammate to get back on her feet!
What happened?
Sonia can make things disappear. C'mon, the game's restarting!

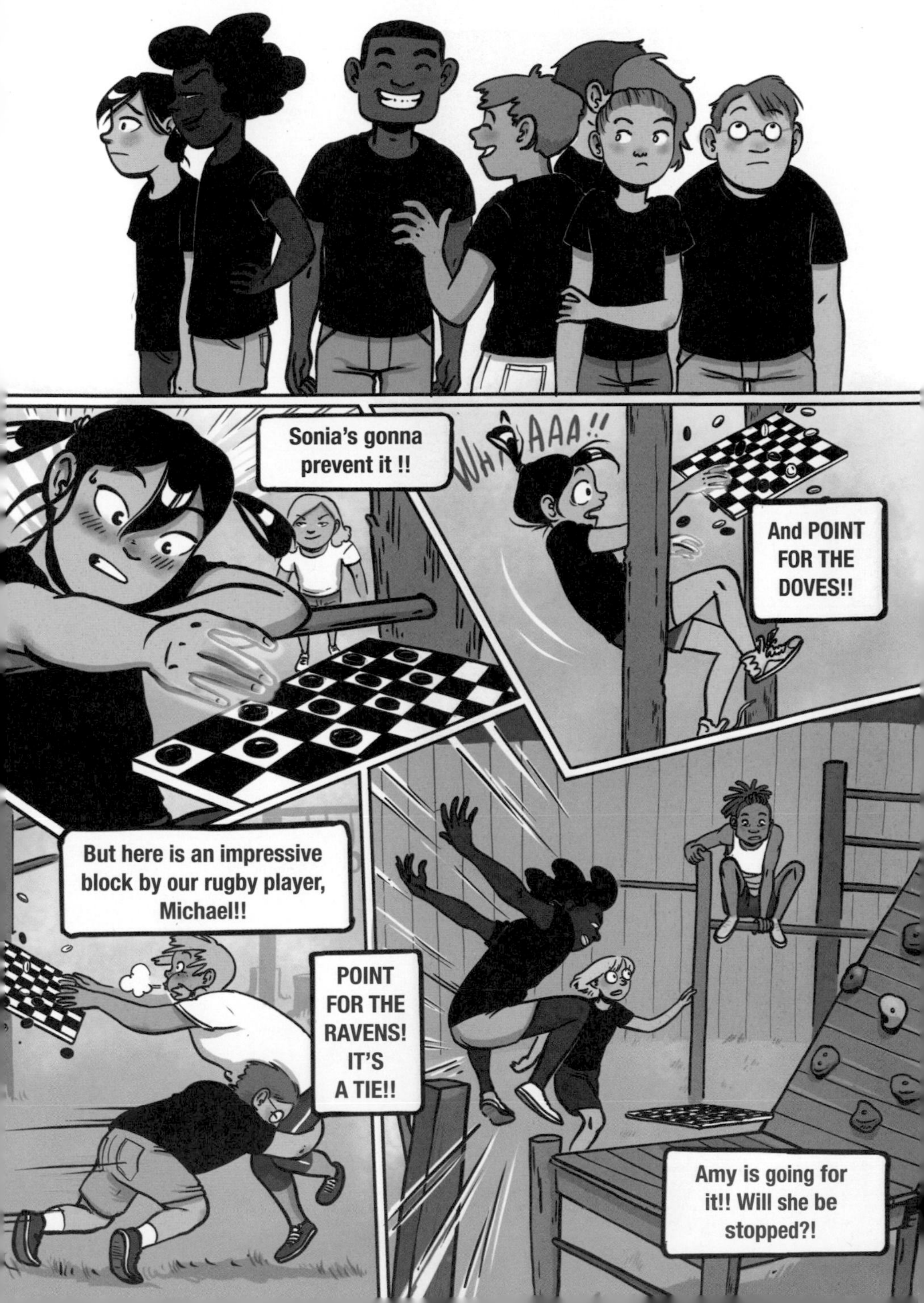
Sonia's gonna prevent it !!
WHAAAA!!
And POINT FOR THE DOVES!!
But here is an impressive block by our rugby player, Michael!!
POINT FOR THE RAVENS! IT'S A TIE!!
Amy is going for it!! Will she be stopped?!

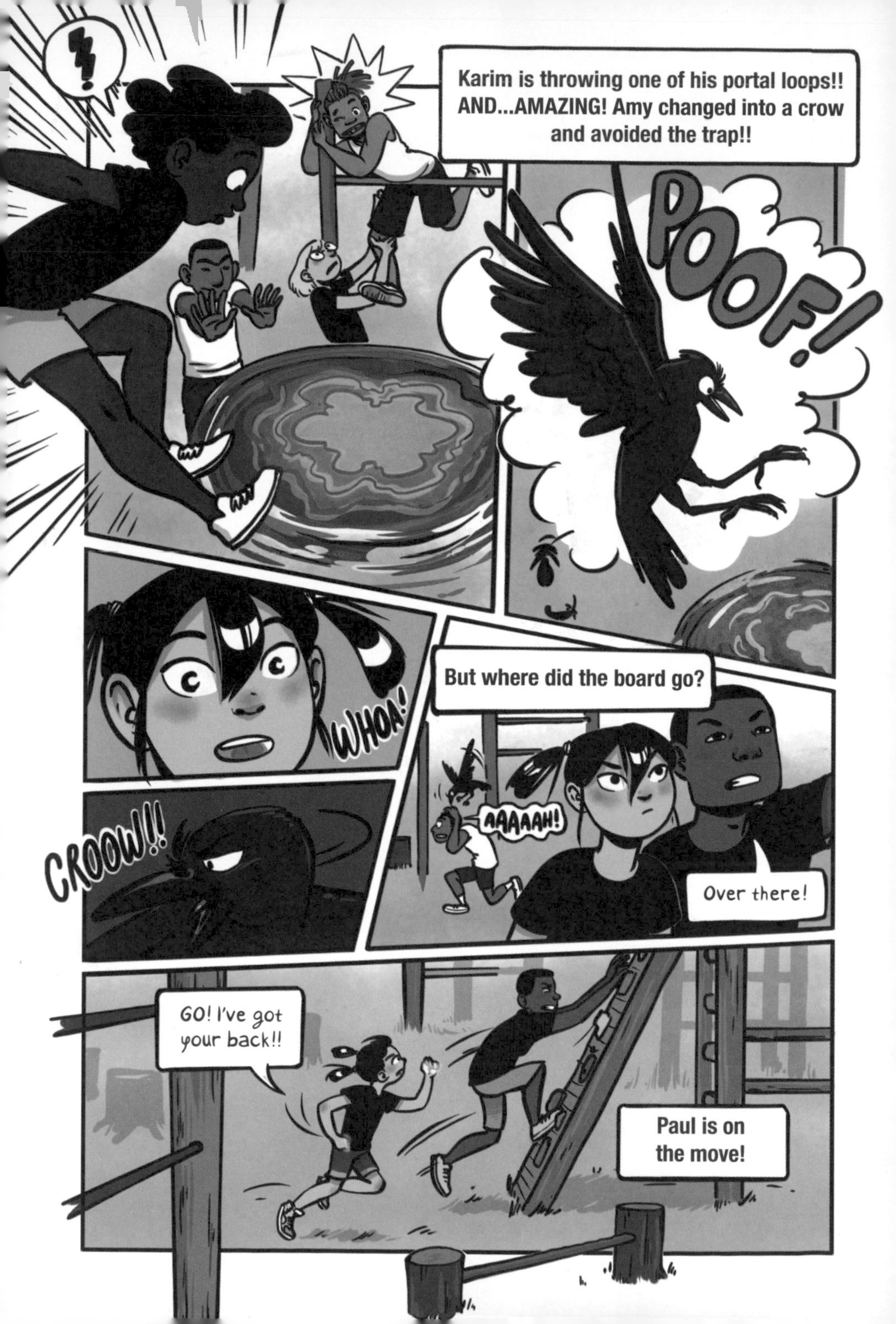

Karim is throwing one of his portal loops!! AND...AMAZING! Amy changed into a crow and avoided the trap!!
POOF!
WHOA!
CROOW!!
But where did the board go?
AAAAAH!
Over there!
GO! I've got your back!!
Paul is on the move!

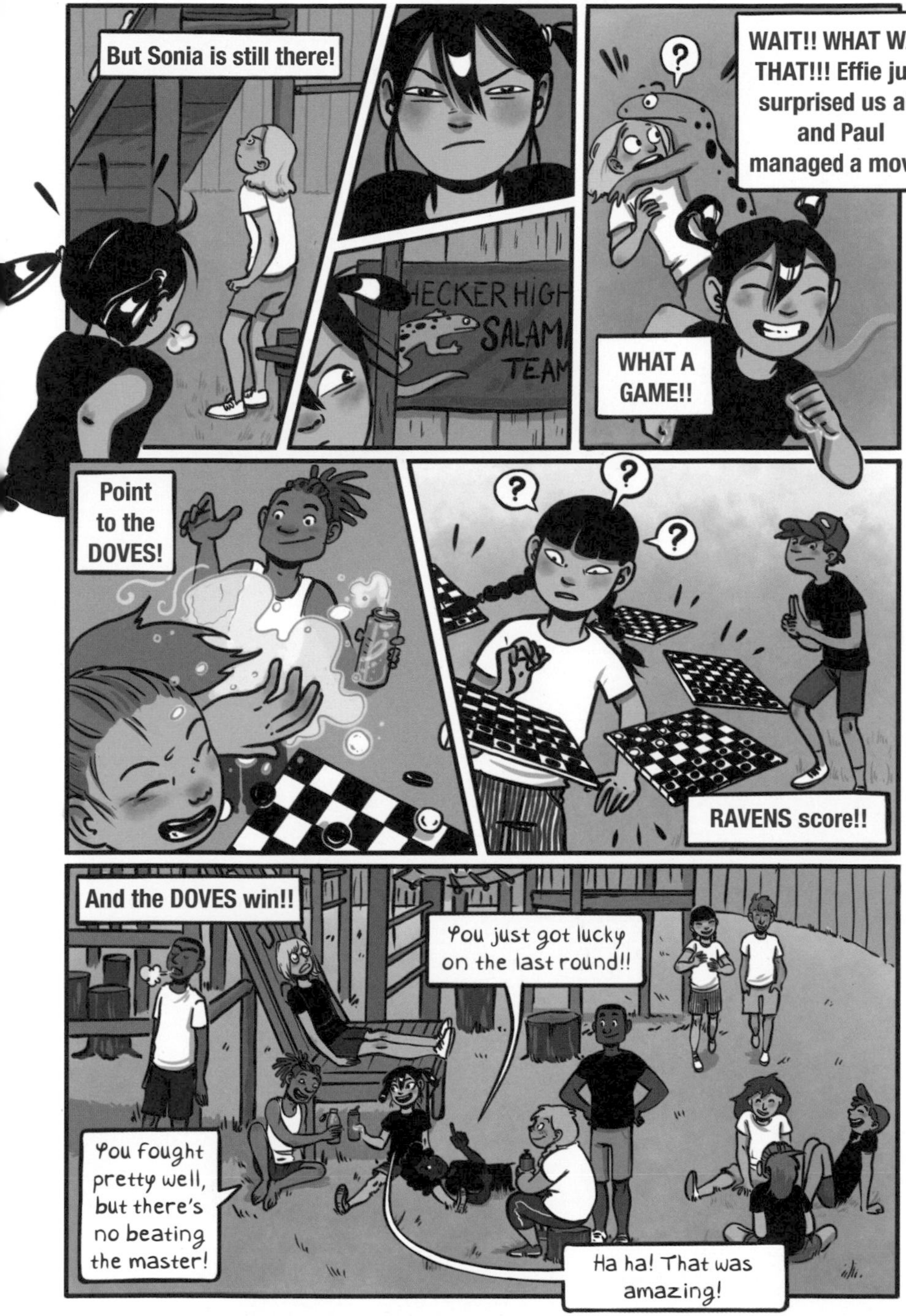

But Sonia is still there!
HECKER HIGH SALAM TEAM
WAIT!! WHAT WAS THAT!!! Effie just surprised us all, and Paul managed a move!
?
WHAT A GAME!!
Point to the DOVES!
?
?
?
RAVENS score!!
And the DOVES win!!
You just got lucky on the last round!!
You fought pretty well, but there's no beating the master!
Ha ha! That was amazing!

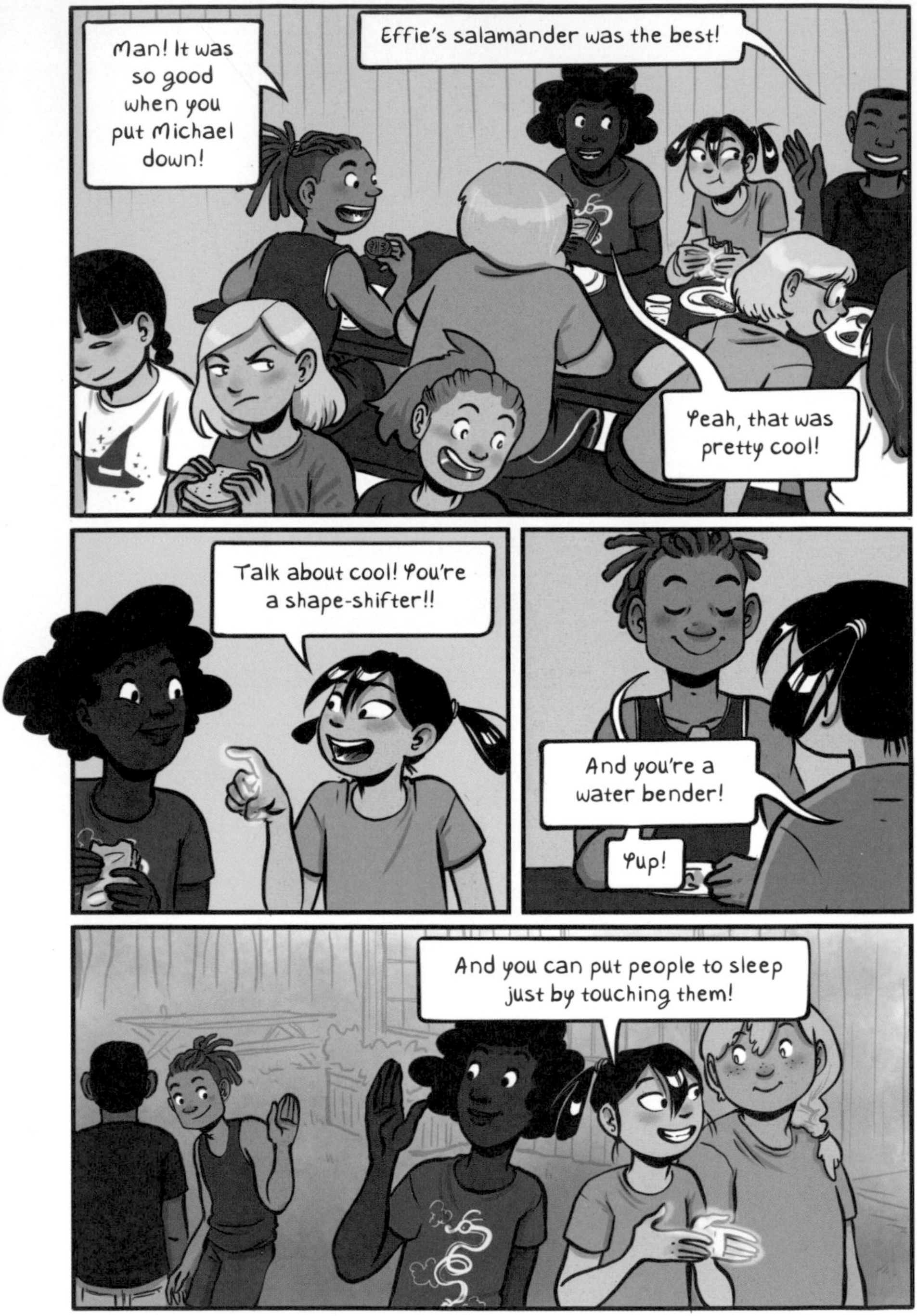
Man! It was so good when you put Michael down!
Effie's salamander was the best!
Yeah, that was pretty cool!
Talk about cool! You're a shape-shifter!!
And you're a water bender!
Yup!
And you can put people to sleep just by touching them!

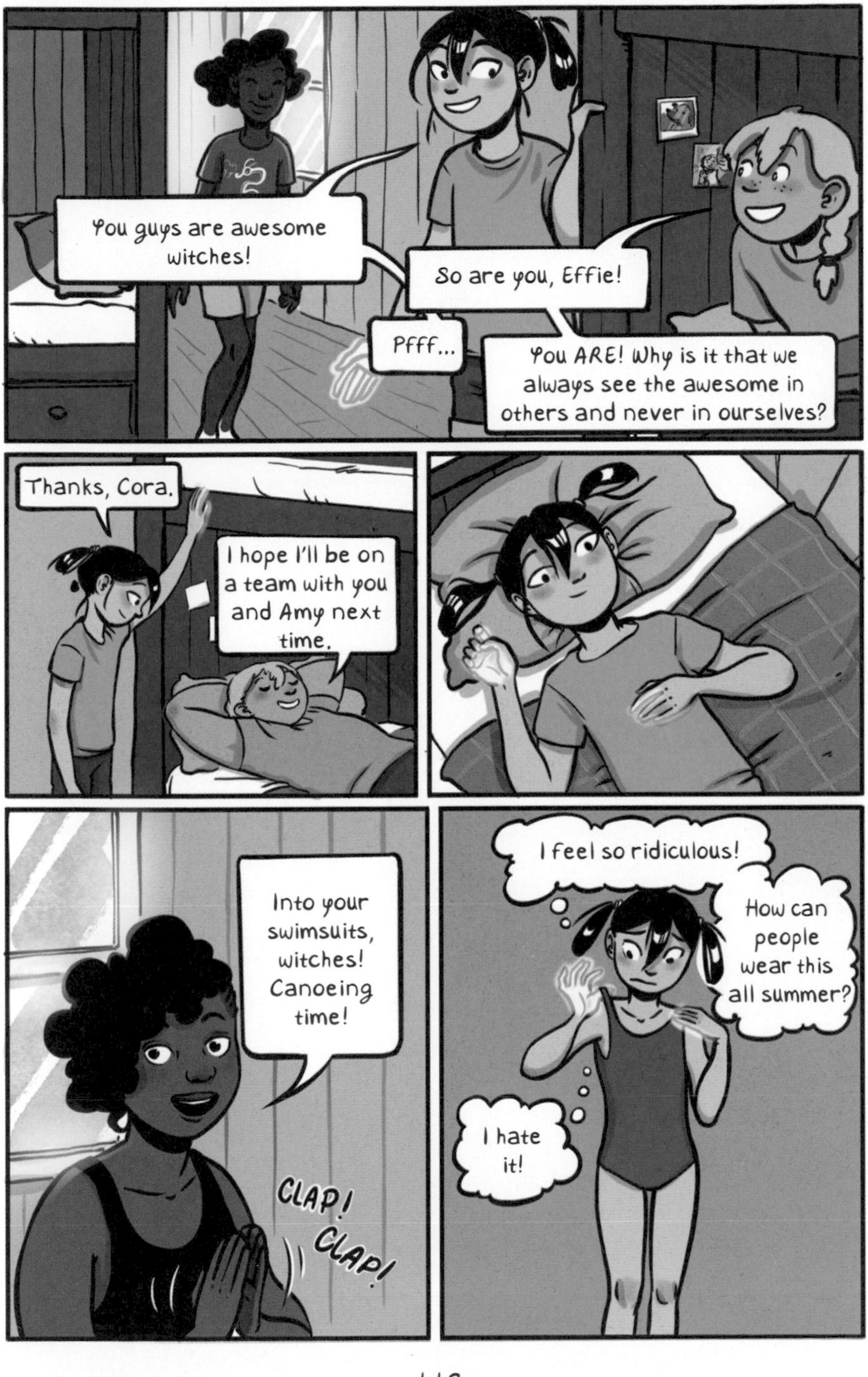

You guys are awesome witches!
So are you, Effie!
Pfff...
You ARE! Why is it that we always see the awesome in others and never in ourselves?
Thanks, Cora.
I hope I'll be on a team with you and Amy next time.
Into your swimsuits, witches! Canoeing time!
CLAP! CLAP!
I feel so ridiculous!
How can people wear this all summer?
I hate it!

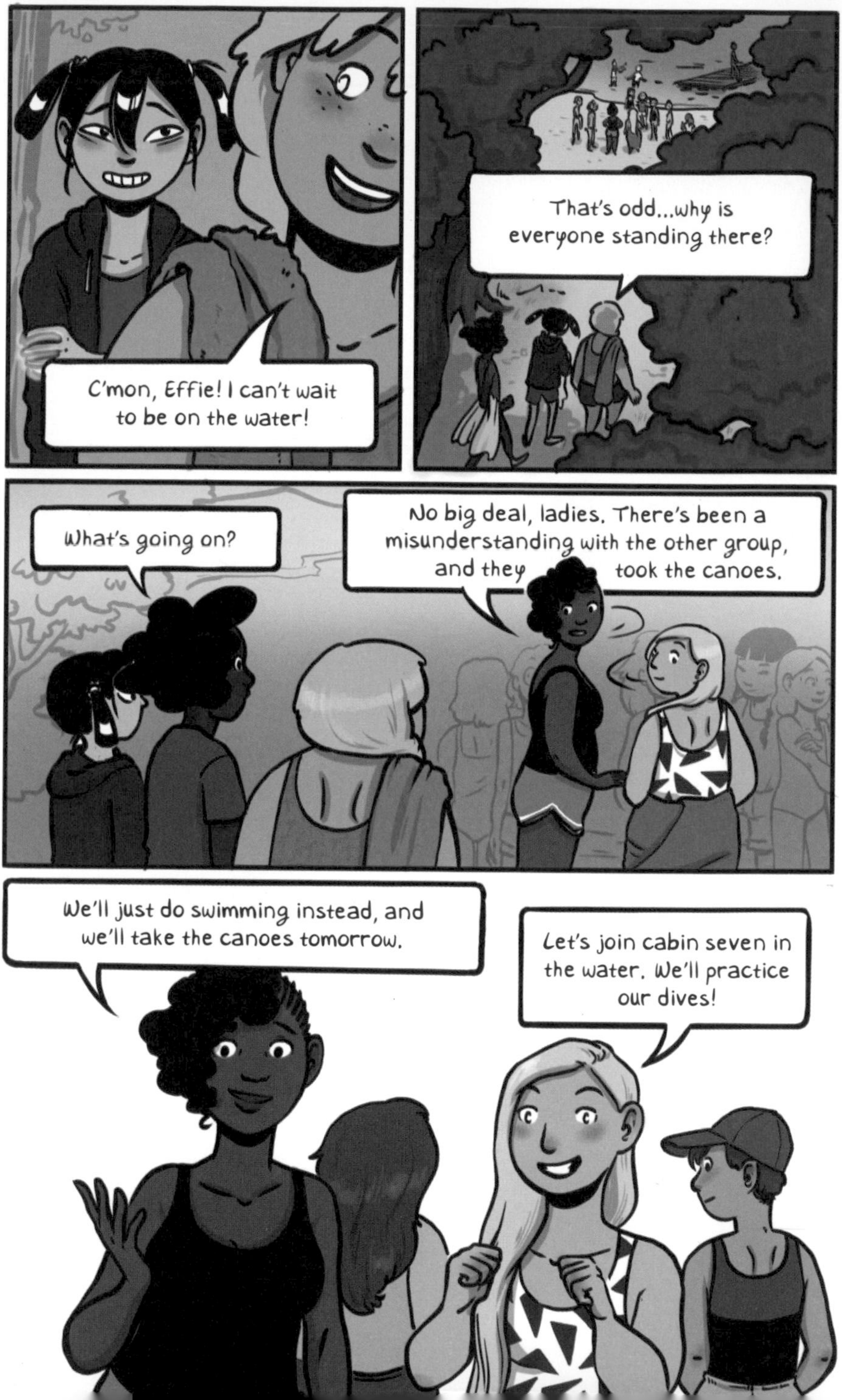
C'mon, Effie! I can't wait to be on the water!
That's odd...why is everyone standing there?
What's going on?
No big deal, ladies. There's been a misunderstanding with the other group, and they took the canoes.
We'll just do swimming instead, and we'll take the canoes tomorrow.
Let's join cabin seven in the water. We'll practice our dives!

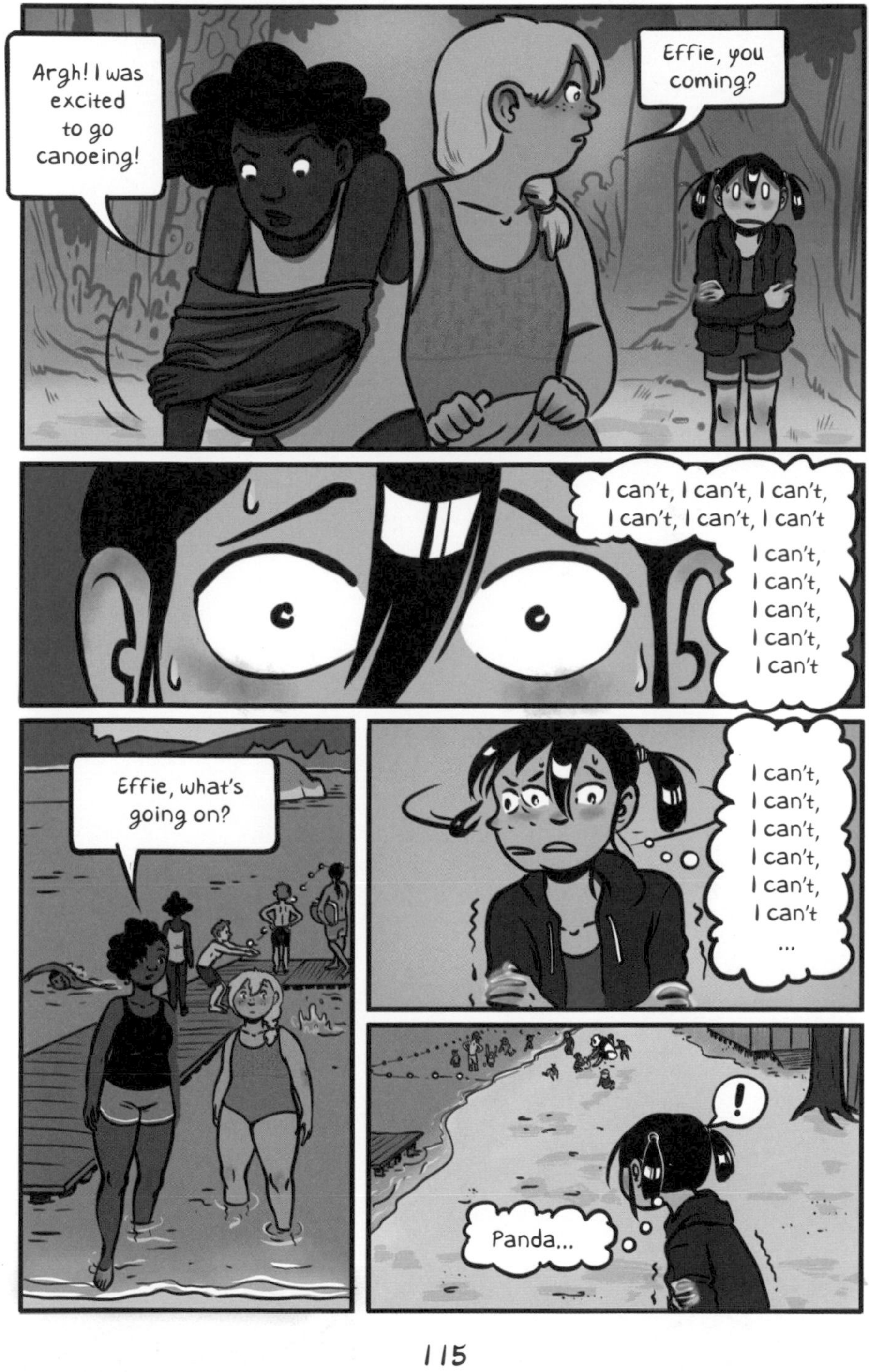
Argh! I was excited to go canoeing!
Effie, you coming?
I can't, I can't, I can't, I can't, I can't, I can't
I can't, I can't, I can't, I can't, I can't
Effie, what's going on?
I can't, I can't, I can't, I can't, I can't, I can't ...
!
Panda...

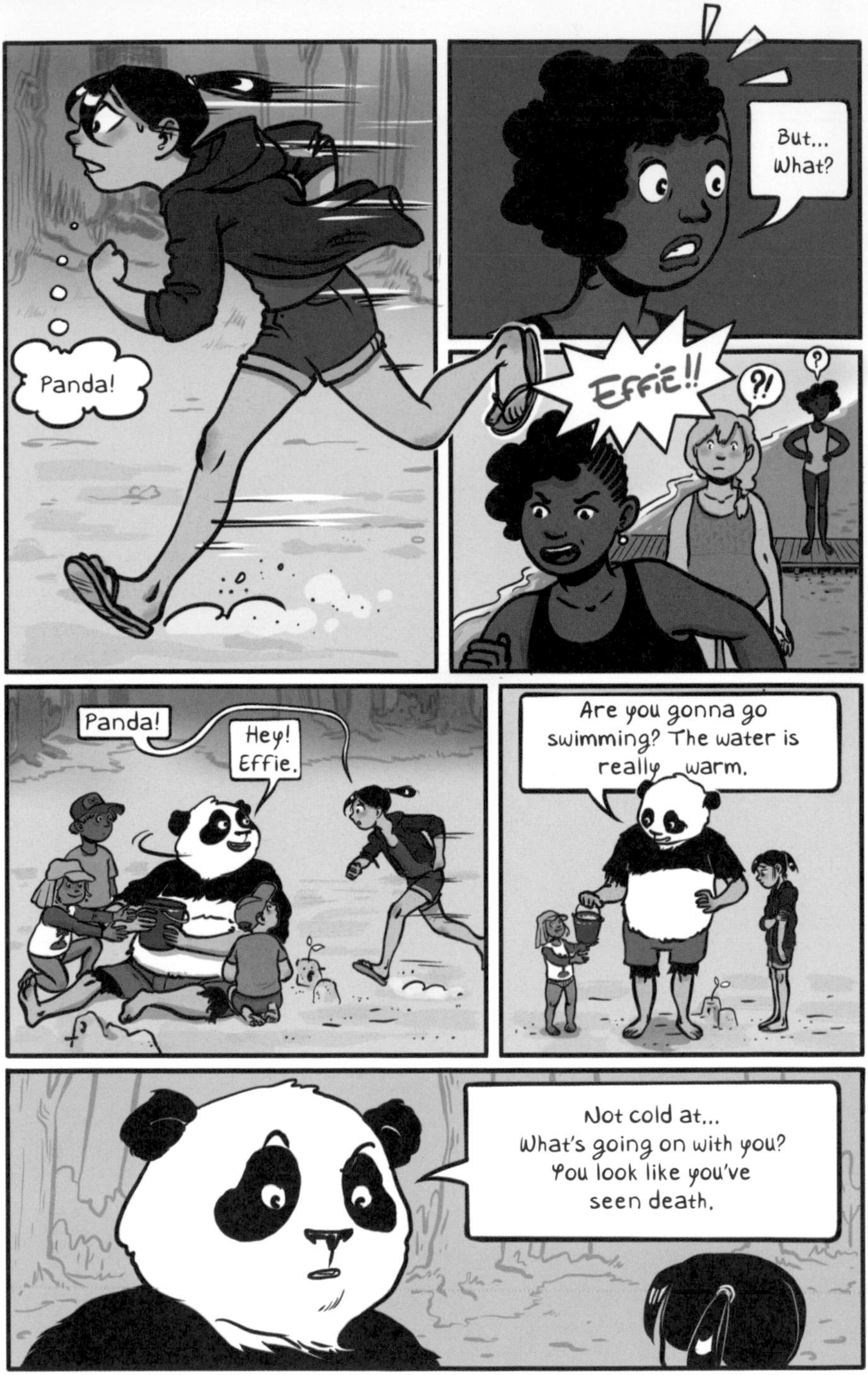

Panda!
But... What?
EFFIE!!
?!
?
Panda!
Hey! Effie.
Are you gonna go swimming? The water is really warm.
Not cold at... What's going on with you? You look like you've seen death.

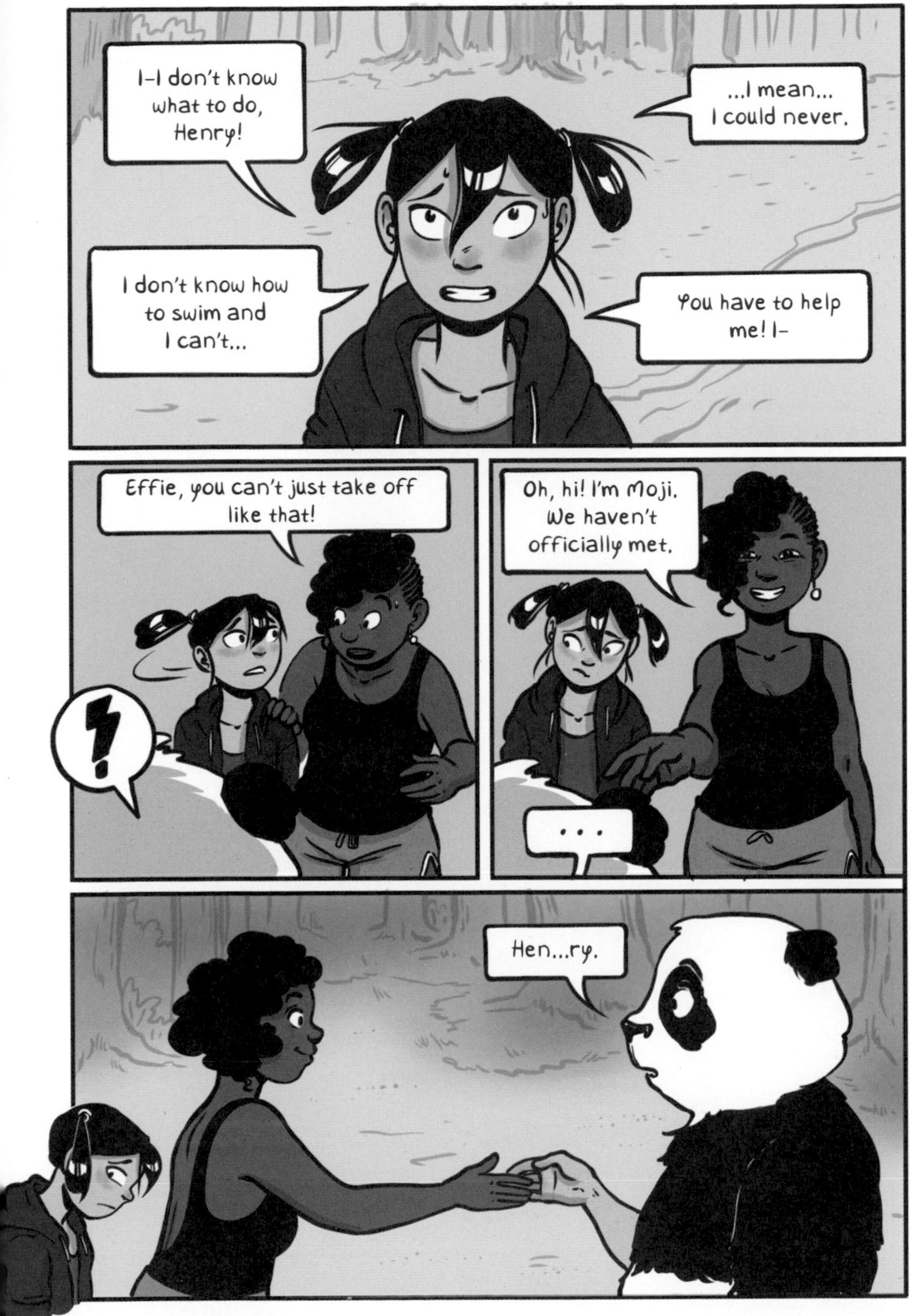
I-I don't know what to do, Henry!
...I mean... I could never.
I don't know how to swim and I can't...
You have to help me! I-
Effie, you can't just take off like that!
!
Oh, hi! I'm Moji. We haven't officially met.
...
Hen...ry.

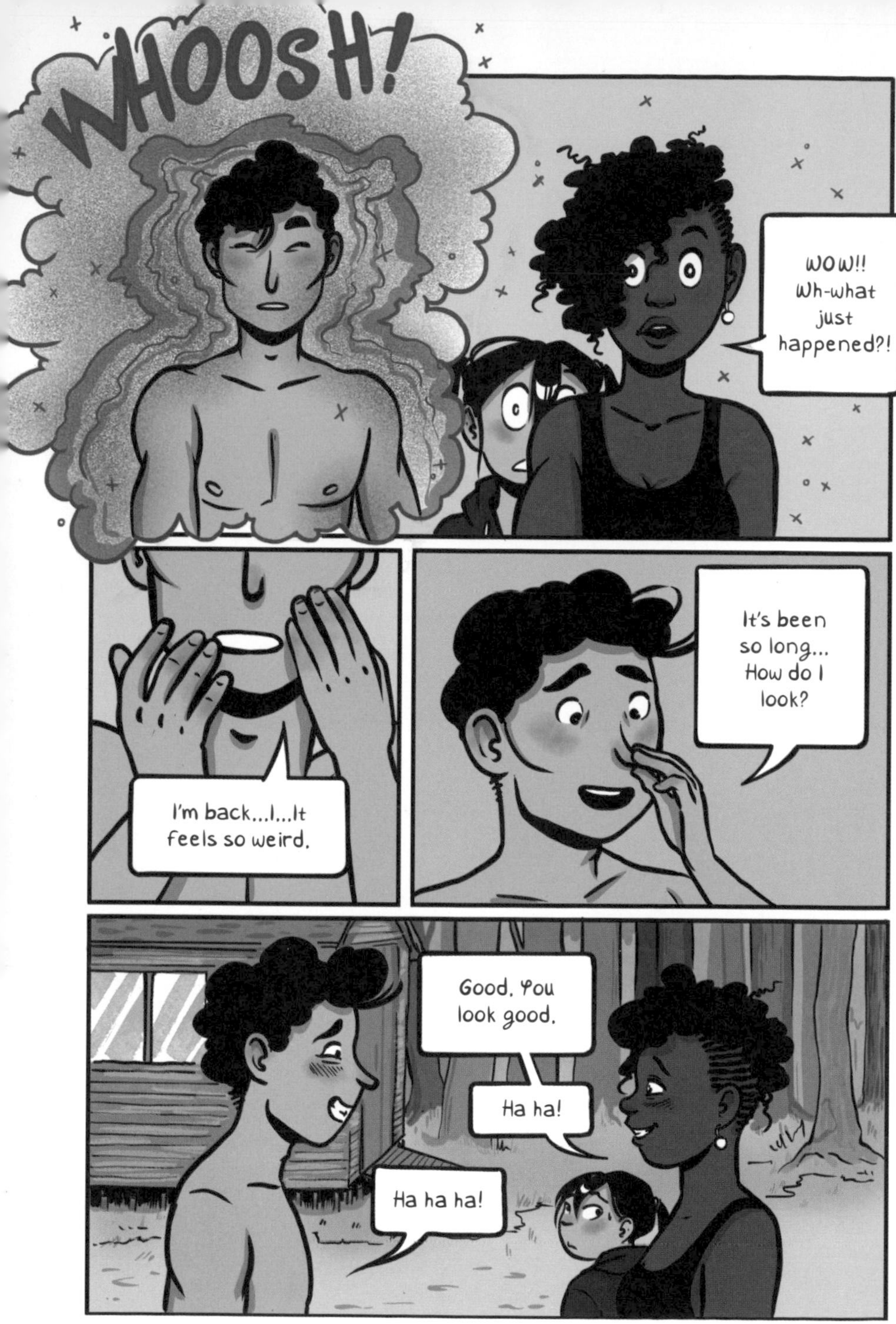
WHOOSH!
WOW!! Wh-what just happened?!
I'm back...I...It feels so weird.
It's been so long... How do I look?
Good. You look good.
Ha ha!
Ha ha ha!

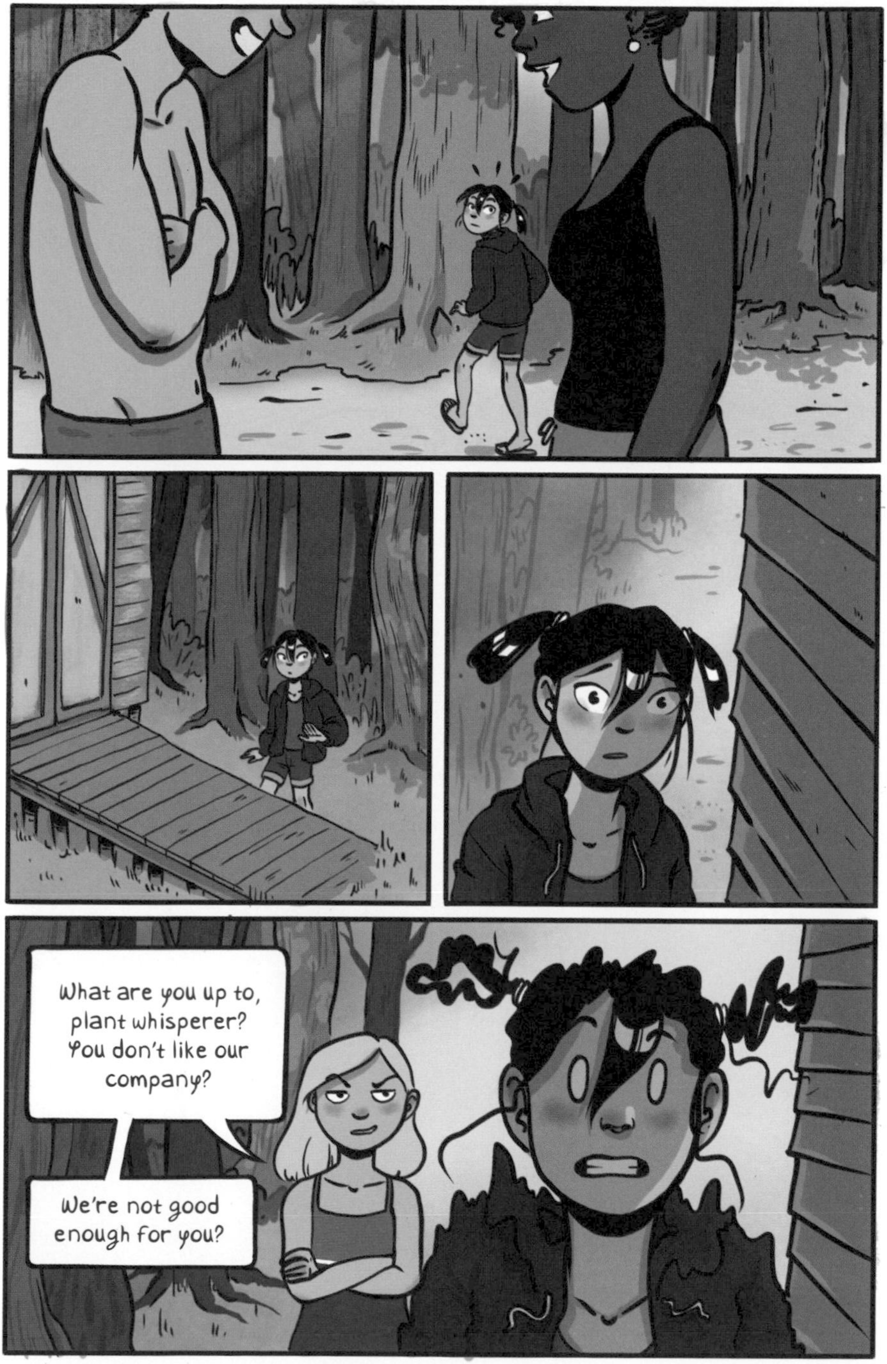
What are you up to, plant whisperer? You don't like our company?
We're not good enough for you?

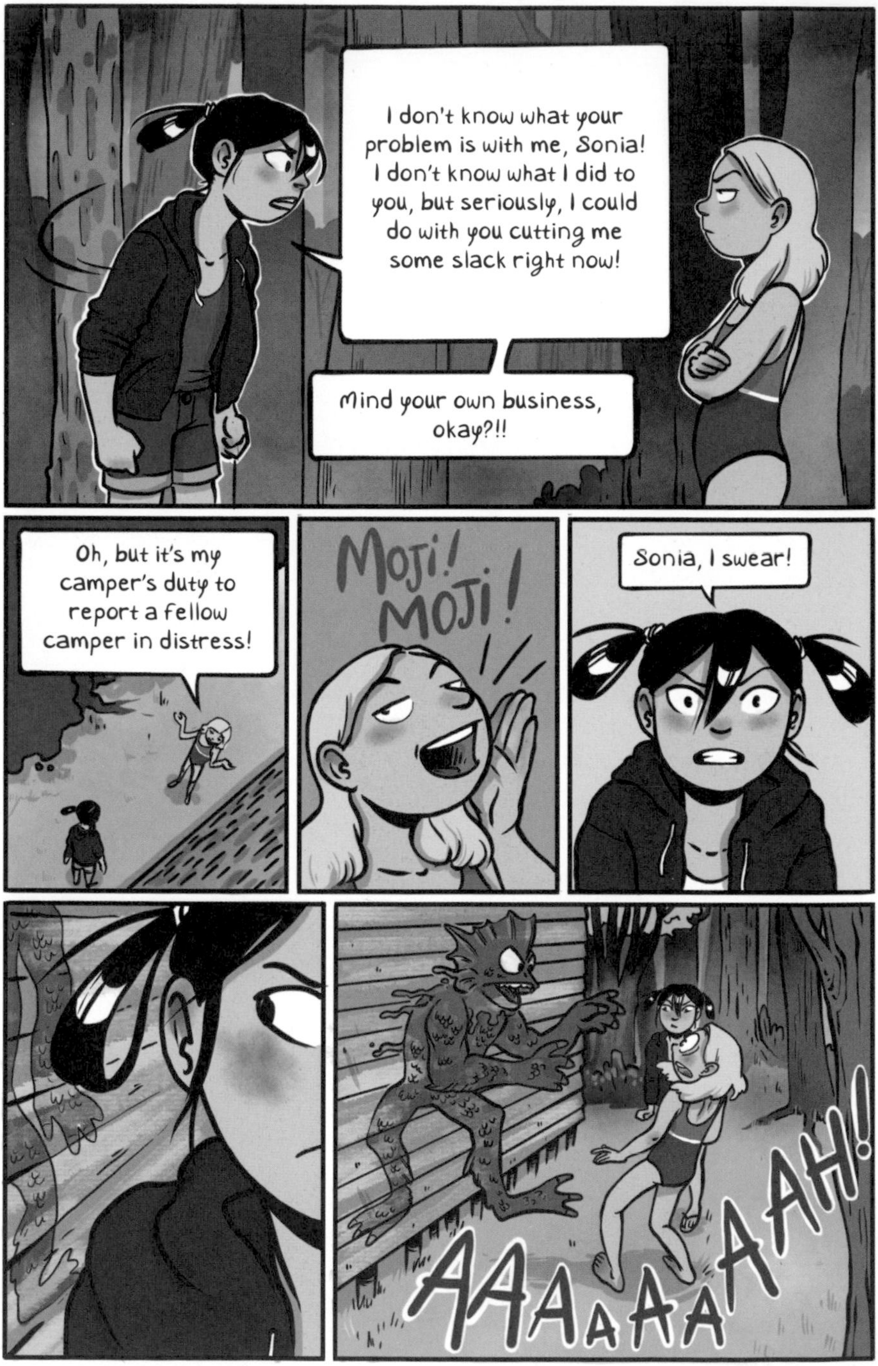

I don't know what your problem is with me, Sonia! I don't know what I did to you, but seriously, I could do with you cutting me some slack right now!
Mind your own business, okay?!!
Oh, but it's my camper's duty to report a fellow camper in distress!
MOJI! MOJI!
Sonia, I swear!
AAAAAAAAH!

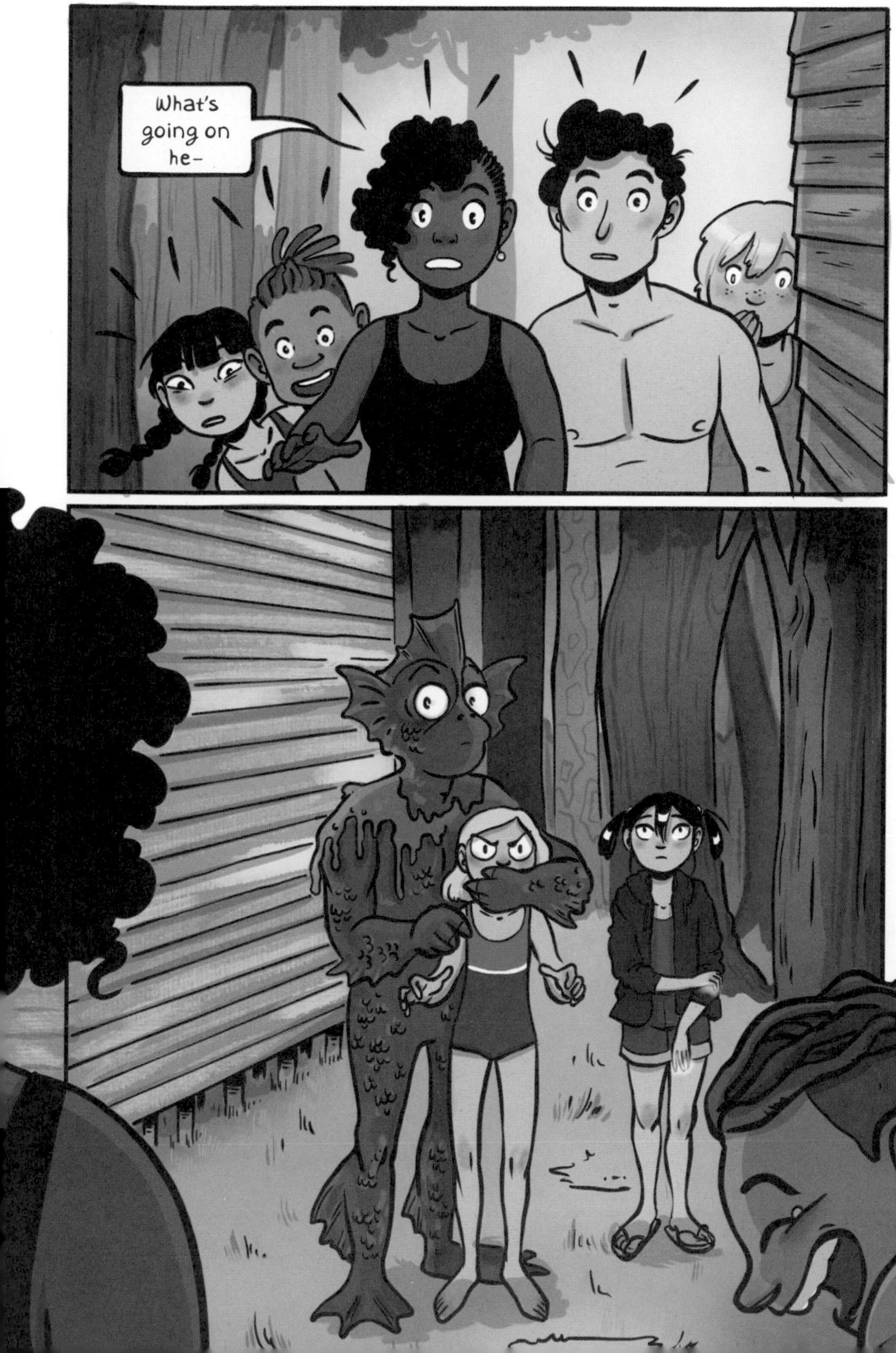
What's going on he-

Chapter 4

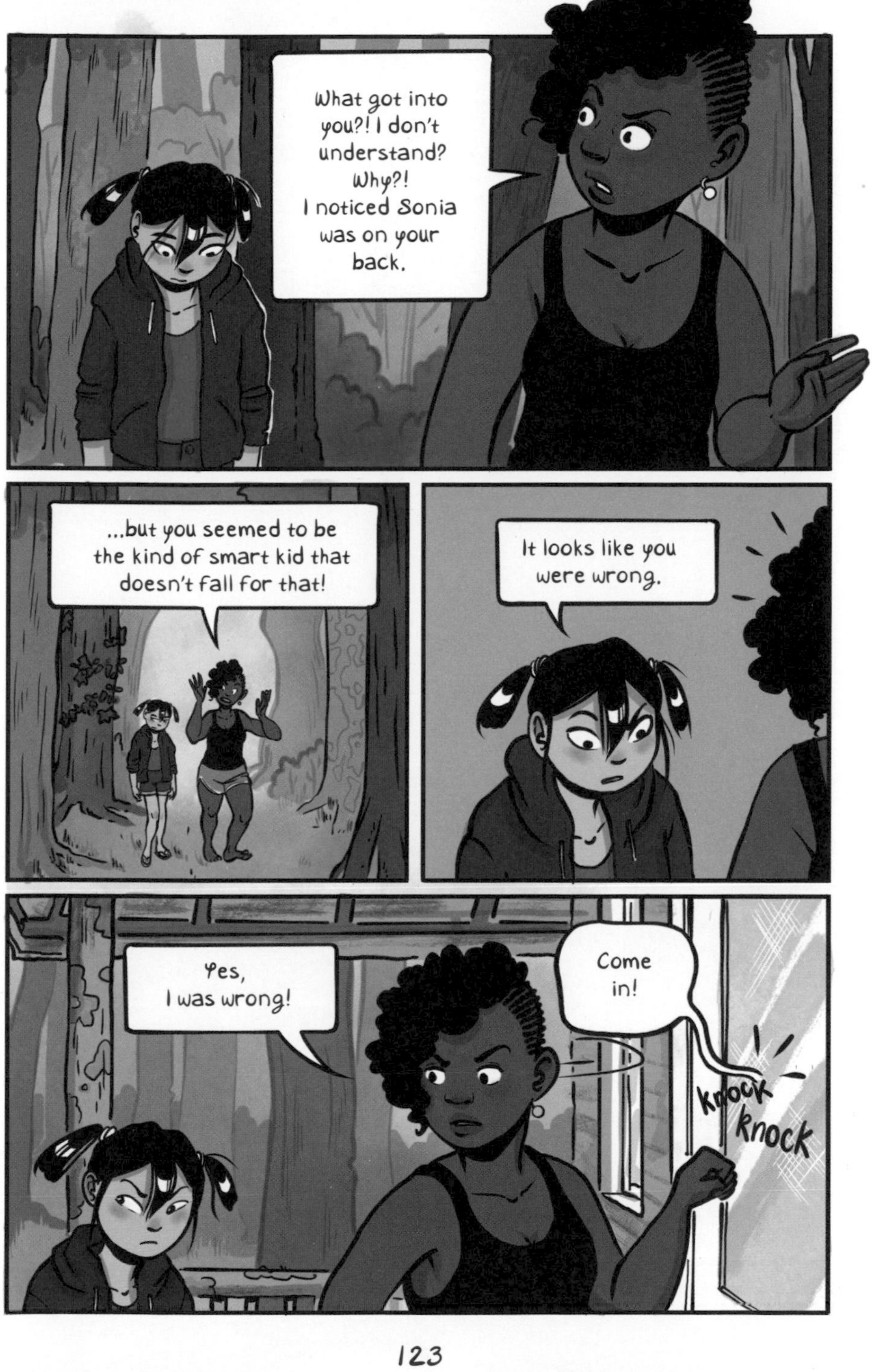
What got into you?! I don't understand? Why?! I noticed Sonia was on your back.
...but you seemed to be the kind of smart kid that doesn't fall for that!
It looks like you were wrong.
Yes, I was wrong!
Come in!
knock knock

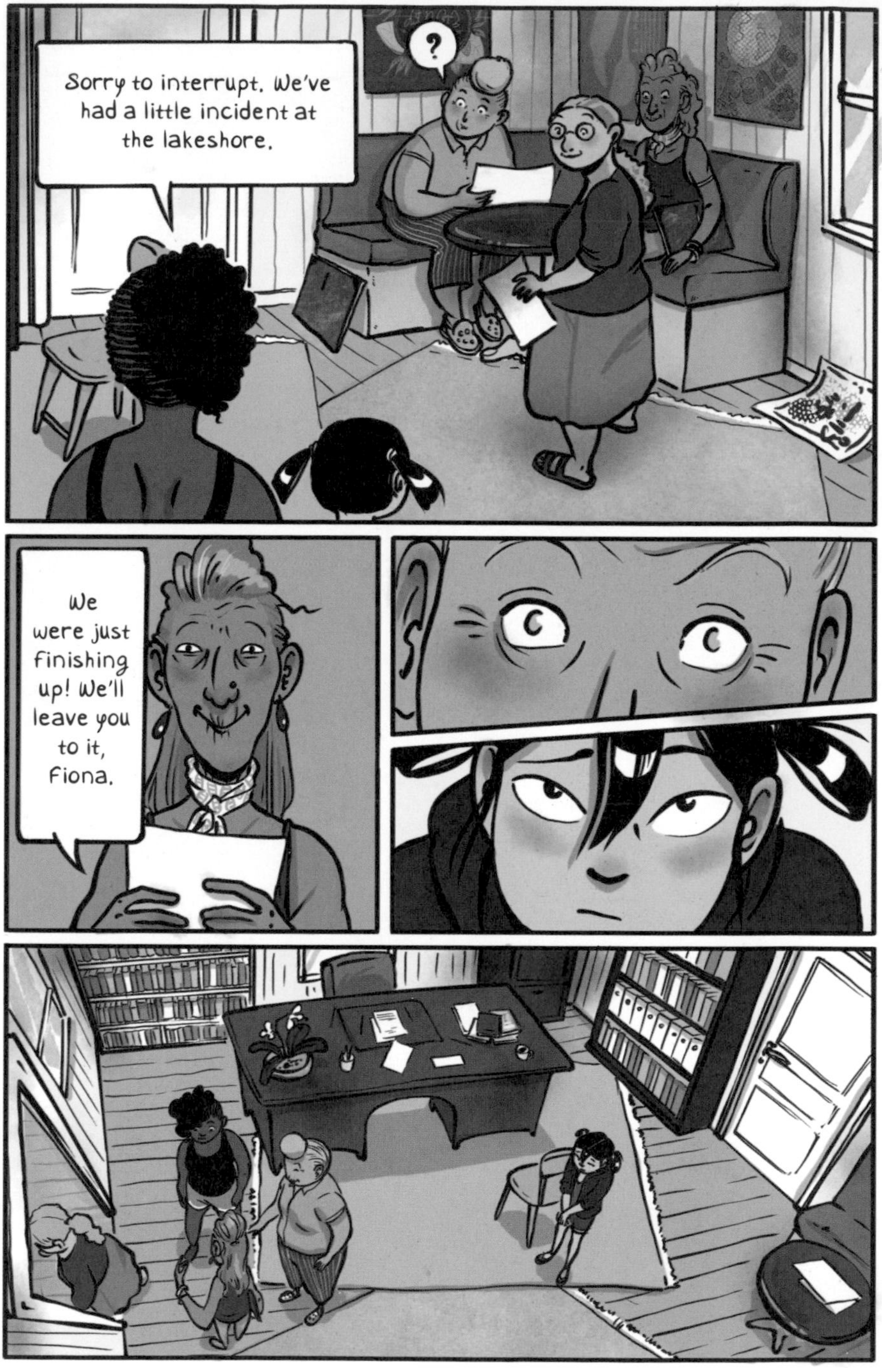
?
Sorry to interrupt. We've had a little incident at the lakeshore.
We were just finishing up! We'll leave you to it, Fiona.

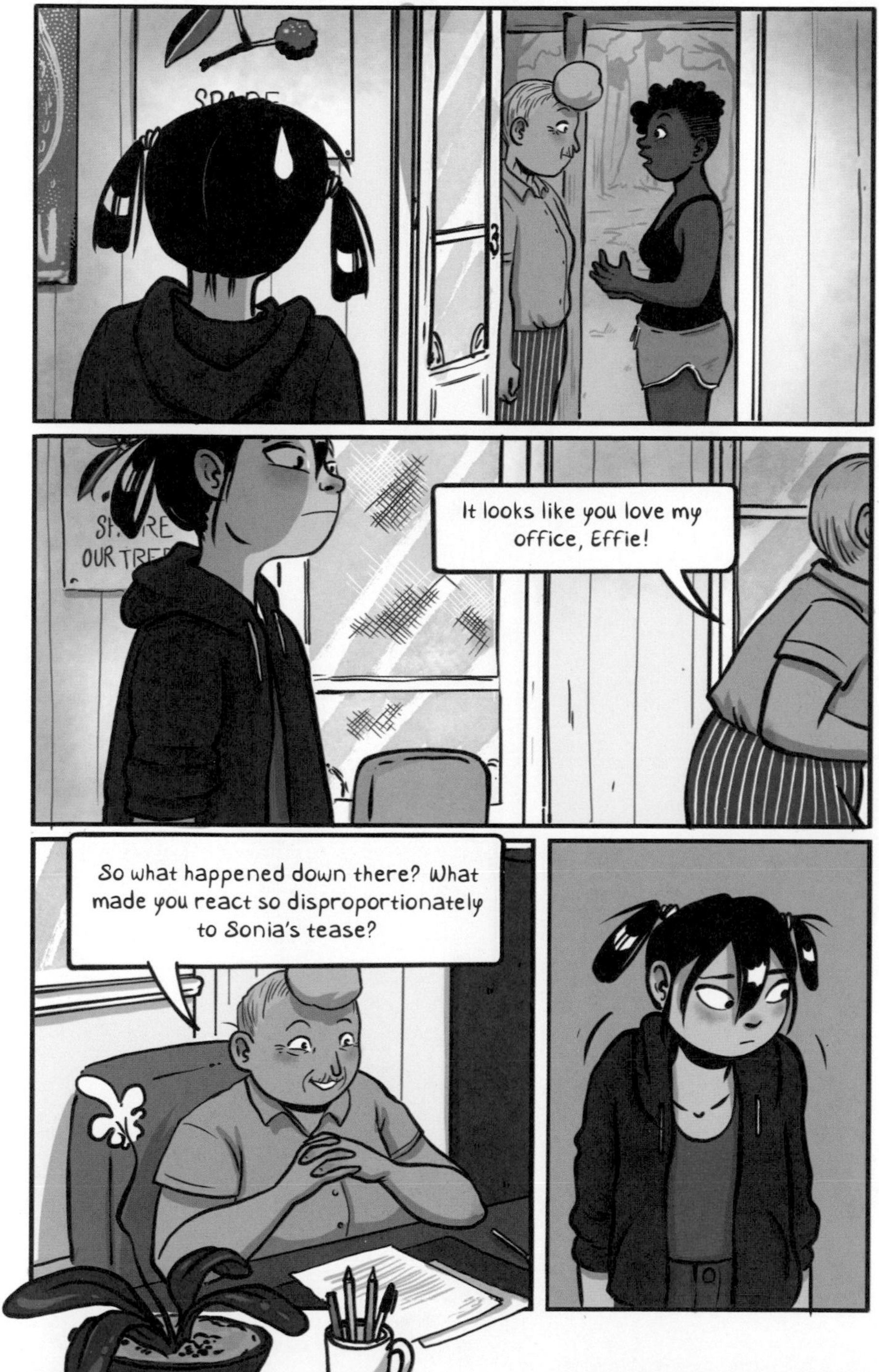

It looks like you love my office, Effie!
So what happened down there? What made you react so disproportionately to Sonia's tease?

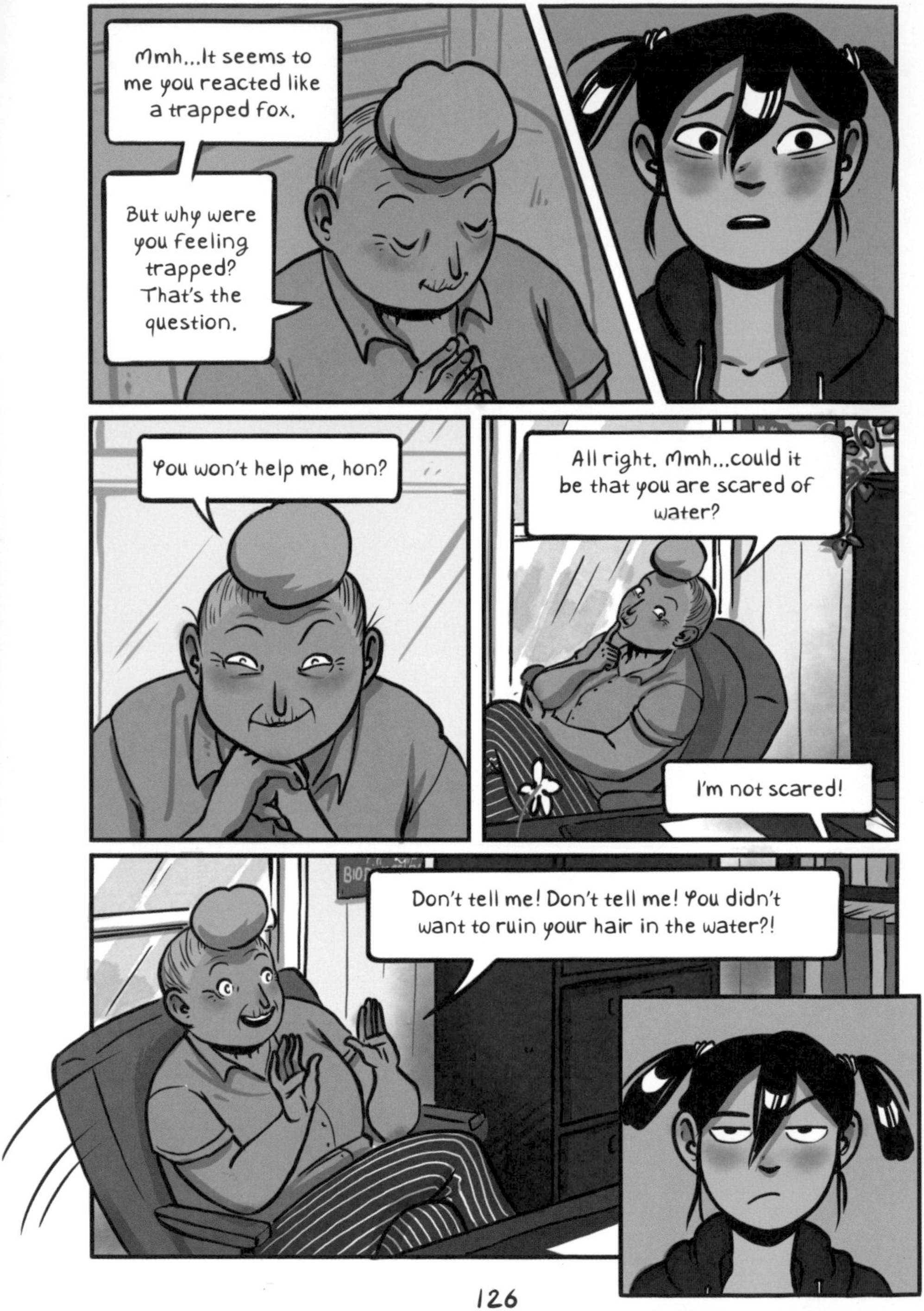
Mmh...It seems to me you reacted like a trapped fox.
But why were you feeling trapped? That's the question.
You won't help me, hon?
All right. Mmh...could it be that you are scared of water?
I'm not scared!
Don't tell me! Don't tell me! You didn't want to ruin your hair in the water?!

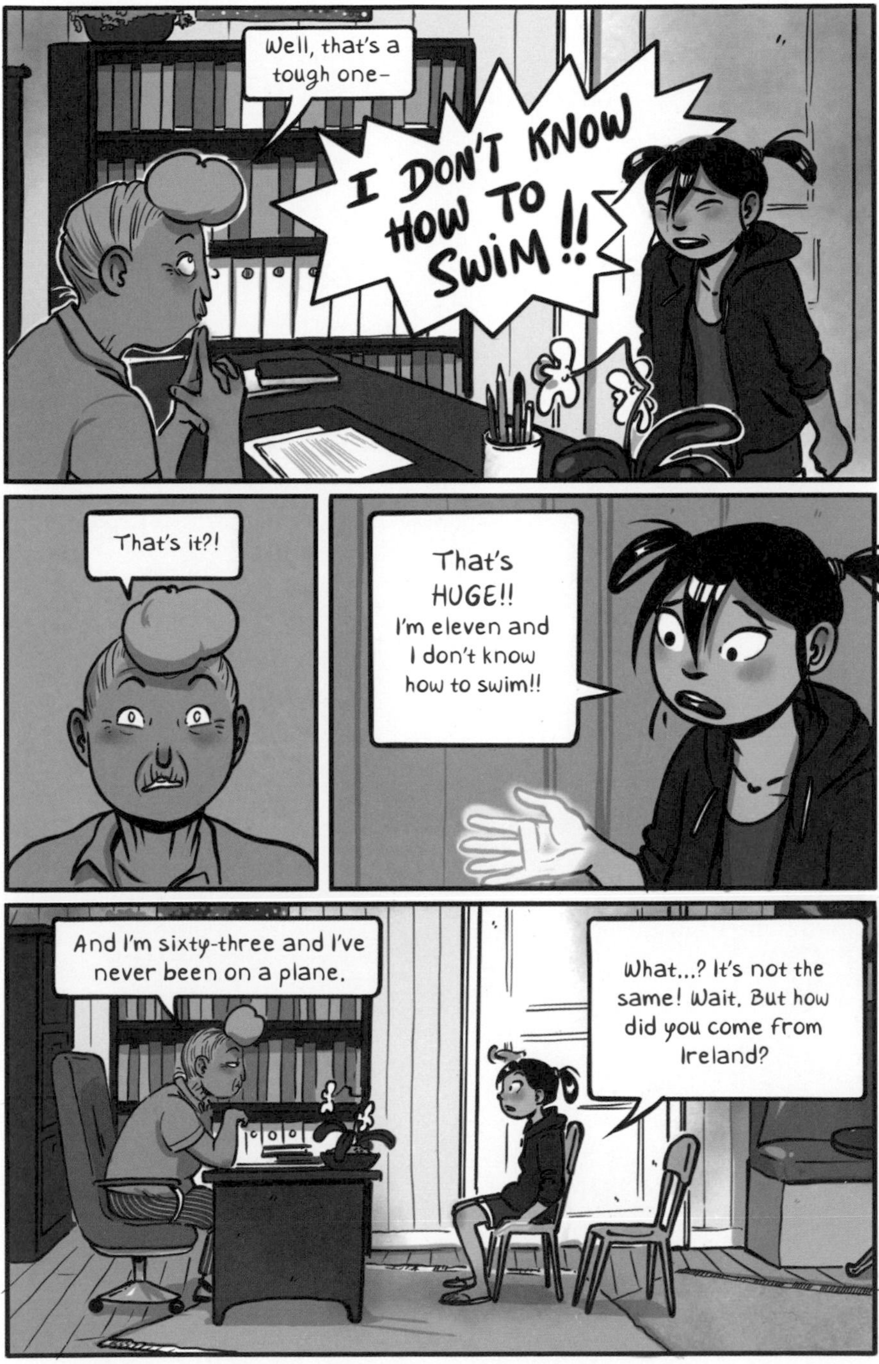
Well, that's a tough one–
I DON'T KNOW HOW TO SWIM!!
That's it?!
That's HUGE!! I'm eleven and I don't know how to swim!!
And I'm sixty-three and I've never been on a plane.
What...? It's not the same! Wait. But how did you come from Ireland?

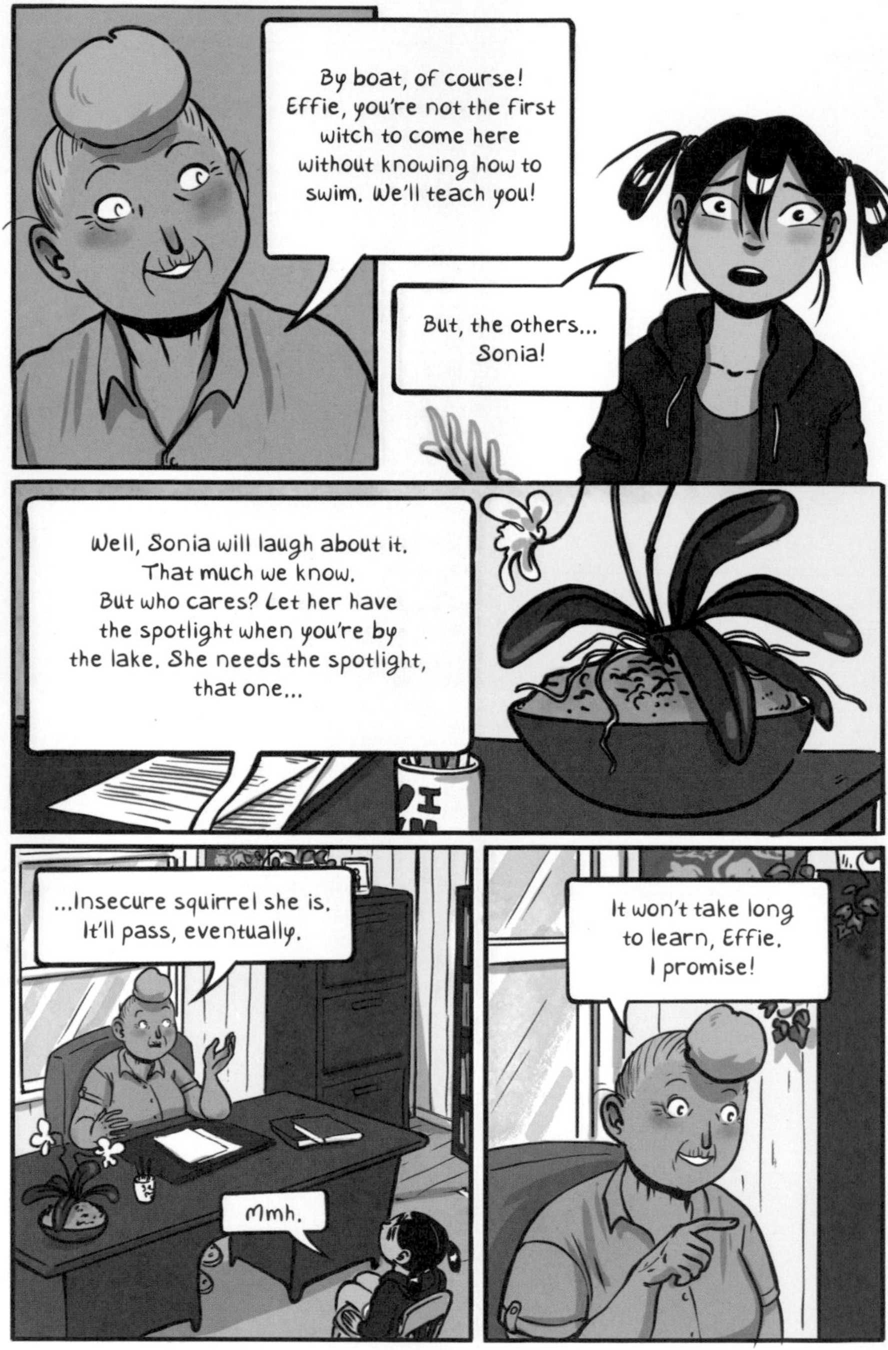
By boat, of course! Effie, you're not the first witch to come here without knowing how to swim. We'll teach you!
But, the others... Sonia!
Well, Sonia will laugh about it. That much we know. But who cares? Let her have the spotlight when you're by the lake. She needs the spotlight, that one...
...Insecure squirrel she is. It'll pass, eventually.
Mmh.
It won't take long to learn, Effie. I promise!

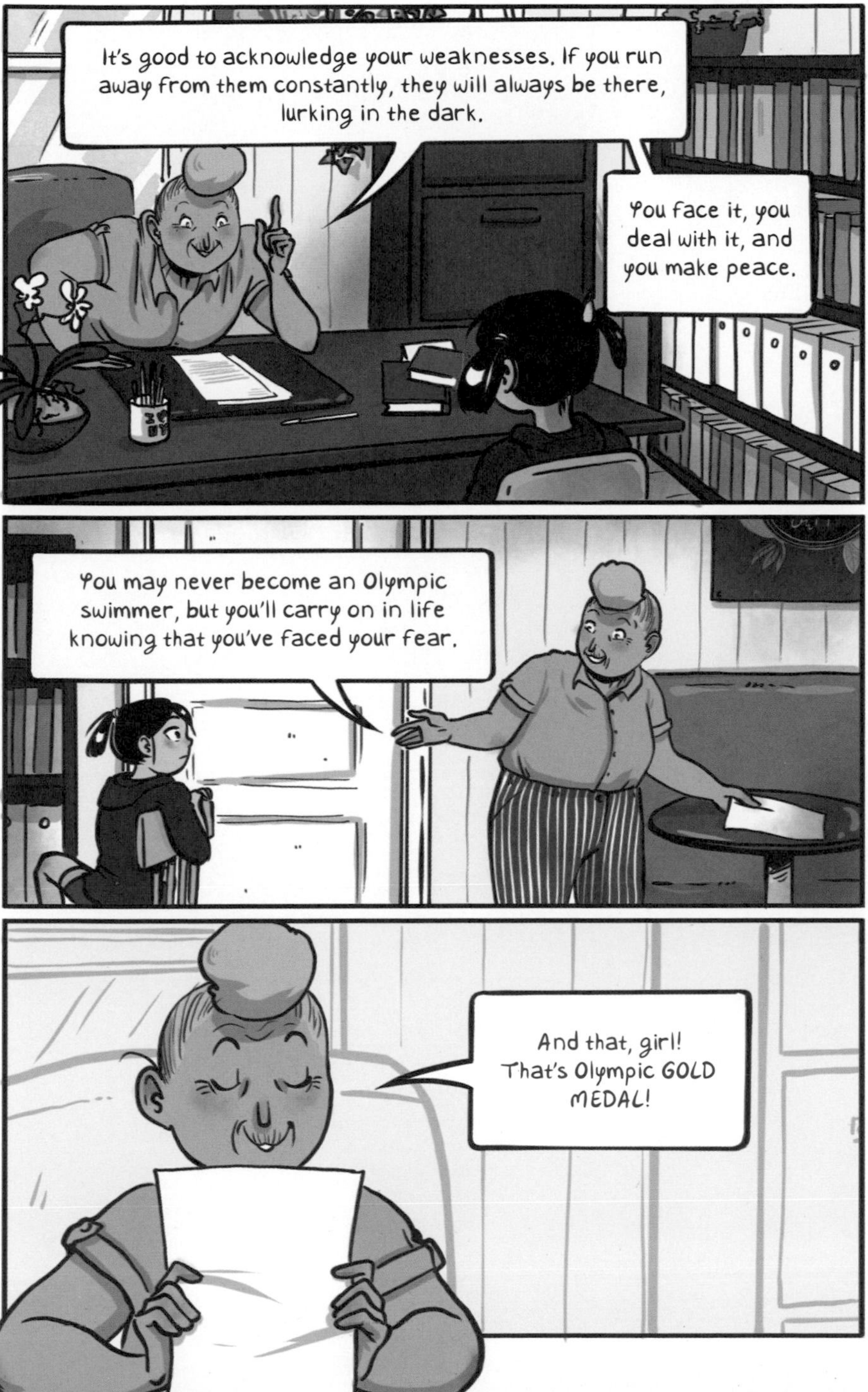
It's good to acknowledge your weaknesses. If you run away from them constantly, they will always be there, lurking in the dark.
You face it, you deal with it, and you make peace.
You may never become an Olympic swimmer, but you'll carry on in life knowing that you've faced your fear.
And that, girl! That's Olympic GOLD MEDAL!

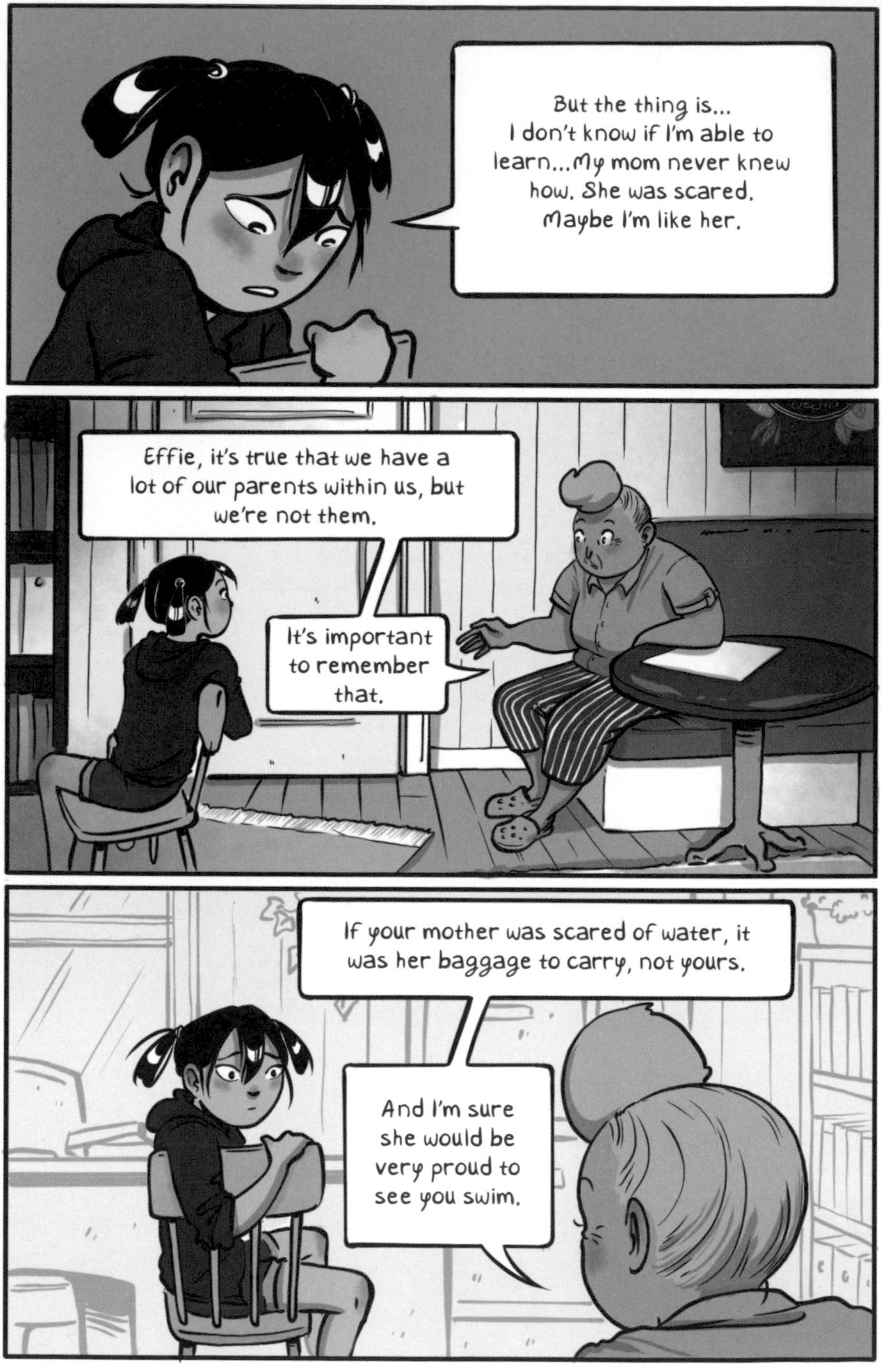
But the thing is... I don't know if I'm able to learn...My mom never knew how. She was scared. Maybe I'm like her.
Effie, it's true that we have a lot of our parents within us, but we're not them.
It's important to remember that.
If your mother was scared of water, it was her baggage to carry, not yours.
And I'm sure she would be very proud to see you swim.

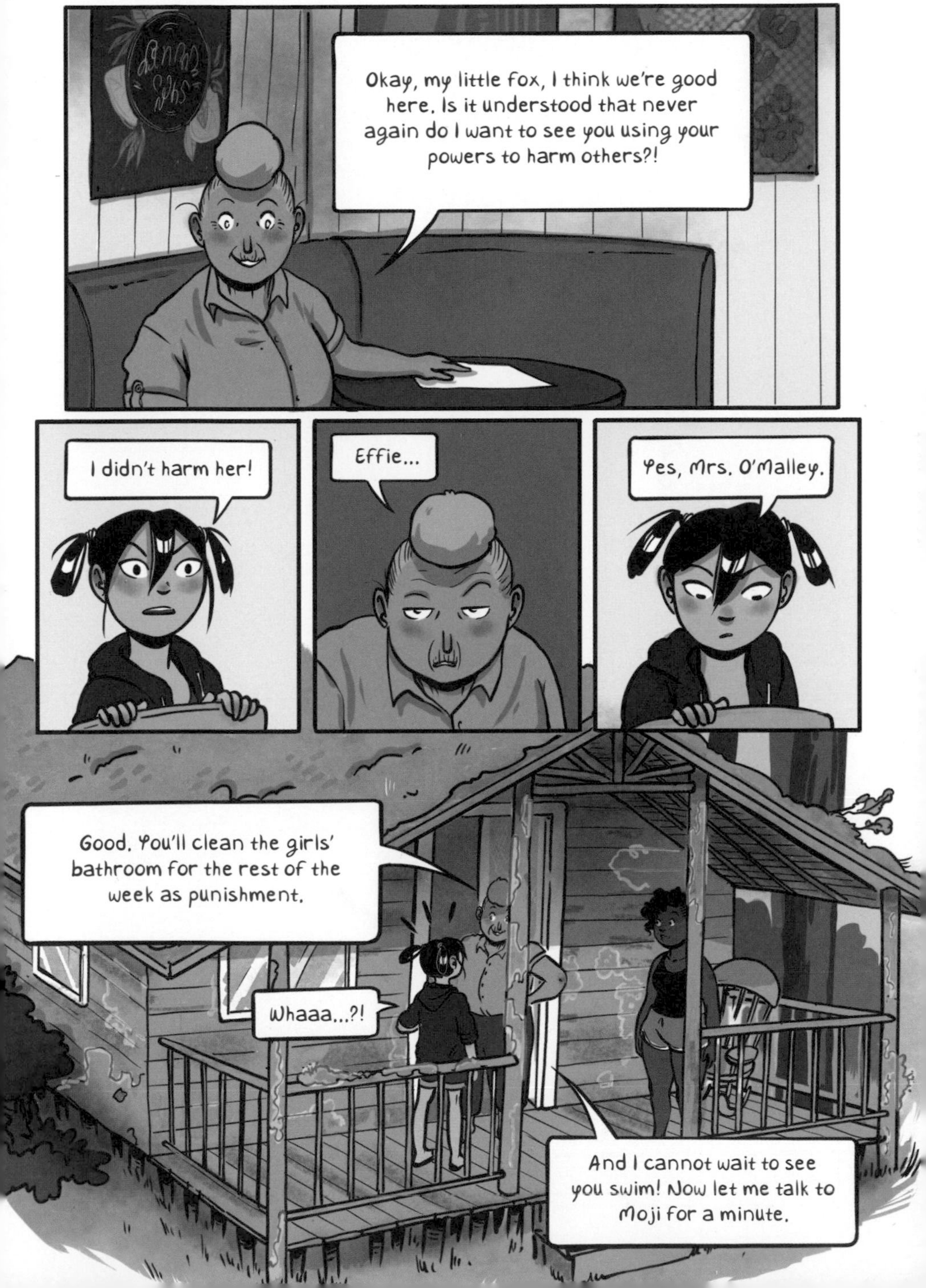
Okay, my little fox, I think we're good here. Is it understood that never again do I want to see you using your powers to harm others?!
I didn't harm her!
Effie...
Yes, Mrs. O'Malley.
Good. You'll clean the girls' bathroom for the rest of the week as punishment.
Whaaa...?!
And I cannot wait to see you swim! Now let me talk to Moji for a minute.

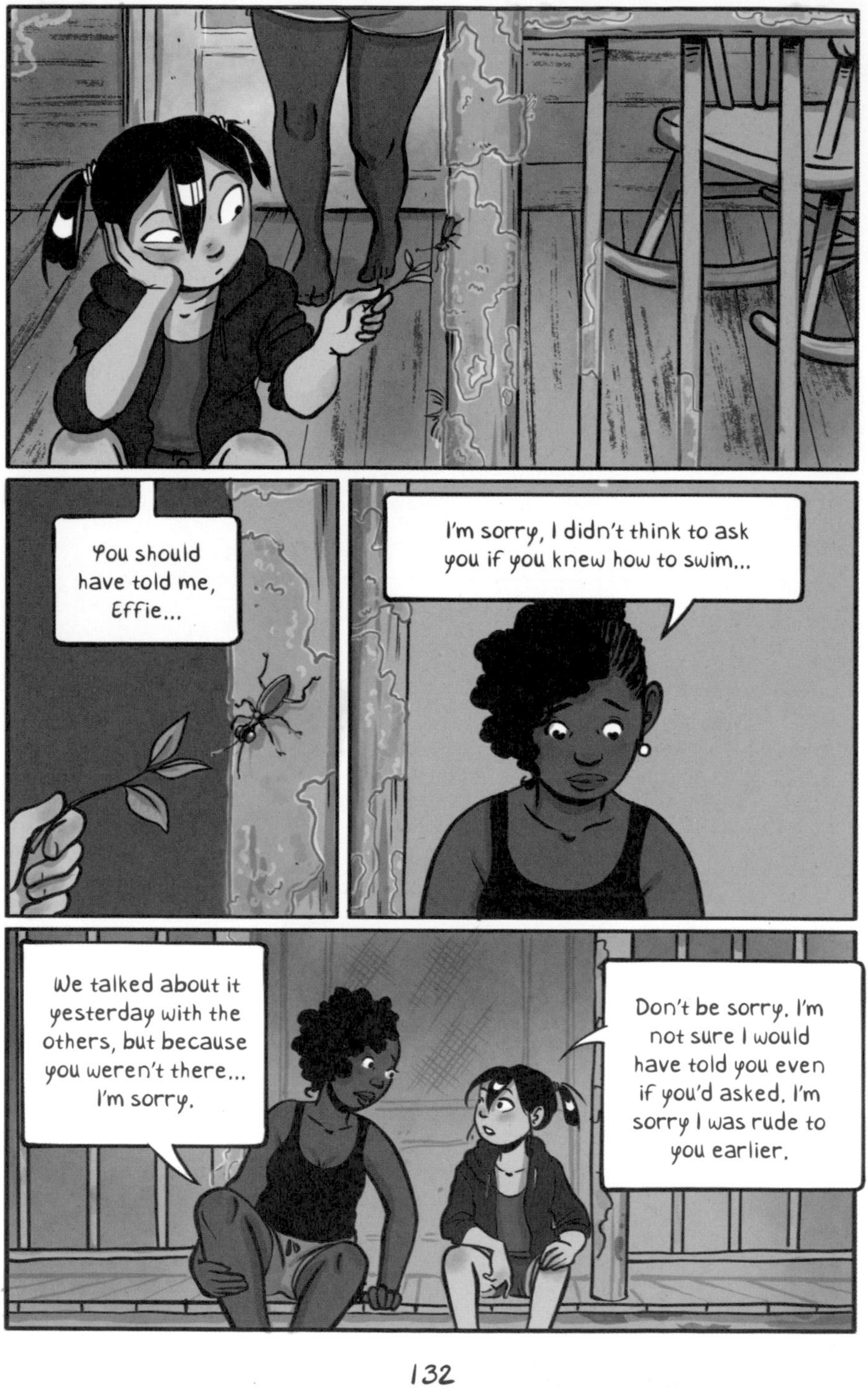
You should have told me, Effie...
I'm sorry, I didn't think to ask you if you knew how to swim...
We talked about it yesterday with the others, but because you weren't there... I'm sorry.
Don't be sorry. I'm not sure I would have told you even if you'd asked. I'm sorry I was rude to you earlier.

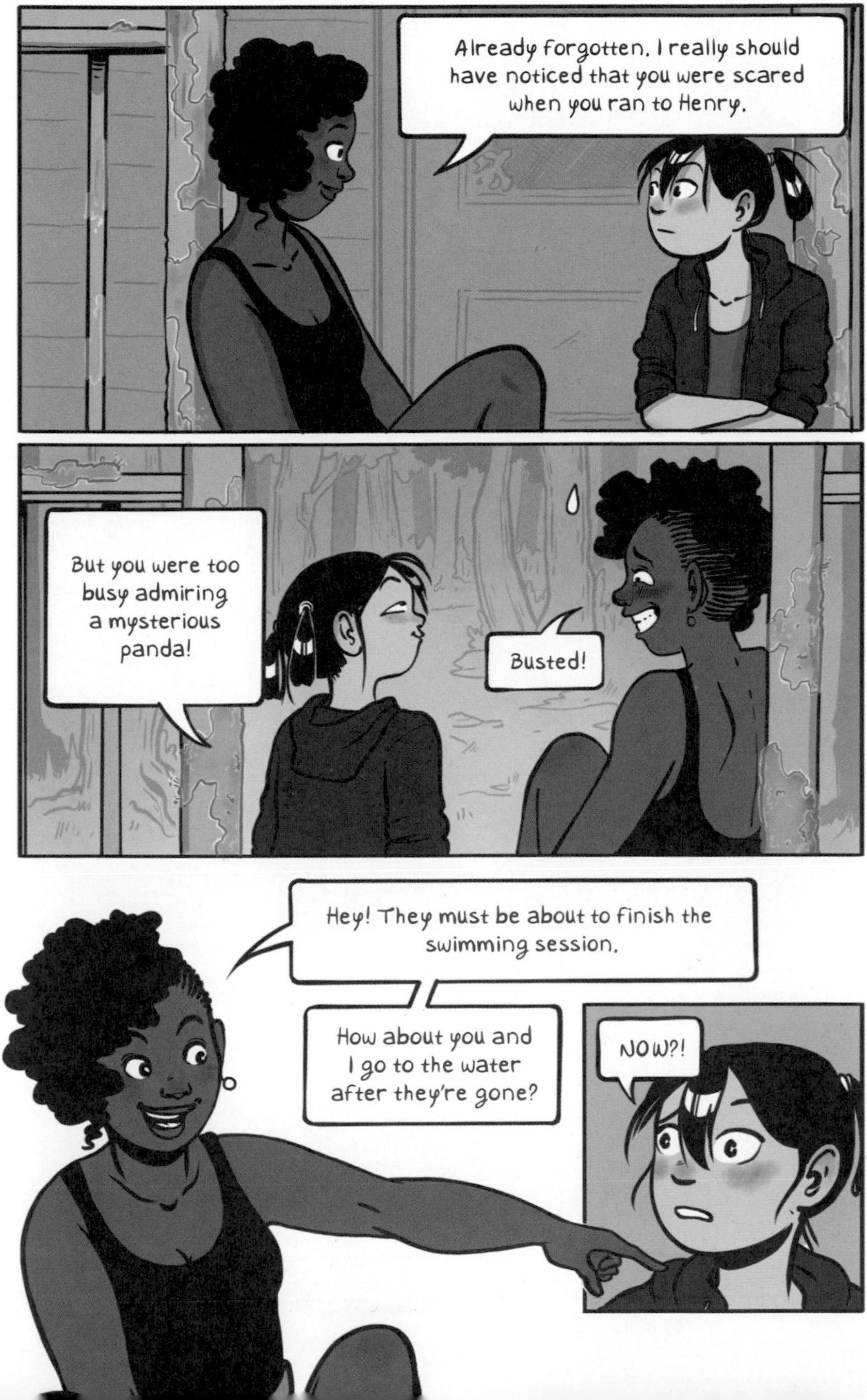

Already forgotten. I really should have noticed that you were scared when you ran to Henry.
But you were too busy admiring a mysterious panda!
Busted!
Hey! They must be about to finish the swimming session.
How about you and I go to the water after they're gone?
NOW?!

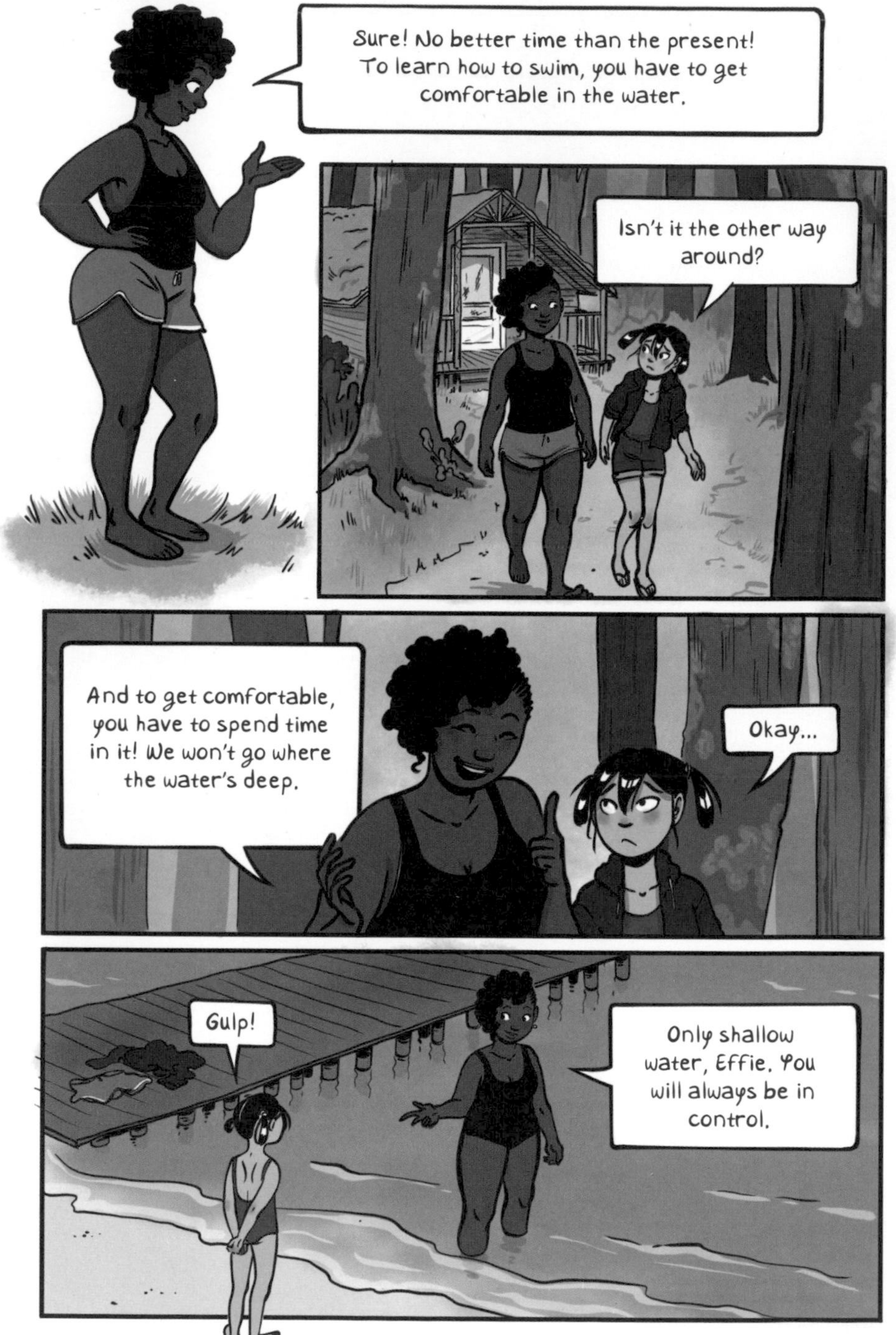
Sure! No better time than the present! To learn how to swim, you have to get comfortable in the water.
Isn't it the other way around?
And to get comfortable, you have to spend time in it! We won't go where the water's deep.
Okay...
Gulp!
Only shallow water, Effie. You will always be in control.

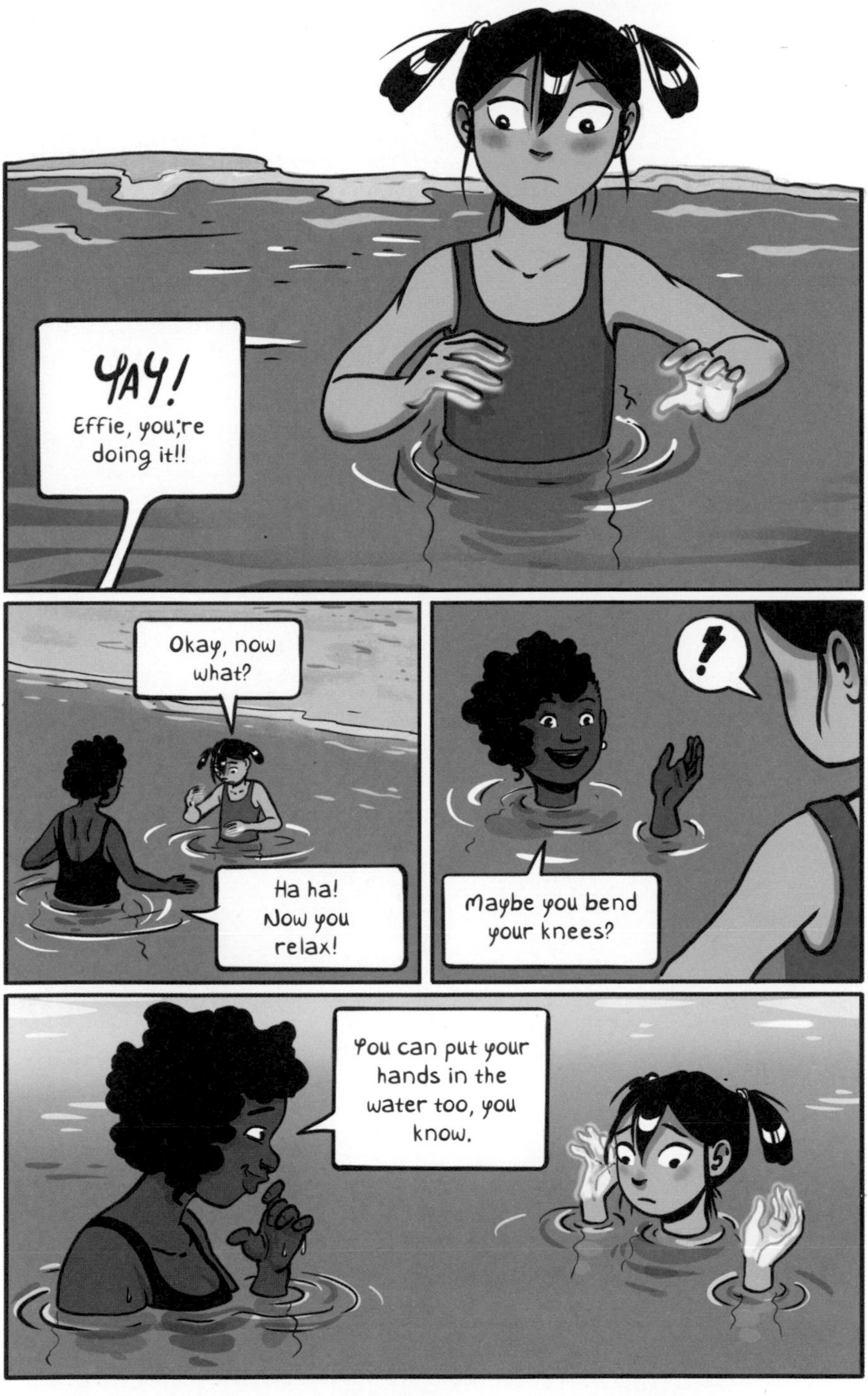
YAY! Effie, you;re doing it!!
Okay, now what?
Ha ha! Now you relax!
!
Maybe you bend your knees?
You can put your hands in the water too, you know.

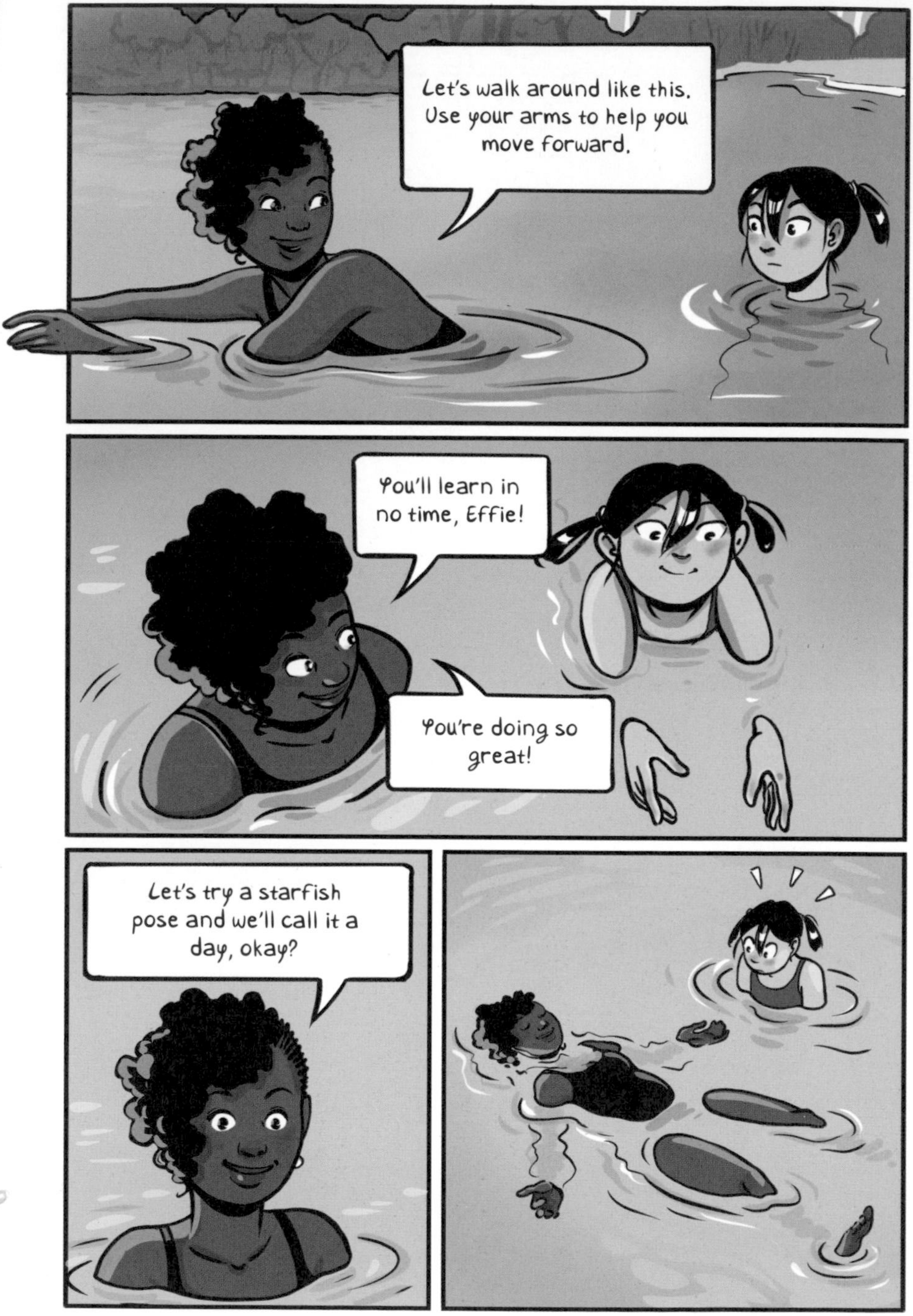
Let's walk around like this. Use your arms to help you move forward.
You'll learn in no time, Effie!
You're doing so great!
Let's try a starfish pose and we'll call it a day, okay?

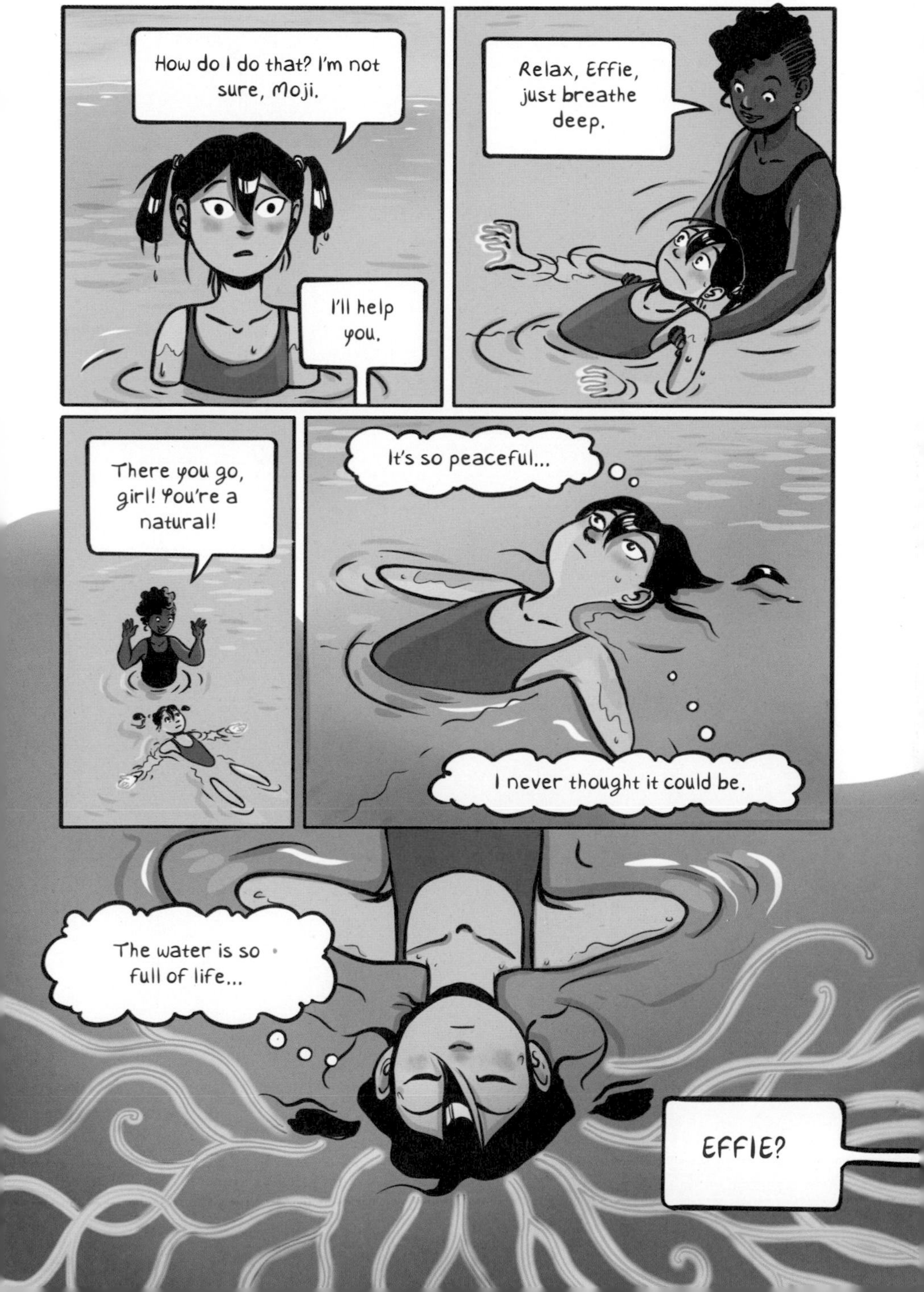
How do I do that? I'm not sure, Moji.
I'll help you.
Relax, Effie, just breathe deep.
There you go, girl! You're a natural!
It's so peaceful...
I never thought it could be.
The water is so full of life...
EFFIE?

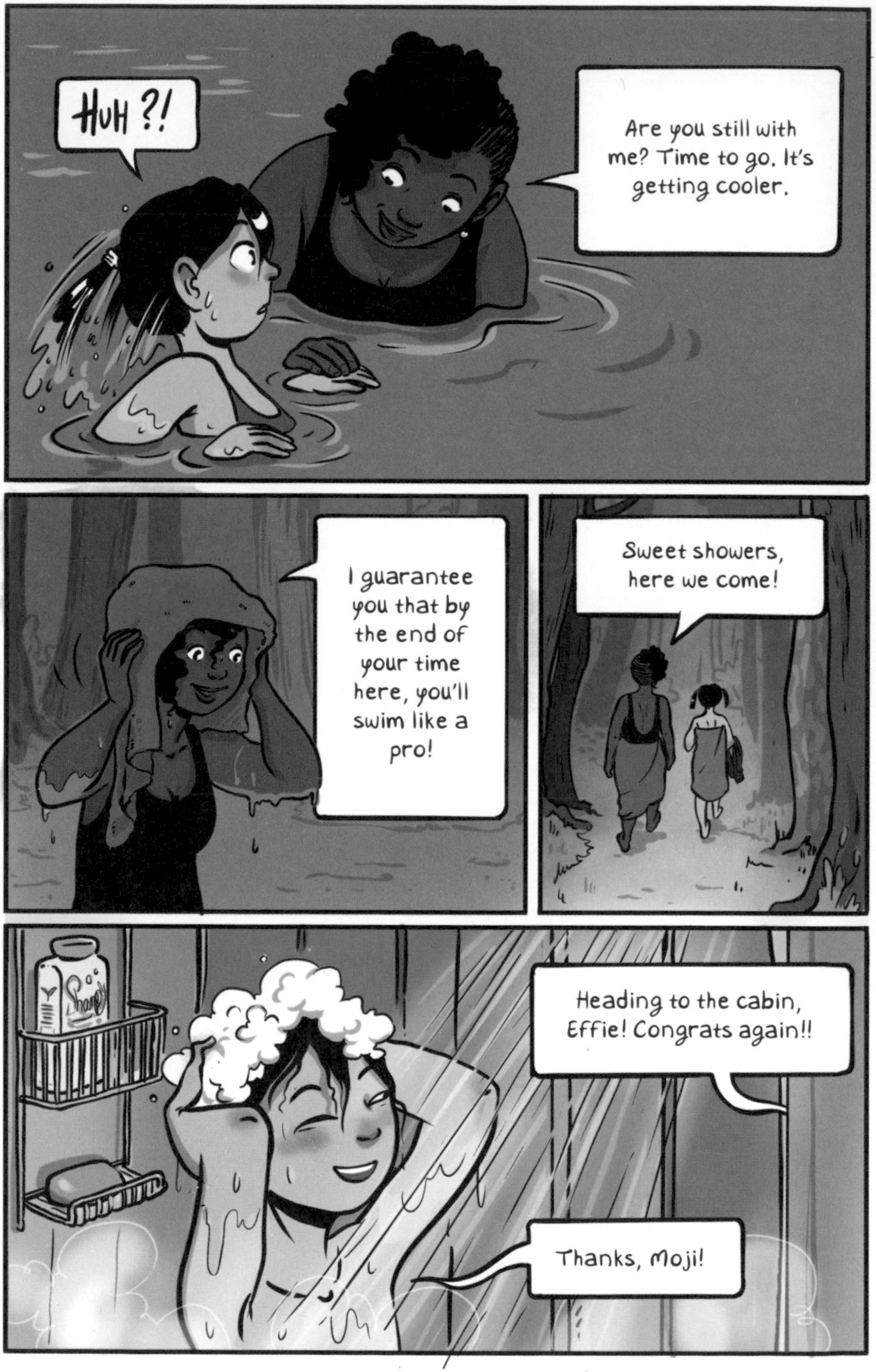
HUH ?!
Are you still with me? Time to go. It's getting cooler.
I guarantee you that by the end of your time here, you'll swim like a pro!
Sweet showers, here we come!
Heading to the cabin, Effie! Congrats again!!
Thanks, Moji!

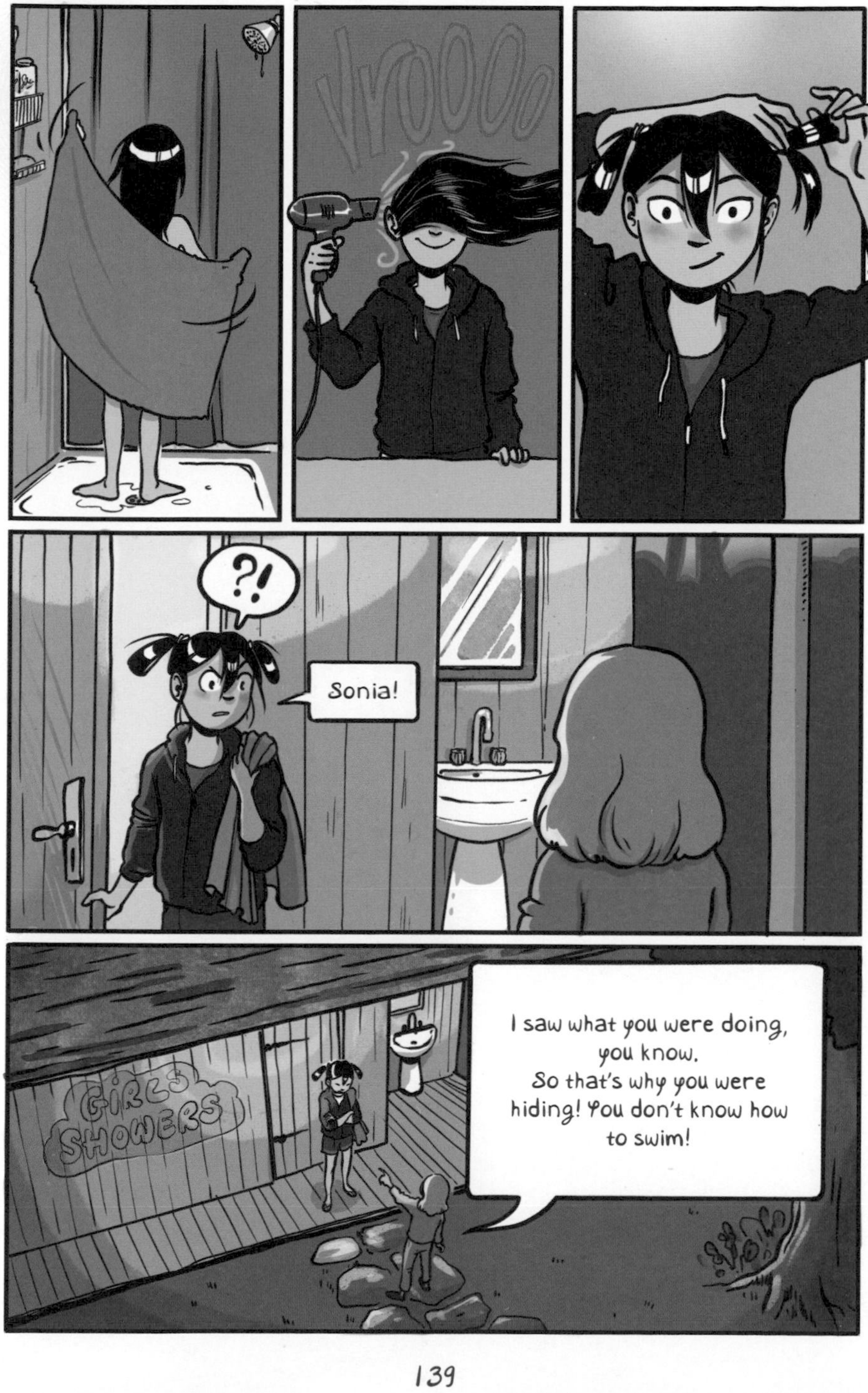
VROOOOO
?!
Sonia!
GIRLS SHOWERS
I saw what you were doing, you know.
So that's why you were hiding! You don't know how to swim!

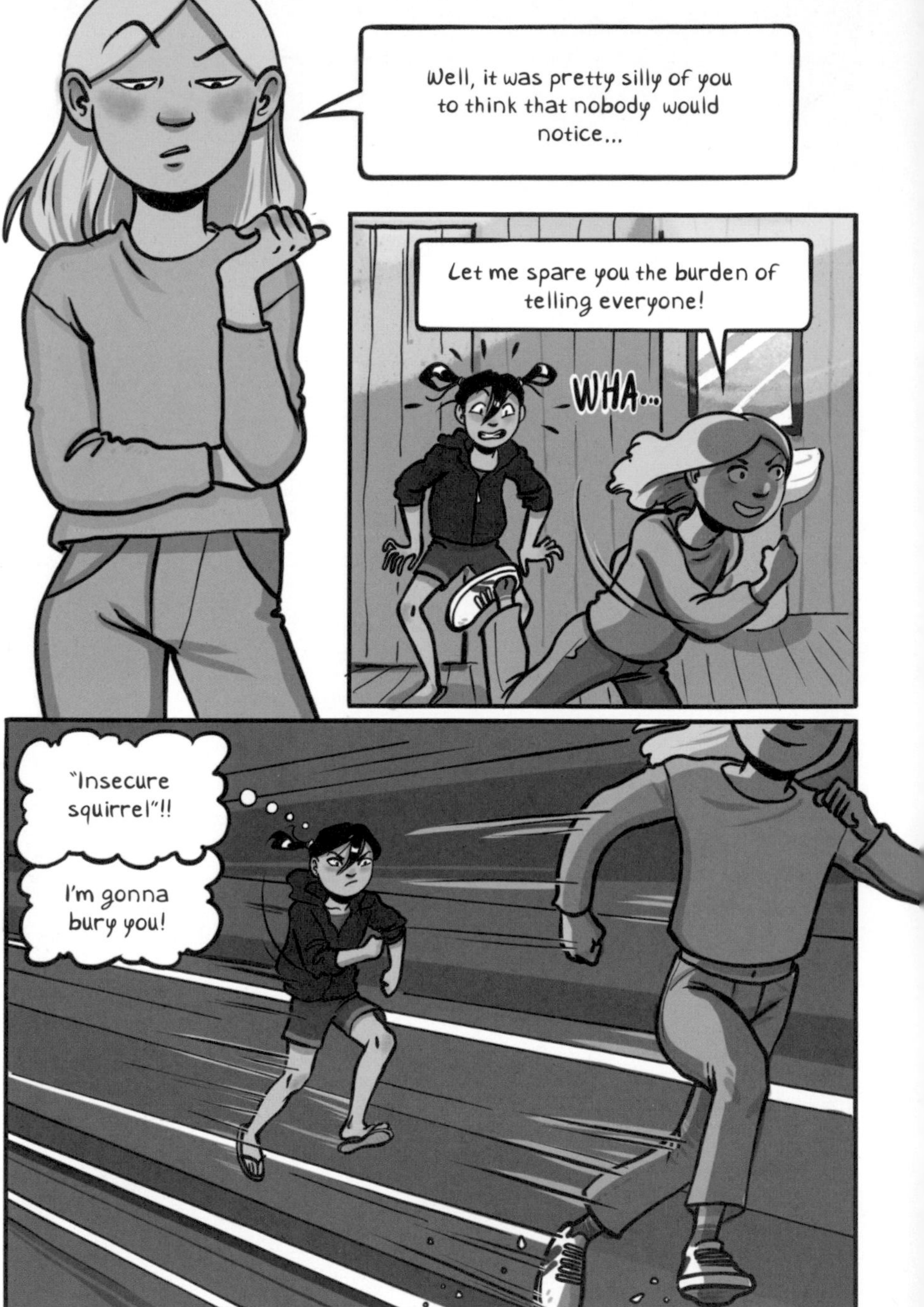
Well, it was pretty silly of you to think that nobody would notice...
Let me spare you the burden of telling everyone!
WHA...
"Insecure squirrel"!!
I'm gonna bury you!

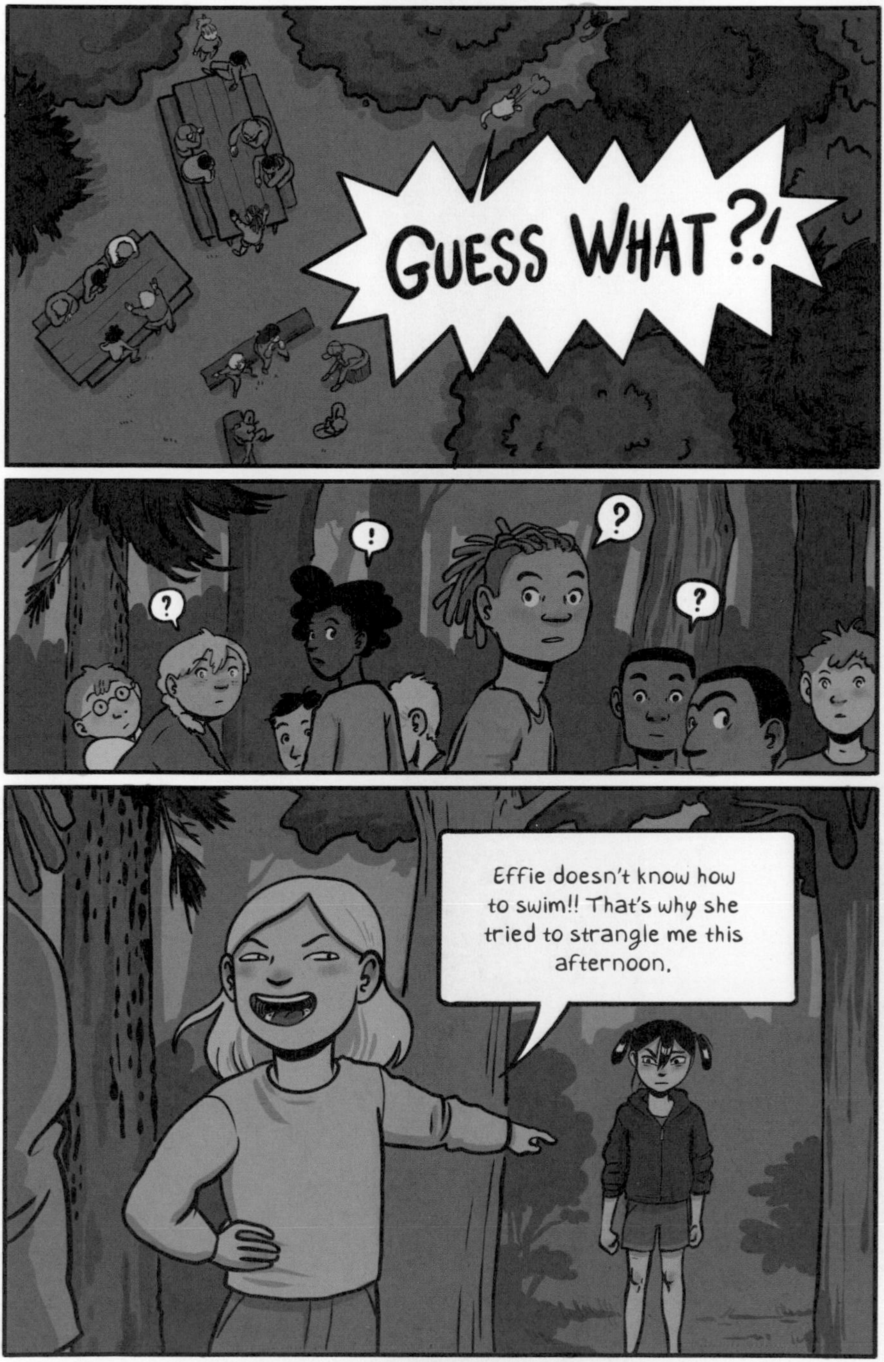
GUESS WHAT?!
?
!
?
?
Effie doesn't know how to swim!! That's why she tried to strangle me this afternoon.

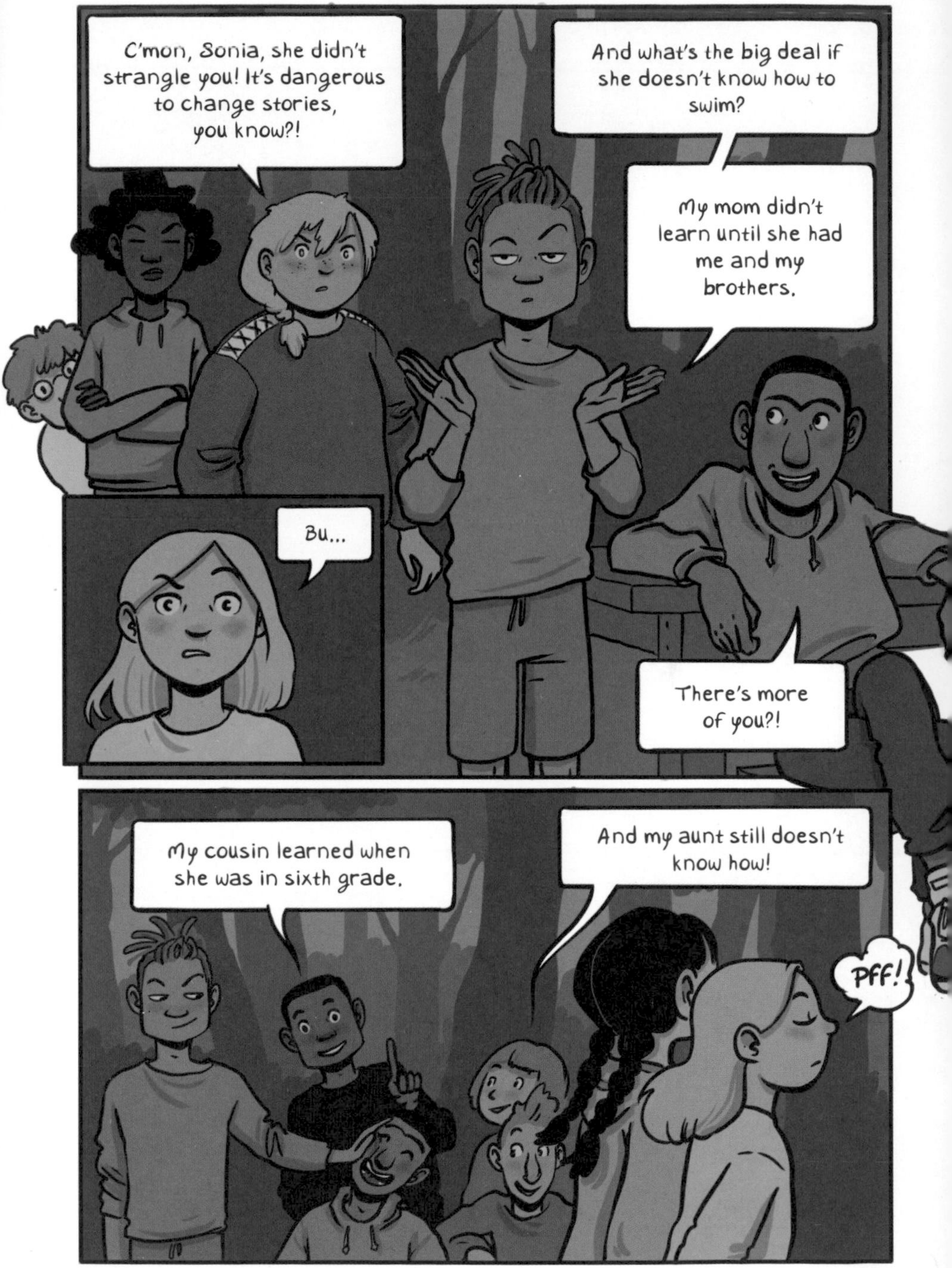
C'mon, Sonia, she didn't strangle you! It's dangerous to change stories, you know?!
And what's the big deal if she doesn't know how to swim?
My mom didn't learn until she had me and my brothers.
Bu...
There's more of you?!
My cousin learned when she was in sixth grade.
And my aunt still doesn't know how!
Pff!

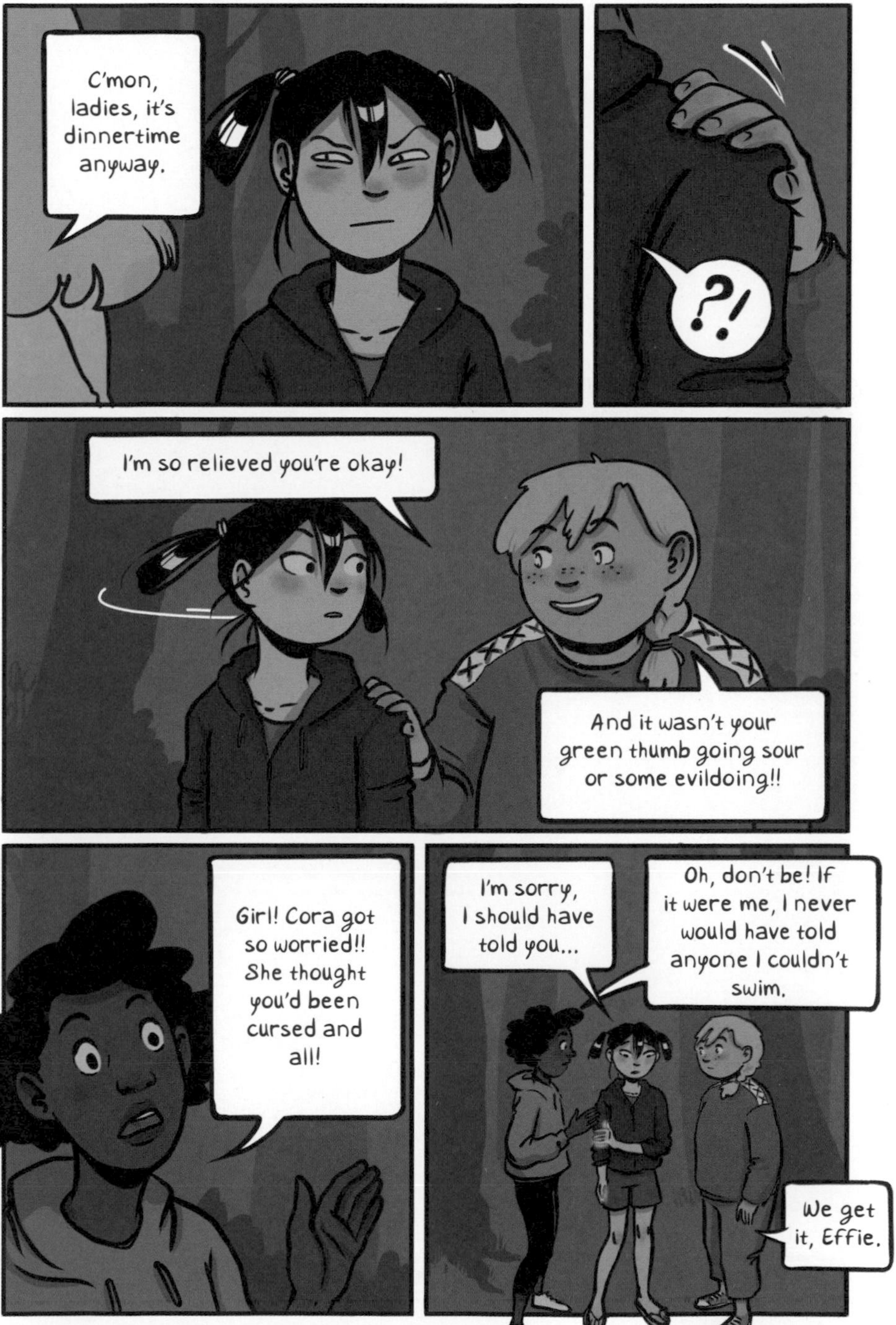
C'mon, ladies, it's dinnertime anyway.
?!
I'm so relieved you're okay!
And it wasn't your green thumb going sour or some evildoing!!
Girl! Cora got so worried!! She thought you'd been cursed and all!
I'm sorry, I should have told you...
Oh, don't be! If it were me, I never would have told anyone I couldn't swim.
We get it, Effie.

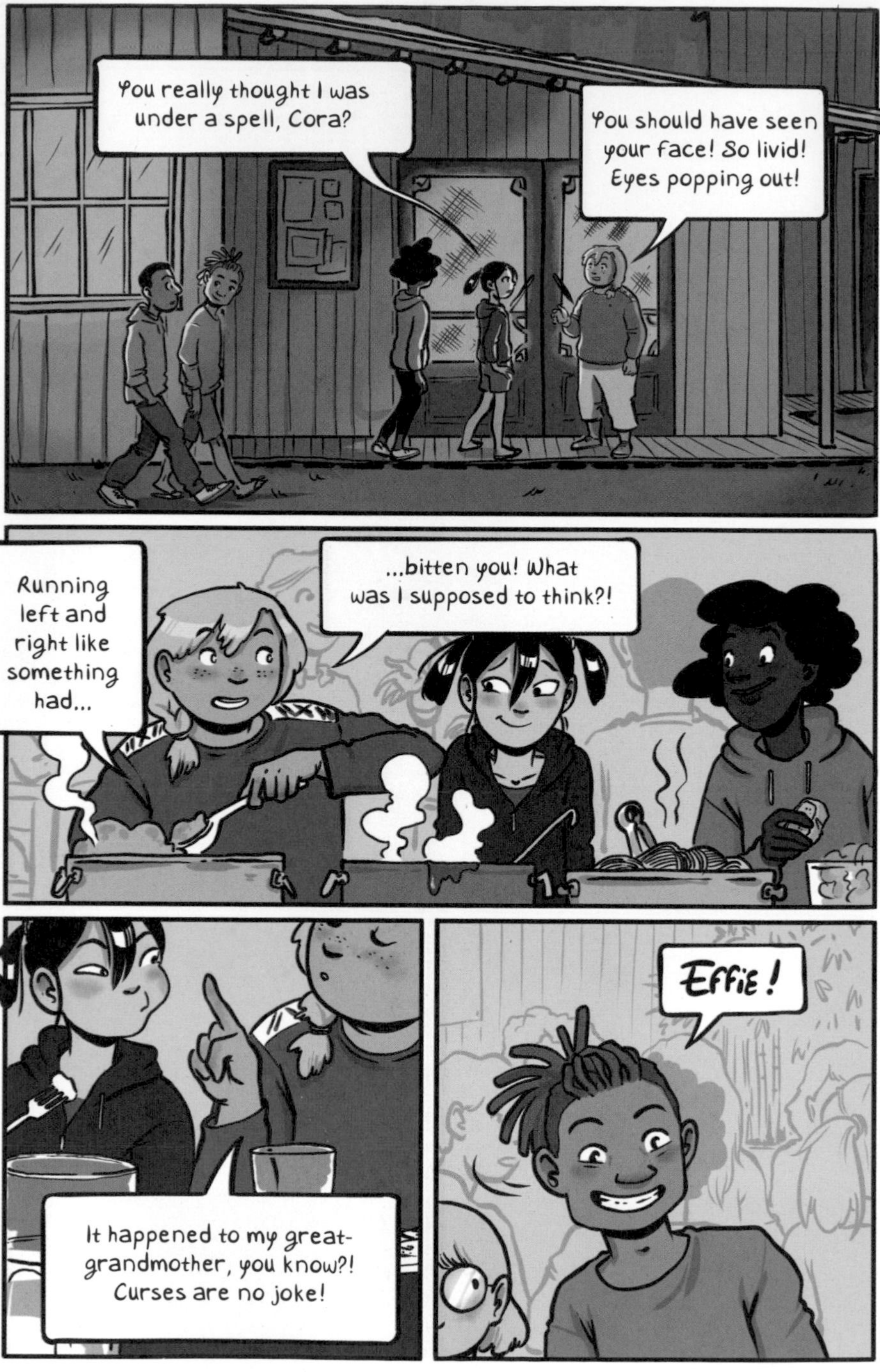
You really thought I was under a spell, Cora?
You should have seen your face! So livid! Eyes popping out!
Running left and right like something had...
...bitten you! What was I supposed to think?!
It happened to my great-grandmother, you know?! Curses are no joke!
Effie!

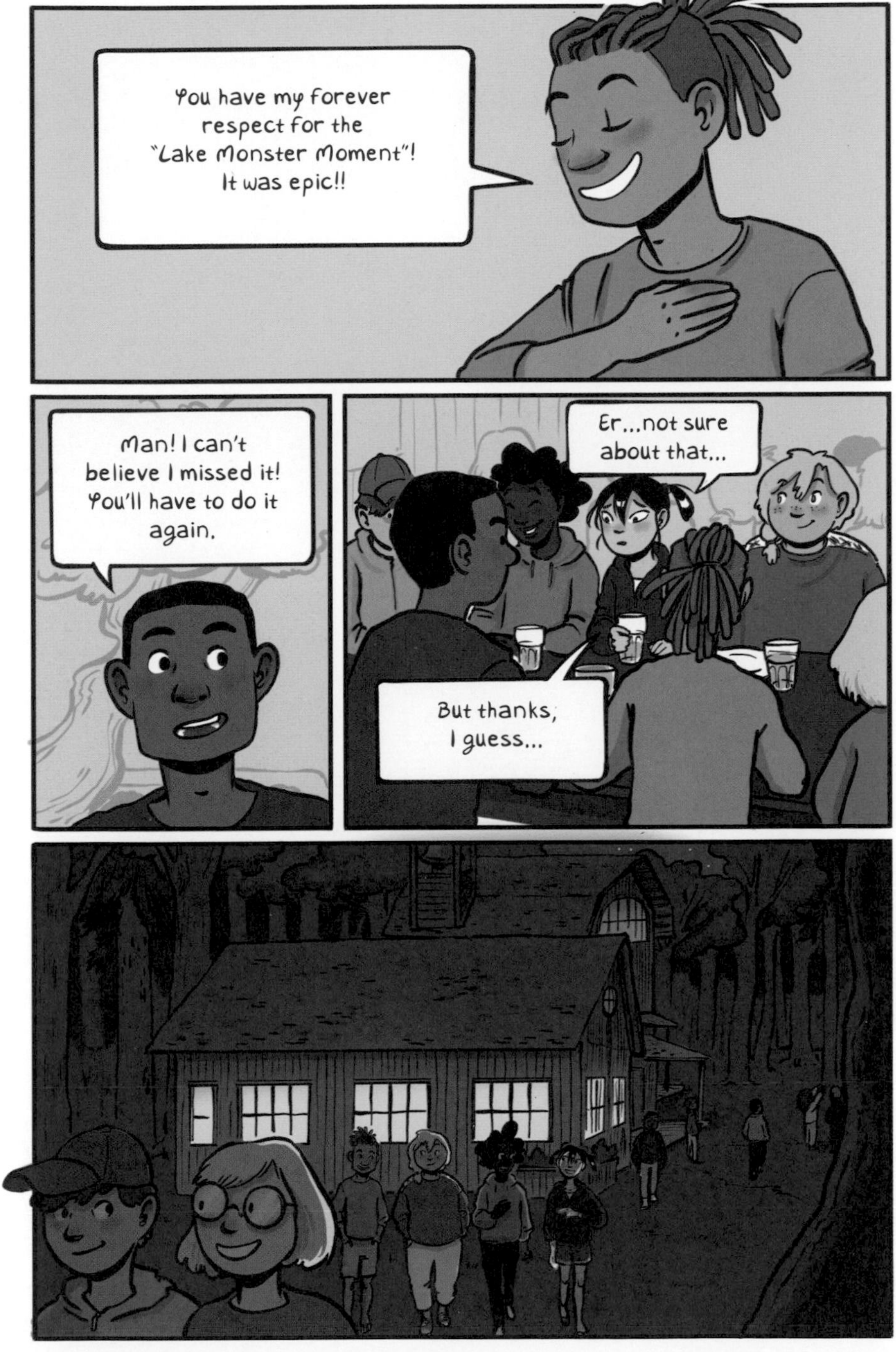
You have my forever respect for the "Lake Monster Moment"! It was epic!!
Man! I can't believe I missed it! You'll have to do it again.
Er...not sure about that...
But thanks, I guess...

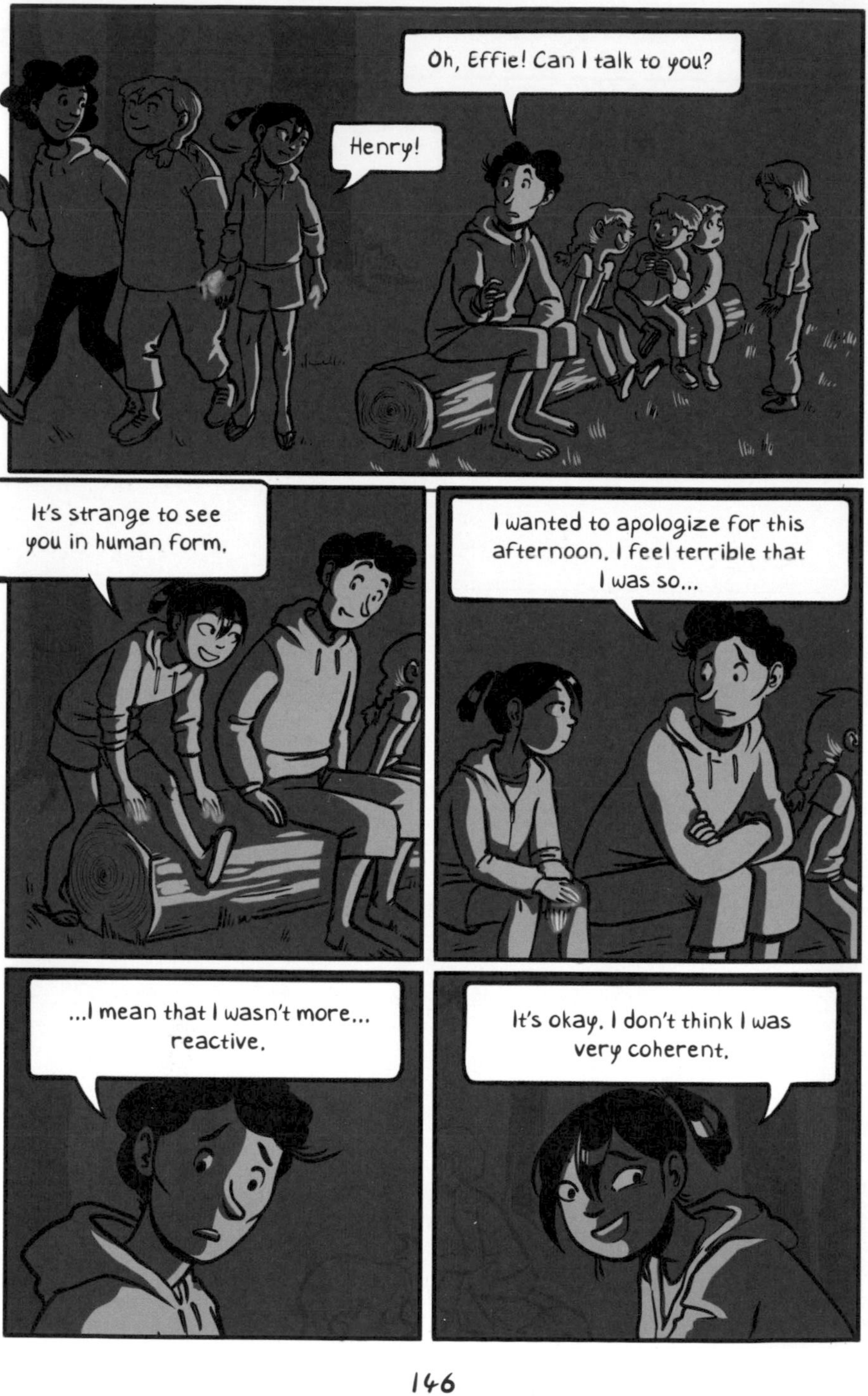
Henry!
Oh, Effie! Can I talk to you?
It's strange to see you in human form.
I wanted to apologize for this afternoon. I feel terrible that I was so...
...I mean that I wasn't more... reactive.
It's okay. I don't think I was very coherent.

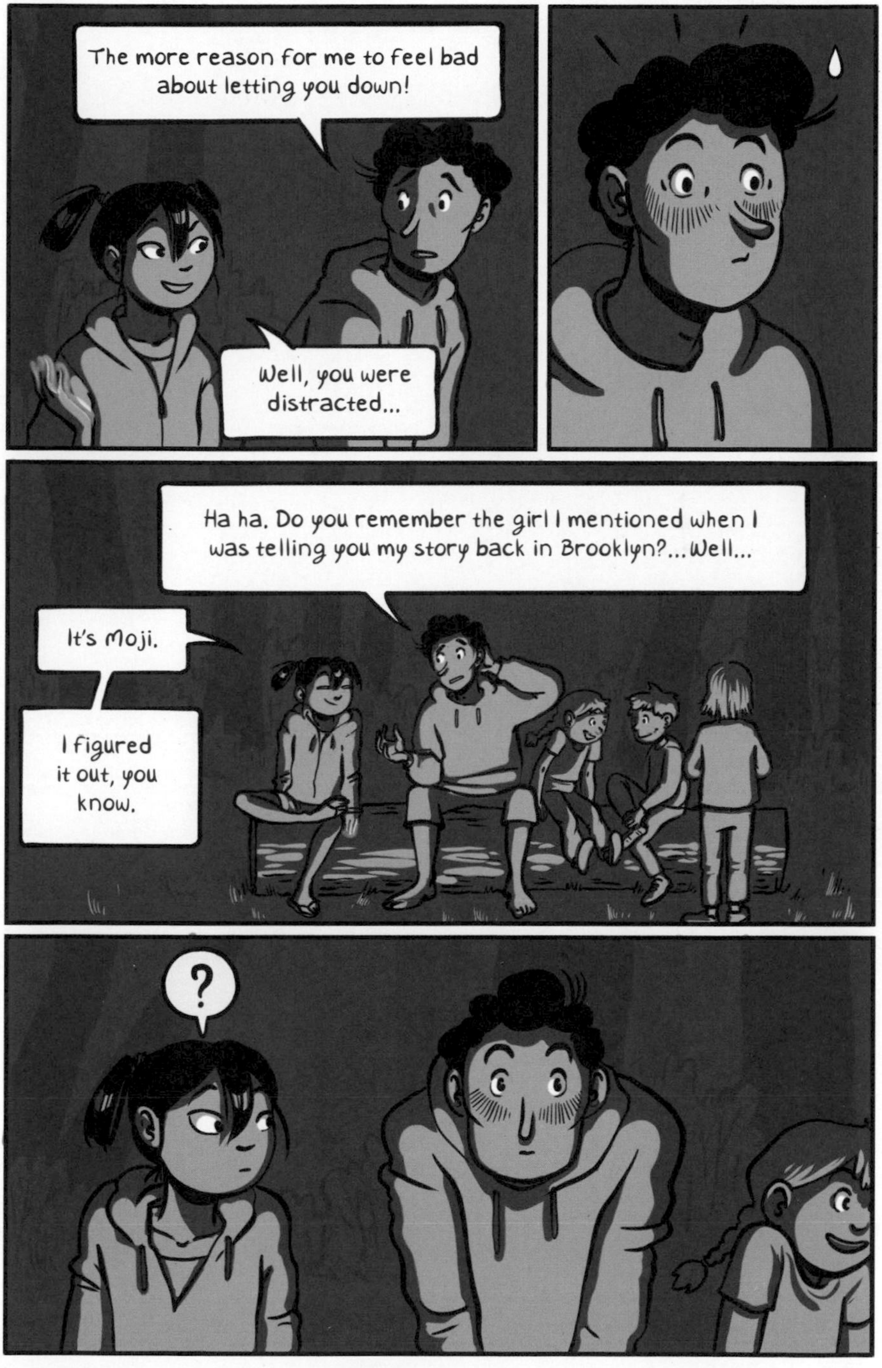
The more reason for me to feel bad about letting you down!
Well, you were distracted...
Ha ha. Do you remember the girl I mentioned when I was telling you my story back in Brooklyn?... Well...
It's Moji.
I figured it out, you know.
?

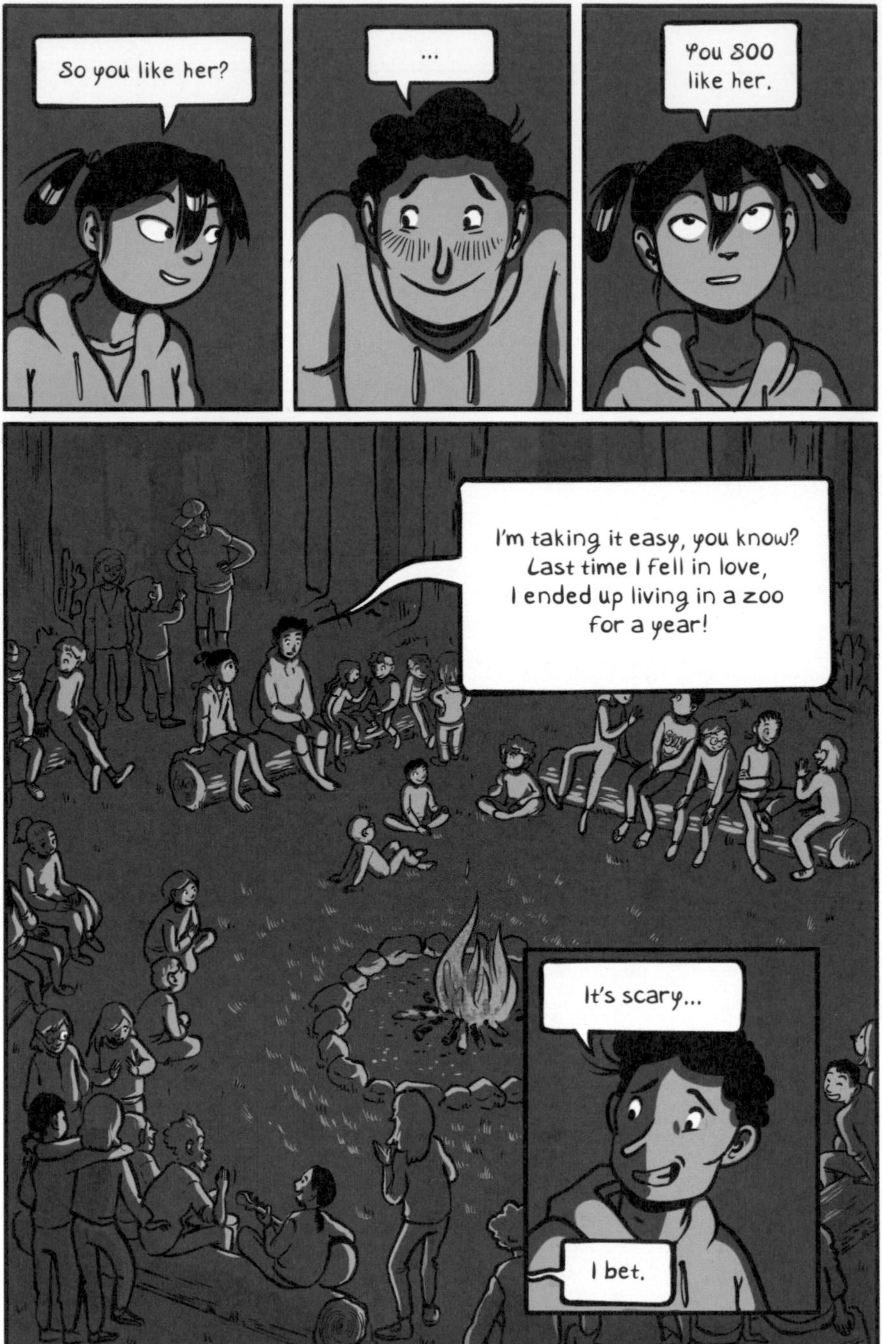

So you like her?
...
You SOO like her.
I'm taking it easy, you know? Last time I fell in love, I ended up living in a zoo for a year!
It's scary...
I bet.

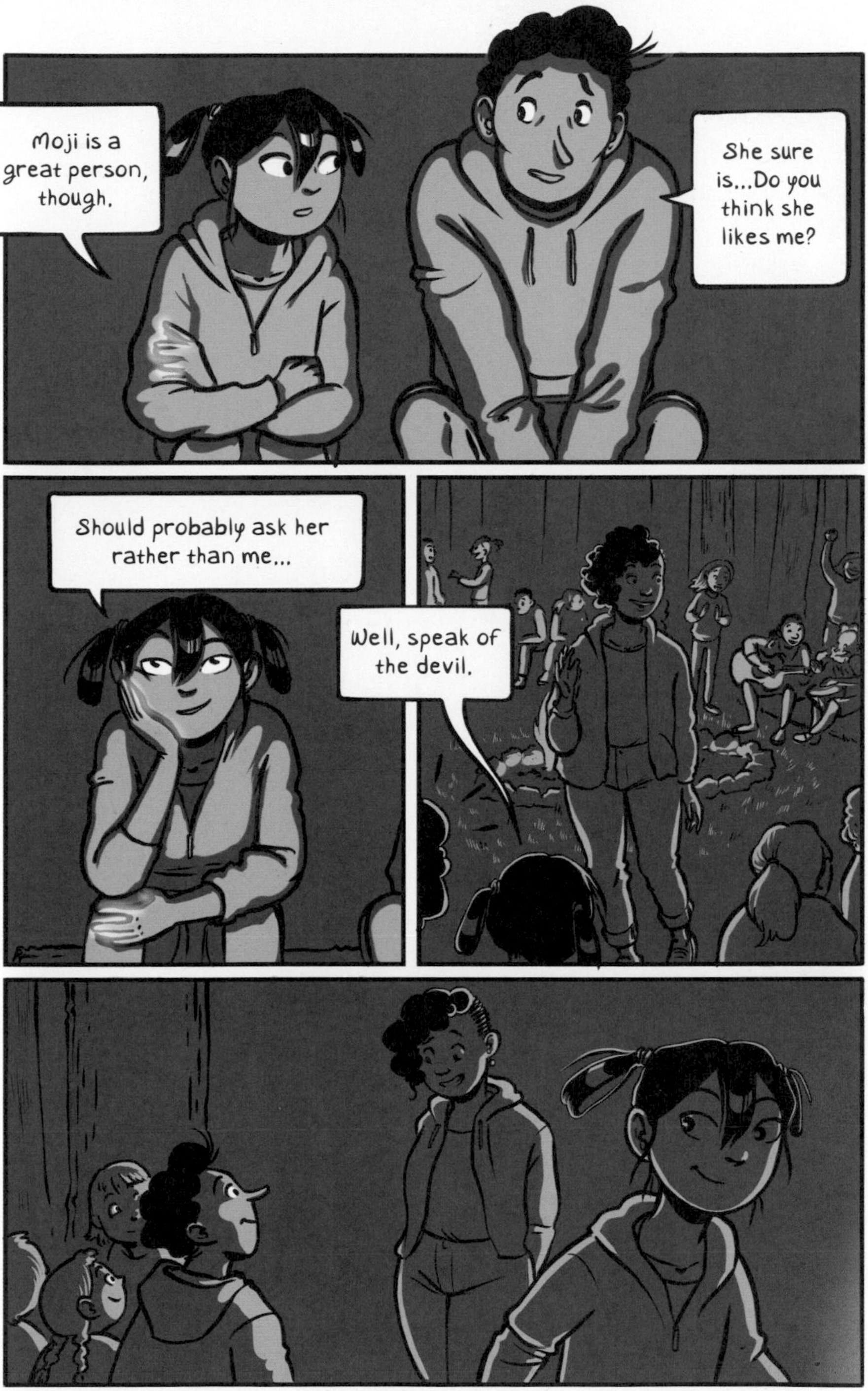
Moji is a great person, though.
She sure is...Do you think she likes me?
Should probably ask her rather than me...
Well, speak of the devil.

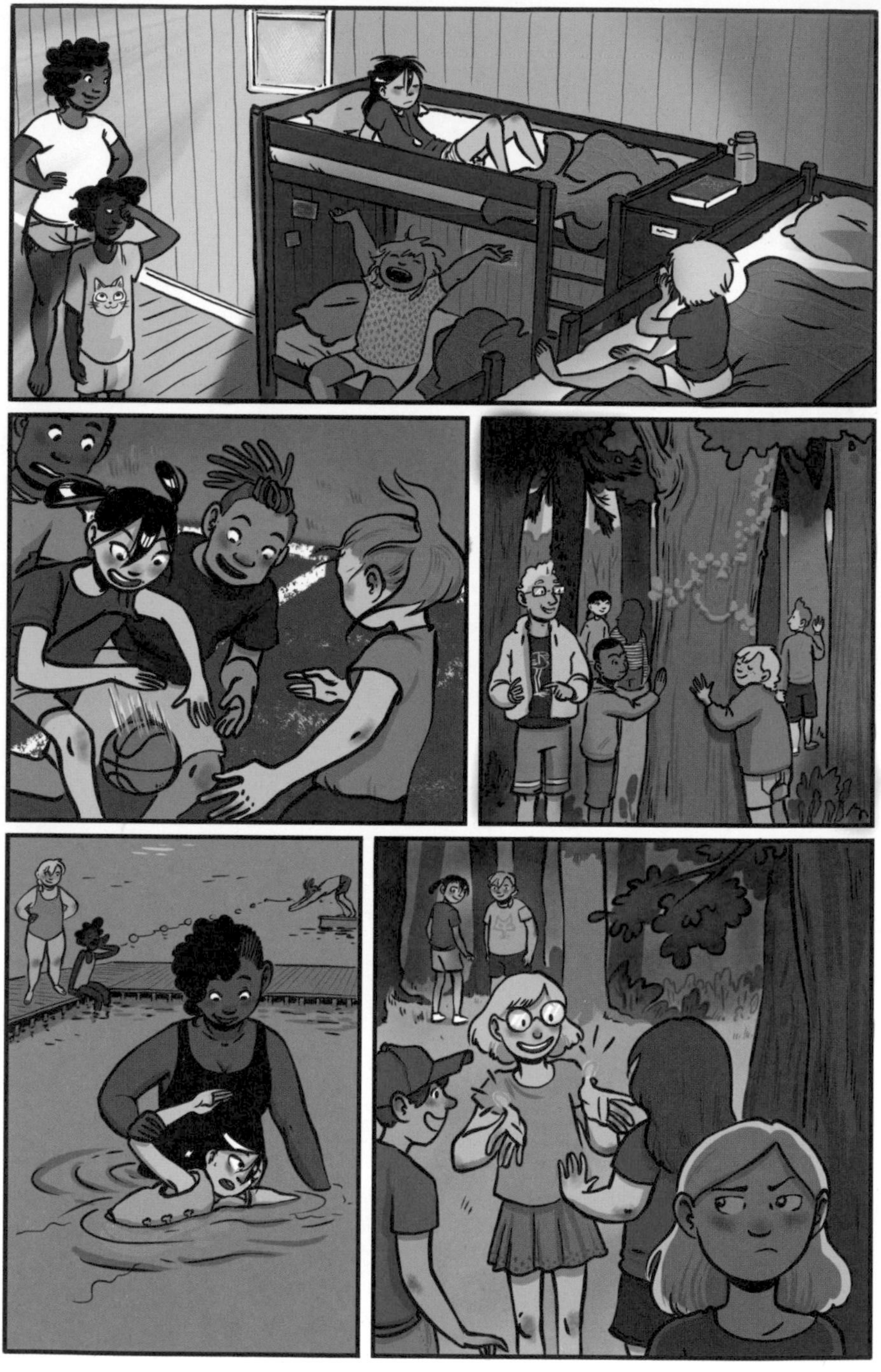

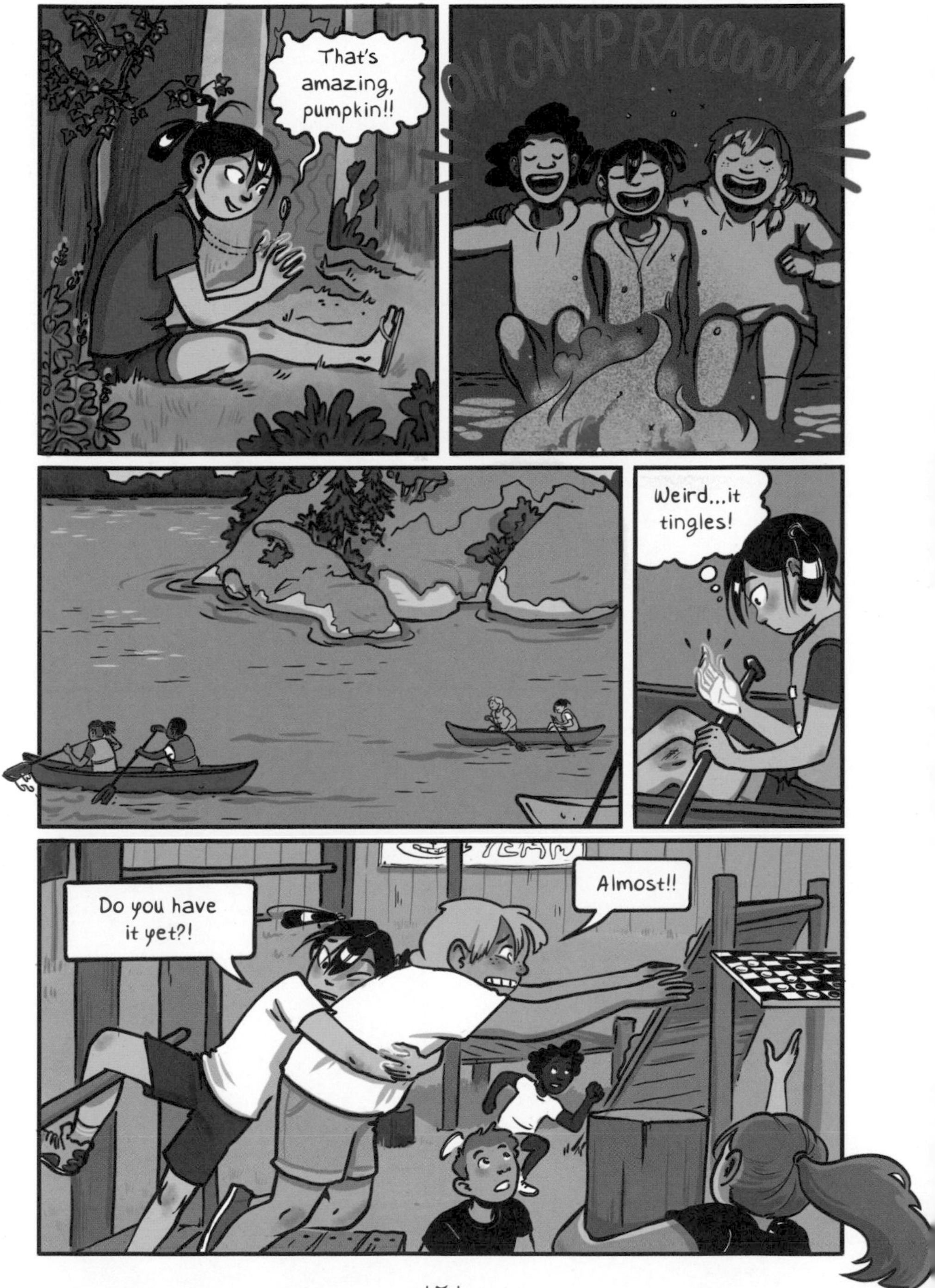
That's amazing, pumpkin!!
OH, CAMP RACCOON!!
Weird...it tingles!
Do you have it yet?!
Almost!!

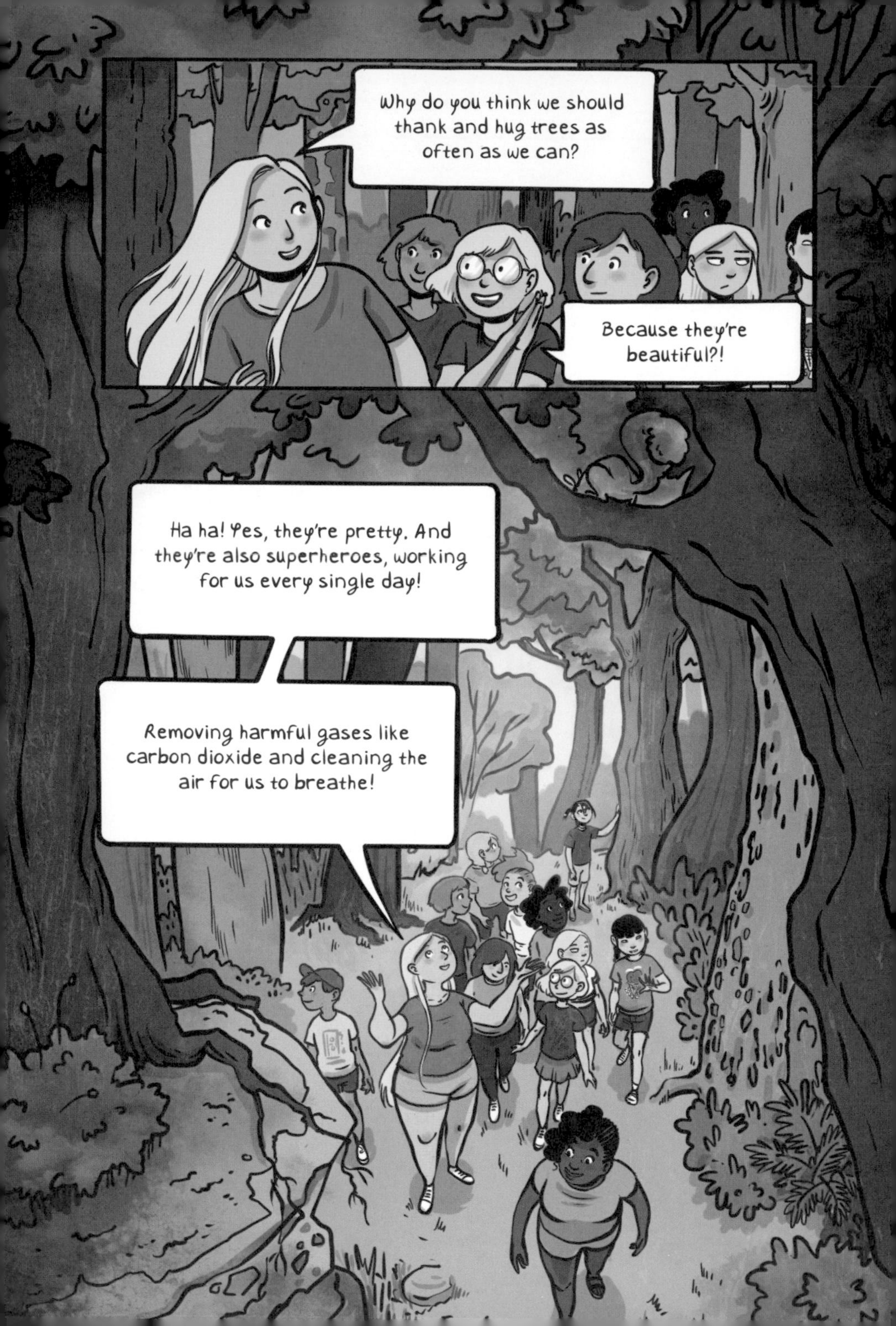

Why do you think we should thank and hug trees as often as we can?
Because they're beautiful?!
Ha ha! Yes, they're pretty. And they're also superheroes, working for us every single day!
Removing harmful gases like carbon dioxide and cleaning the air for us to breathe!

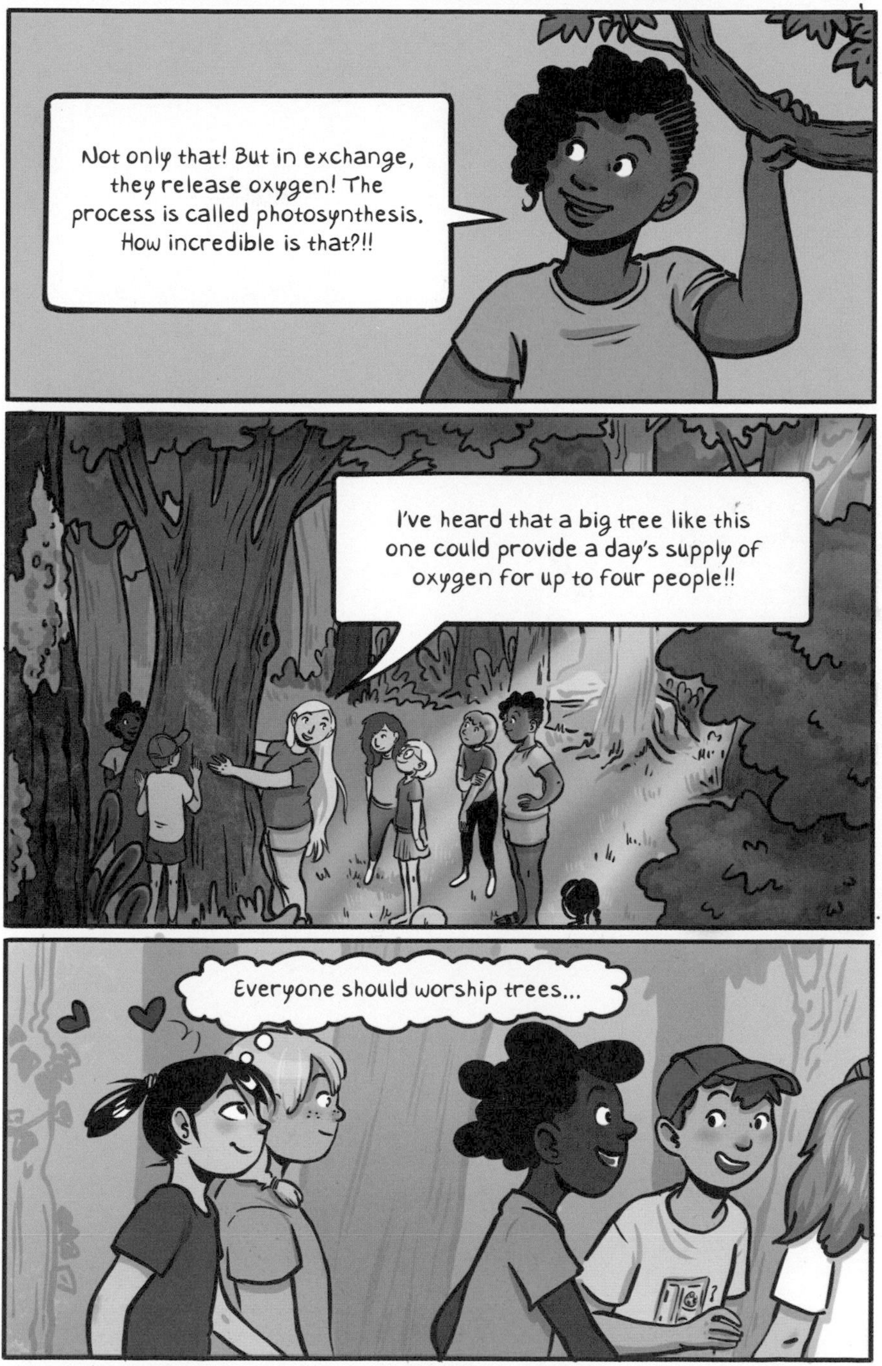
Not only that! But in exchange, they release oxygen! The process is called photosynthesis. How incredible is that?!!
I've heard that a big tree like this one could provide a day's supply of oxygen for up to four people!!
Everyone should worship trees...

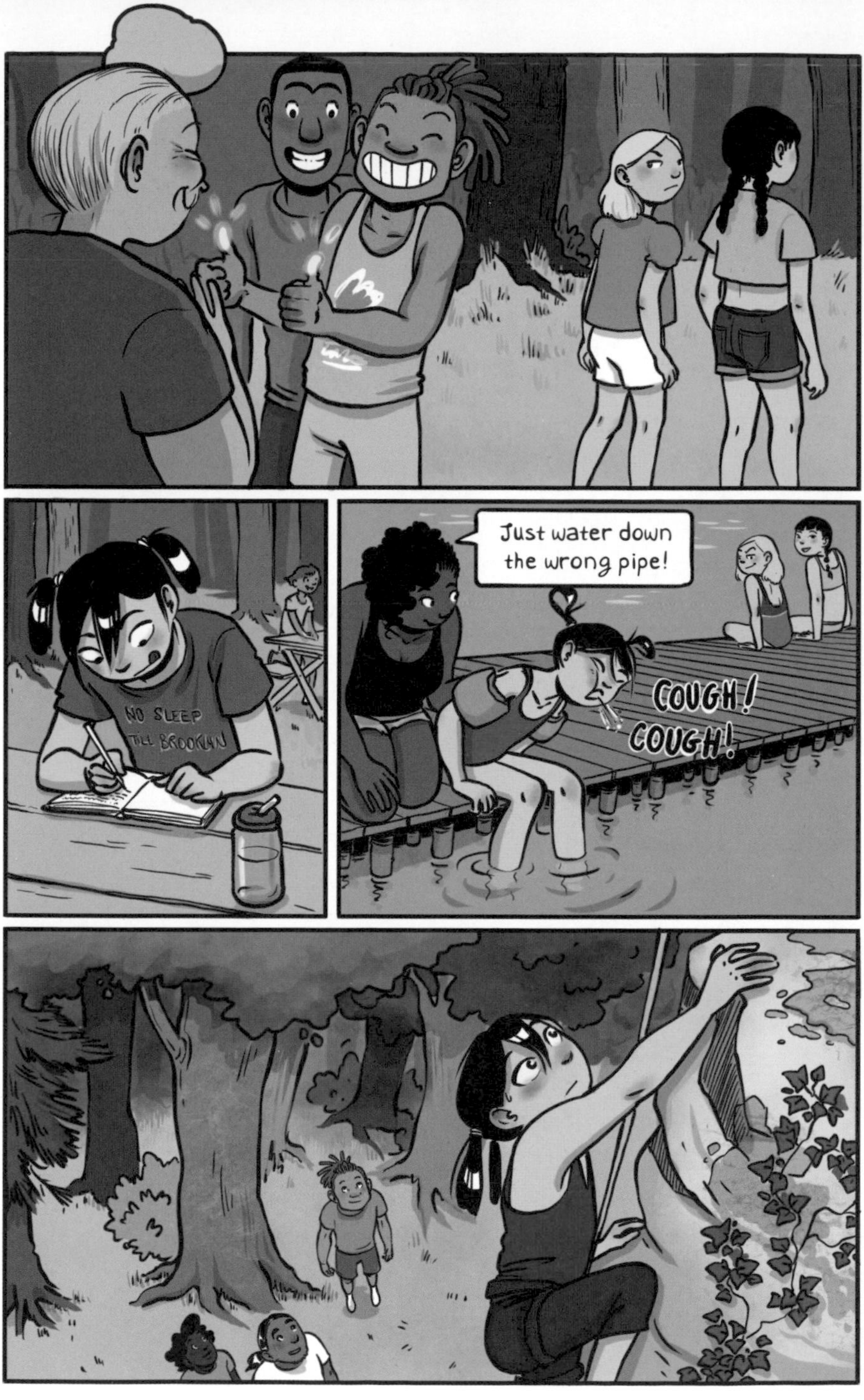
NO SLEEP TILL BROOKLYN
Just water down the wrong pipe!
COUGH! COUGH!

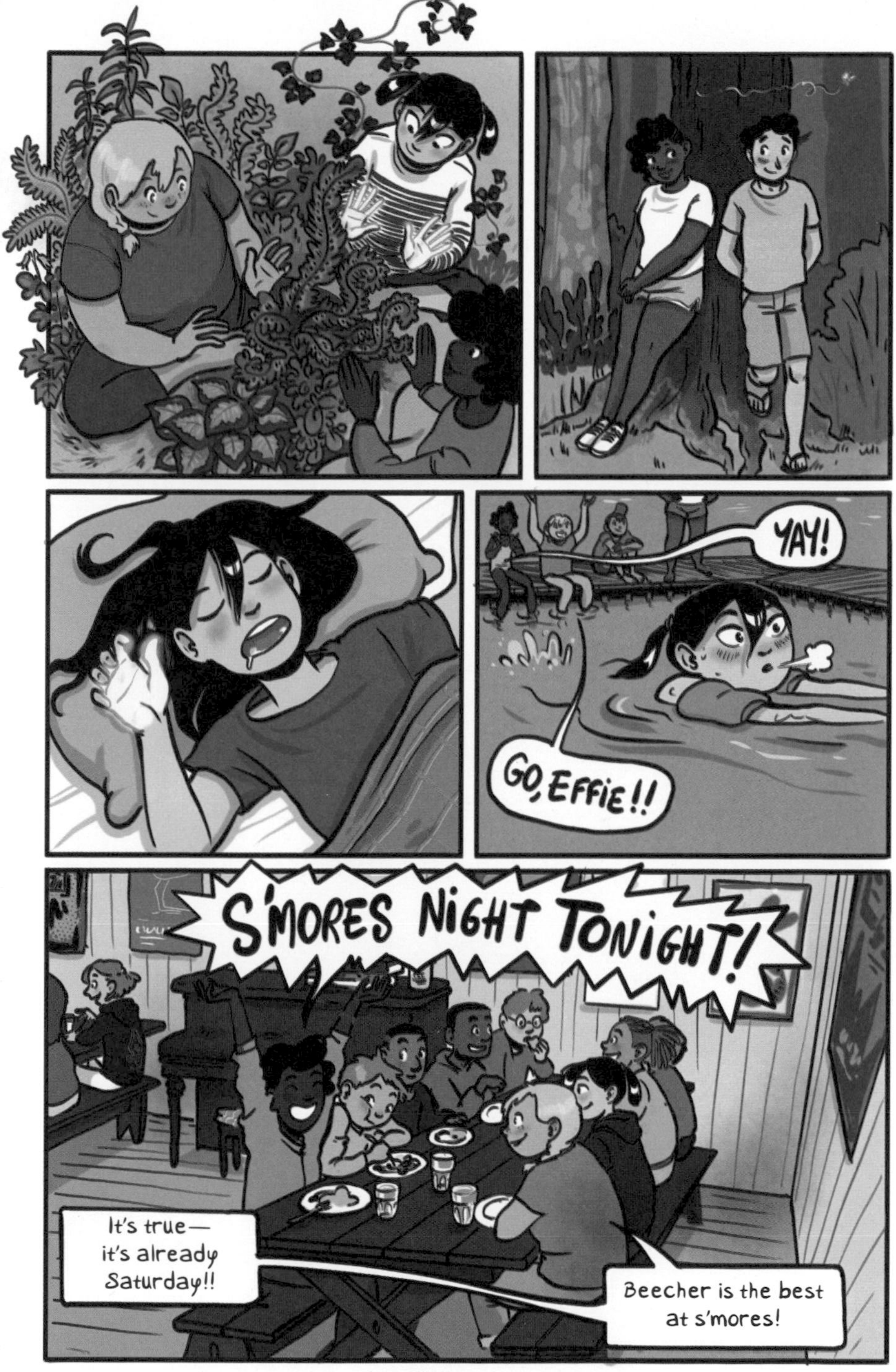
YAY!
GO, EFFIE!!
S'MORES NIGHT TONIGHT!
It's true— it's already Saturday!!
Beecher is the best at s'mores!

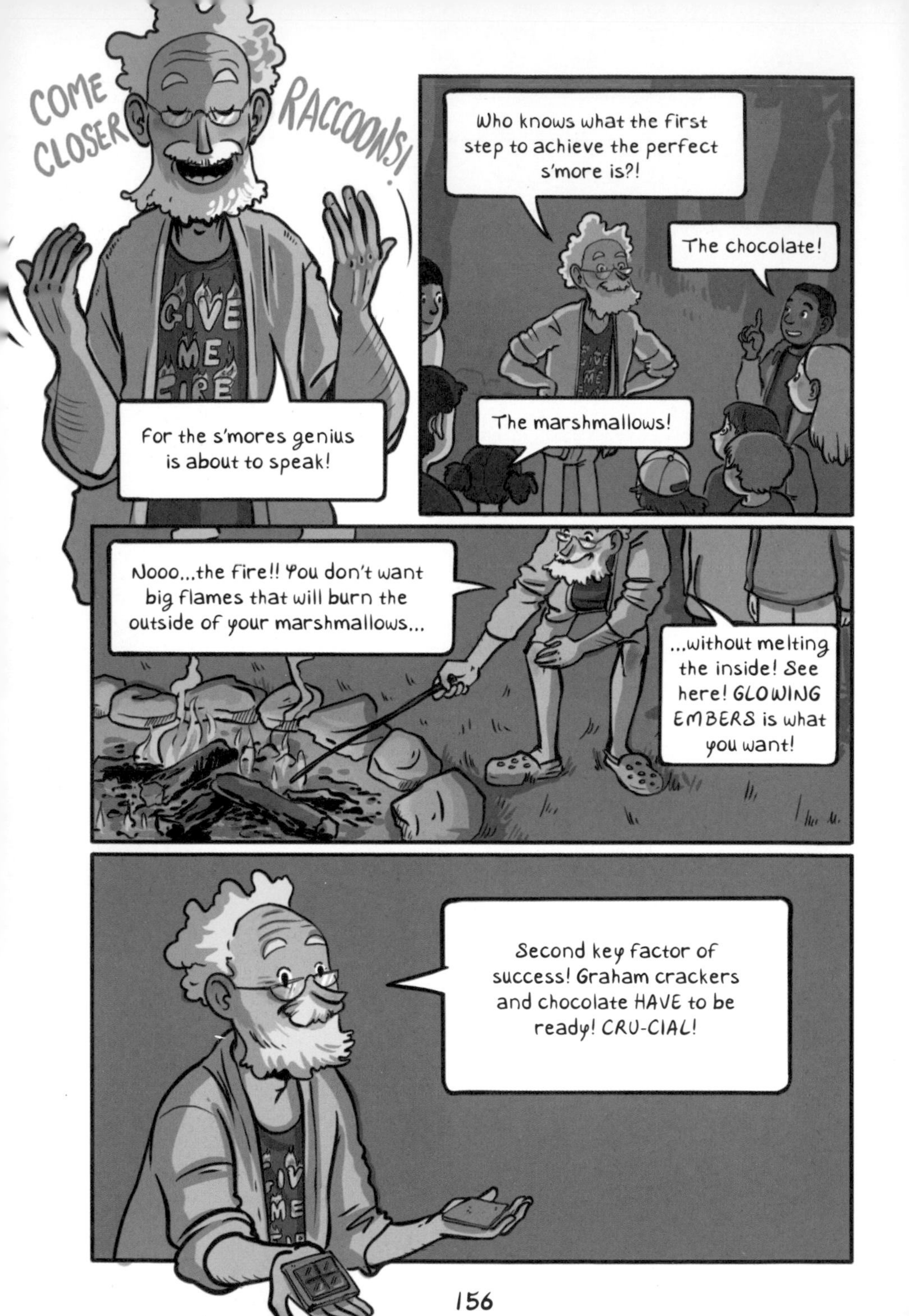
COME CLOSER RACCOONS!
For the s'mores genius is about to speak!
Who knows what the first step to achieve the perfect s'more is?!
The chocolate!
The marshmallows!
Nooo...the fire!! You don't want big flames that will burn the outside of your marshmallows...
...without melting the inside! See here! GLOWING EMBERS is what you want!
Second key factor of success! Graham crackers and chocolate HAVE to be ready! CRU-CIAL!

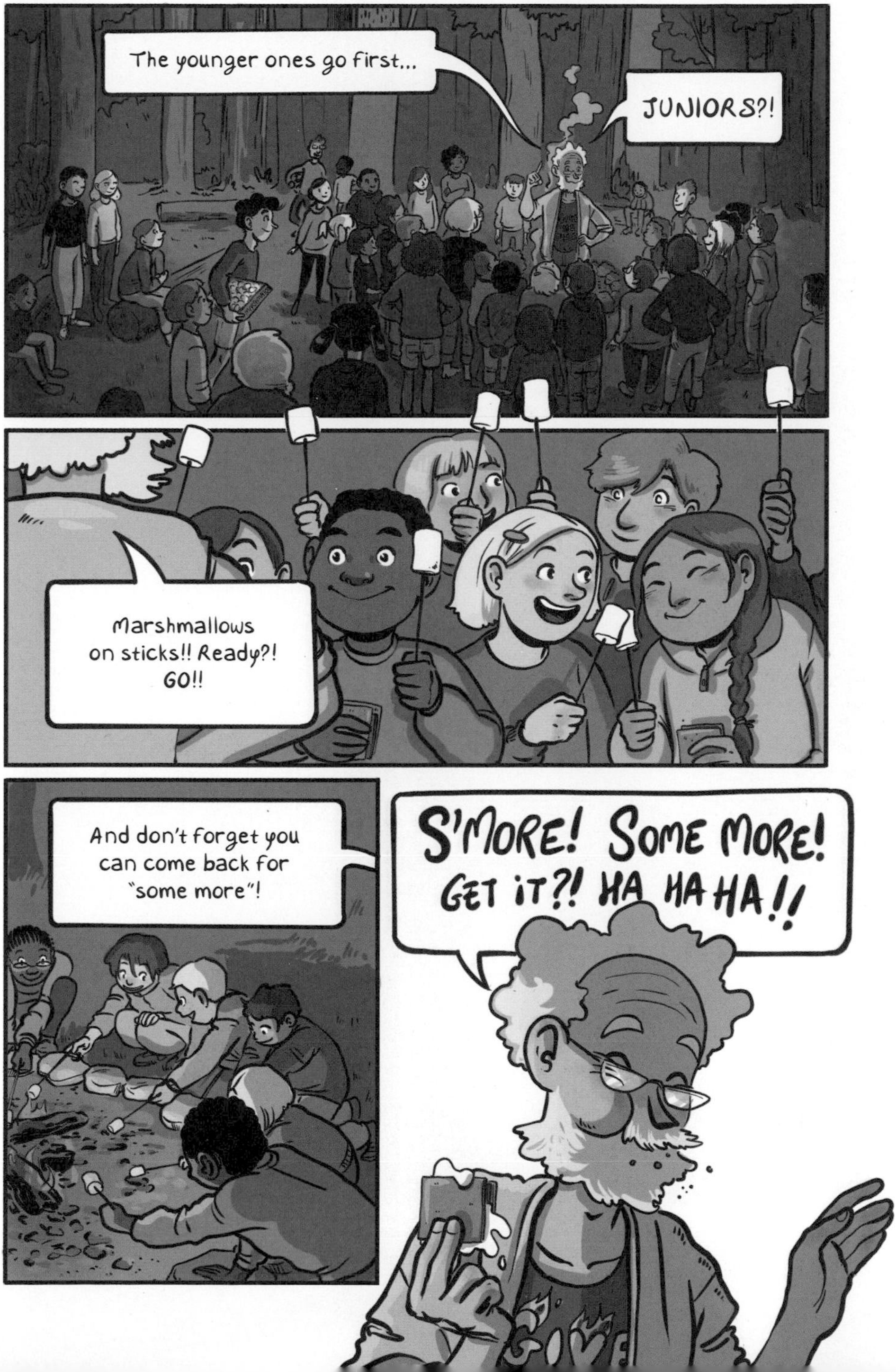
The younger ones go first...
JUNIORS?!
Marshmallows on sticks!! Ready?! GO!!
And don't forget you can come back for "some more"!
S'MORE! SOME MORE! GET IT?! HA HA HA!!

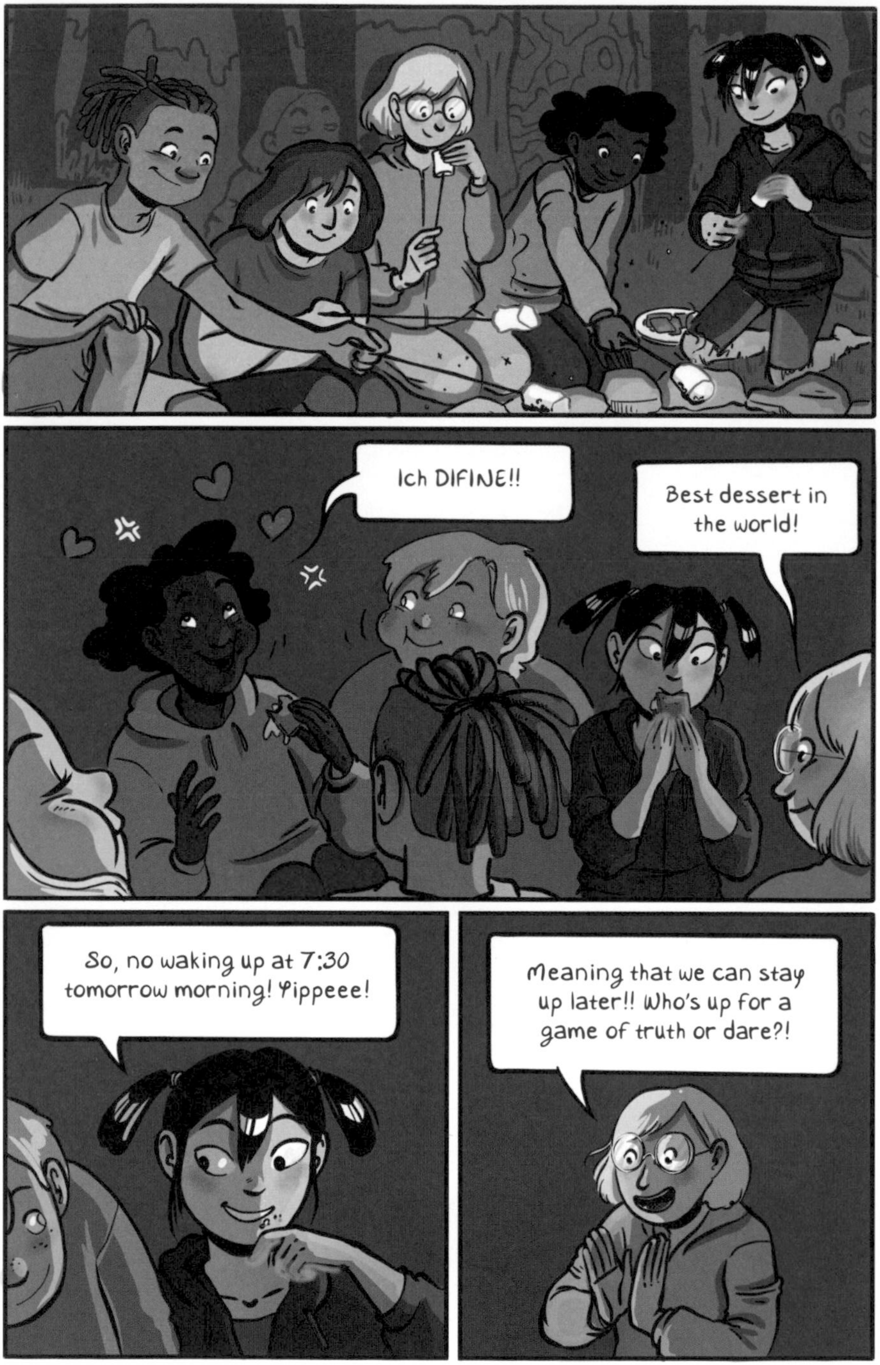
Ich DIFINE!!
Best dessert in the world!
So, no waking up at 7:30 tomorrow morning! Yippeee!
Meaning that we can stay up later!! Who's up for a game of truth or dare?!

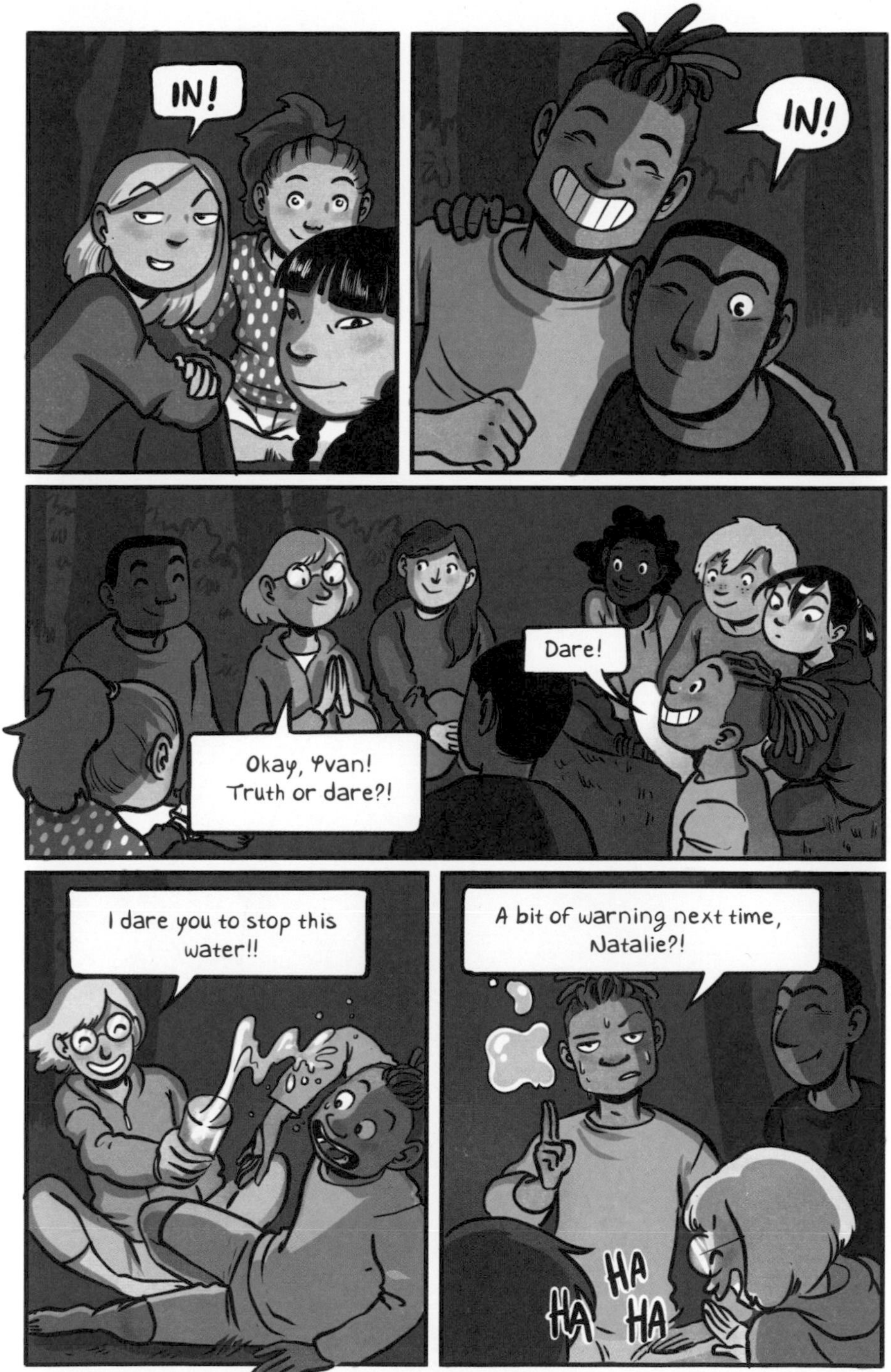
IN!
IN!
Okay, Yvan! Truth or dare?!
Dare!
I dare you to stop this water!!
A bit of warning next time, Natalie?!
HA HA HA HA

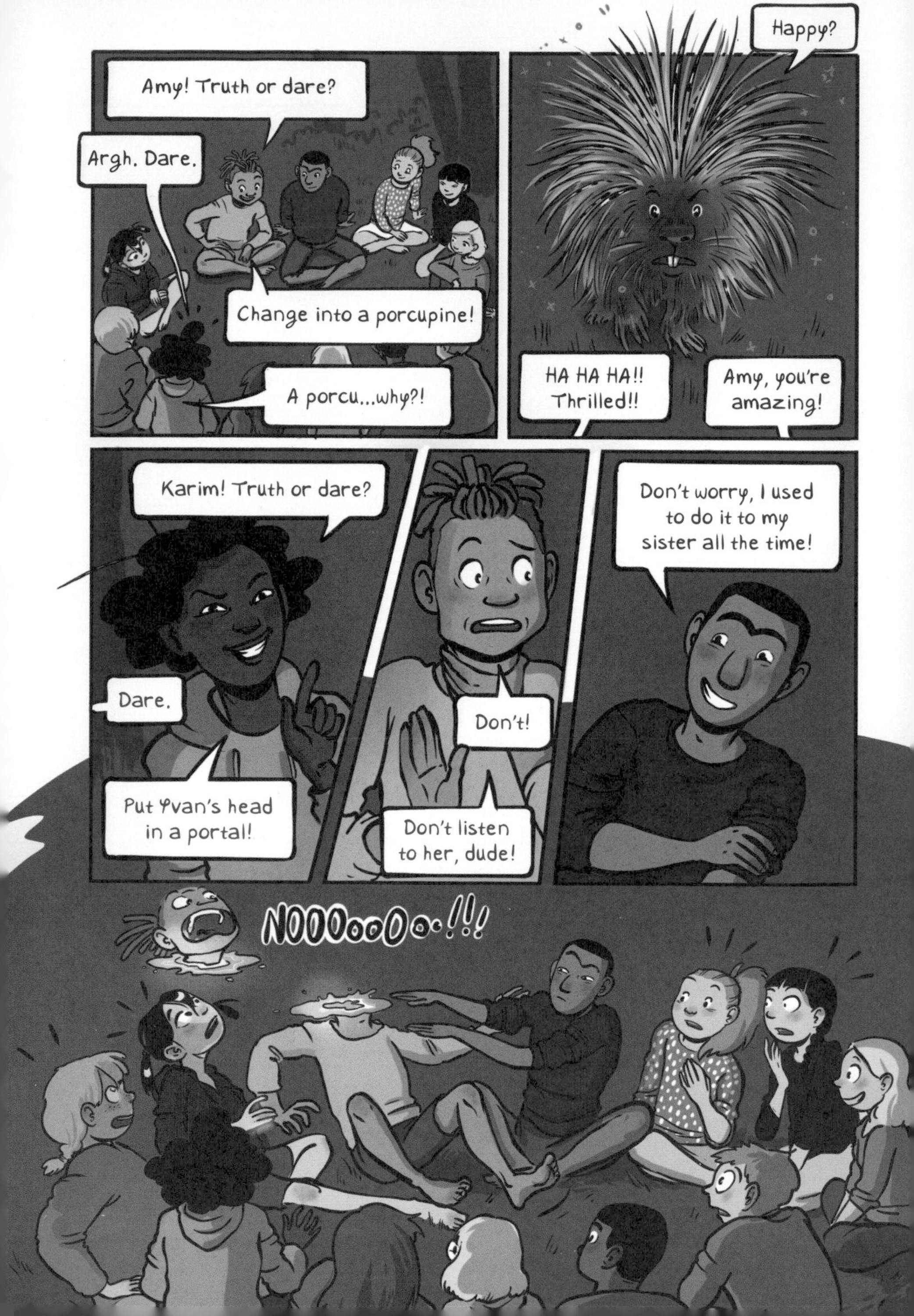
Amy! Truth or dare?
Argh. Dare.
Change into a porcupine!
A porcu...why?!
Happy?
HA HA HA!! Thrilled!!
Amy, you're amazing!
Karim! Truth or dare?
Dare.
Put Yvan's head in a portal!
Don't!
Don't listen to her, dude!
Don't worry, I used to do it to my sister all the time!
NOOOooOo..!!!

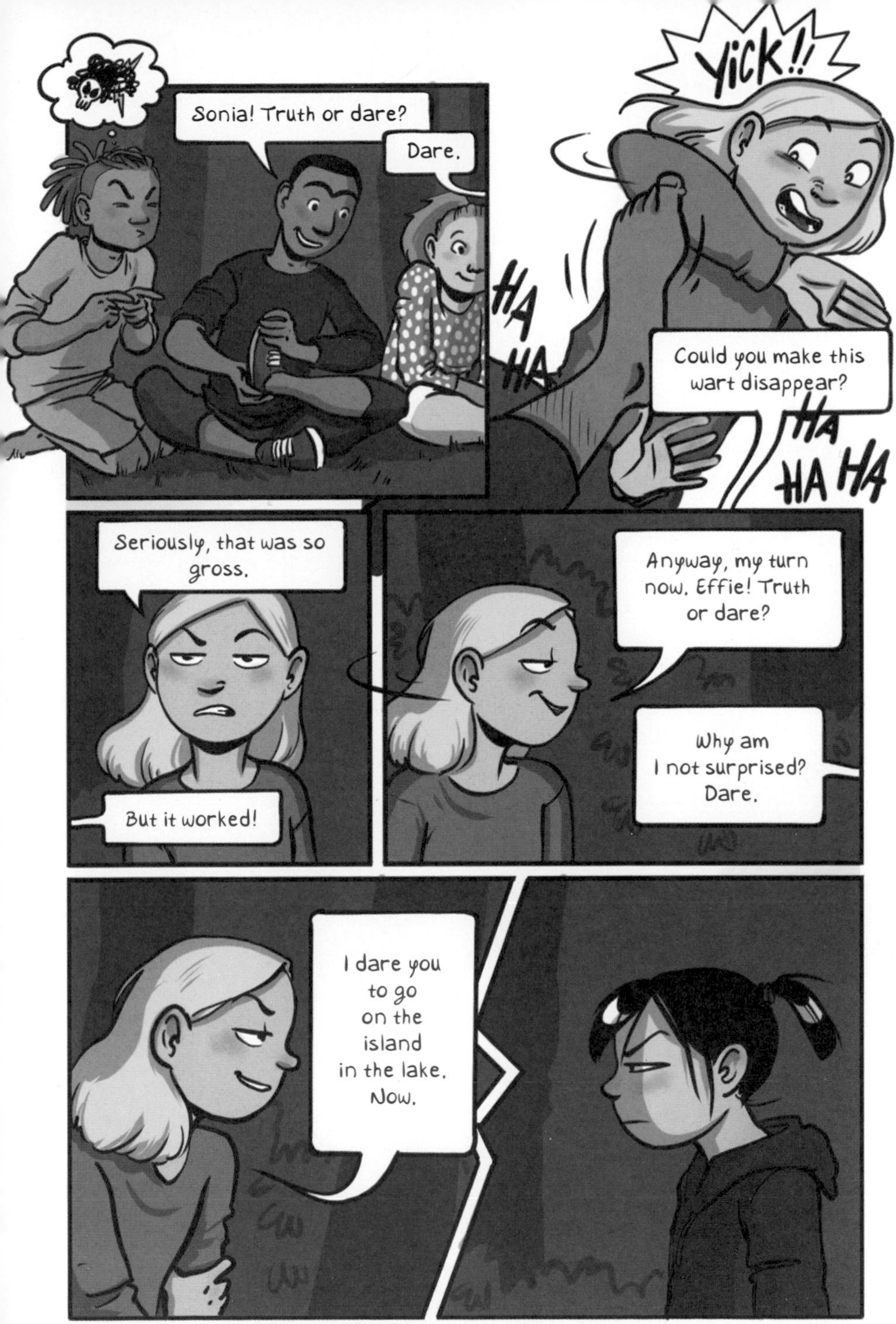
Sonia! Truth or dare?
Dare.
YICK!!
HA HA
Could you make this wart disappear?
HA HA HA
Seriously, that was so gross.
But it worked!
Anyway, my turn now. Effie! Truth or dare?
Why am I not surprised? Dare.
I dare you to go on the island in the lake. Now.

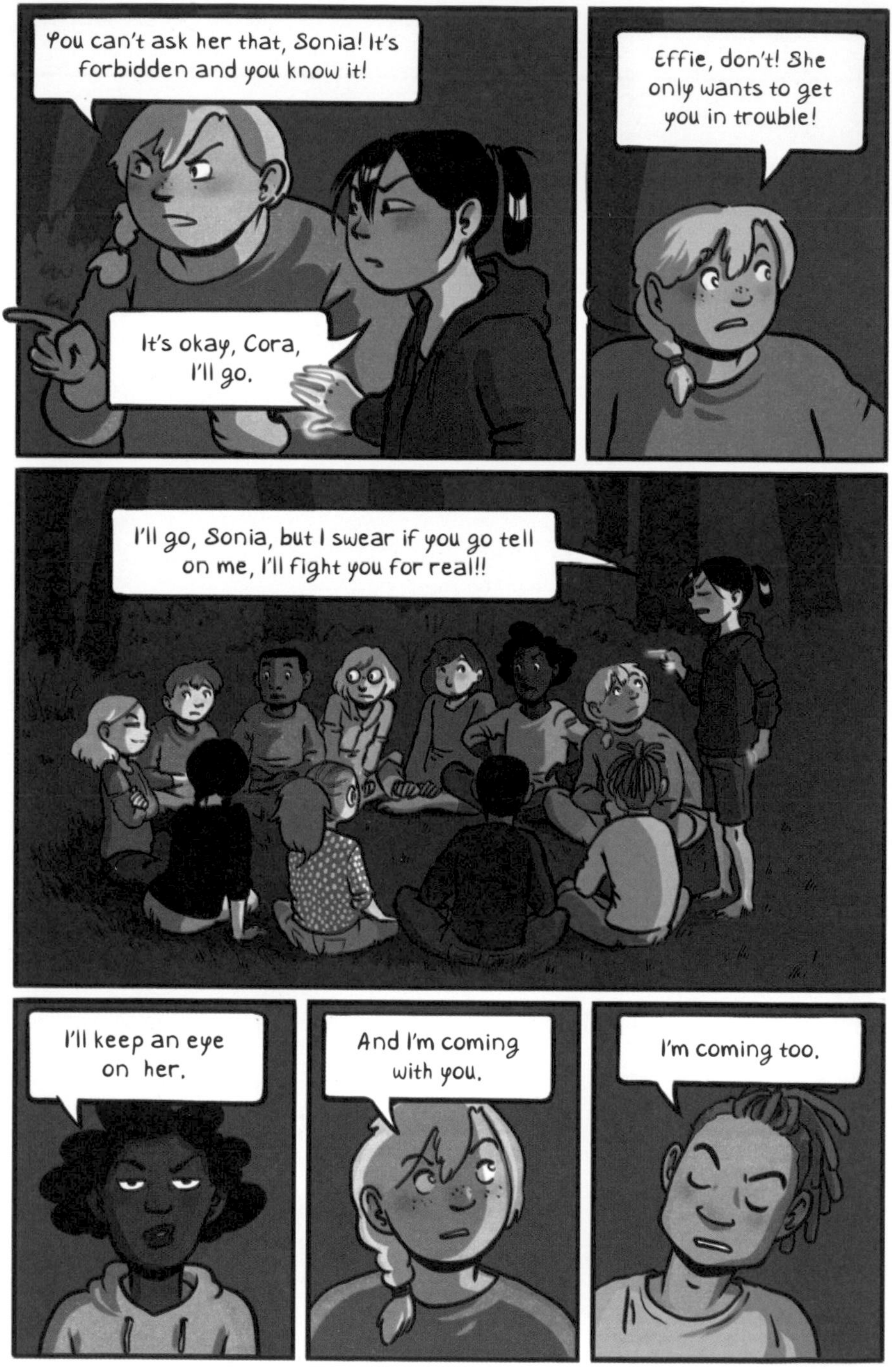
You can't ask her that, Sonia! It's forbidden and you know it!
It's okay, Cora, I'll go.
Effie, don't! She only wants to get you in trouble!
I'll go, Sonia, but I swear if you go tell on me, I'll fight you for real!!
I'll keep an eye on her.
And I'm coming with you.
I'm coming too.

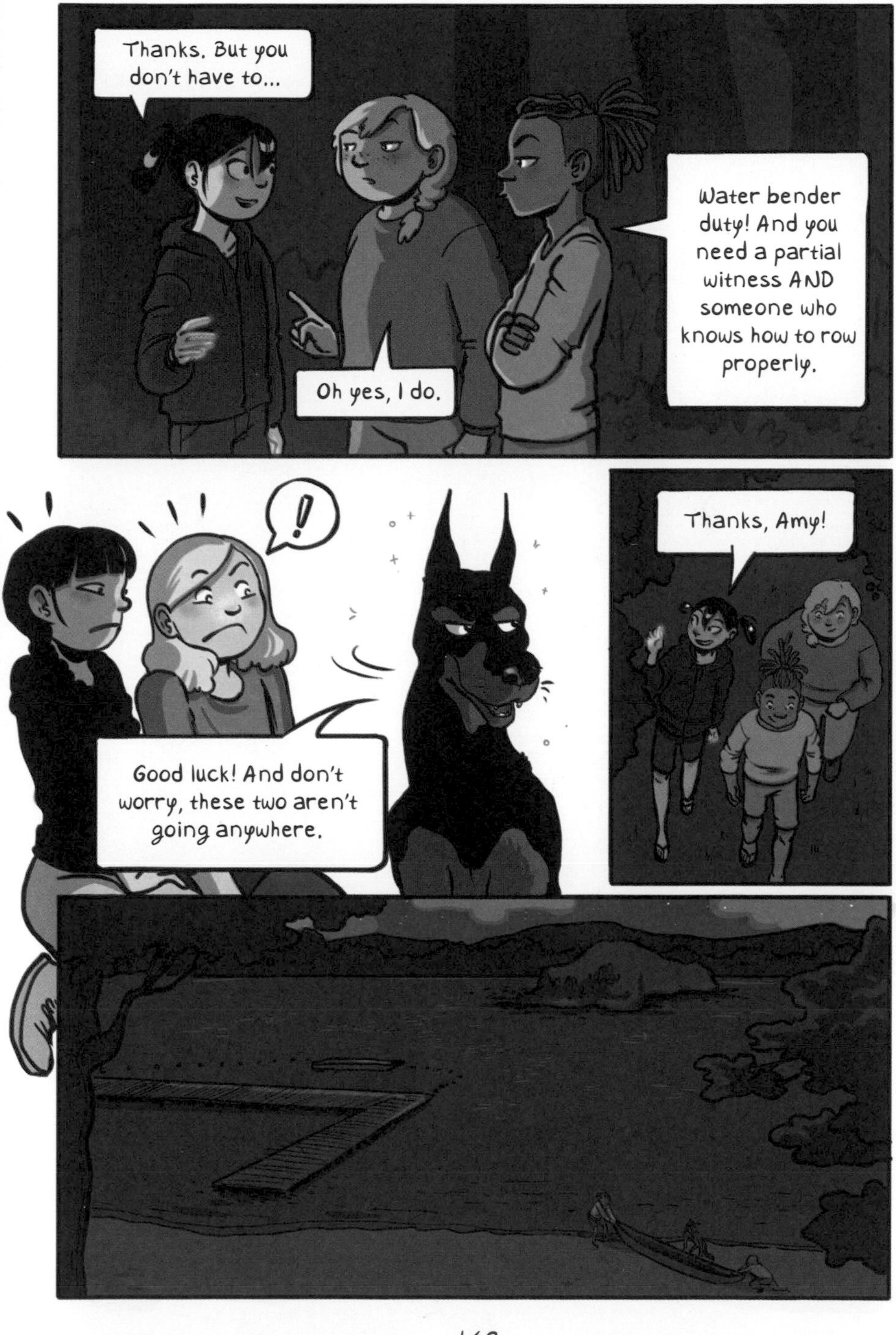
Thanks. But you don't have to...
Oh yes, I do.
Water bender duty! And you need a partial witness AND someone who knows how to row properly.
!
Good luck! And don't worry, these two aren't going anywhere.
Thanks, Amy!

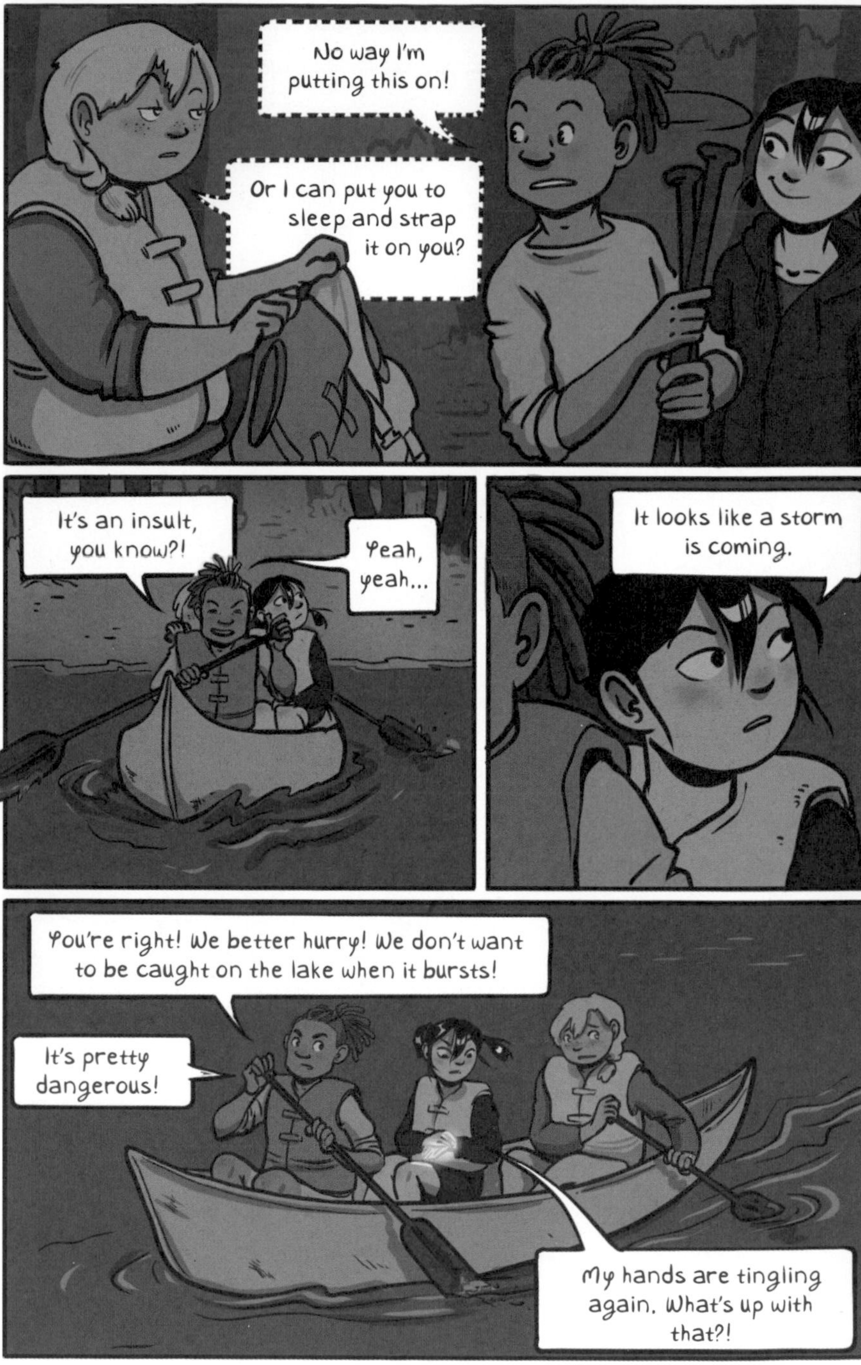
No way I'm putting this on!
Or I can put you to sleep and strap it on you?
It's an insult, you know?!
Yeah, yeah...
It looks like a storm is coming.
You're right! We better hurry! We don't want to be caught on the lake when it bursts!
It's pretty dangerous!
My hands are tingling again. What's up with that?!

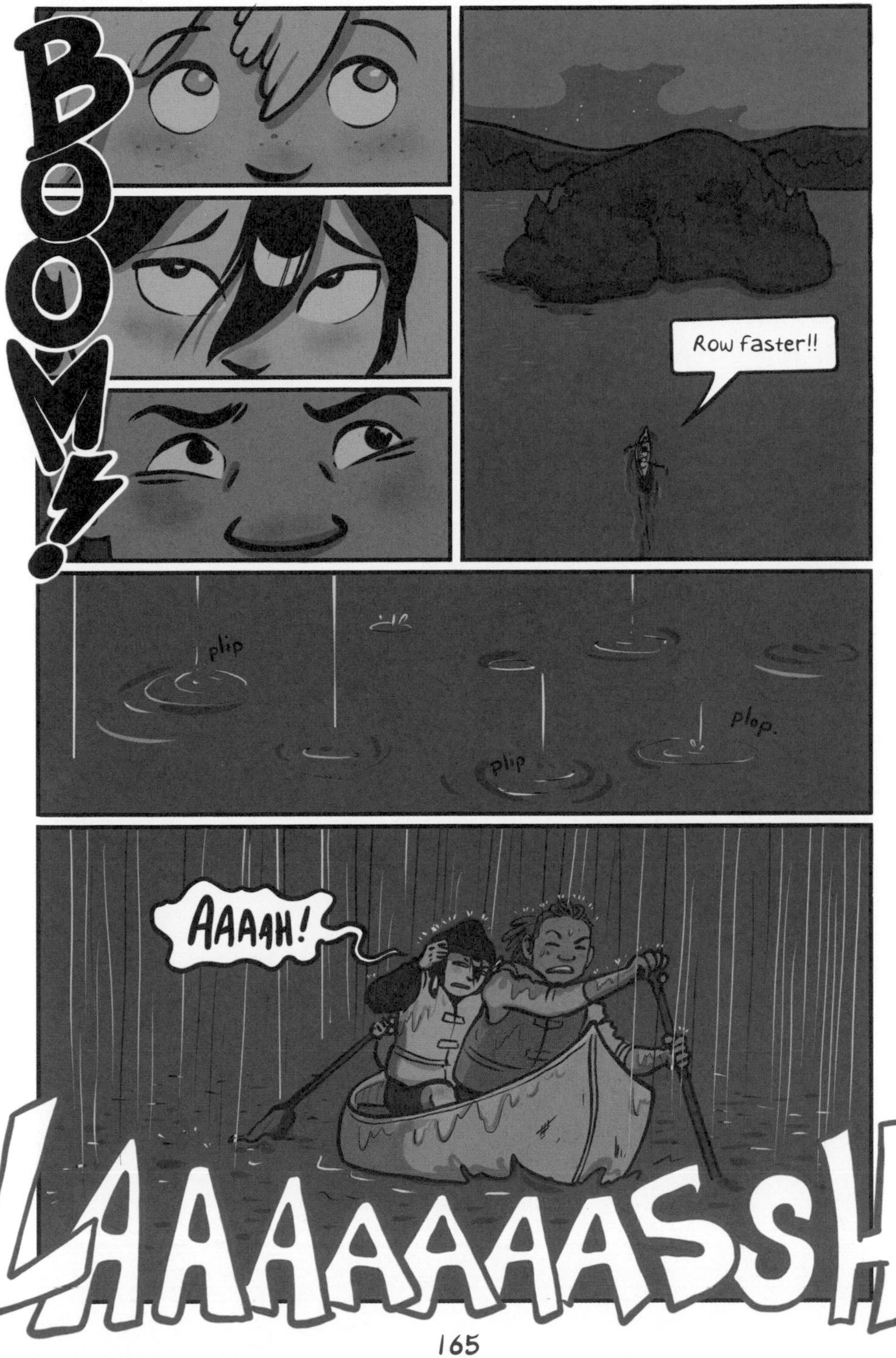
BOOOM!
Row faster!!
plip
plop.
plip
AAAAH!
LAAAAAASSH

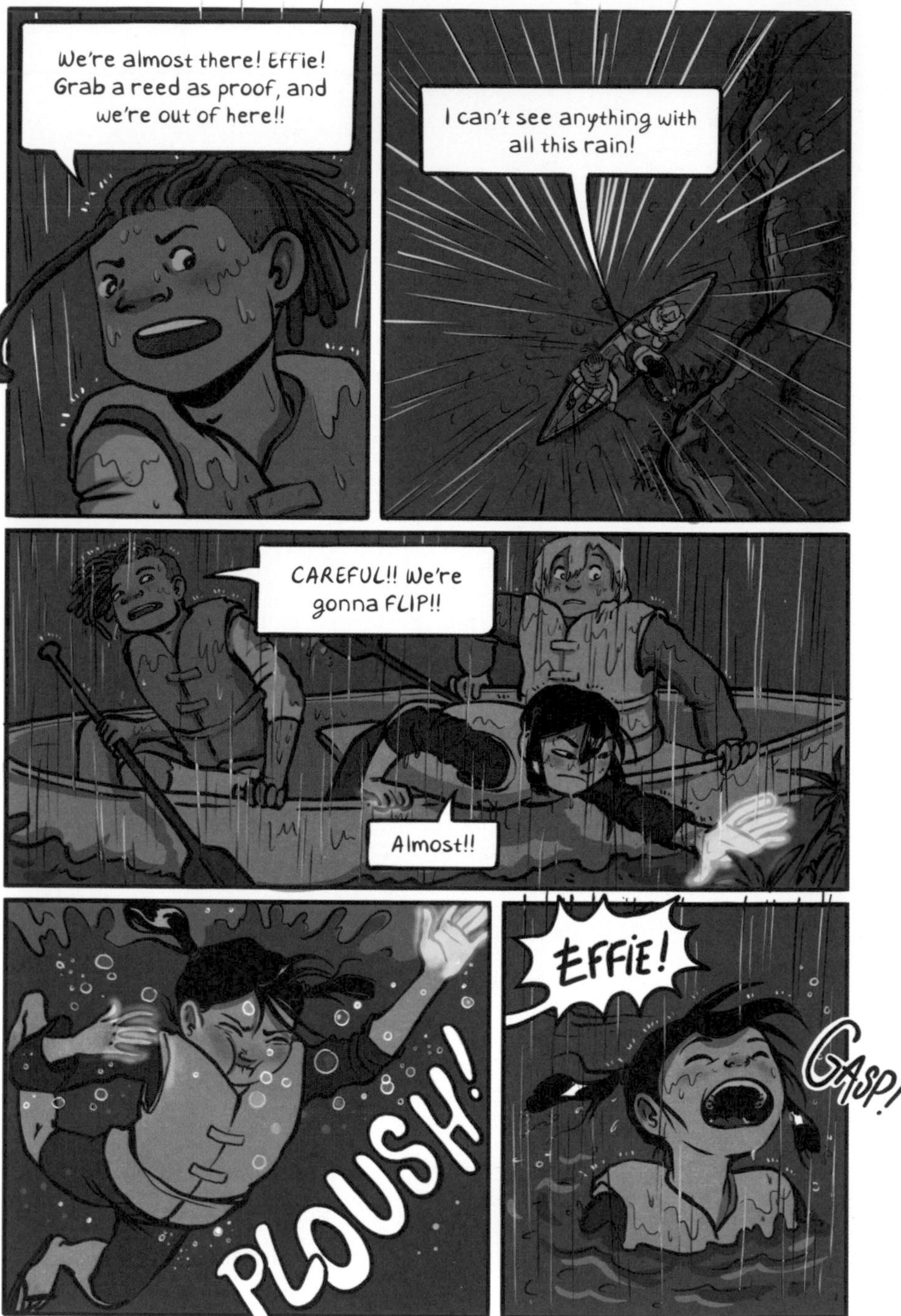
We're almost there! Effie! Grab a reed as proof, and we're out of here!!
I can't see anything with all this rain!
CAREFUL!! We're gonna FLIP!!
Almost!!
PLOUSH!
EFFIE!
GASP!

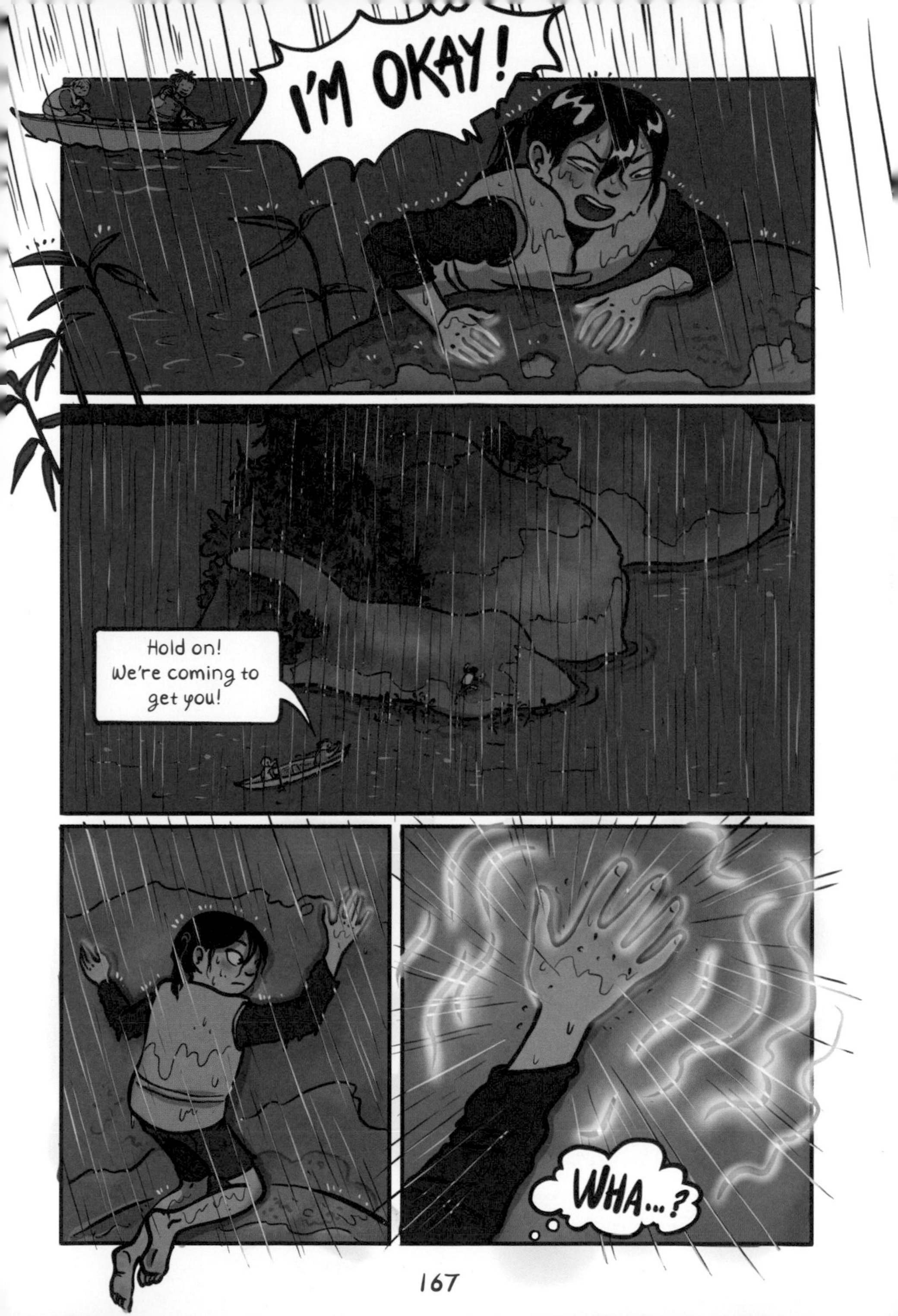
I'M OKAY!
Hold on! We're coming to get you!
WHA...?

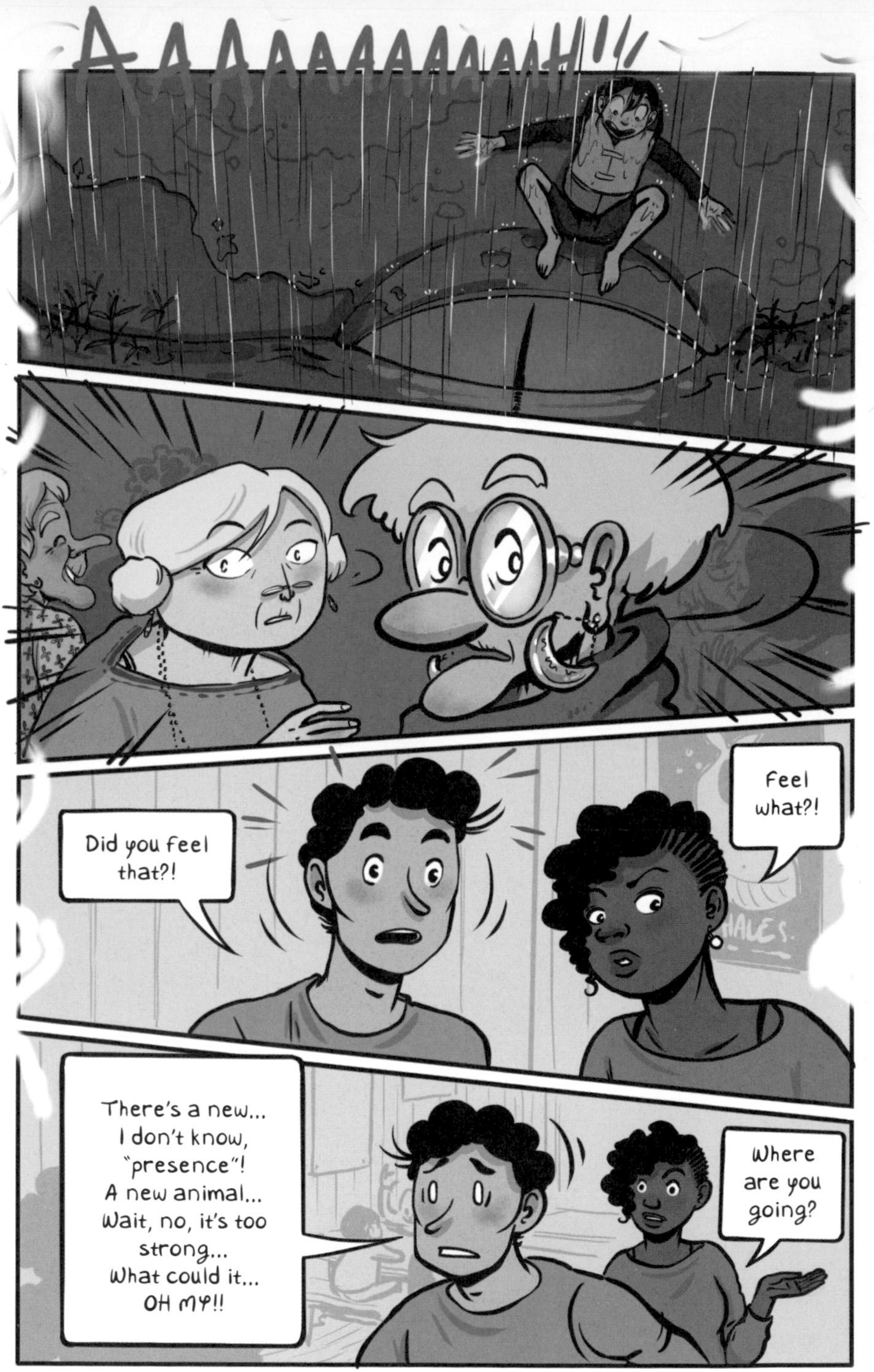
AAAAAAAAAAH!!!
Did you feel that?!
Feel what?!
There's a new... I don't know, "presence"! A new animal... Wait, no, it's too strong... What could it... OH MY!!
Where are you going?

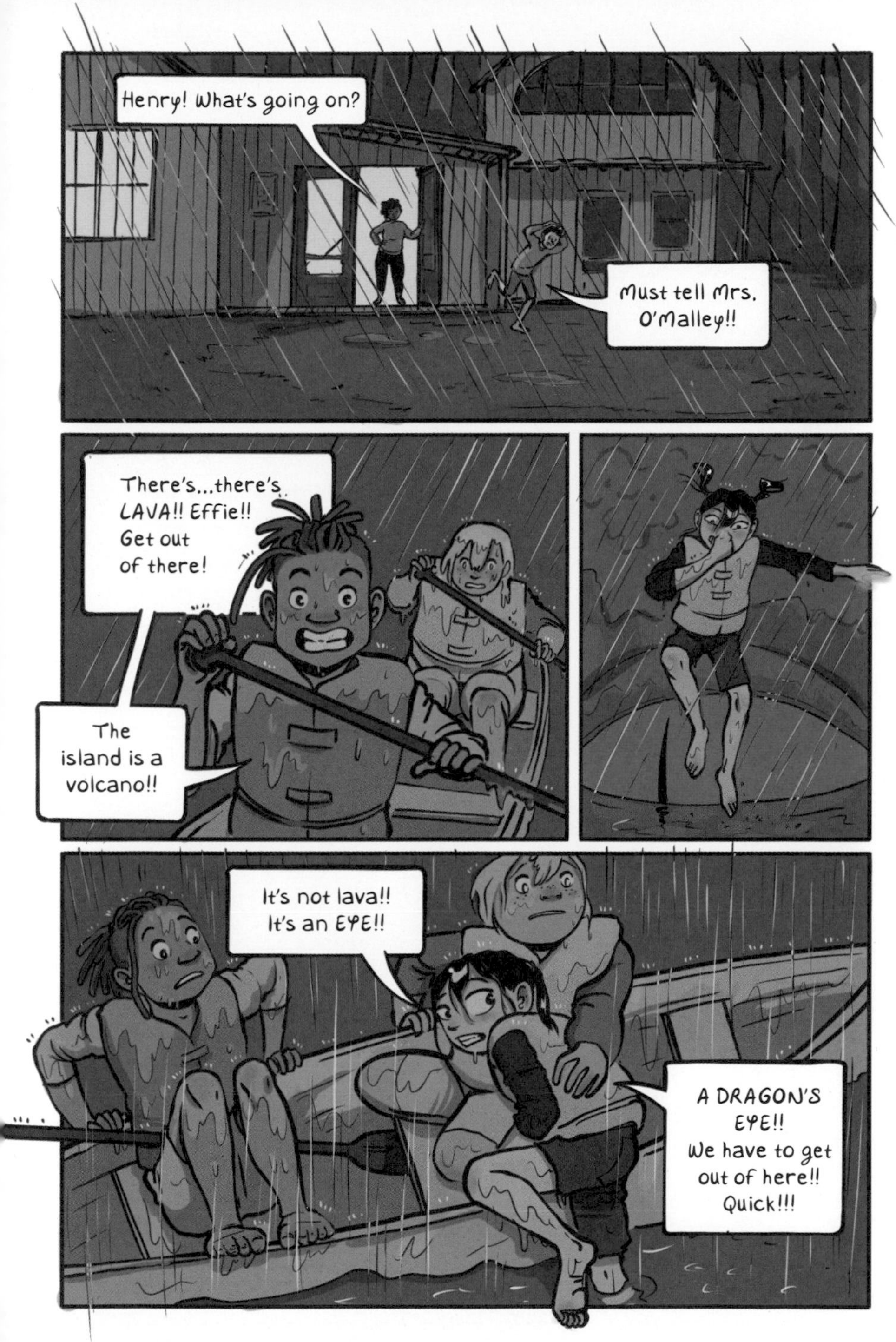
Henry! What's going on?
Must tell Mrs. O'Malley!!
There's...there's LAVA!! Effie!! Get out of there!
The island is a volcano!!
It's not lava!! It's an EYE!!
A DRAGON'S EYE!! We have to get out of here!! Quick!!!

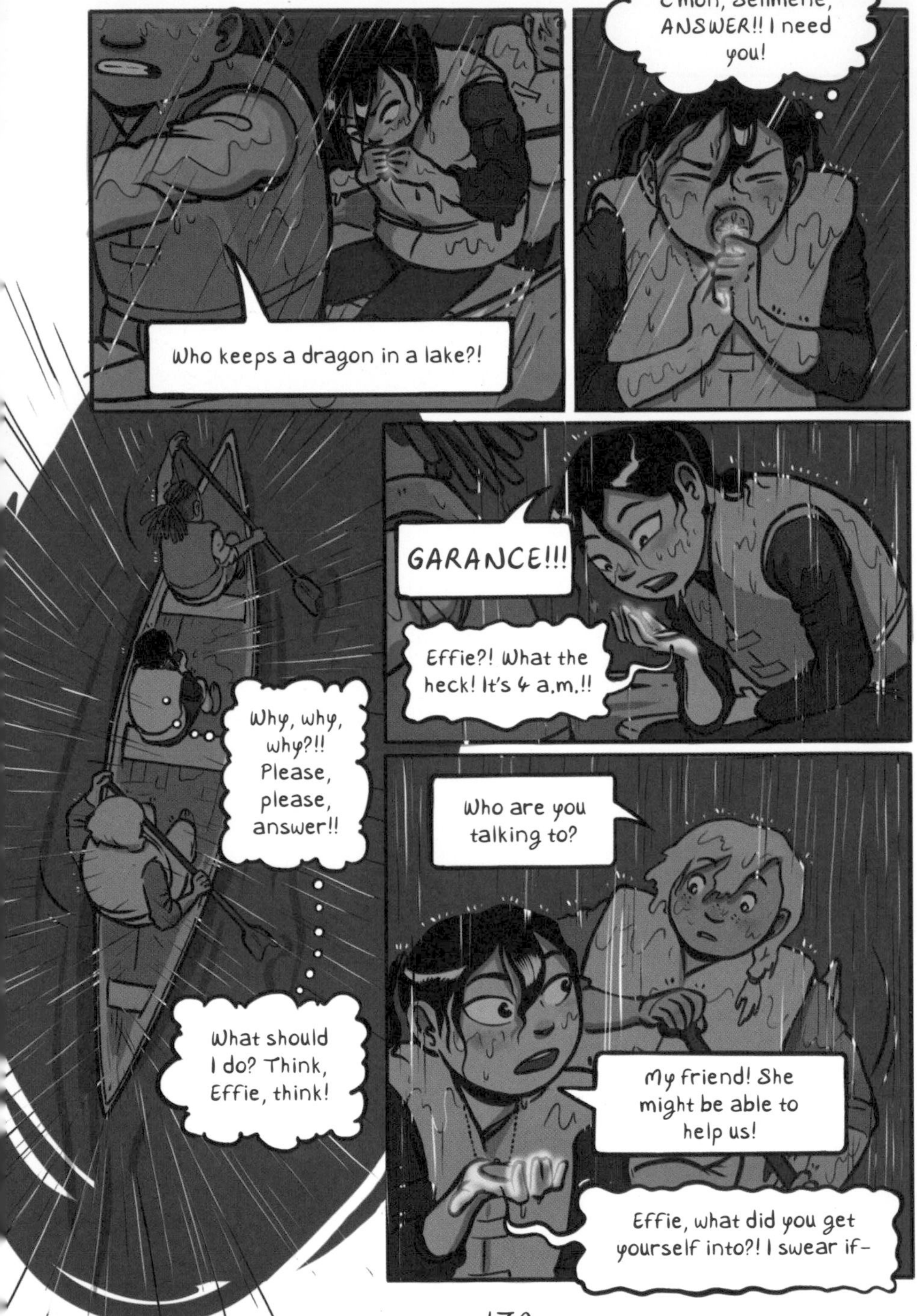
Who keeps a dragon in a lake?!
C'mon, Selimene, ANSWER!! I need you!
GARANCE!!!
Effie?! What the heck! It's 4 a.m.!!
Why, why, why?!! Please, please, answer!!
What should I do? Think, Effie, think!
Who are you talking to?
My friend! She might be able to help us!
Effie, what did you get yourself into?! I swear if-

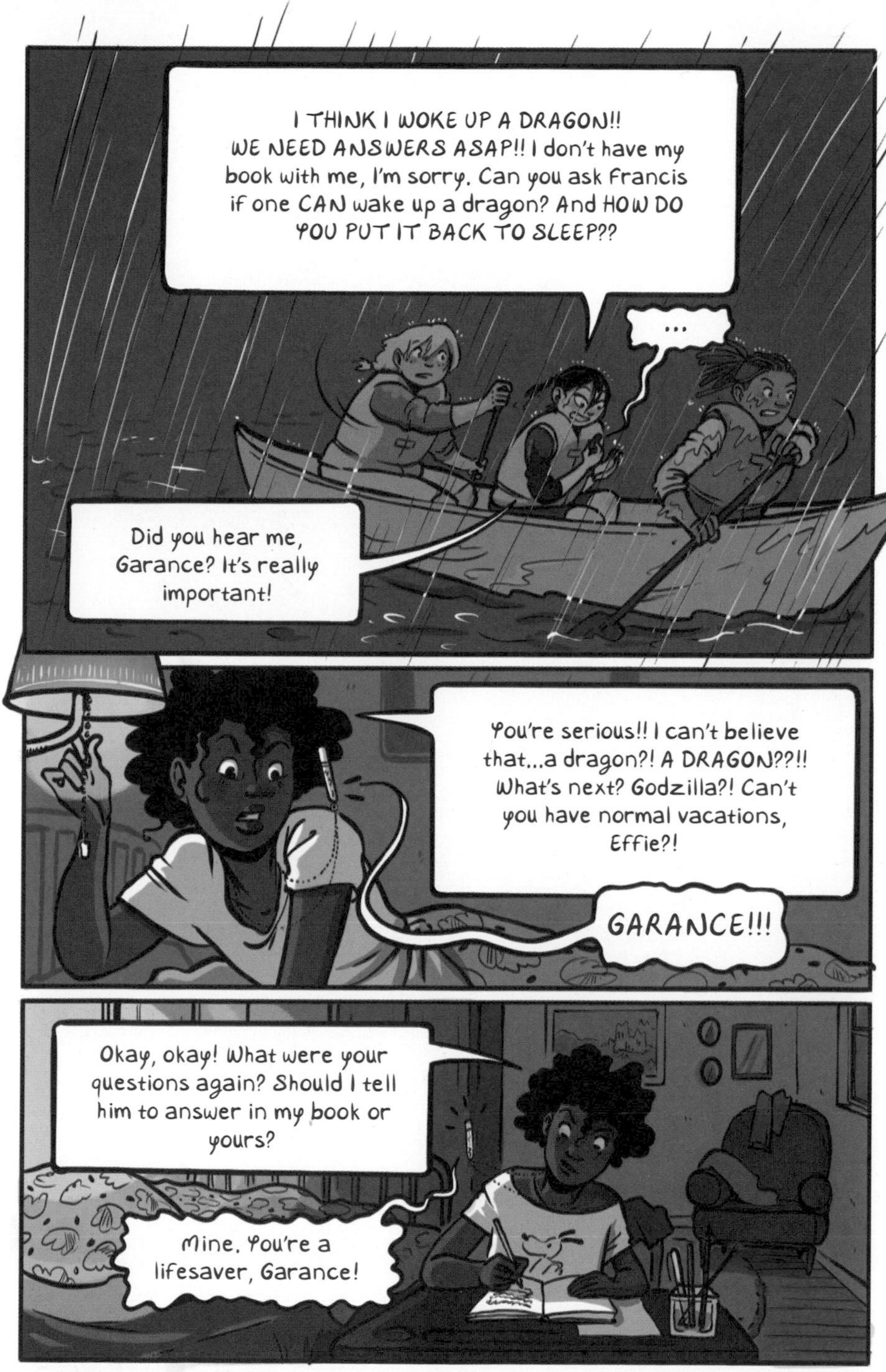
I THINK I WOKE UP A DRAGON!! WE NEED ANSWERS ASAP!! I don't have my book with me, I'm sorry. Can you ask Francis if one CAN wake up a dragon? And HOW DO YOU PUT IT BACK TO SLEEP??
...
Did you hear me, Garance? It's really important!
You're serious!! I can't believe that...a dragon?! A DRAGON??!! What's next? Godzilla?! Can't you have normal vacations, Effie?!
GARANCE!!!
Okay, okay! What were your questions again? Should I tell him to answer in my book or yours?
Mine. You're a lifesaver, Garance!

Chapter 5

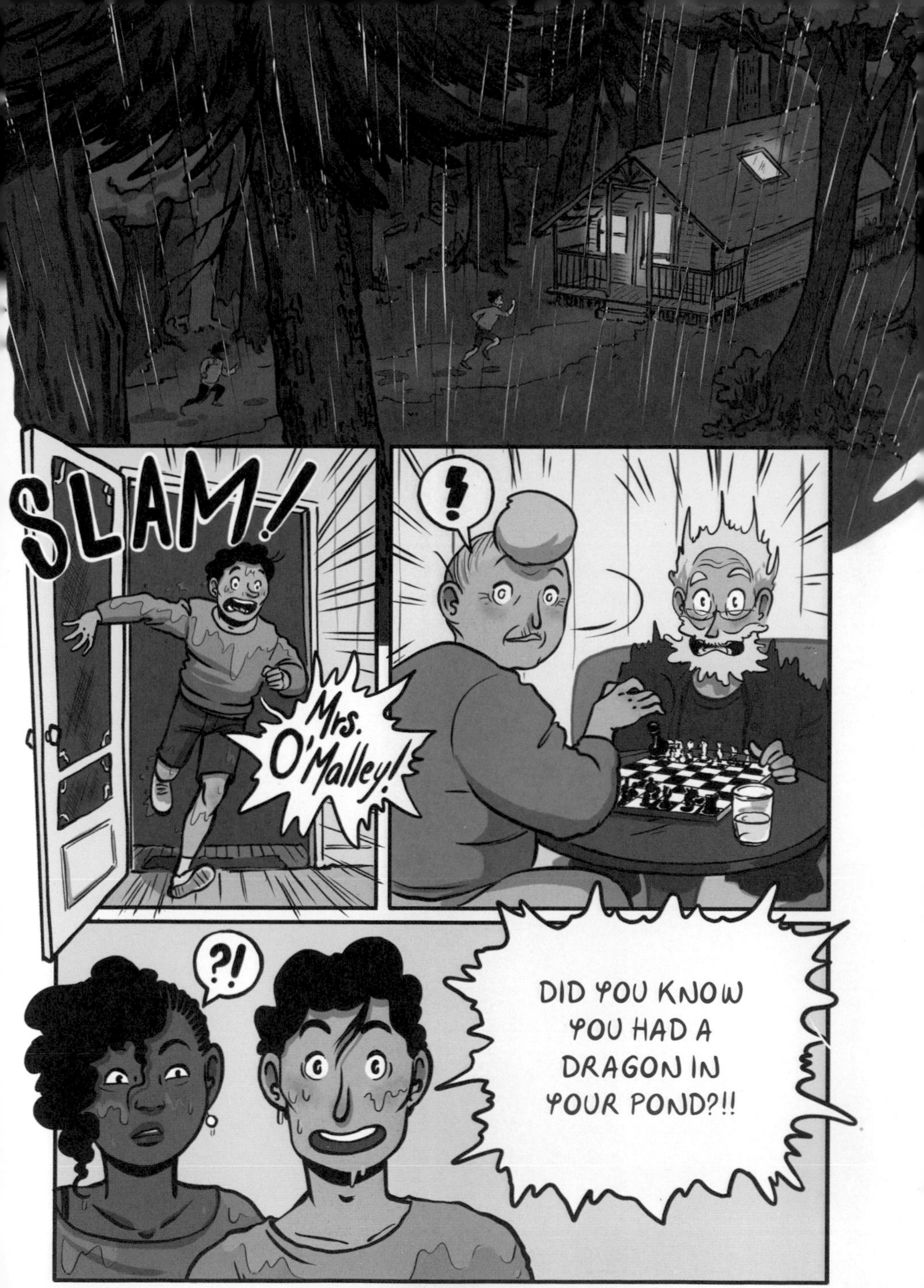
SLAM!
!
Mrs. O'Malley!
?!
DID YOU KNOW YOU HAD A DRAGON IN YOUR POND?!!

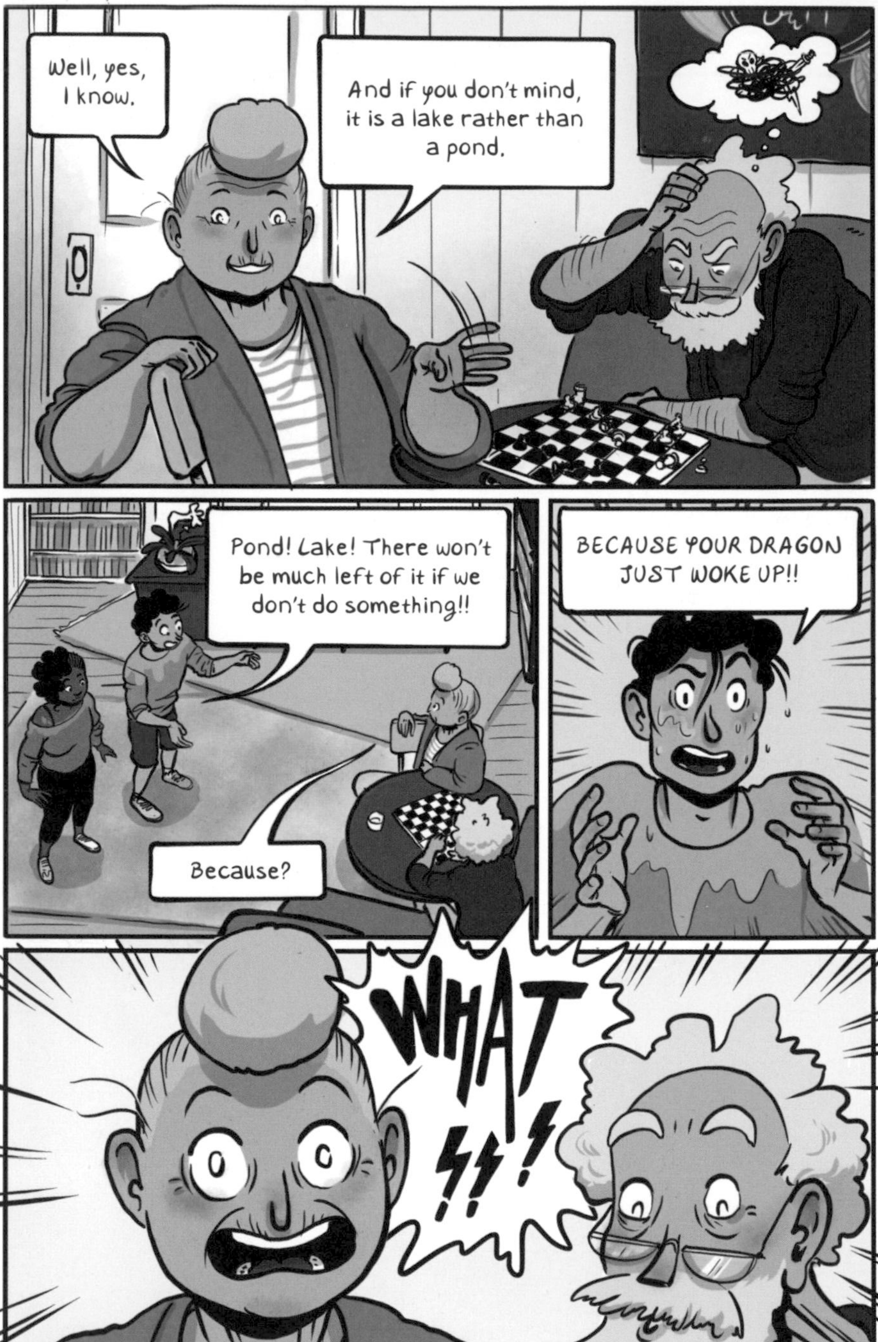
Well, yes, I know.
And if you don't mind, it is a lake rather than a pond.
Pond! Lake! There won't be much left of it if we don't do something!!
Because?
BECAUSE YOUR DRAGON JUST WOKE UP!!
WHAT!!

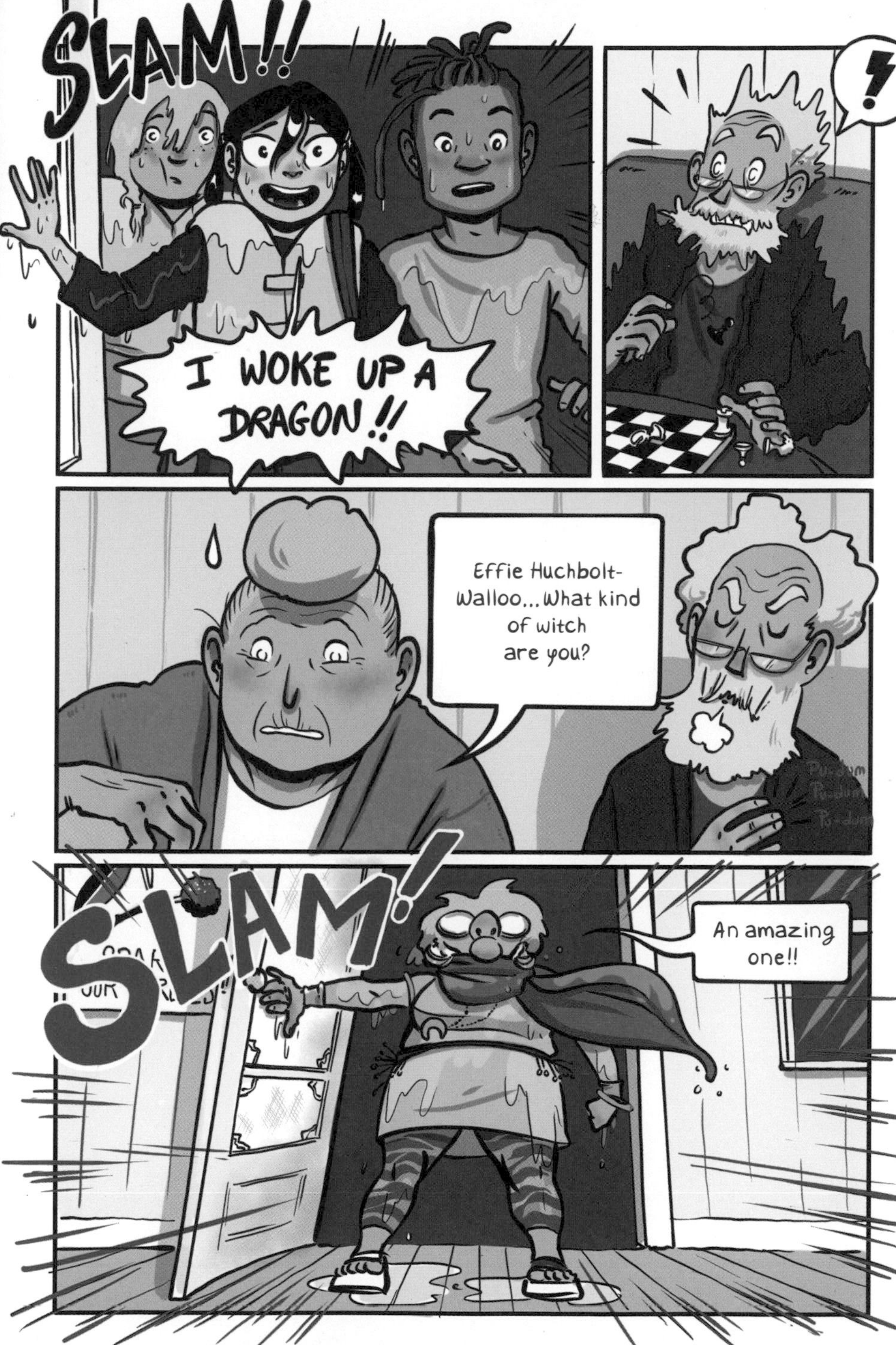
SLAM!!
I WOKE UP A DRAGON!!
!
Effie Huchbolt-Walloo... What kind of witch are you?
SLAM!
An amazing one!!

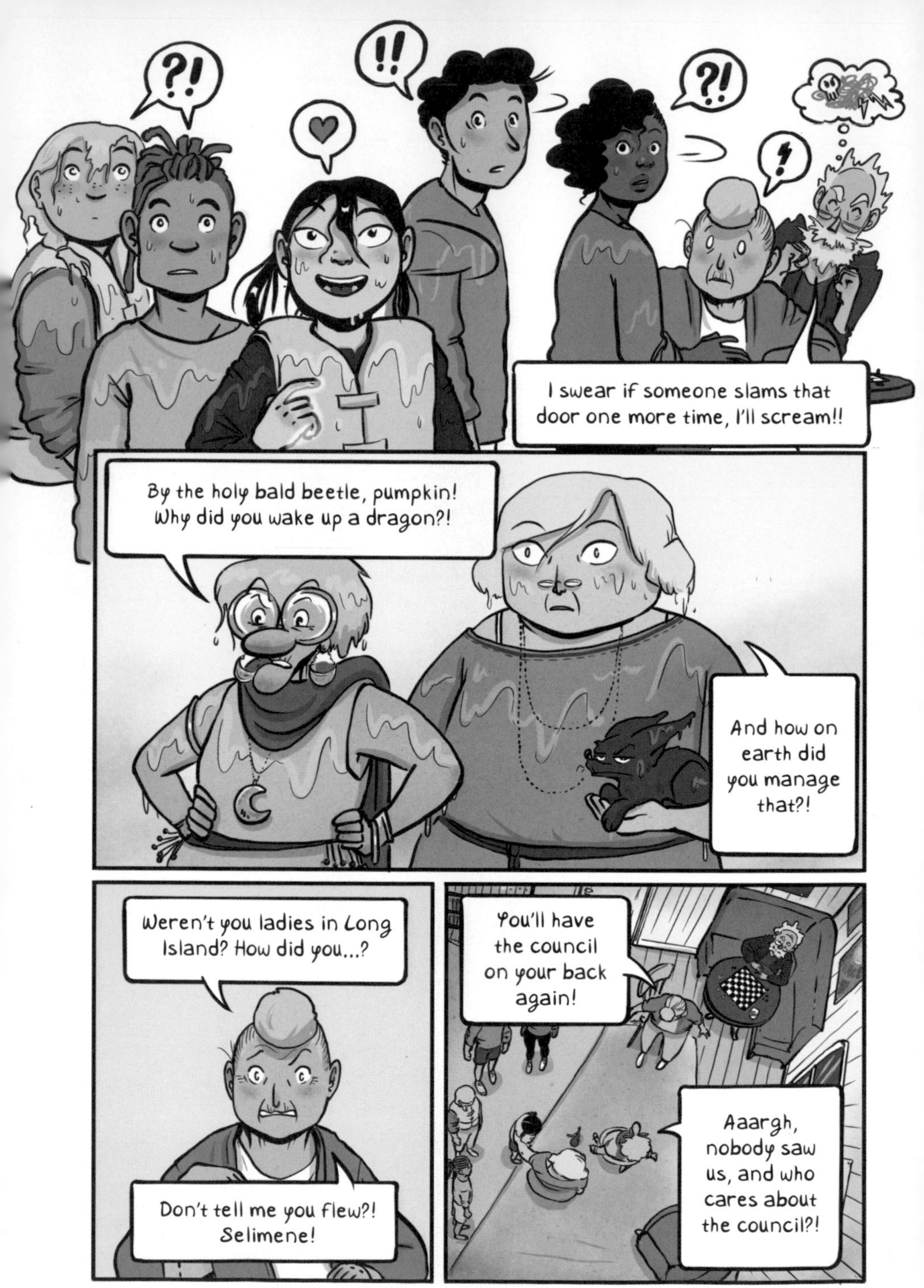
?!
♥
!!
?!
!
I swear if someone slams that door one more time, I'll scream!!
By the holy bald beetle, pumpkin! Why did you wake up a dragon?!
And how on earth did you manage that?!
Weren't you ladies in Long Island? How did you...?
Don't tell me you flew?! Selimene!
You'll have the council on your back again!
Aaargh, nobody saw us, and who cares about the council?!

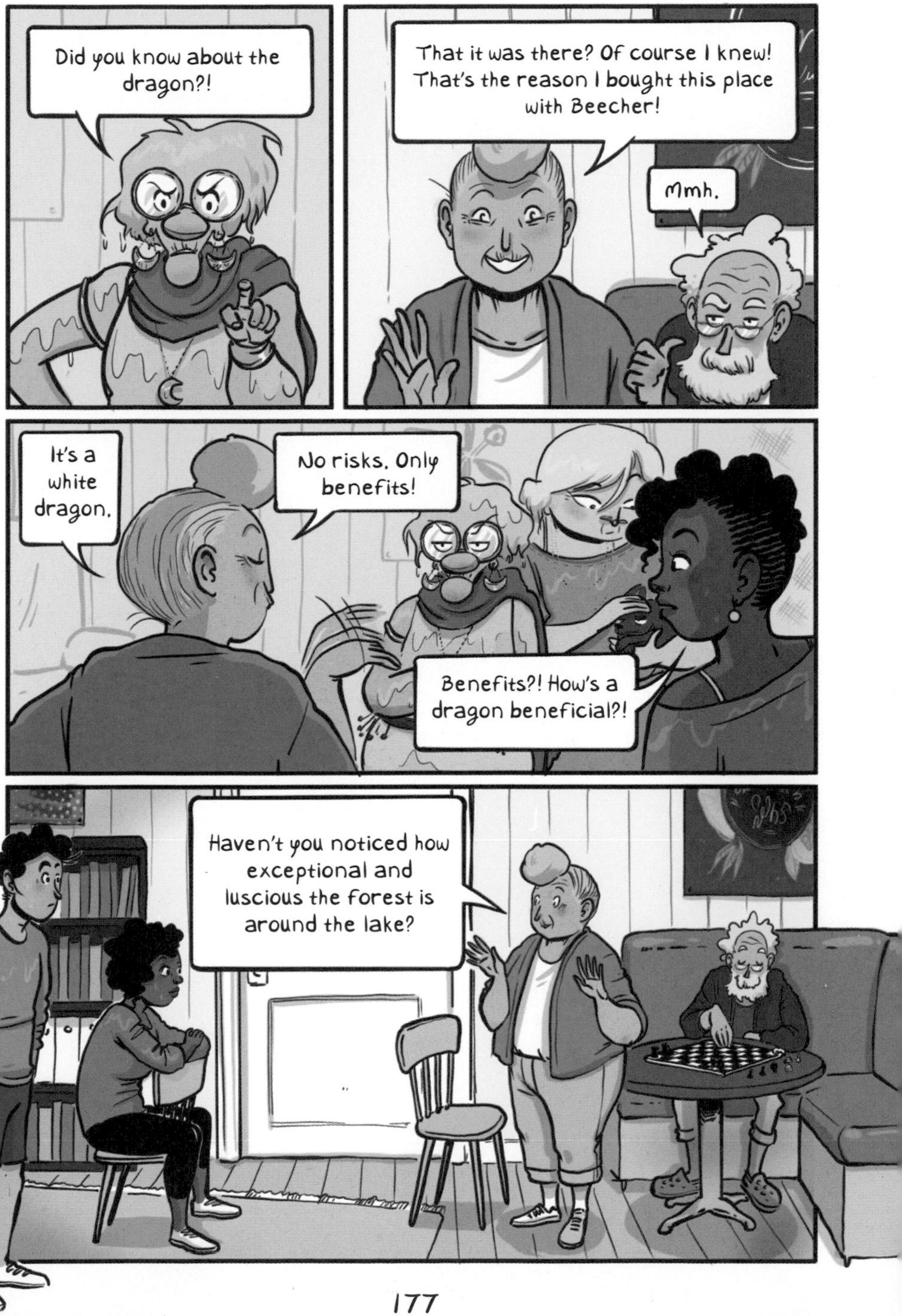
Did you know about the dragon?!
That it was there? Of course I knew! That's the reason I bought this place with Beecher!
Mmh.
It's a white dragon.
No risks. Only benefits!
Benefits?! How's a dragon beneficial?!
Haven't you noticed how exceptional and luscious the forest is around the lake?

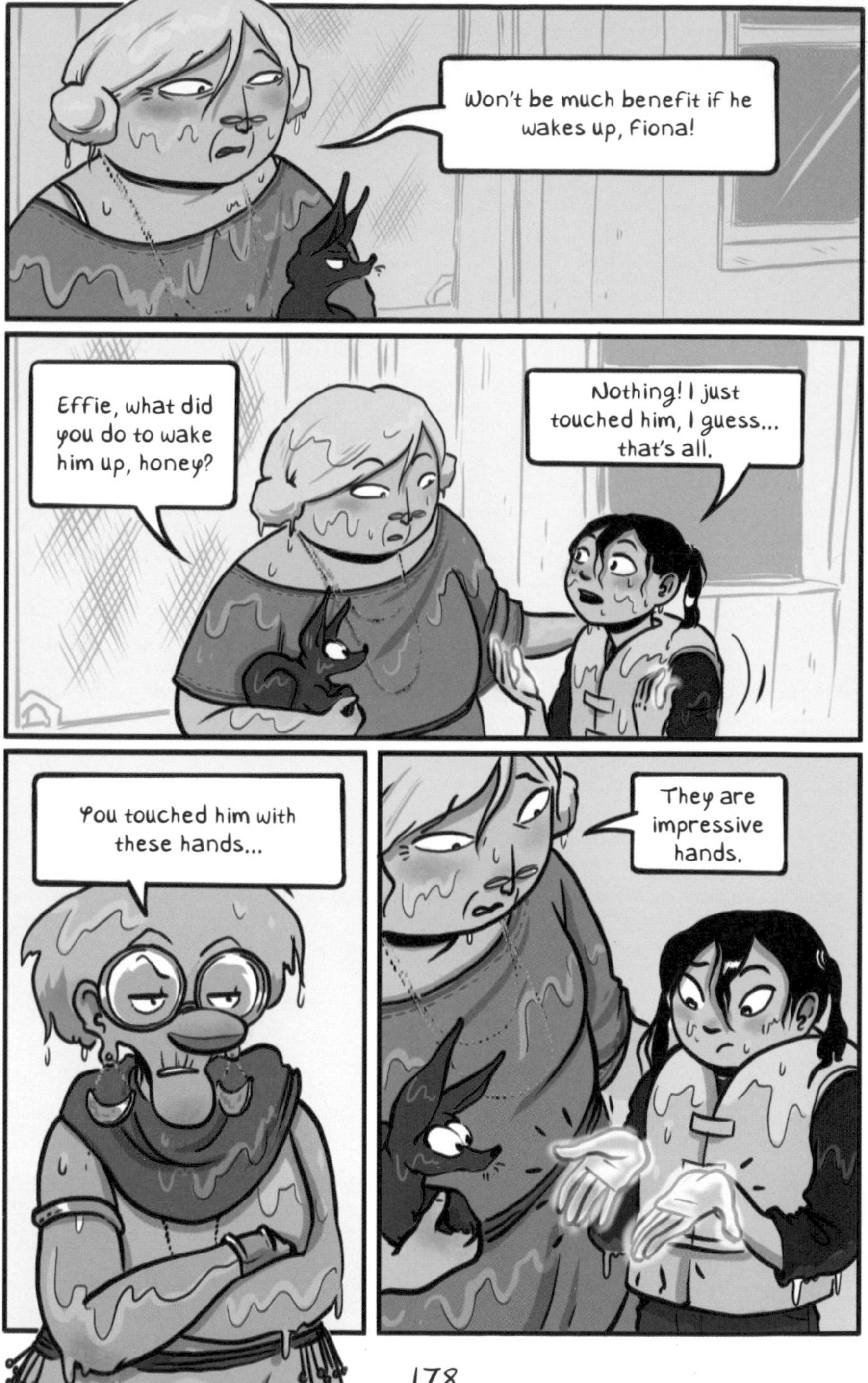
Won't be much benefit if he wakes up, Fiona!
Effie, what did you do to wake him up, honey?
Nothing! I just touched him, I guess... that's all.
You touched him with these hands...
They are impressive hands.

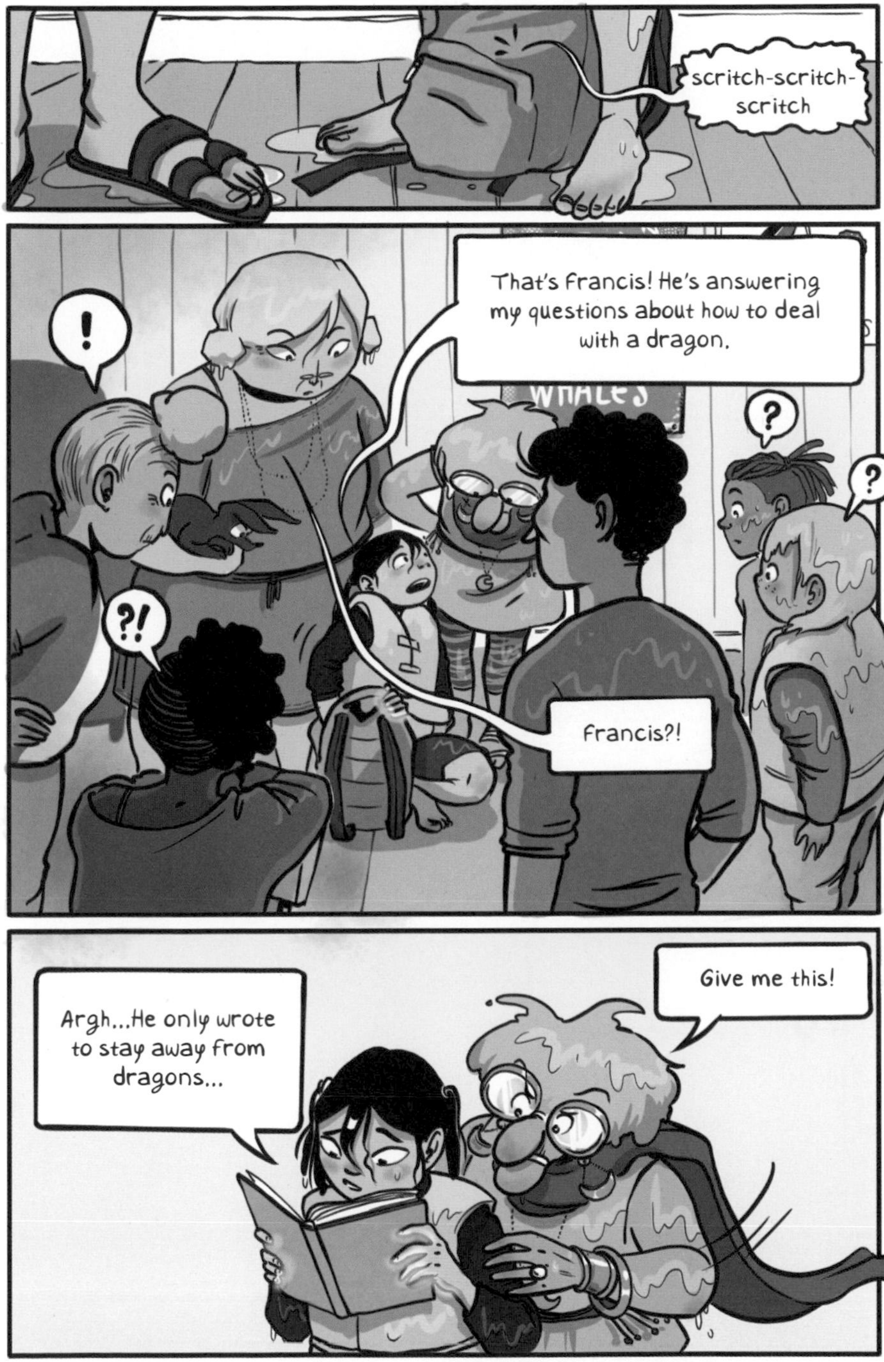
scritch-scritch-scritch
!
That's Francis! He's answering my questions about how to deal with a dragon.
WHALES
?
?
?!
Francis?!
Argh...He only wrote to stay away from dragons...
Give me this!

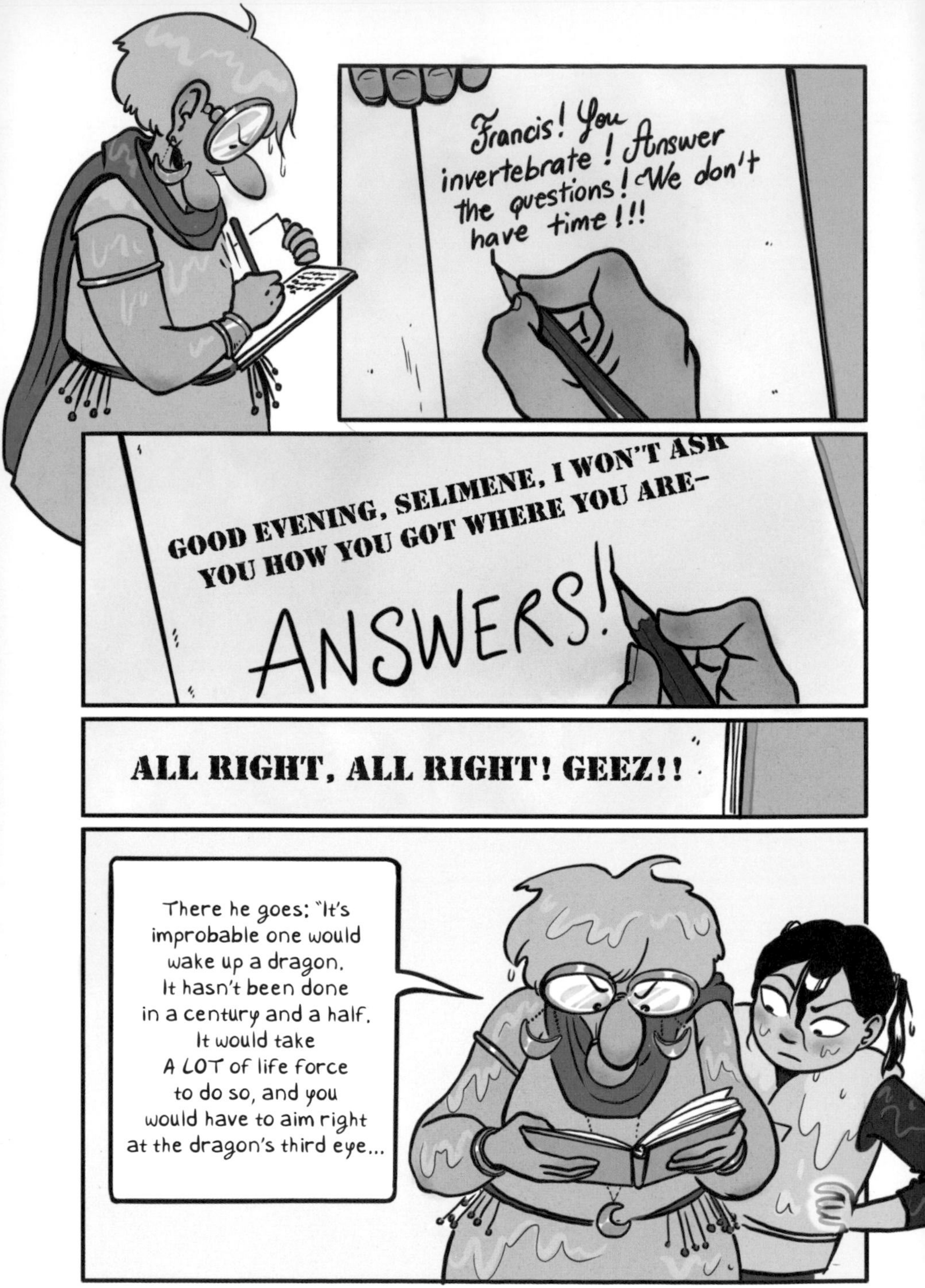
Francis! You invertebrate! Answer the questions! We don't have time!!!
GOOD EVENING, SELIMENE, I WON'T ASK YOU HOW YOU GOT WHERE YOU ARE–
ANSWERS!
ALL RIGHT, ALL RIGHT! GEEZ!!
There he goes: "It's improbable one would wake up a dragon. It hasn't been done in a century and a half. It would take A LOT of life force to do so, and you would have to aim right at the dragon's third eye...

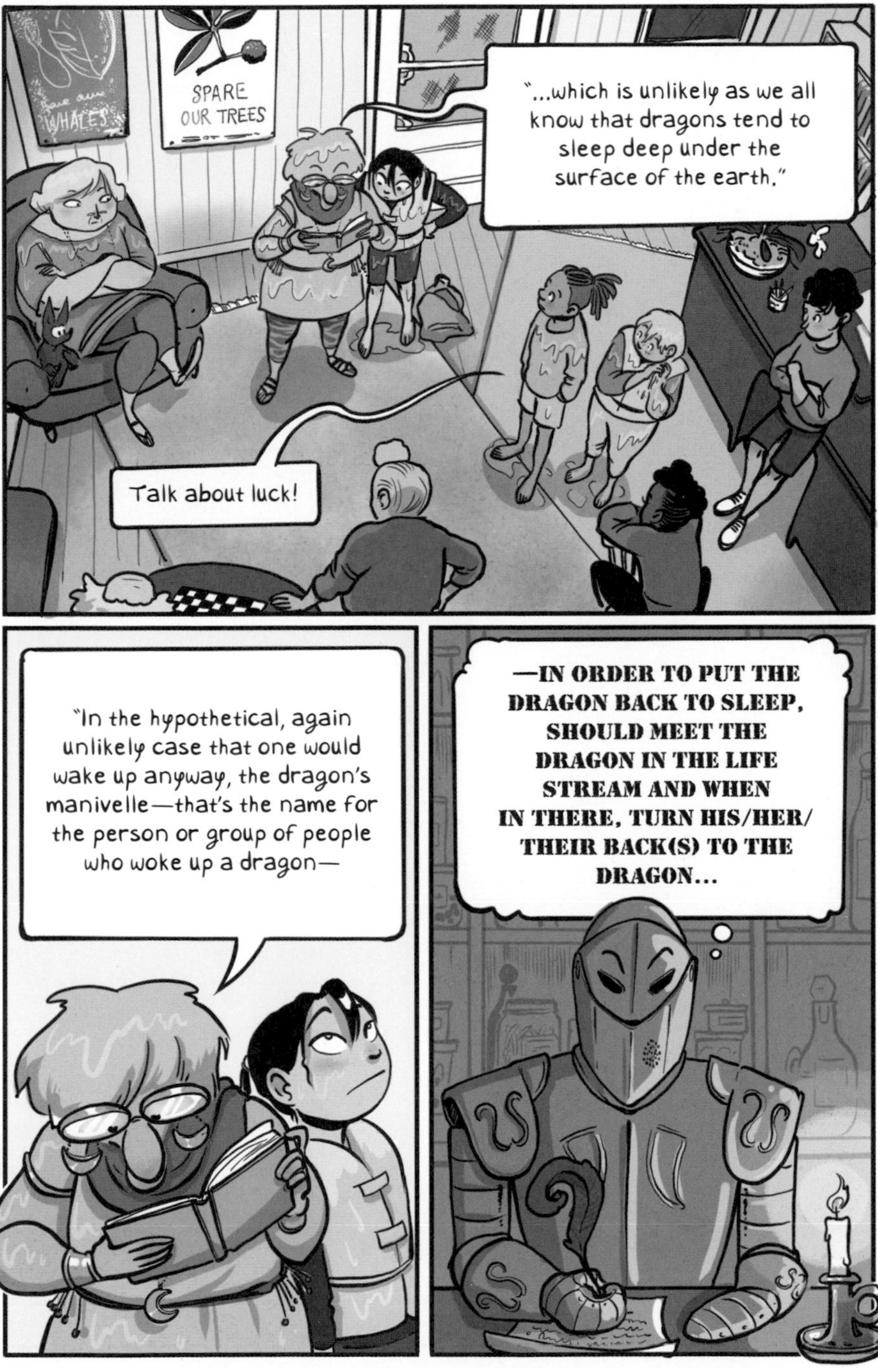
SPARE OUR TREES
"...which is unlikely as we all know that dragons tend to sleep deep under the surface of the earth."
Talk about luck!
"In the hypothetical, again unlikely case that one would wake up anyway, the dragon's manivelle—that's the name for the person or group of people who woke up a dragon—
—IN ORDER TO PUT THE DRAGON BACK TO SLEEP, SHOULD MEET THE DRAGON IN THE LIFE STREAM AND WHEN IN THERE, TURN HIS/HER/ THEIR BACK(S) TO THE DRAGON...

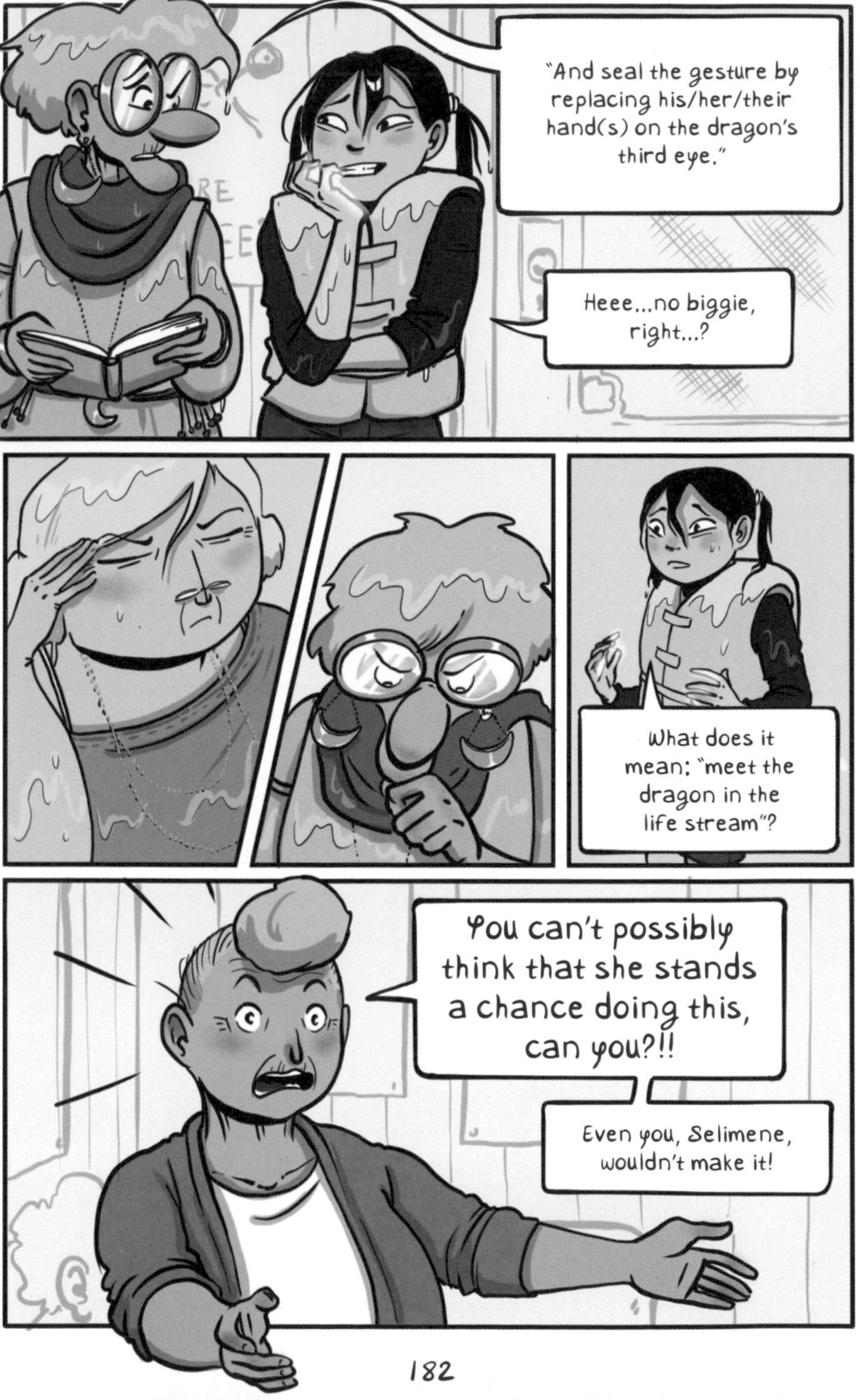
"And seal the gesture by replacing his/her/their hand(s) on the dragon's third eye."
Heee...no biggie, right...?
What does it mean: "meet the dragon in the life stream"?
You can't possibly think that she stands a chance doing this, can you?!!
Even you, Selimene, wouldn't make it!

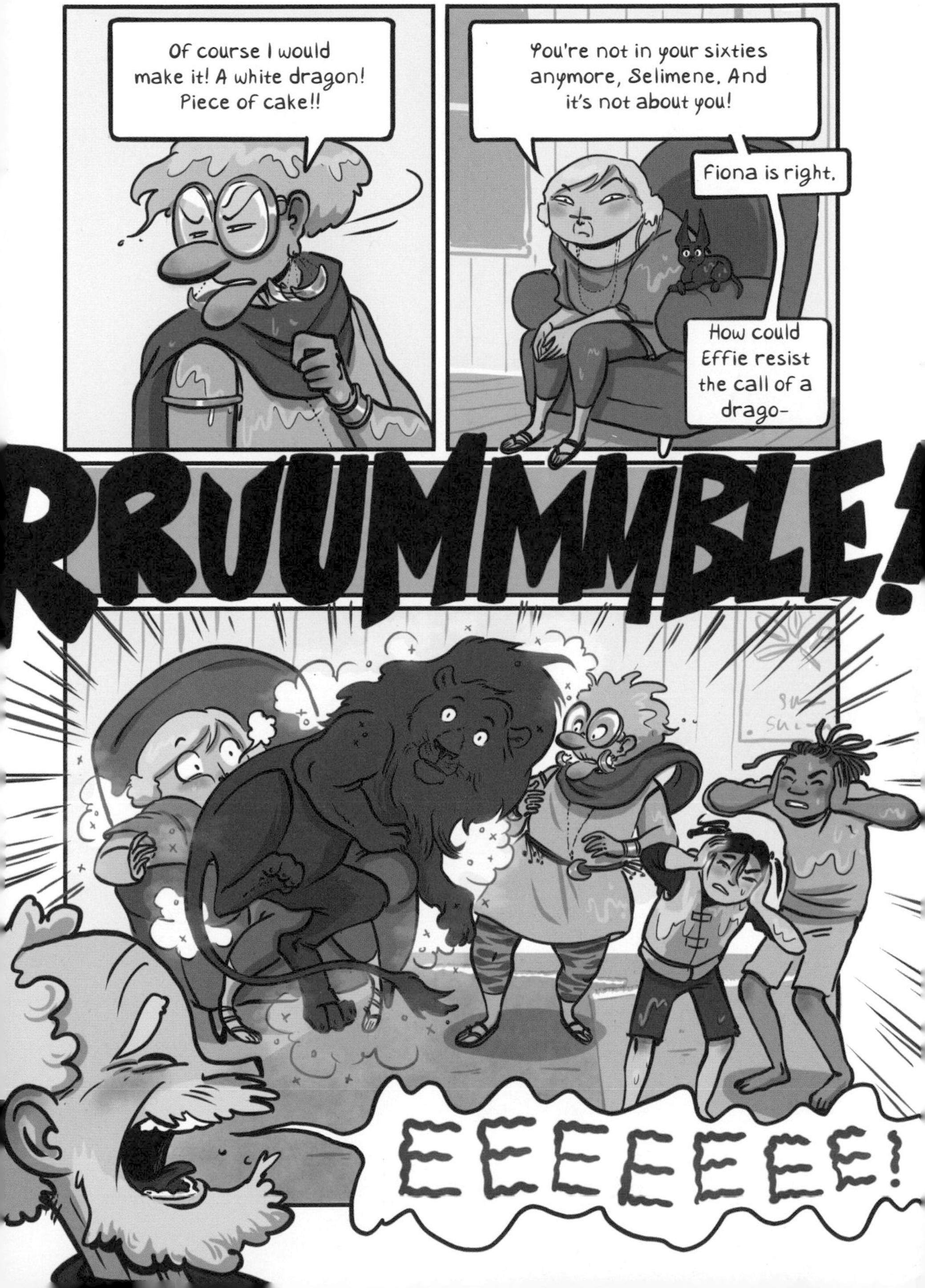
Of course I would make it! A white dragon! Piece of cake!!
You're not in your sixties anymore, Selimene. And it's not about you!
Fiona is right.
How could Effie resist the call of a drago-
RRUUMMMBLE!
EEEEEEE!

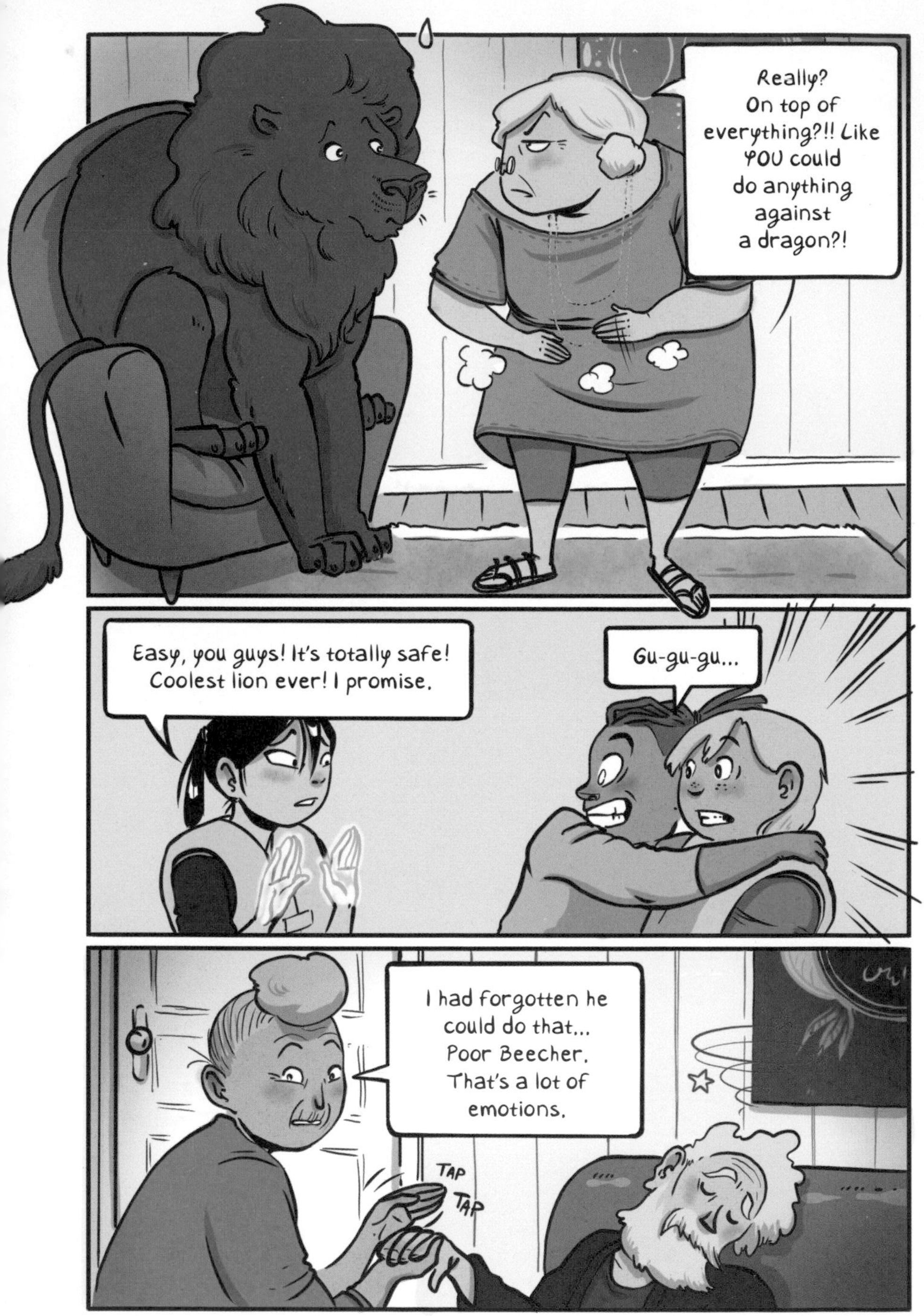
Really? On top of everything?!! Like YOU could do anything against a dragon?!
Easy, you guys! It's totally safe! Coolest lion ever! I promise.
Gu-gu-gu...
I had forgotten he could do that... Poor Beecher. That's a lot of emotions.
TAP
TAP

RRUUUMBLE!

AAAAH!!

It doesn't look like we have a choice, does it?

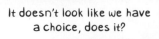

I did this. I need to fix it.

Carlota is right, Effie. You may not have the strength to do this...

The life force of a dragon...

...it's something beyond what you can imagine! It will pull you so strongly that...you won't be able to resist...

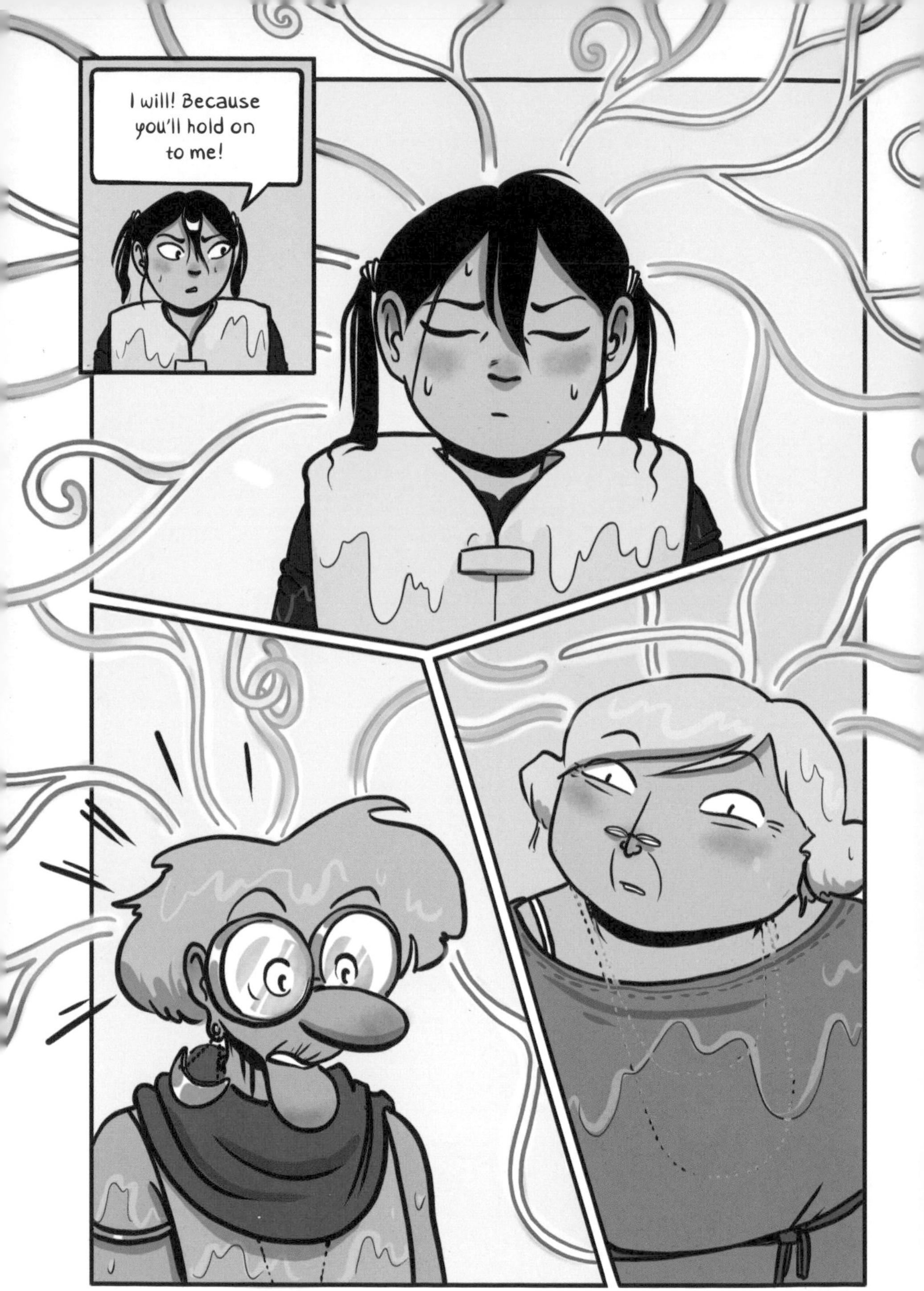
I will! Because you'll hold on to me!

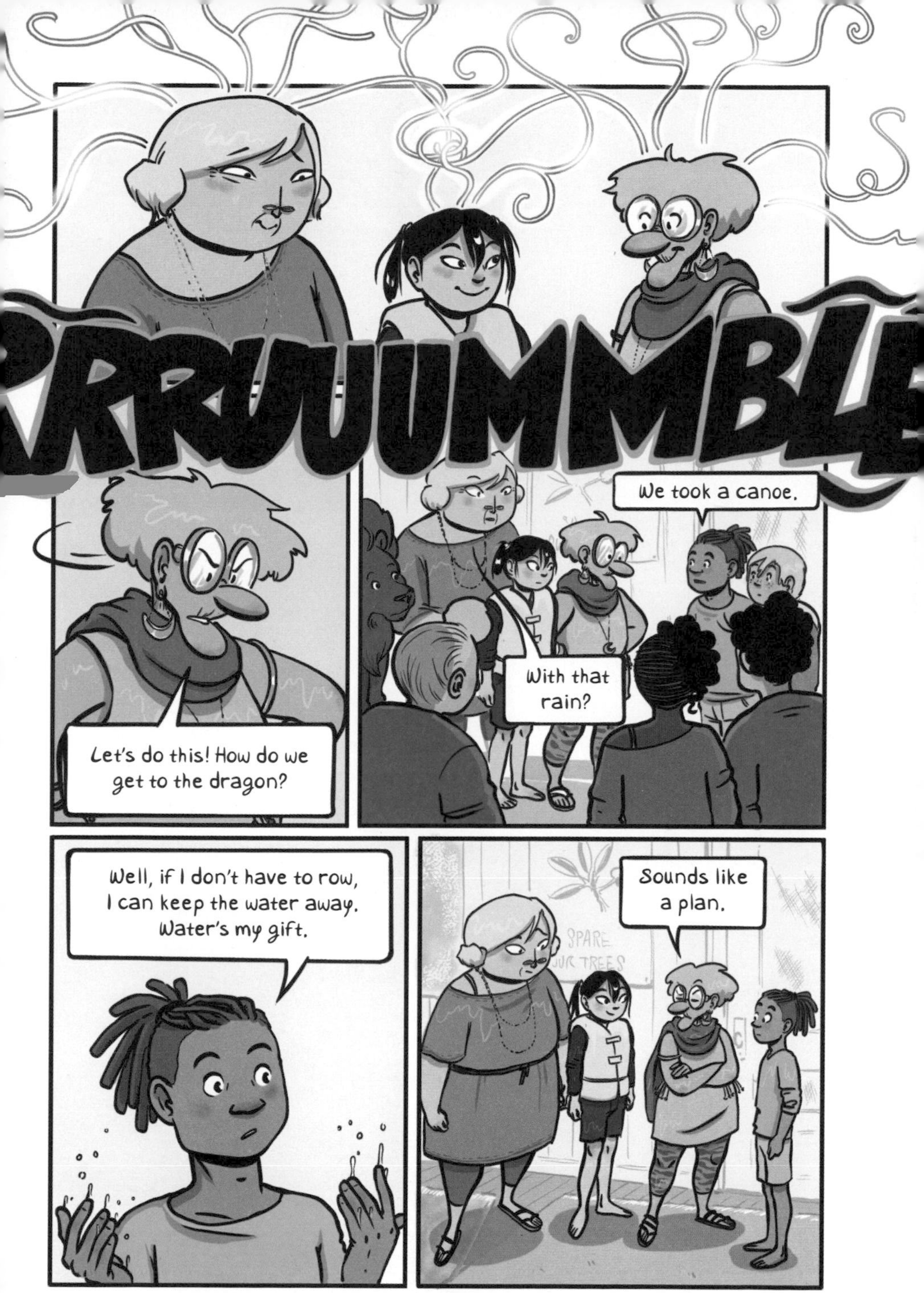

RRUUMMBLE
Let's do this! How do we get to the dragon?
We took a canoe.
With that rain?
Well, if I don't have to row, I can keep the water away. Water's my gift.
Sounds like a plan.
SPARE
UR TREES

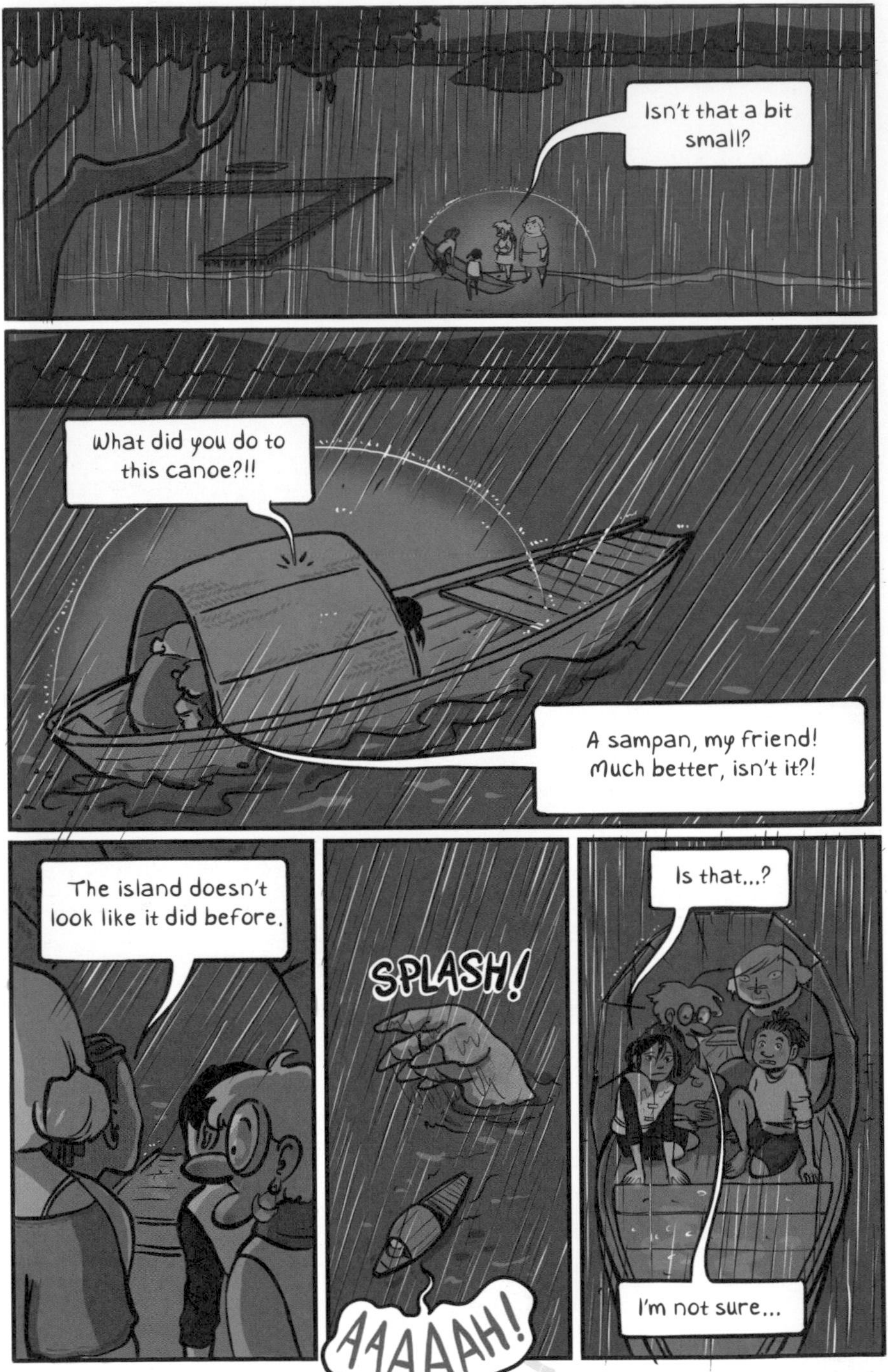
Isn't that a bit small?
What did you do to this canoe?!!
A sampan, my friend! Much better, isn't it?!
The island doesn't look like it did before.
SPLASH!
AAAAAH!
Is that...?
I'm not sure...

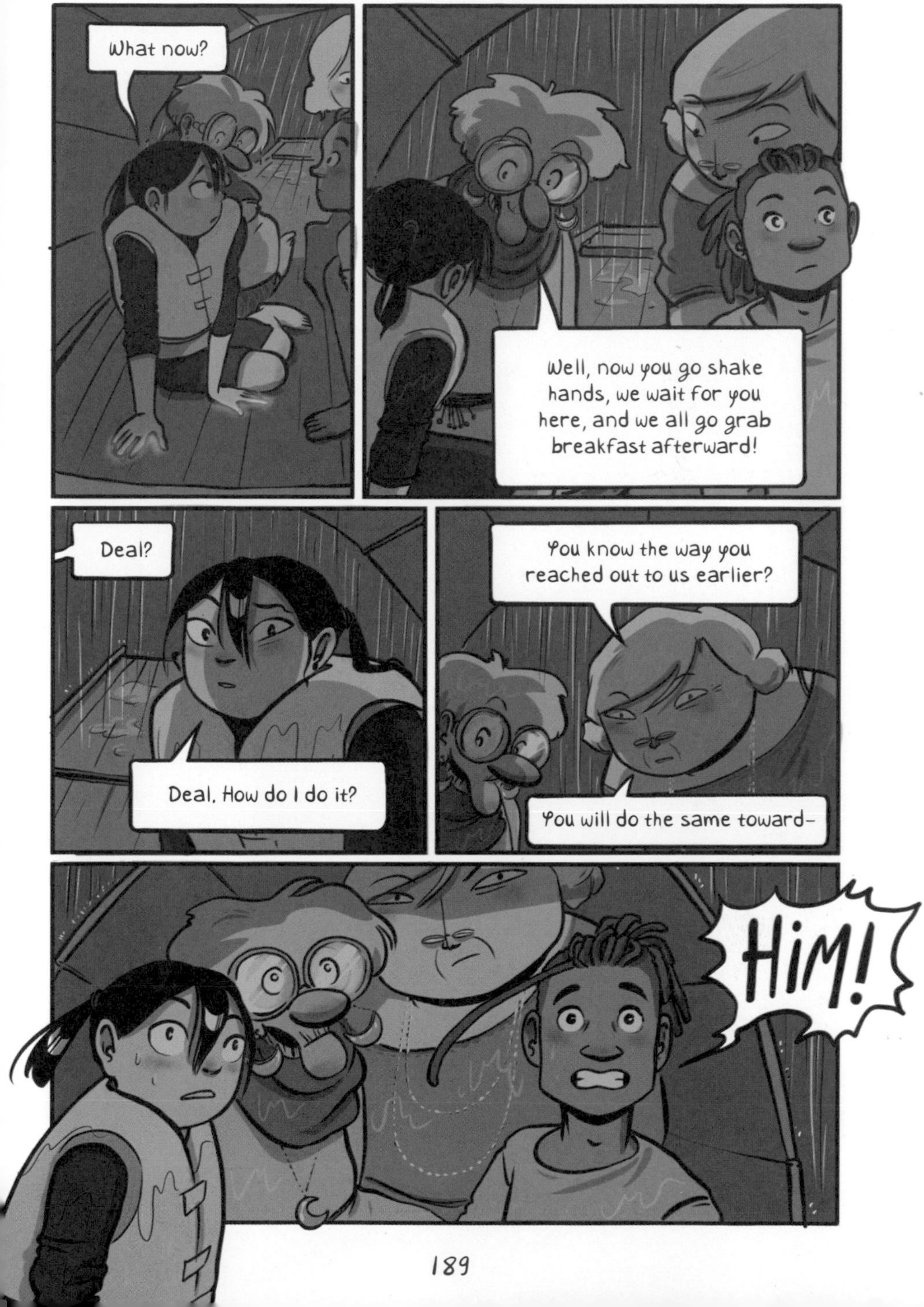
What now?
Well, now you go shake hands, we wait for you here, and we all go grab breakfast afterward!
Deal?
Deal. How do I do it?
You know the way you reached out to us earlier?
You will do the same toward–
HIM!

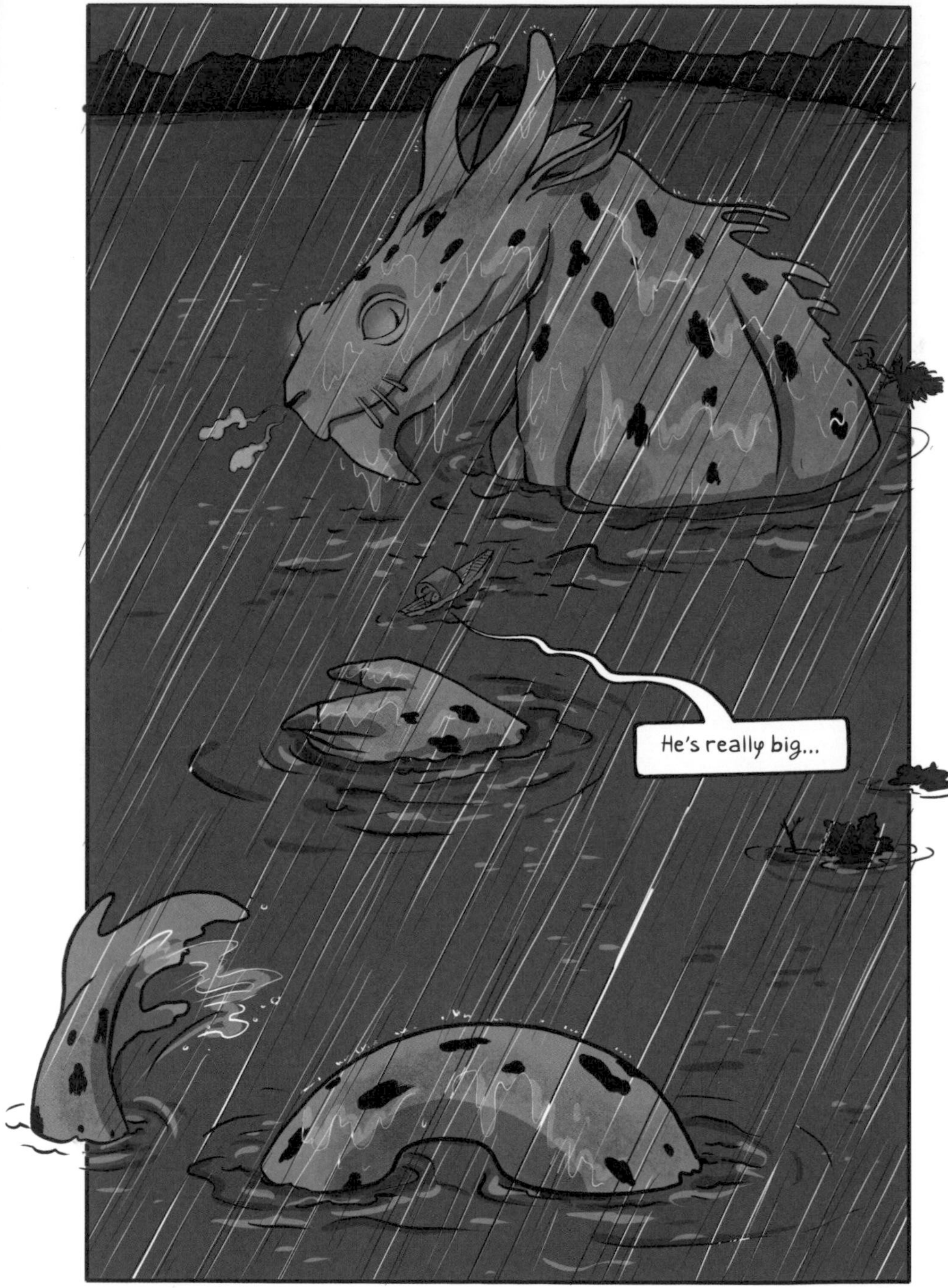
He's really big...

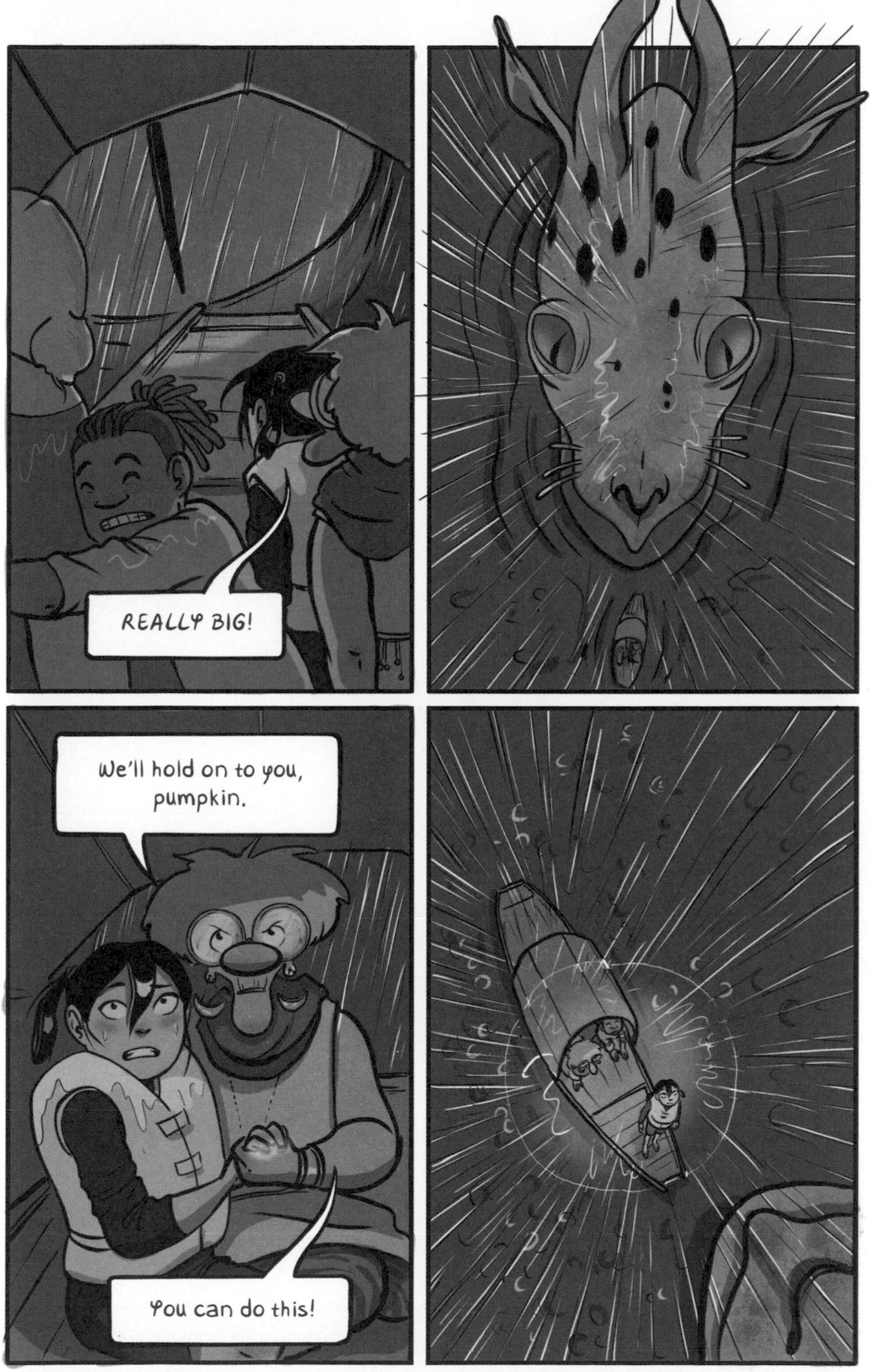
REALLY BIG!
We'll hold on to you, pumpkin.
You can do this!

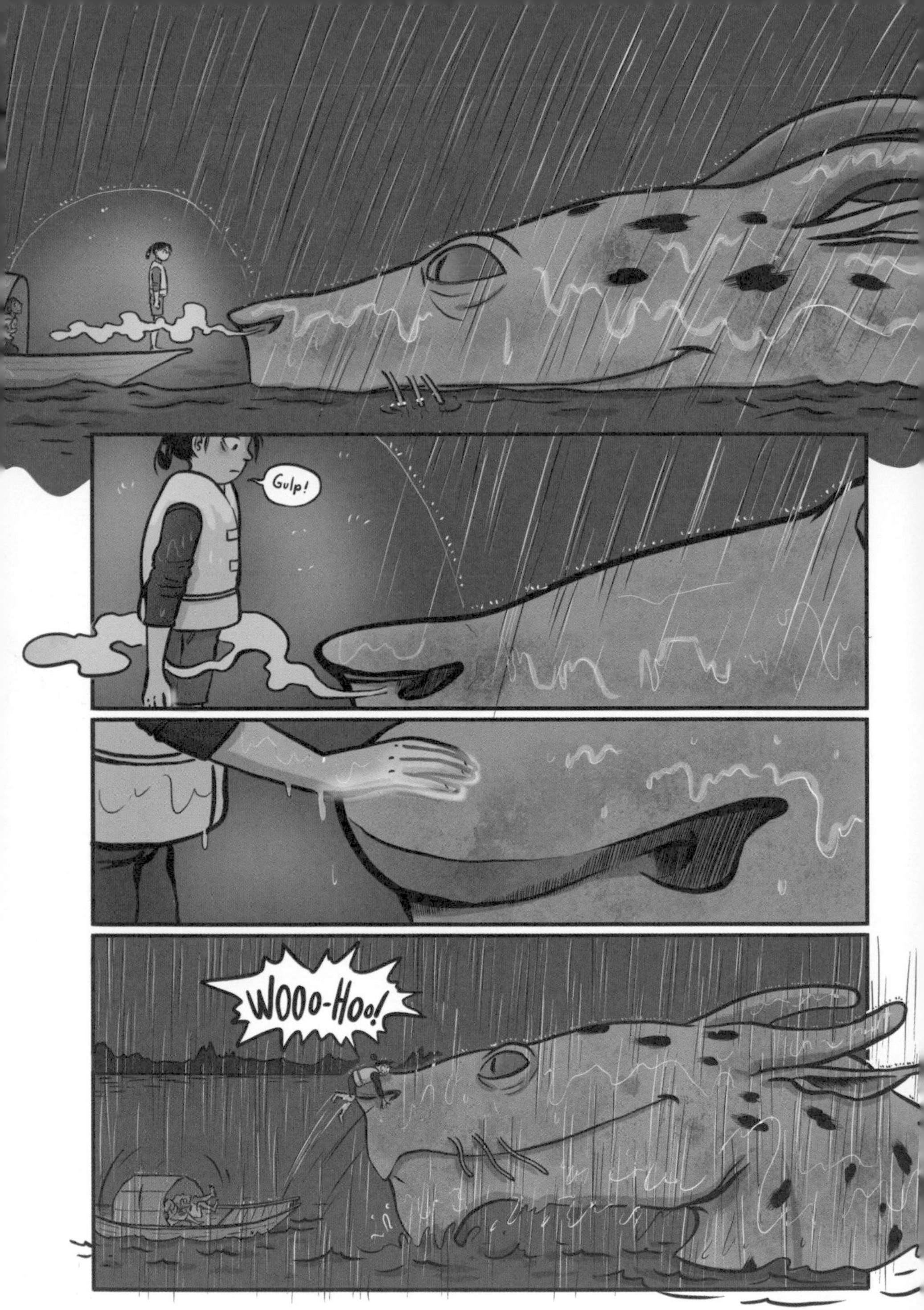
Gulp!
WOOO-HOO!

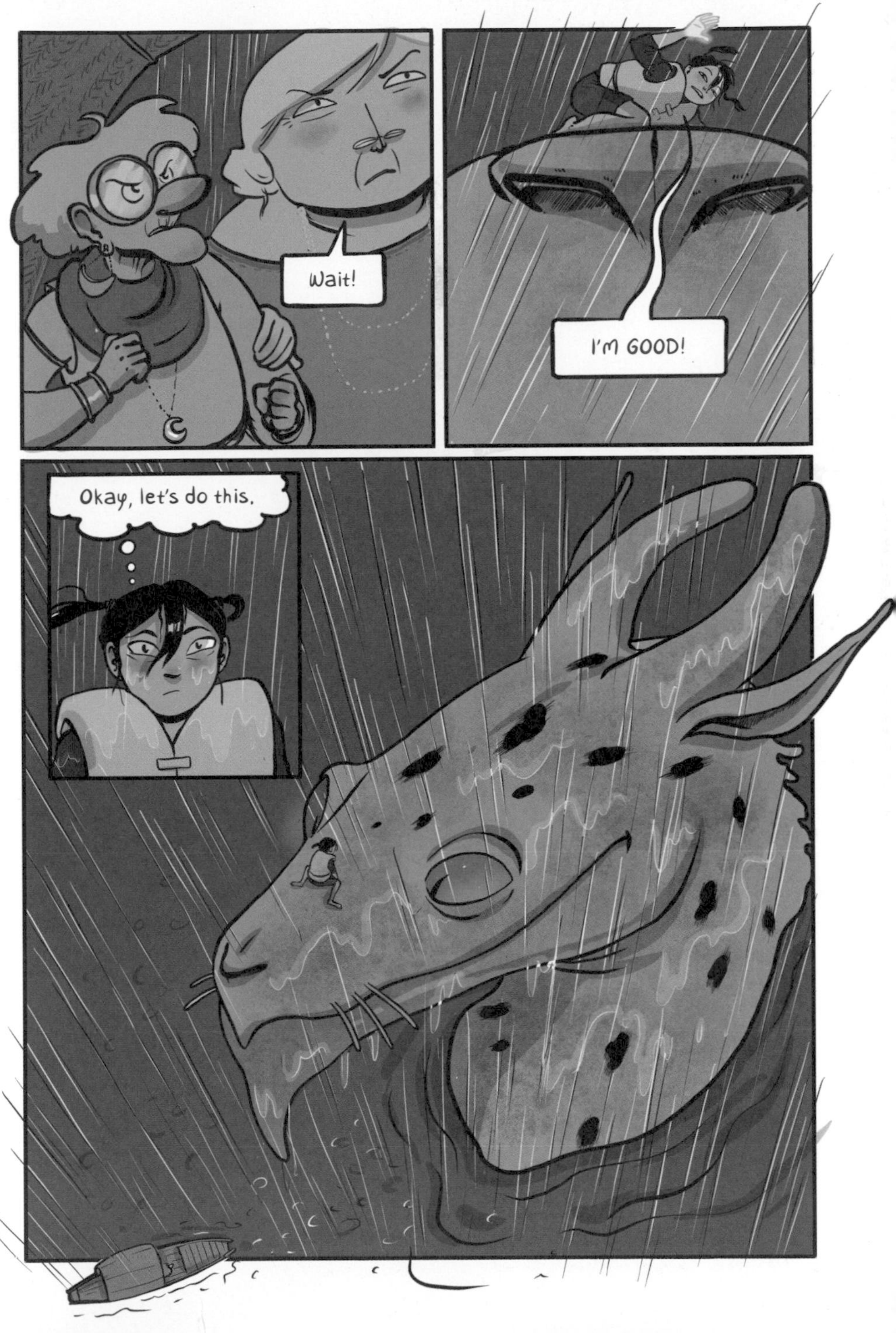
Wait!
I'M GOOD!
Okay, let's do this.

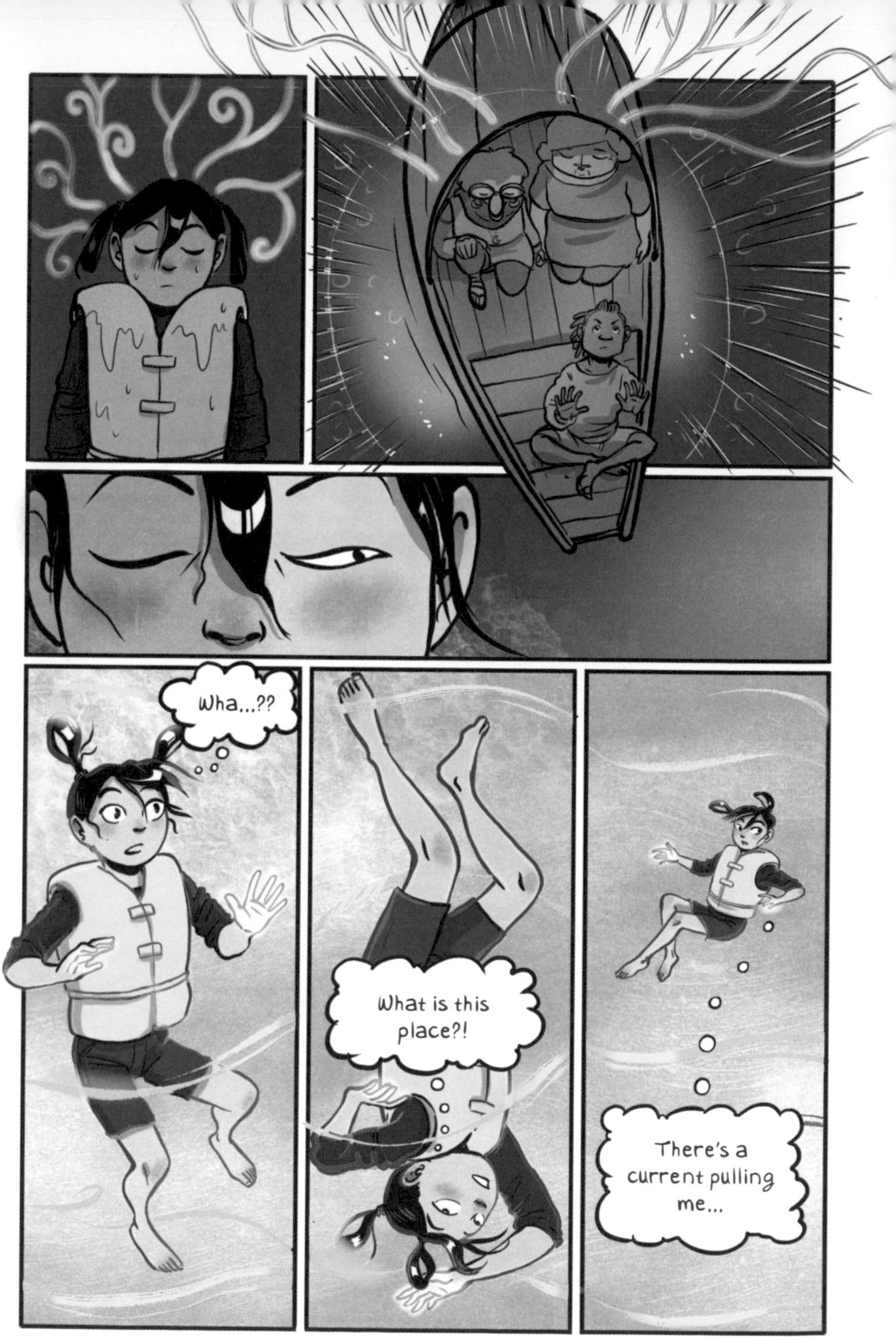
Wha...??
What is this place?!
There's a current pulling me...

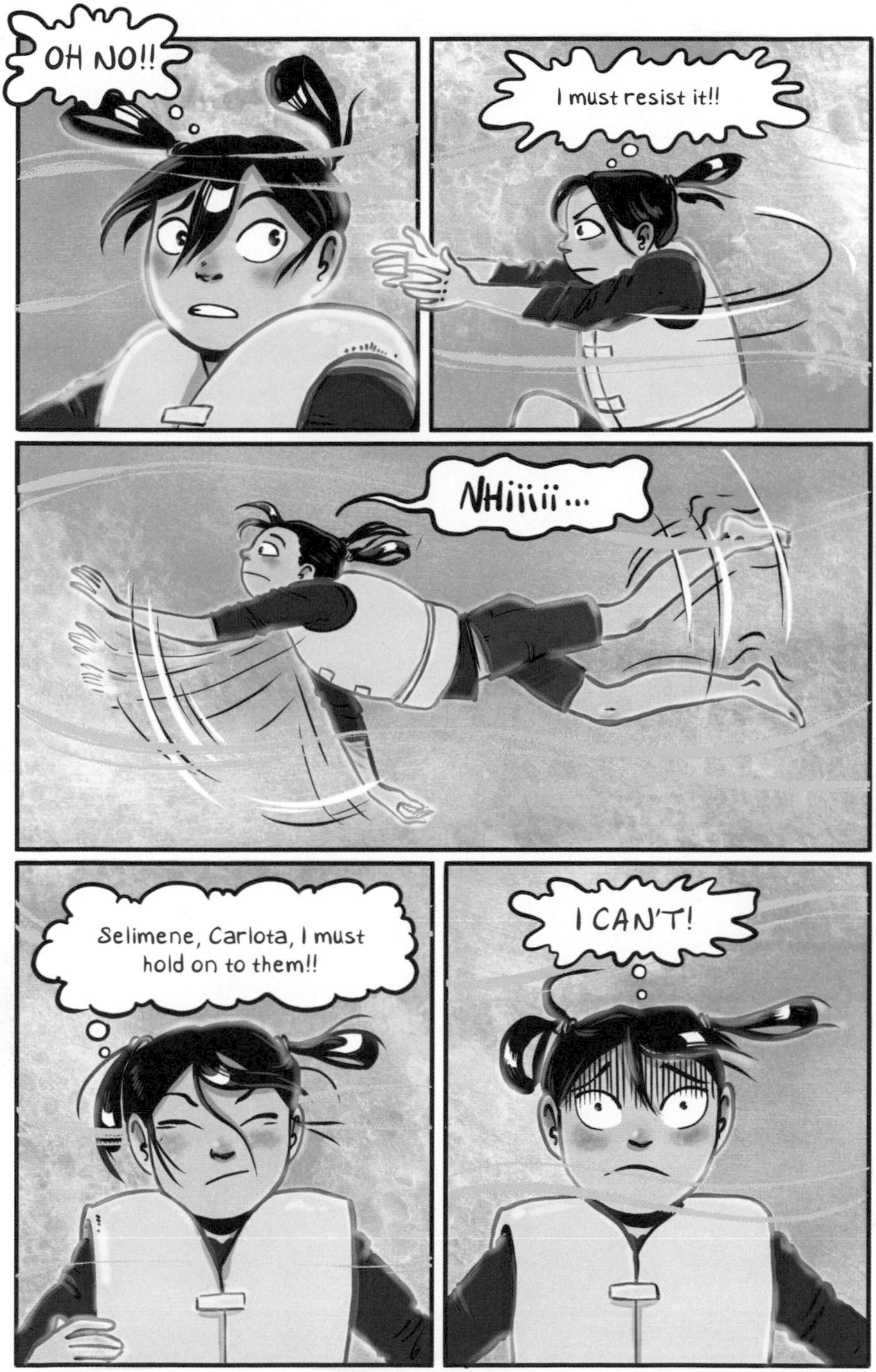
OH NO!!
I must resist it!!
NHiiiii...
Selimene, Carlota, I must hold on to them!!
I CAN'T!

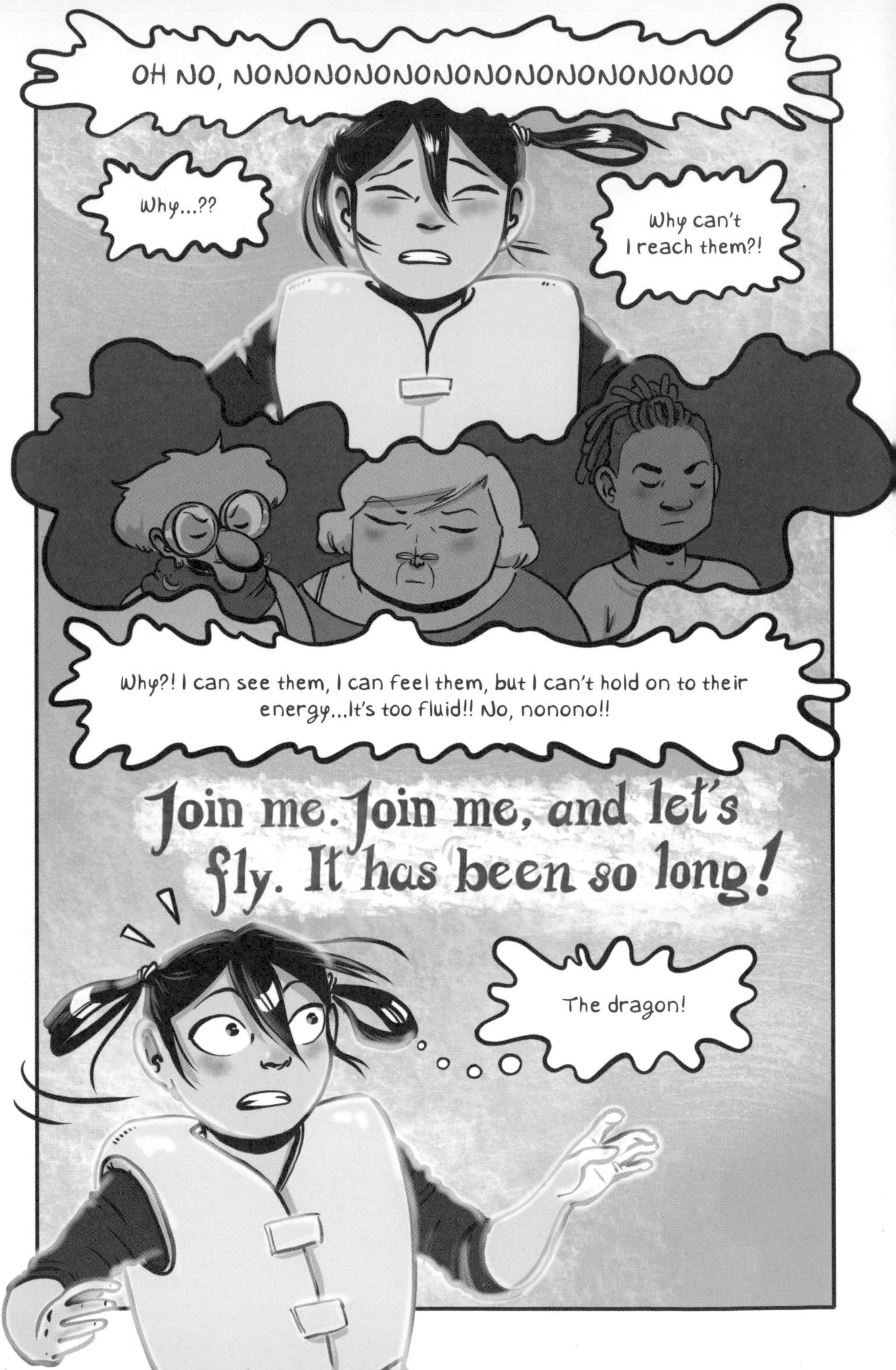
OH NO, NONONONONONONONONONONONONOO
Why...??
Why can't I reach them?!
Why?! I can see them, I can feel them, but I can't hold on to their energy...It's too fluid!! No, nonono!!
Join me. Join me, and let's fly. It has been so long!
The dragon!

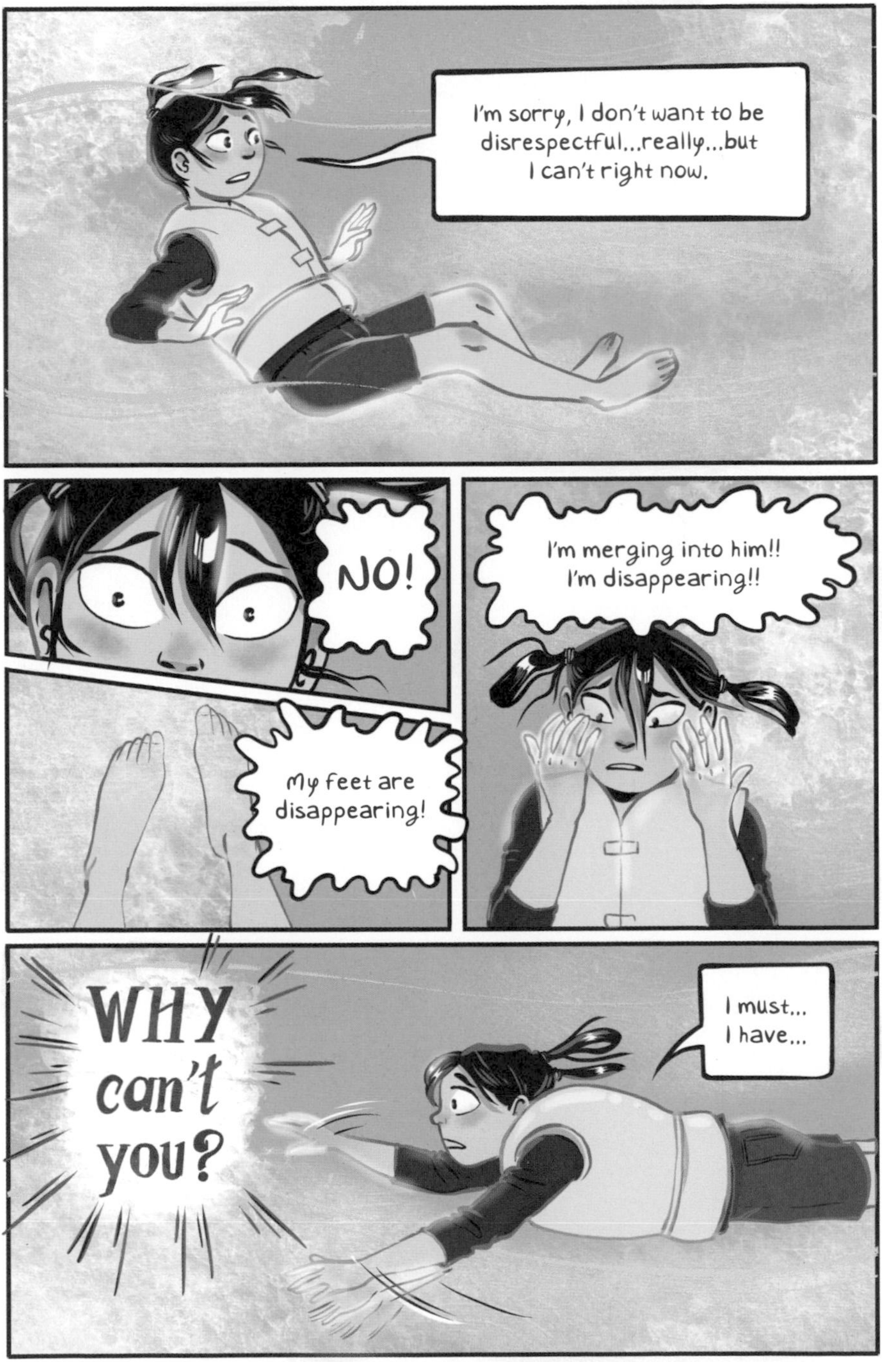

I'm sorry, I don't want to be disrespectful...really...but I can't right now.
NO!
I'm merging into him!! I'm disappearing!!
My feet are disappearing!
WHY can't you?
I must... I have...

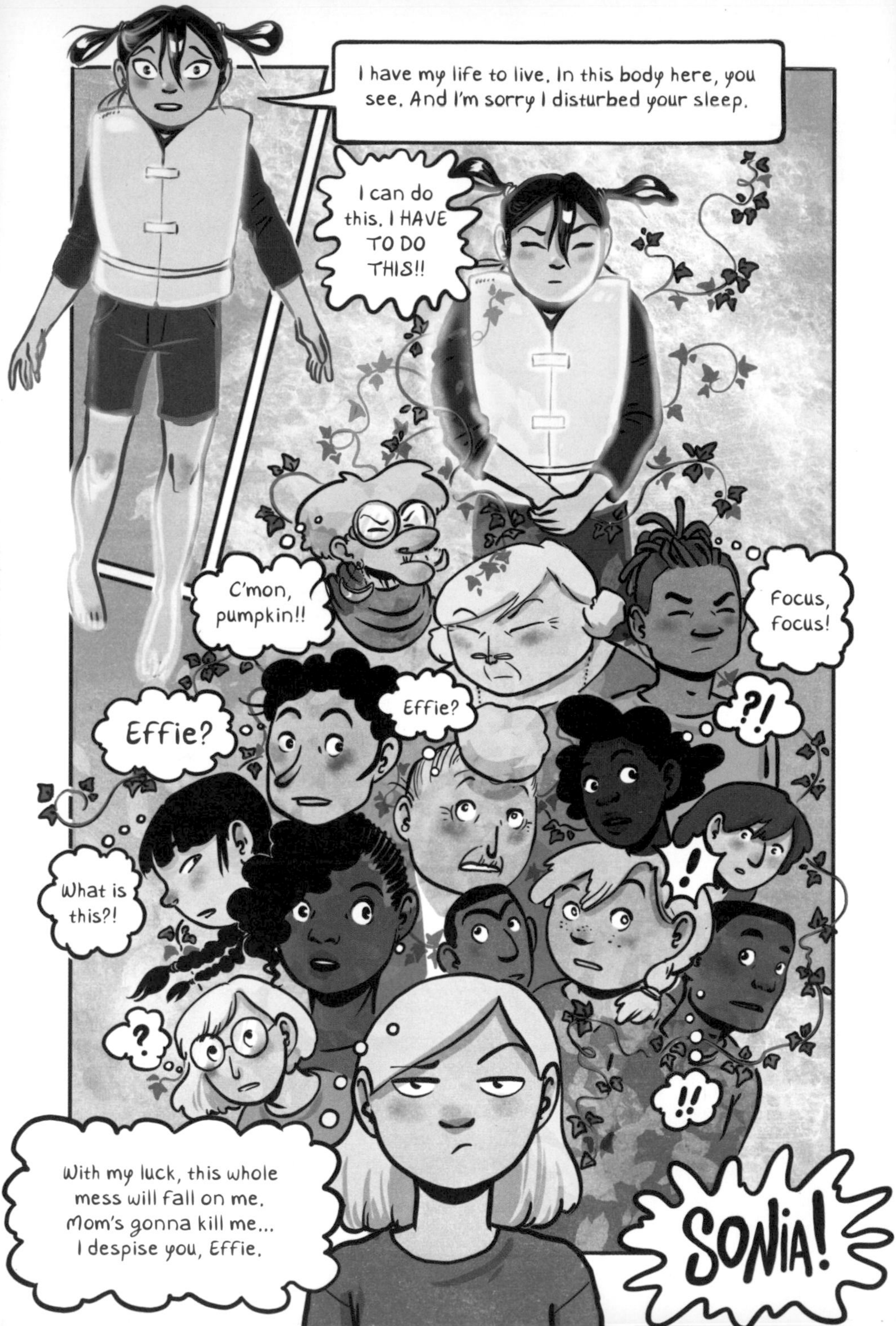

I have my life to live. In this body here, you see. And I'm sorry I disturbed your sleep.
I can do this. I HAVE TO DO THIS!!
C'mon, pumpkin!!
Focus, focus!
Effie?
Effie?
?!
What is this?!
!
?
!!
With my luck, this whole mess will fall on me. Mom's gonna kill me... I despise you, Effie.
SONIA!

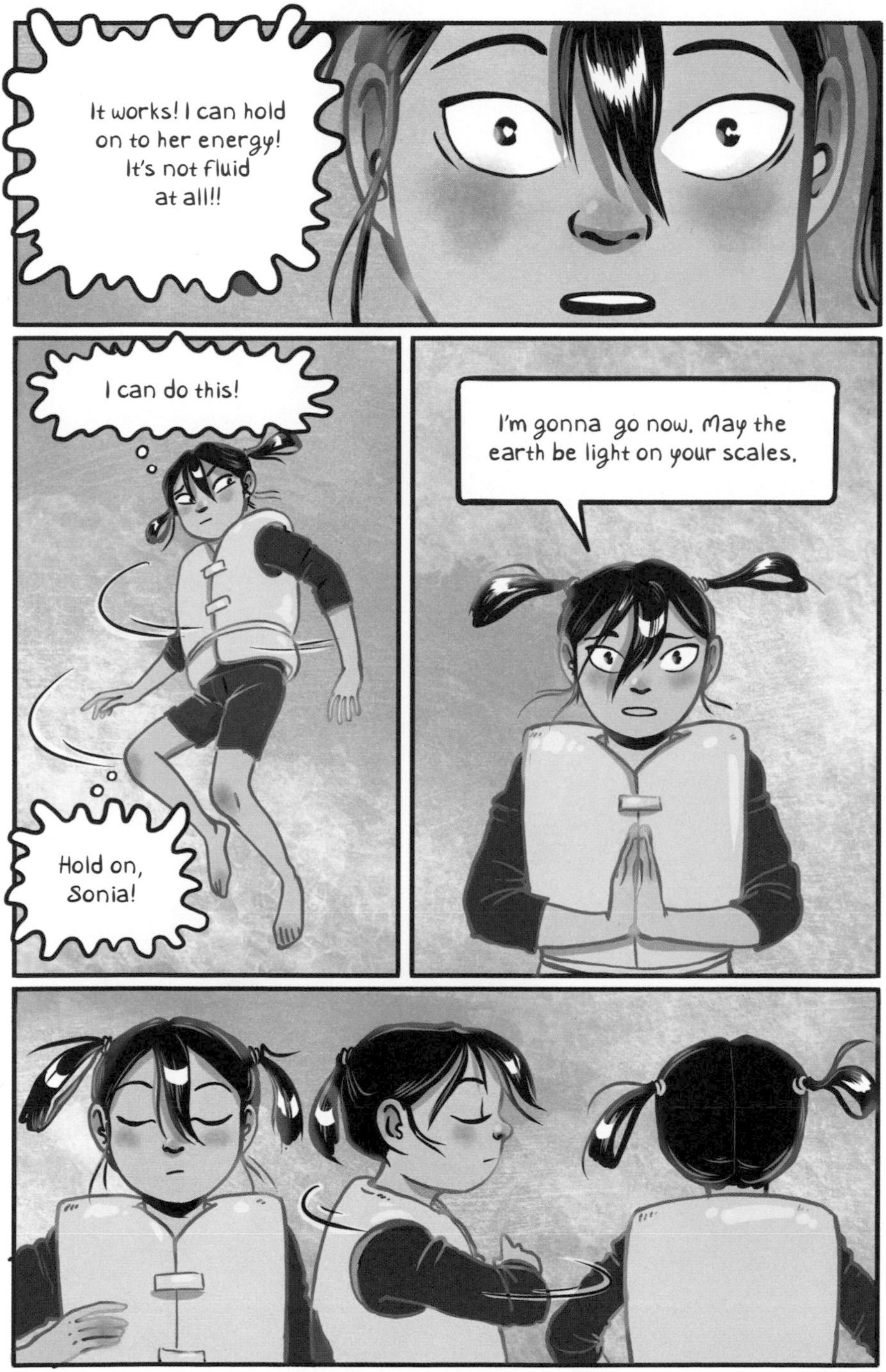
It works! I can hold on to her energy! It's not fluid at all!!
I can do this!
Hold on, Sonia!
I'm gonna go now. May the earth be light on your scales.

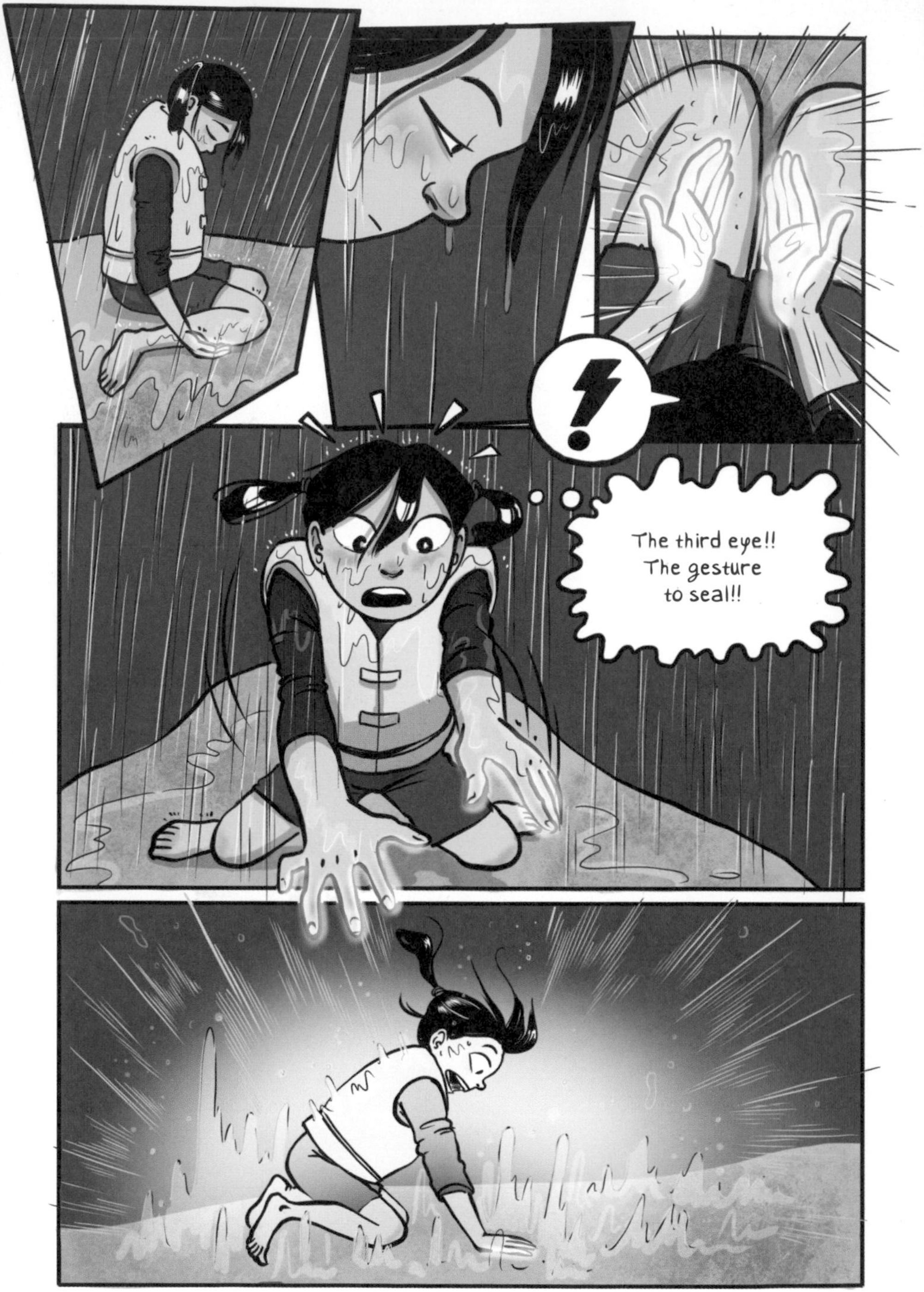
!
The third eye!! The gesture to seal!!

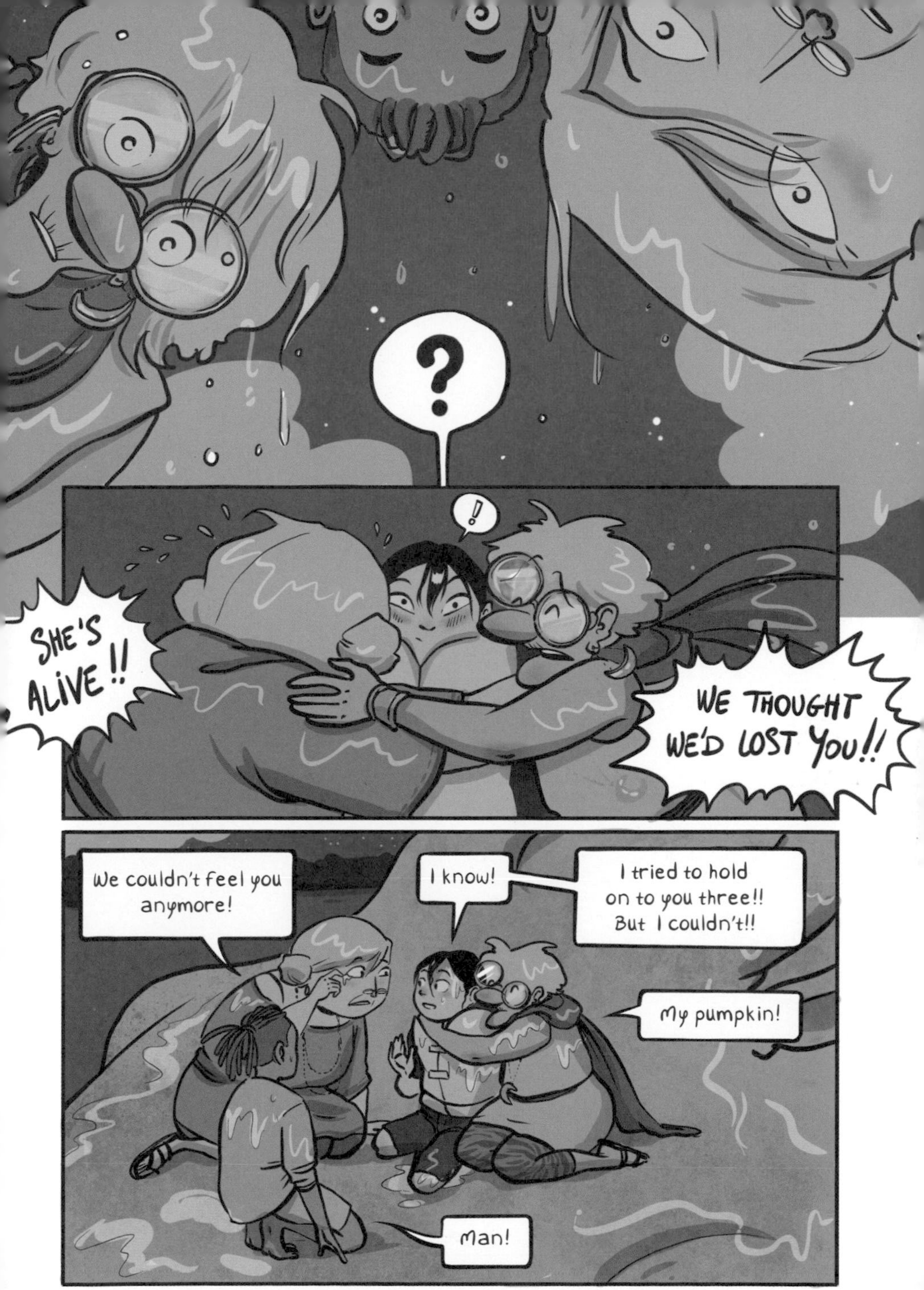
?
!
SHE'S ALIVE!!
WE THOUGHT WE'D LOST YOU!!
We couldn't feel you anymore!
I know!
I tried to hold on to you three!! But I couldn't!!
My pumpkin!
Man!

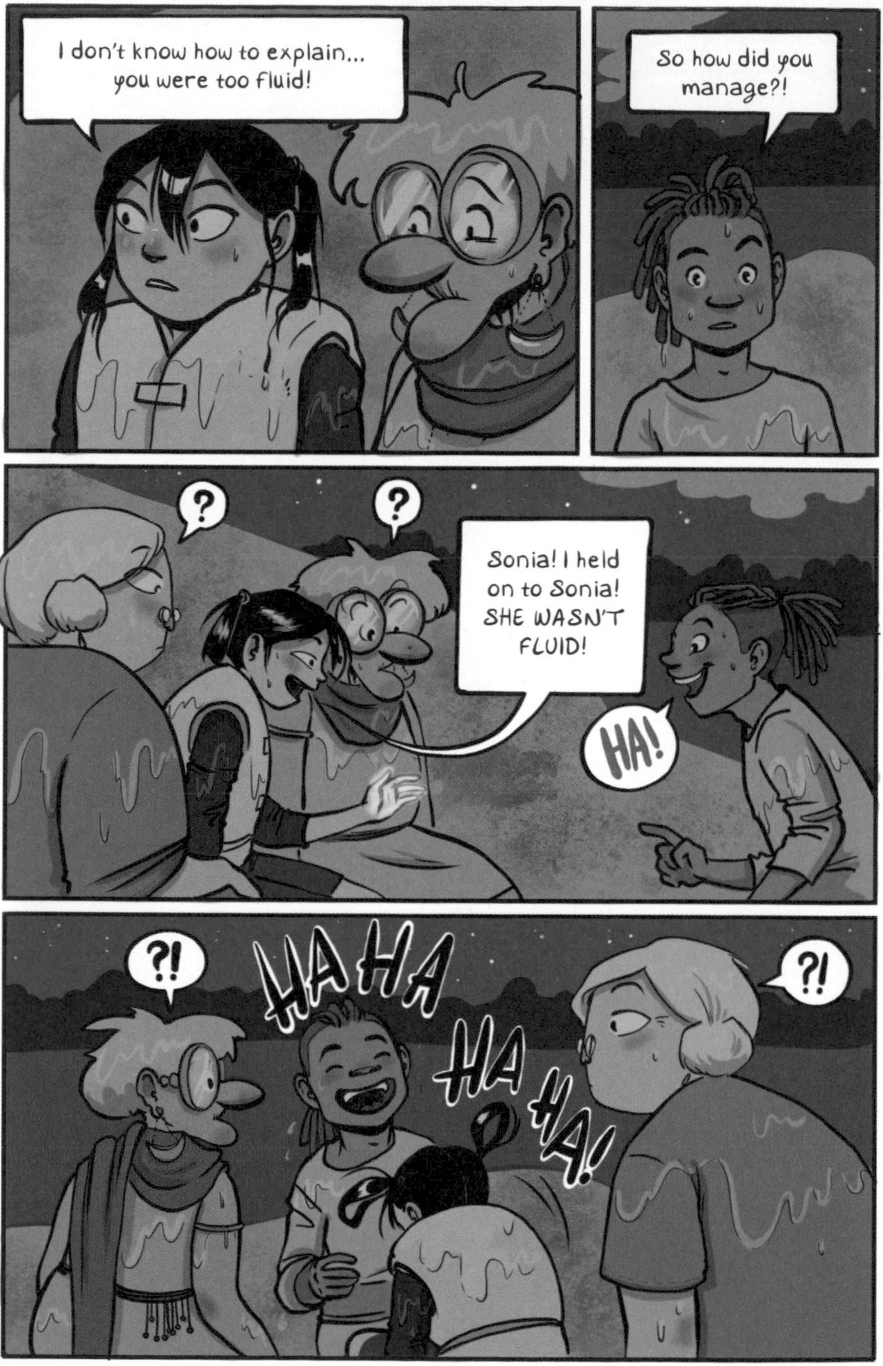
I don't know how to explain... you were too fluid!
So how did you manage?!
?
?
Sonia! I held on to Sonia! SHE WASN'T FLUID!
HA!
?!
HA HA
HA HA HA!
?!

HA! HA! HA!
HA HA HA HA HA HA! HA HA!
HA HA HA HA HA HA! HA HA!
We should probably head back.
Argh, there's no rush. We can take a little nap! Look at this sky!

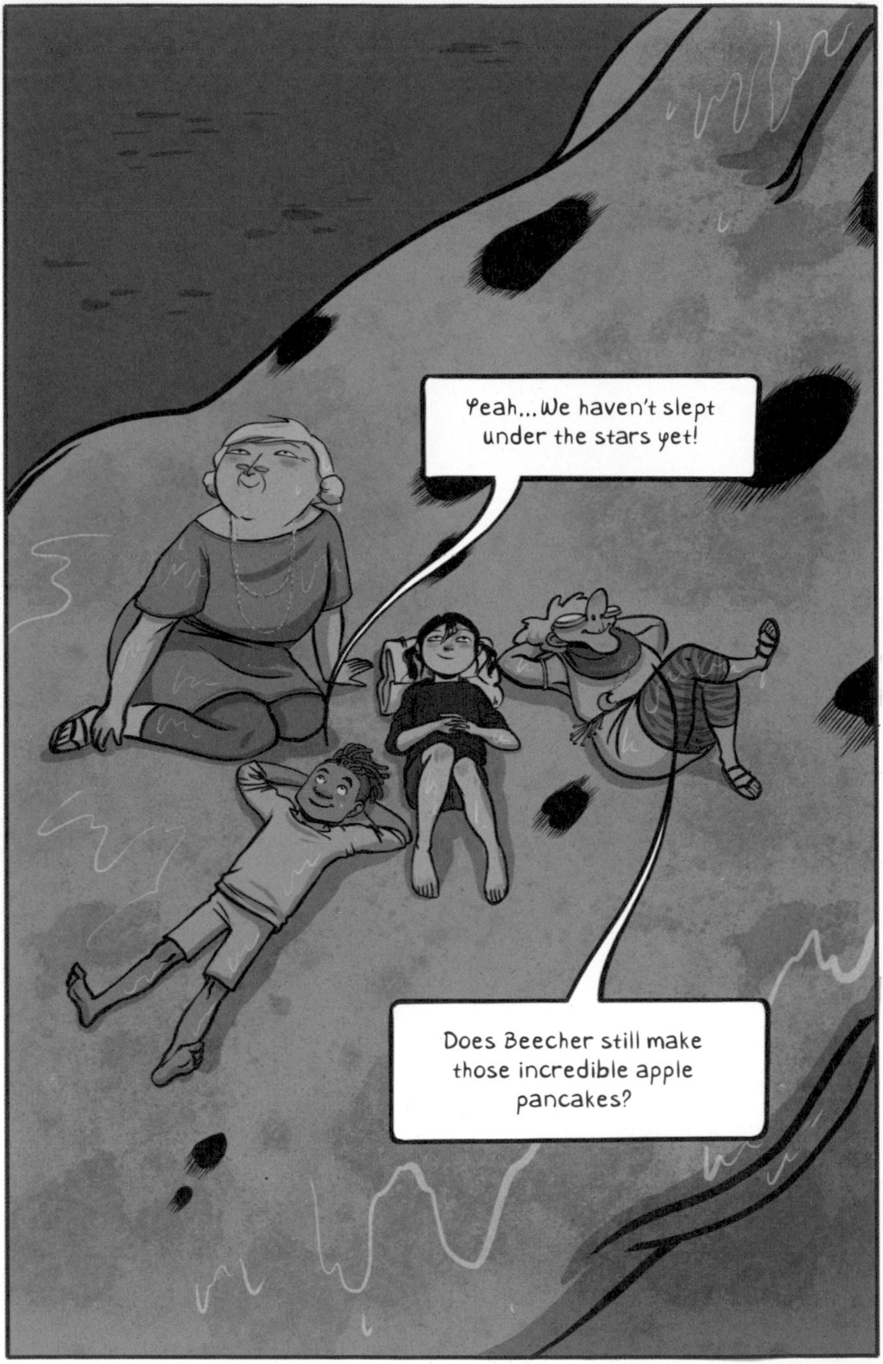
Yeah... We haven't slept under the stars yet!
Does Beecher still make those incredible apple pancakes?

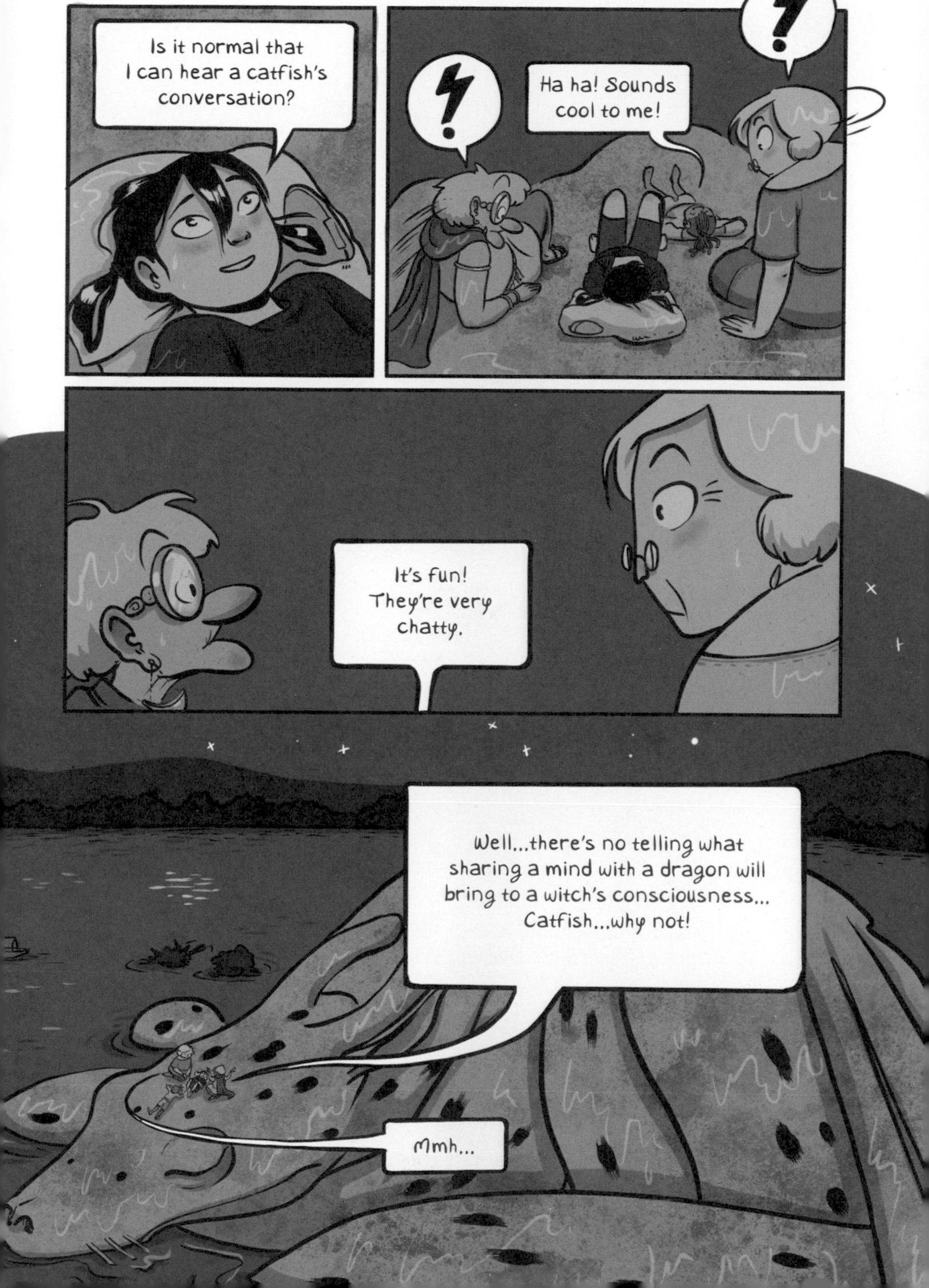
Is it normal that I can hear a catfish's conversation?
Ha ha! Sounds cool to me!
It's fun! They're very chatty.
Well...there's no telling what sharing a mind with a dragon will bring to a witch's consciousness... Catfish...why not!
Mmh...

Epilogue

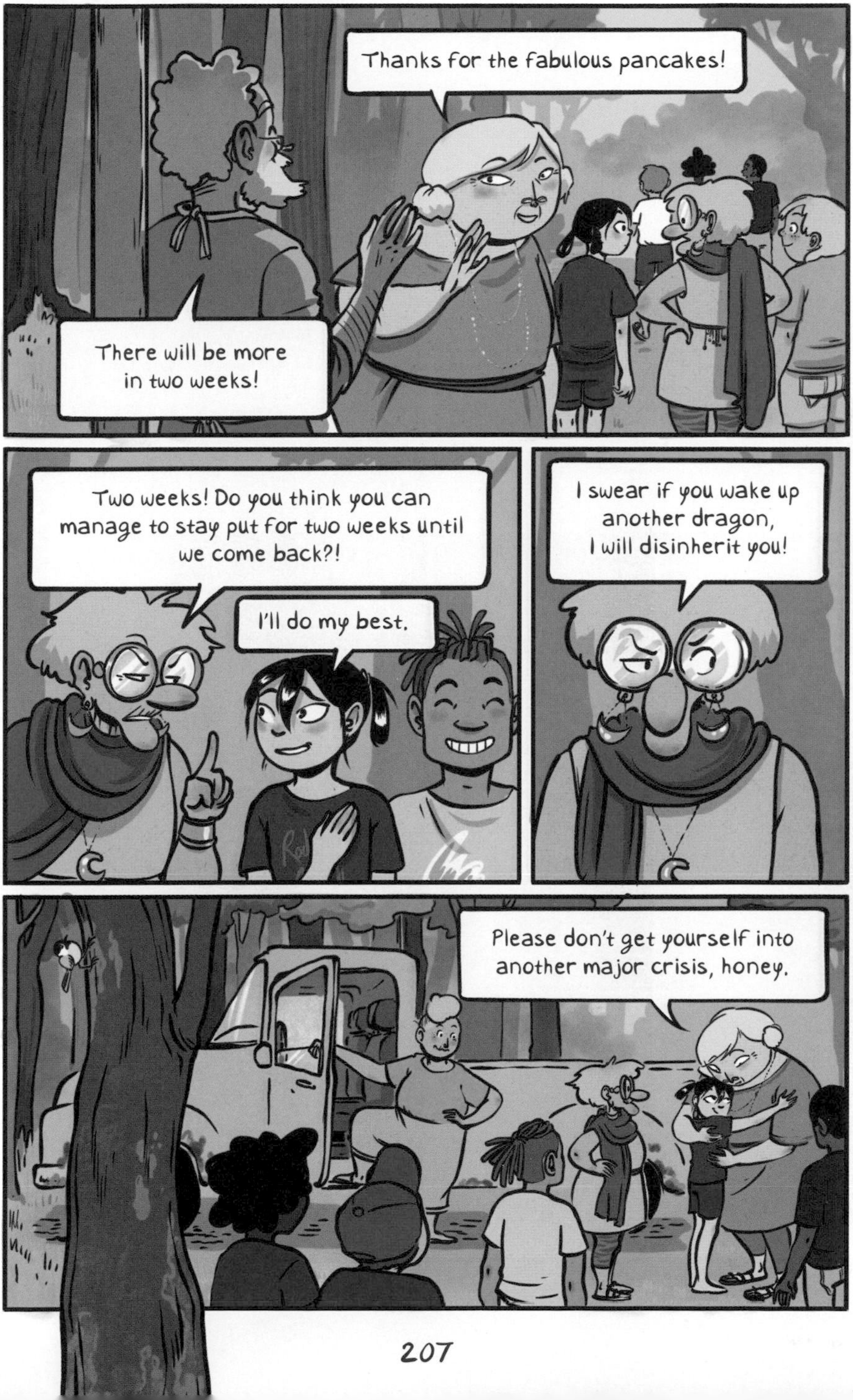
Thanks for the fabulous pancakes!
There will be more in two weeks!
Two weeks! Do you think you can manage to stay put for two weeks until we come back?!
I'll do my best.
I swear if you wake up another dragon, I will disinherit you!
Please don't get yourself into another major crisis, honey.

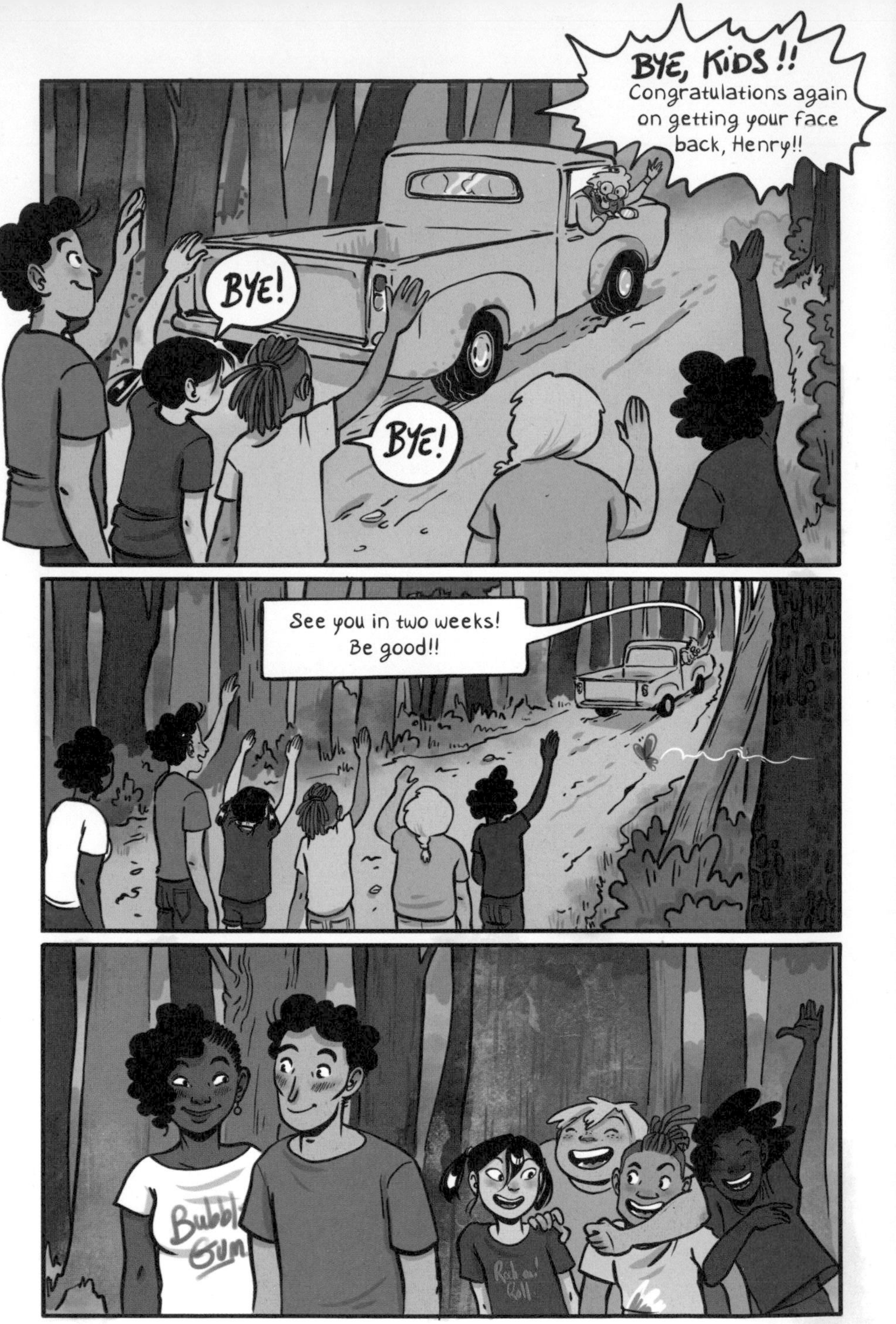
BYE, KIDS!!
Congratulations again on getting your face back, Henry!!
BYE!
BYE!
See you in two weeks! Be good!!
Bubble Gum
Rock n' Roll

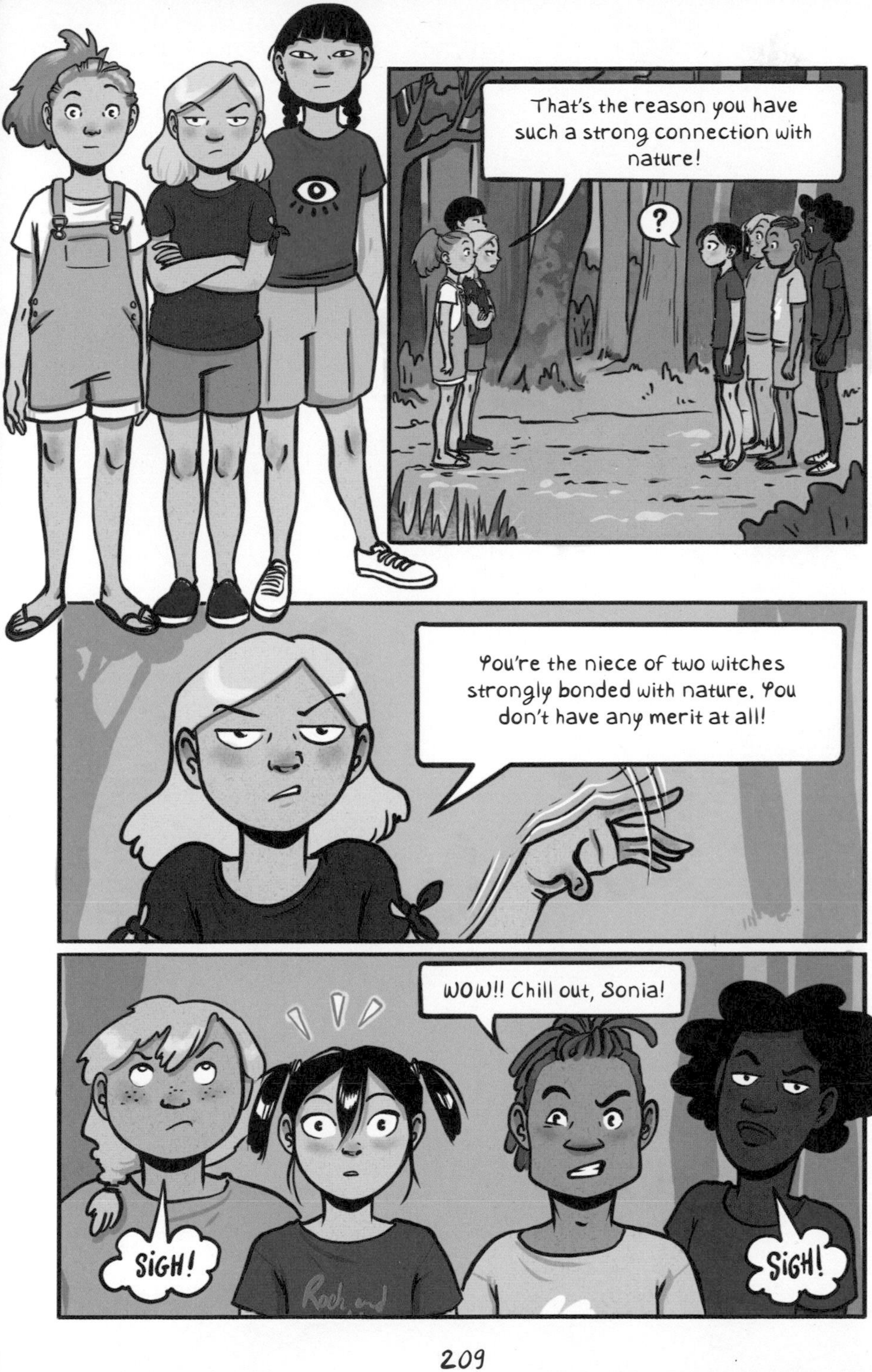
That's the reason you have such a strong connection with nature!
?
You're the niece of two witches strongly bonded with nature. You don't have any merit at all!
WOW!! Chill out, Sonia!
SIGH!
SIGH!

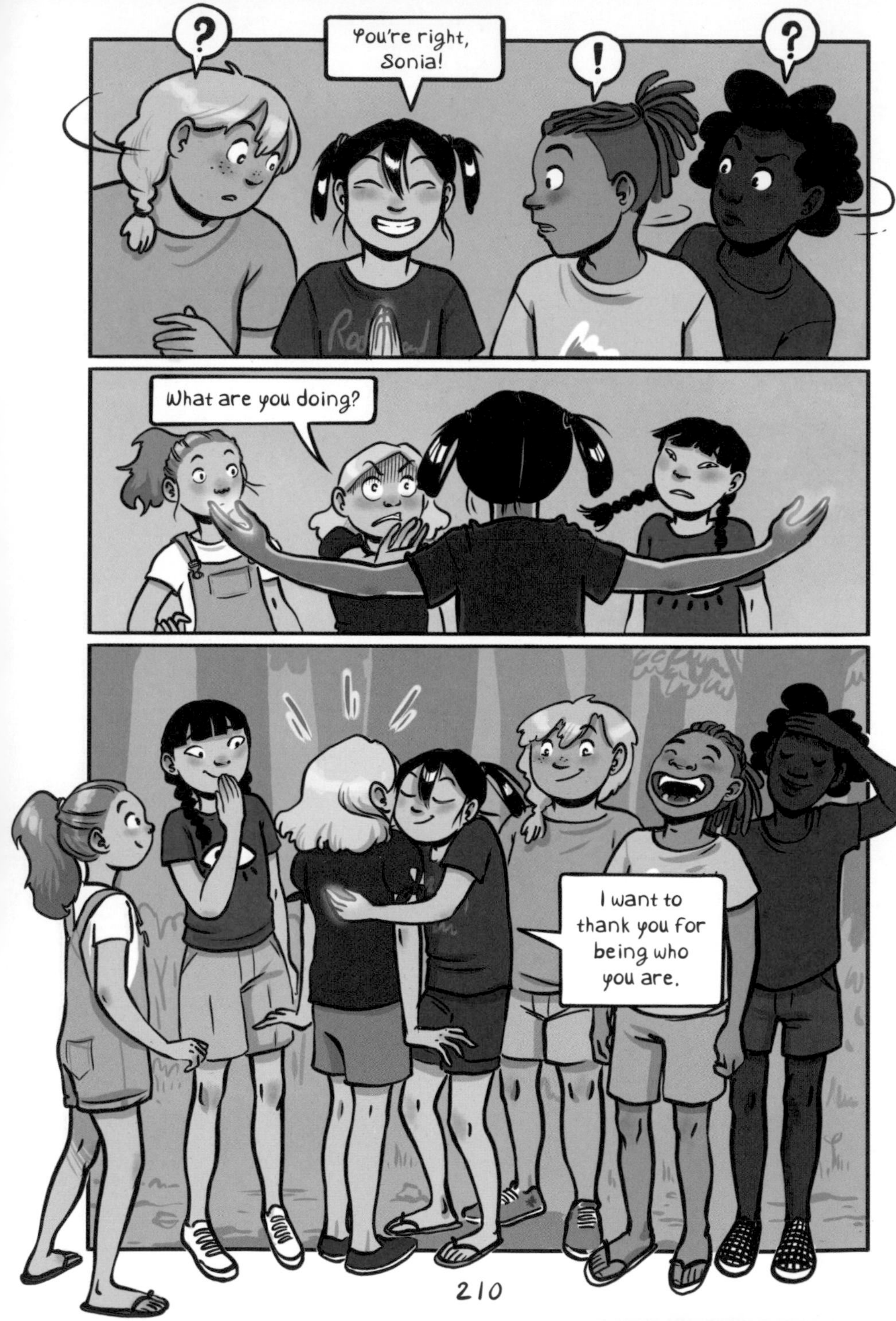
?
You're right, Sonia!
!
?
What are you doing?
I want to thank you for being who you are.

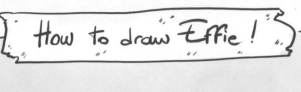

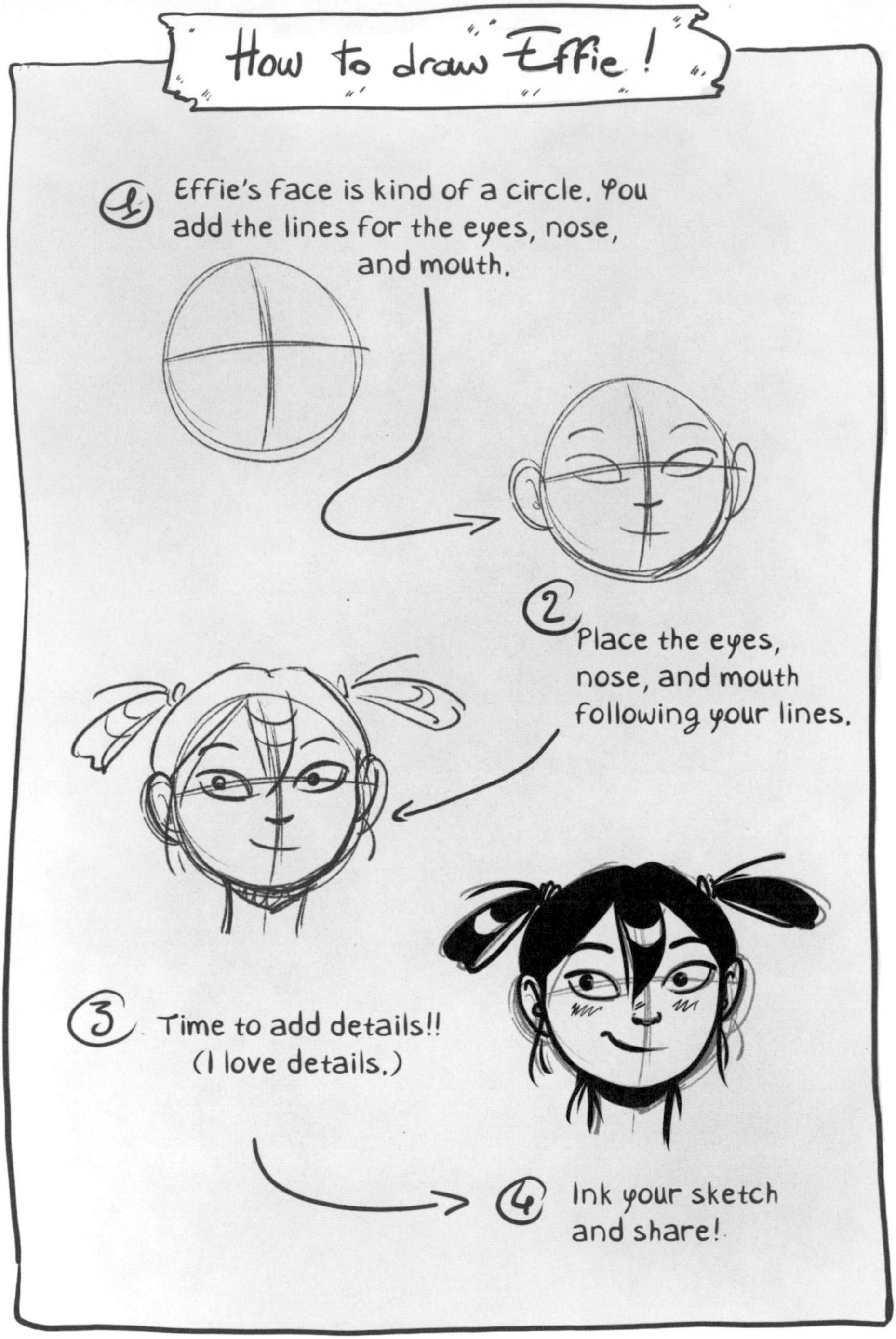

How to draw Effie!

① Effie's face is kind of a circle. You add the lines for the eyes, nose, and mouth.

② Place the eyes, nose, and mouth following your lines.

③ Time to add details!! (I love details.)

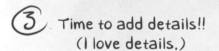

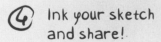

④ Ink your sketch and share!

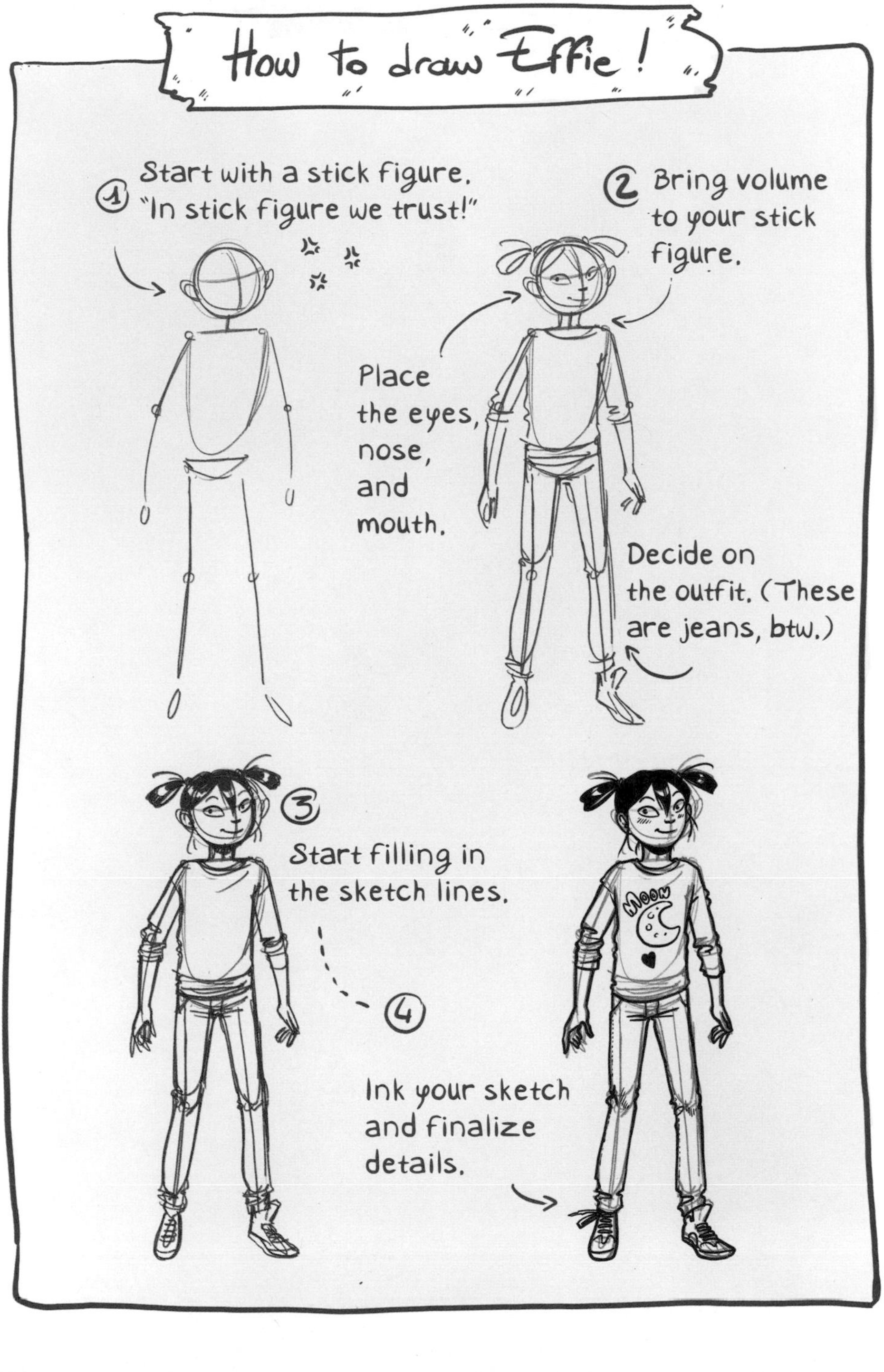
How to draw Effie!
① Start with a stick figure. "In stick figure we trust!"
② Bring volume to your stick figure.
Place the eyes, nose, and mouth.
Decide on the outfit. (These are jeans, btw.)
③ Start filling in the sketch lines.
④
Ink your sketch and finalize details.
MOON

How to draw Selimene!

① Start with two ovals for the glasses, then the nose and chin.

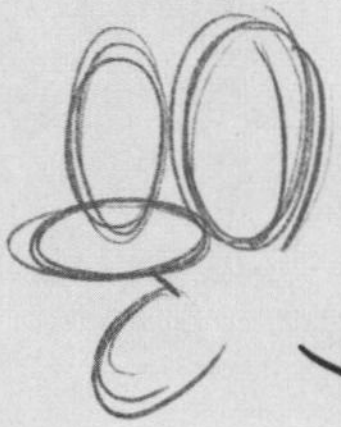

② Next come the hair and eyes. The ear and the big earrings, of course!

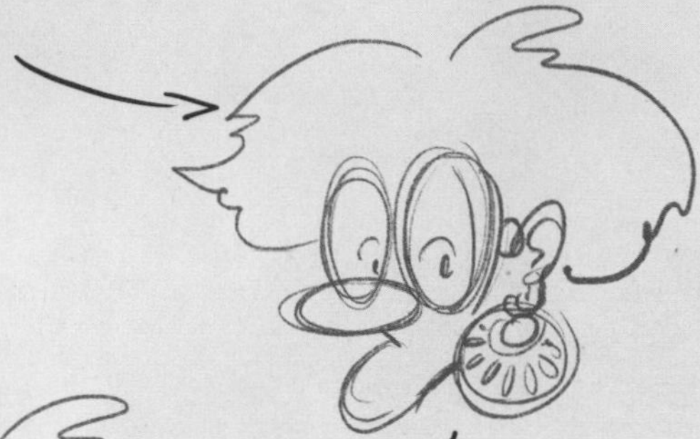

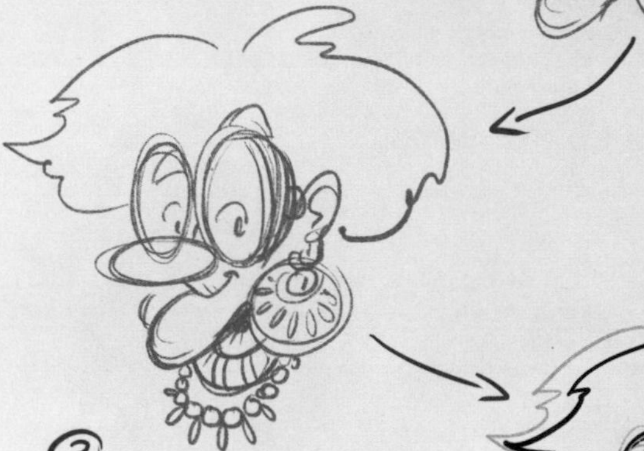

③ Keep adding details, like the eyebrows, mouth, and necklaces.

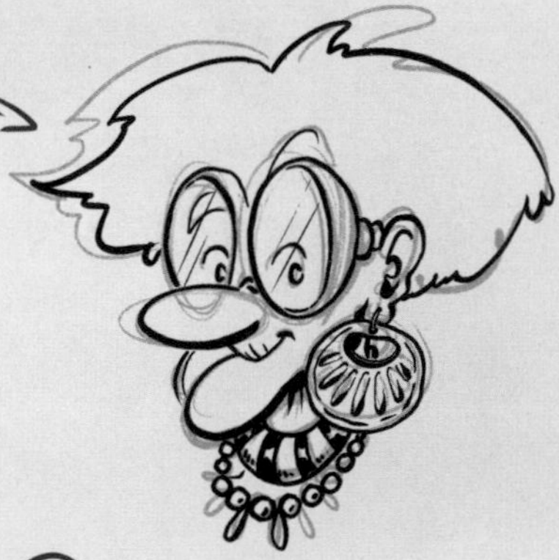

④ Finally, we ink!

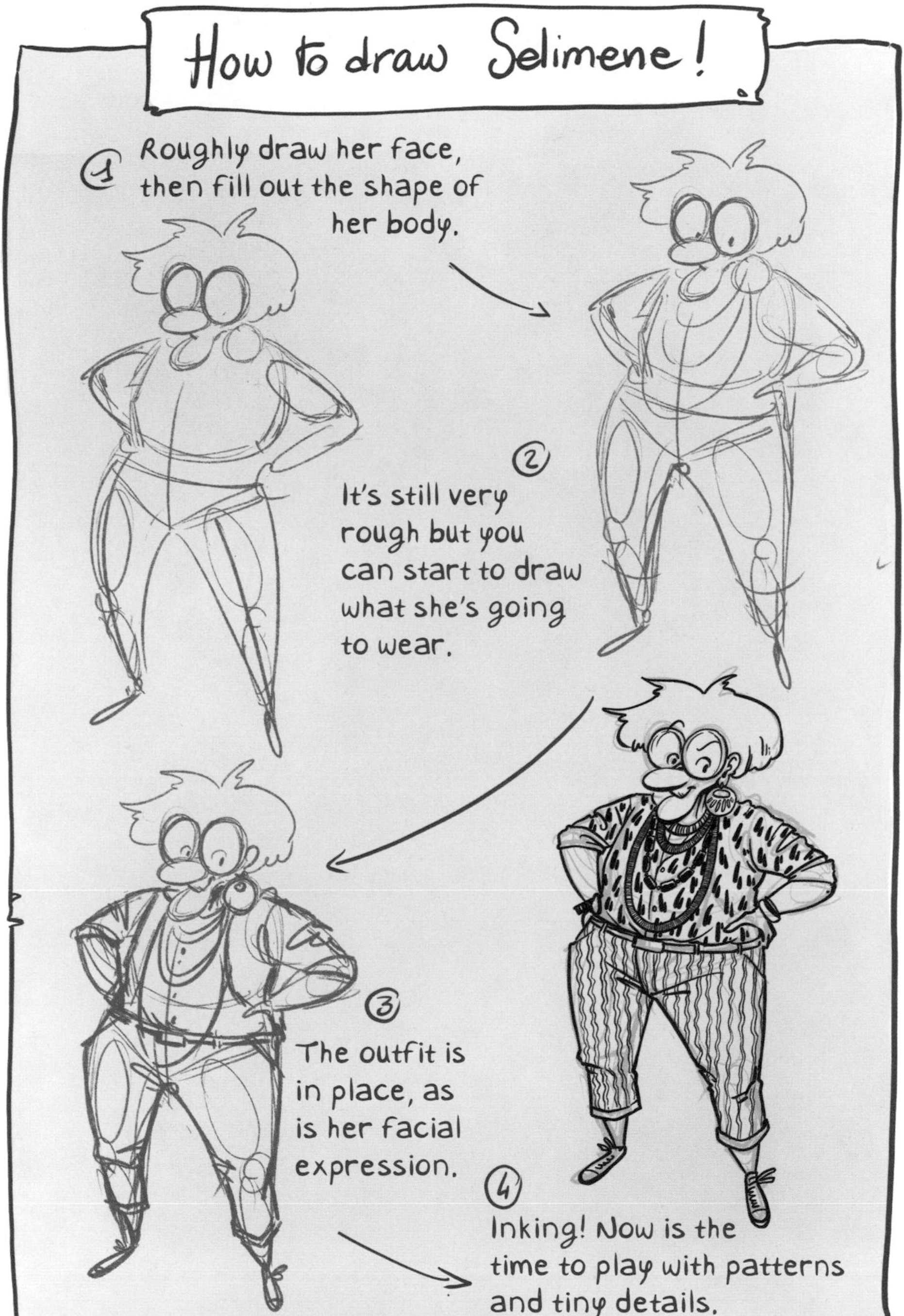
How to draw Selimene!
1 Roughly draw her face, then fill out the shape of her body.
2 It's still very rough but you can start to draw what she's going to wear.
3 The outfit is in place, as is her facial expression.
4 Inking! Now is the time to play with patterns and tiny details.

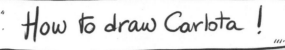

① Carlota's face is pretty rectangular, with the circles of her buns on each side and the lines for the eyes and nose placement.

② Draw the almond-shaped eyes, the mouth, and nose, and give the hair more volume.

③ Add the last details like the wrinkles, pupils, and earrings.

④ Ready?
Steady?
INK!!

As with the other two witches, start with the stick figure and then fill out the shapes...

...and slowly but surely add the details.

The Witches of Brooklyn have
numerous traditions.
Some are more important than
others, of course, but there is one
in April they never miss.

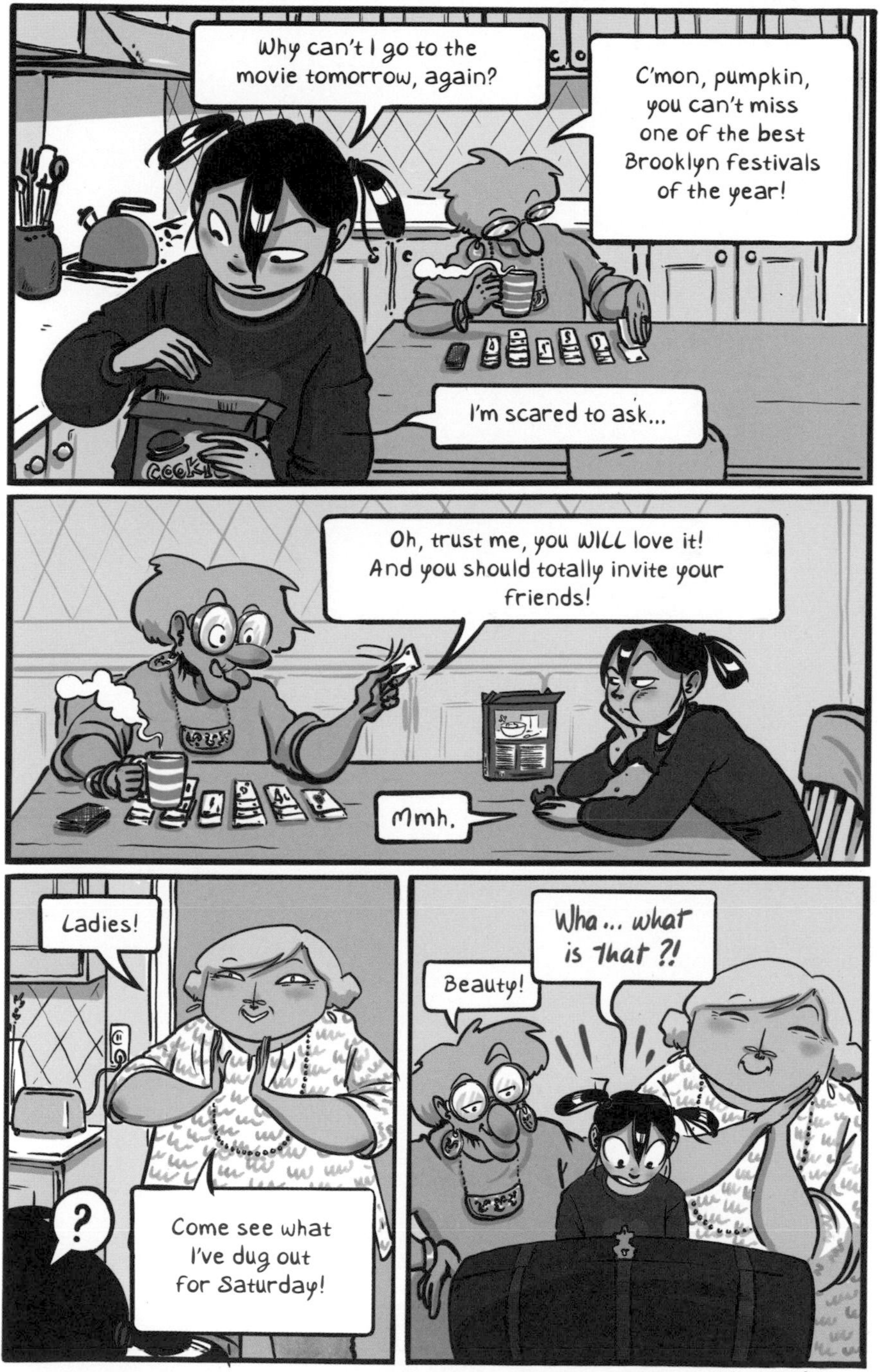
Why can't I go to the movie tomorrow, again?
C'mon, pumpkin, you can't miss one of the best Brooklyn festivals of the year!
I'm scared to ask...
Oh, trust me, you WILL love it! And you should totally invite your friends!
Mmh.
Ladies!
?
Come see what I've dug out for Saturday!
Beauty!
Wha... what is that ?!

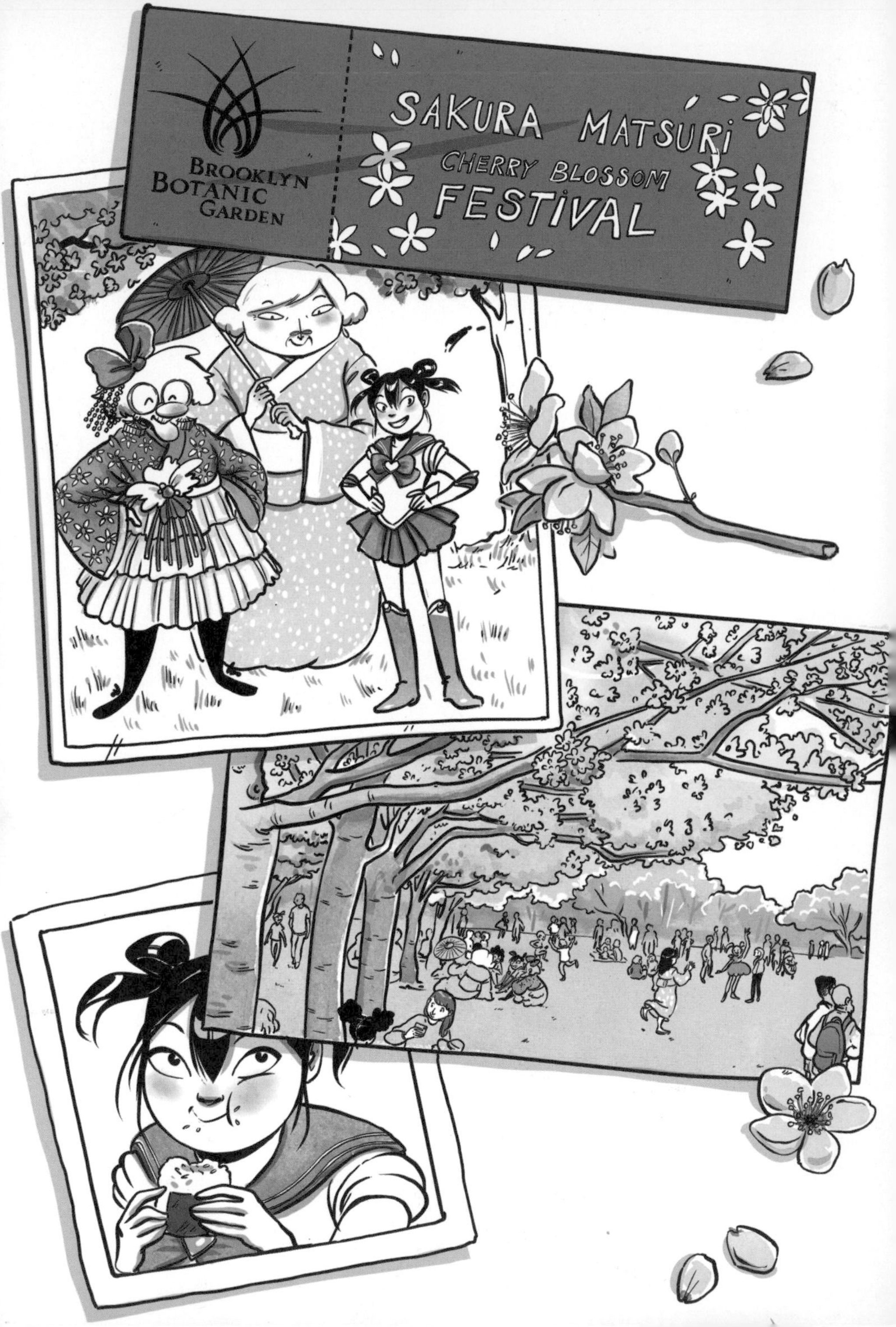
BROOKLYN BOTANIC GARDEN
SAKURA MATSURI
CHERRY BLOSSOM
FESTIVAL

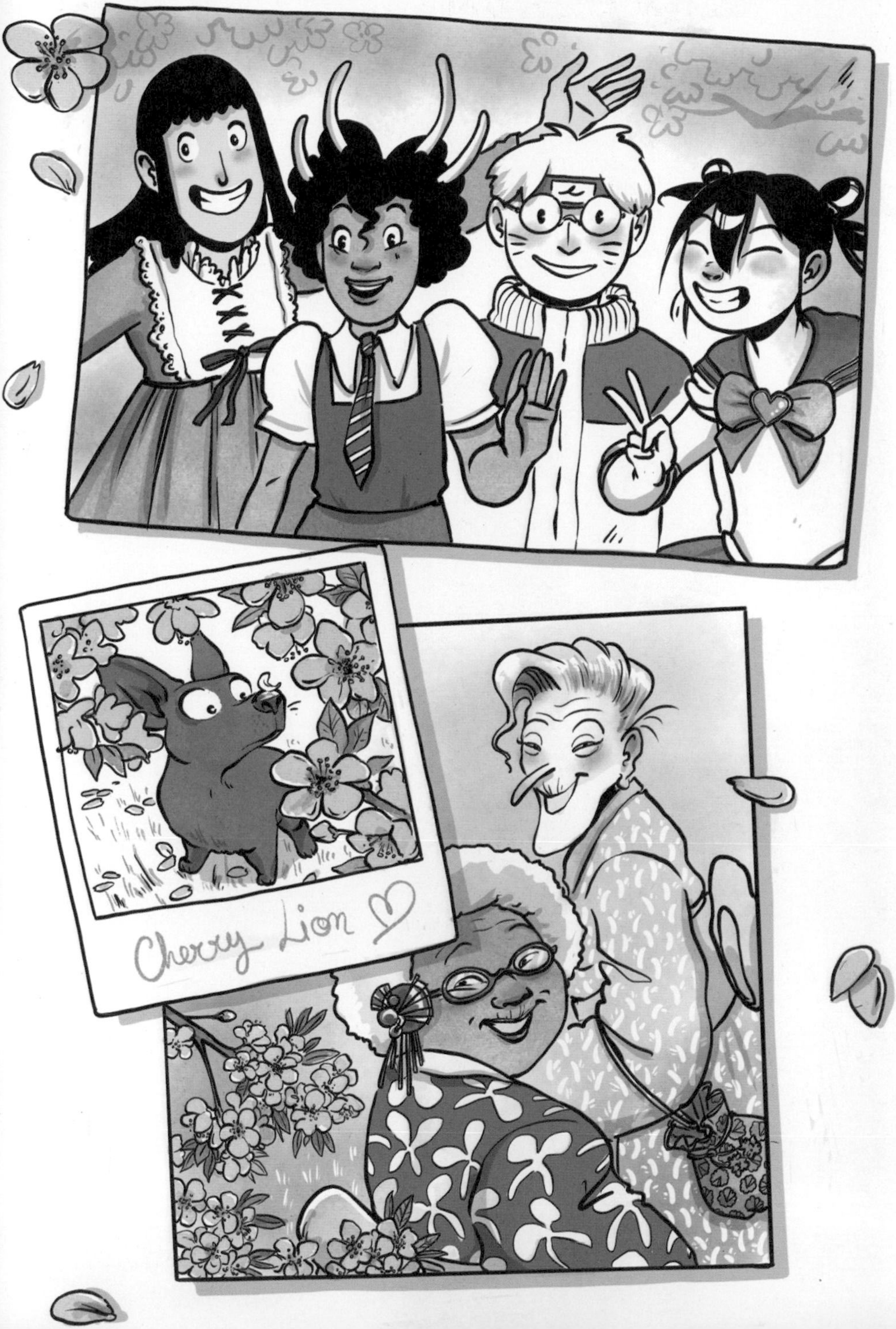
Cherry Lion

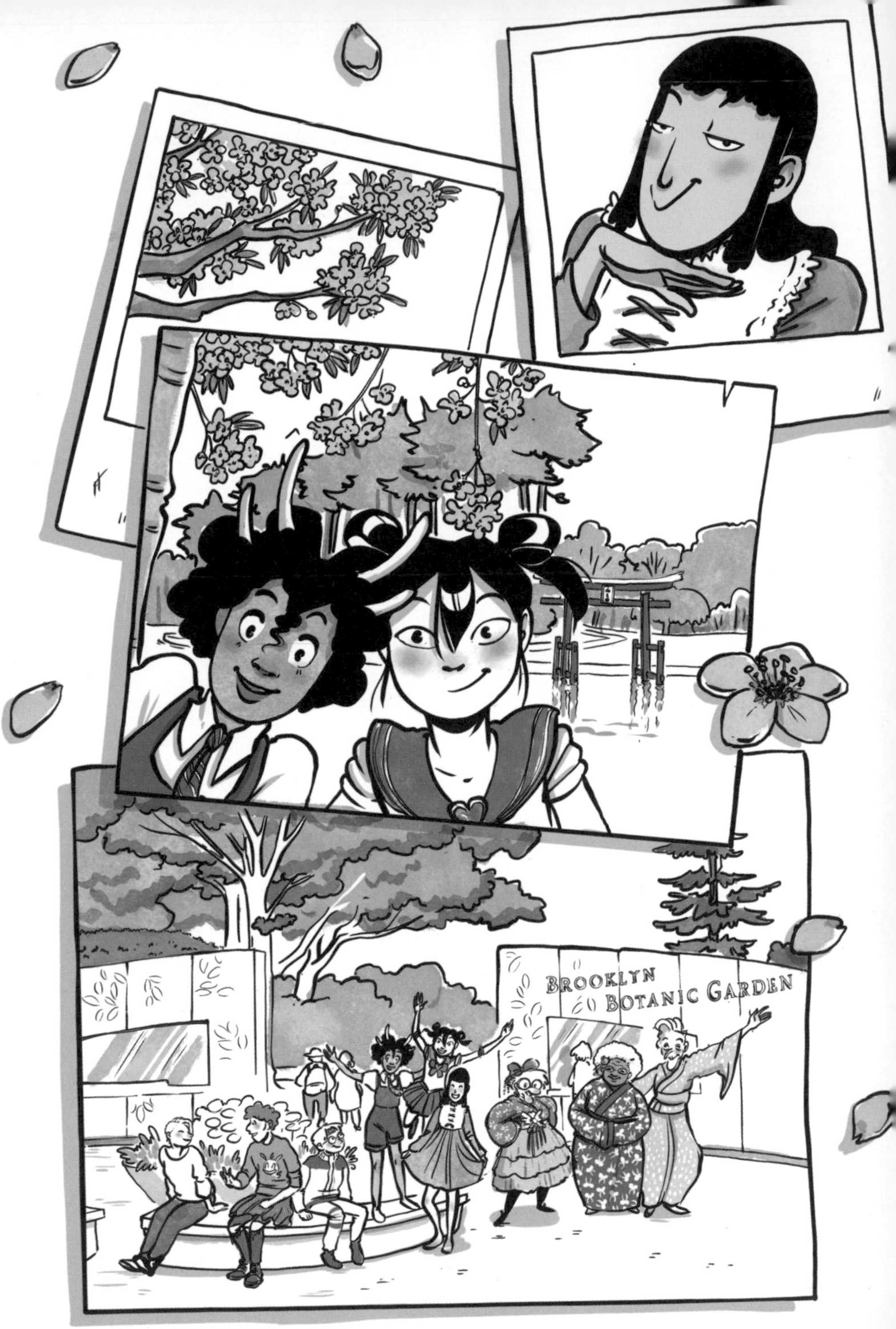
BROOKLYN
BOTANIC GARDEN

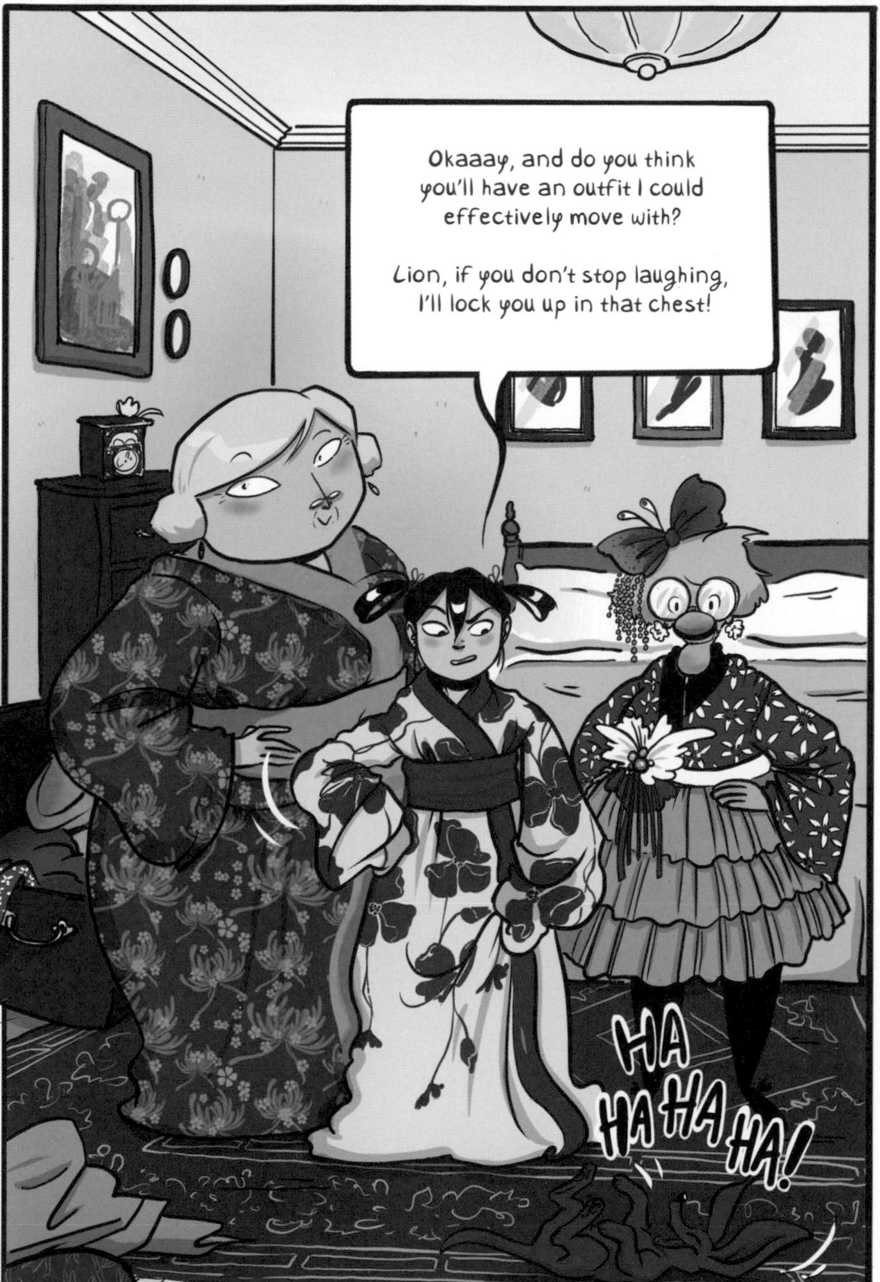
Okaaay, and do you think you'll have an outfit I could effectively move with?
Lion, if you don't stop laughing, I'll lock you up in that chest!
HA HA HA HA HA!

Gardening Tip:
♡ The layering technique

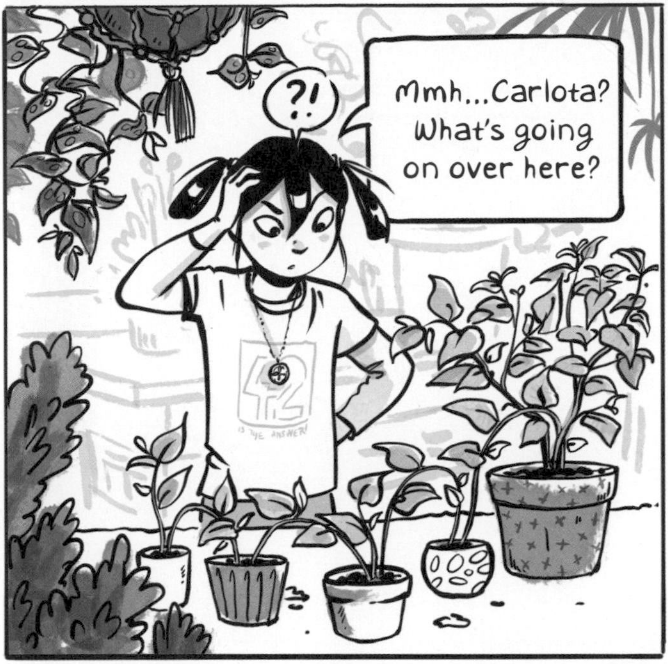
?!
Mmh...Carlota? What's going on over here?
42 IS THE ANSWER!

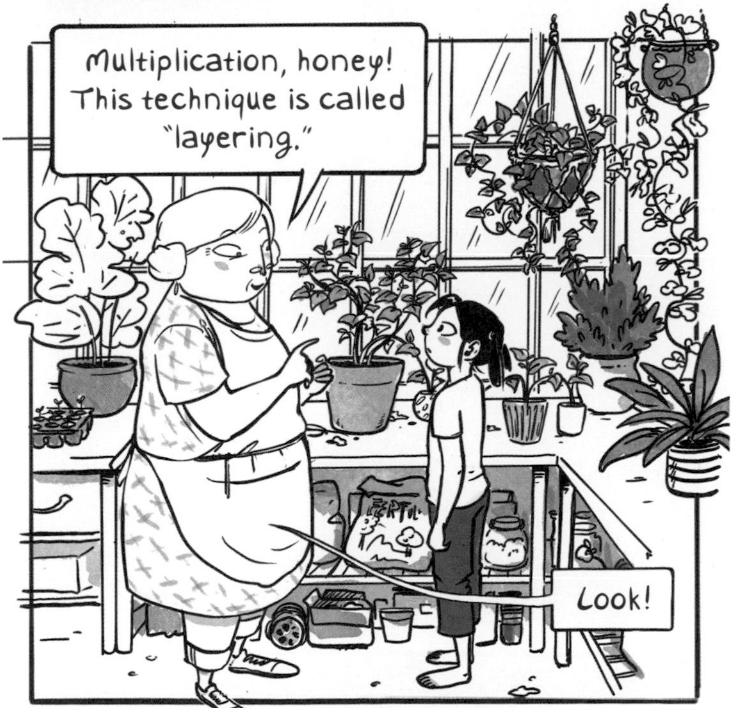
Multiplication, honey! This technique is called "layering."
Look!

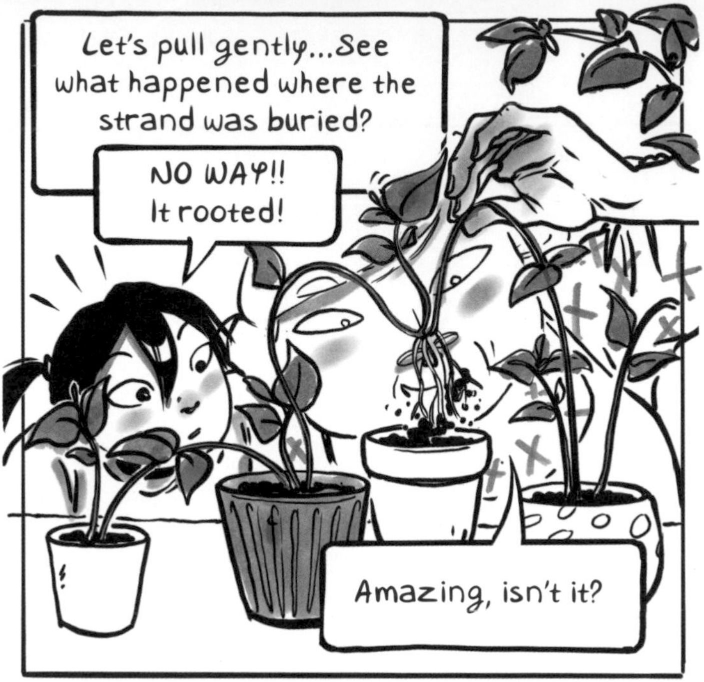
Let's pull gently...See what happened where the strand was buried?
NO WAY!! It rooted!
Amazing, isn't it?

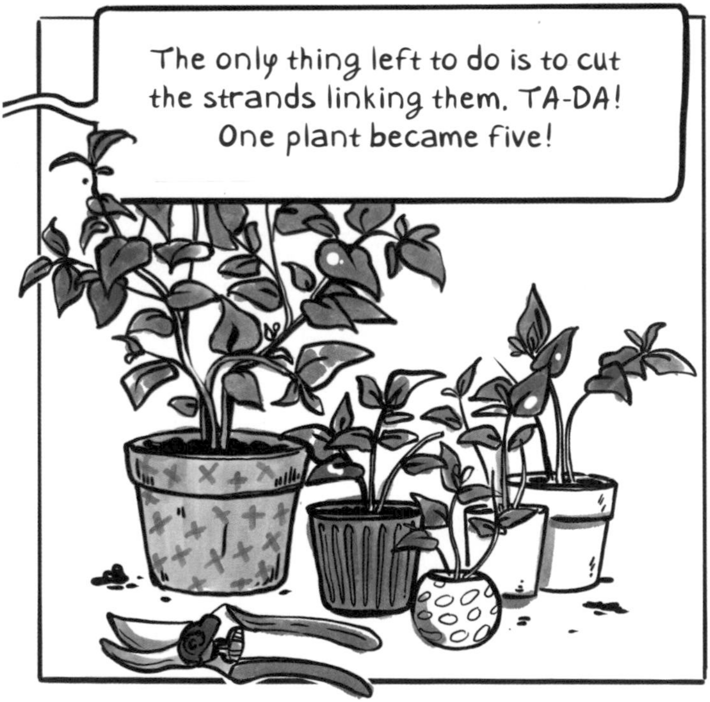
The only thing left to do is to cut the strands linking them. TA-DA! One plant became five!

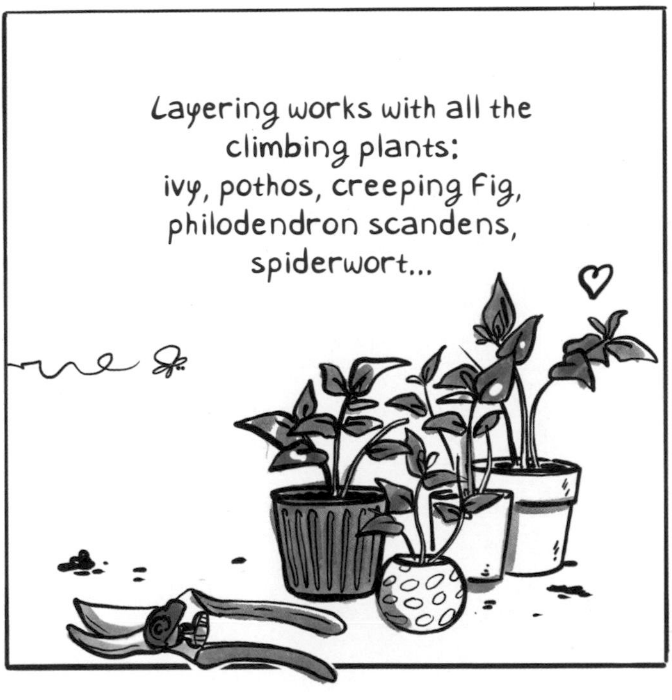
Layering works with all the climbing plants:
ivy, pothos, creeping fig, philodendron scandens, spiderwort...

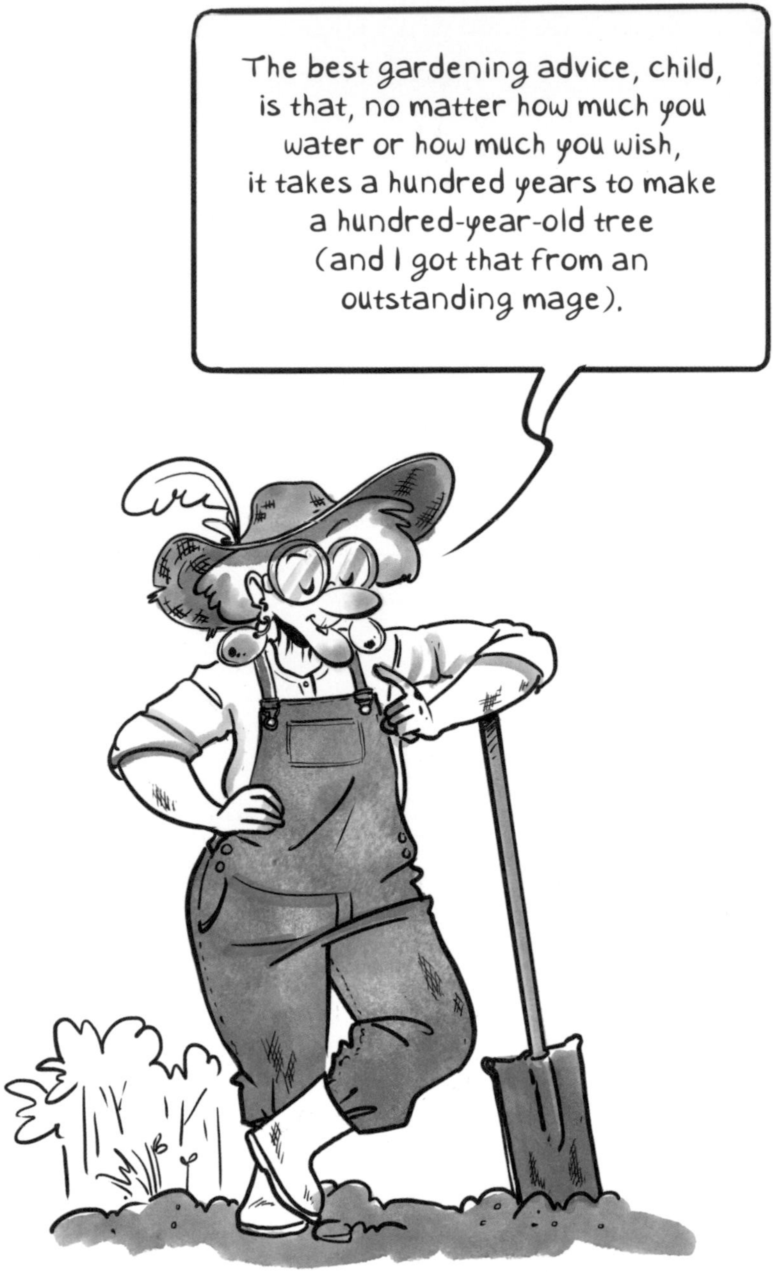
The best gardening advice, child, is that, no matter how much you water or how much you wish, it takes a hundred years to make a hundred-year-old tree (and I got that from an outstanding mage).

Cabin 5

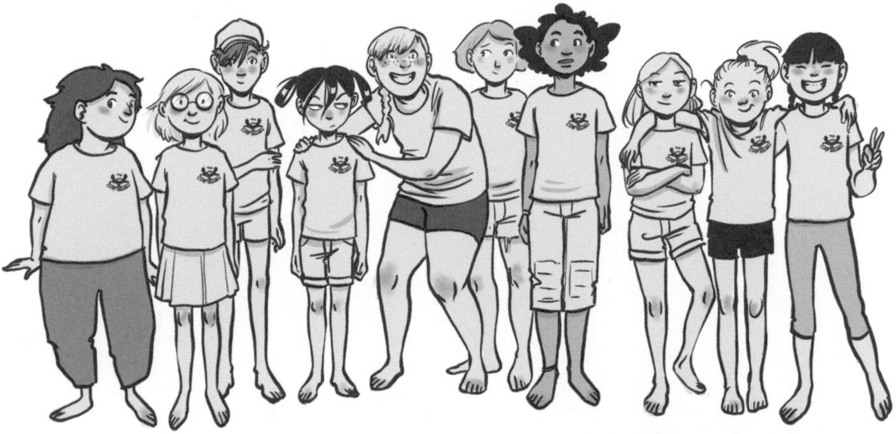

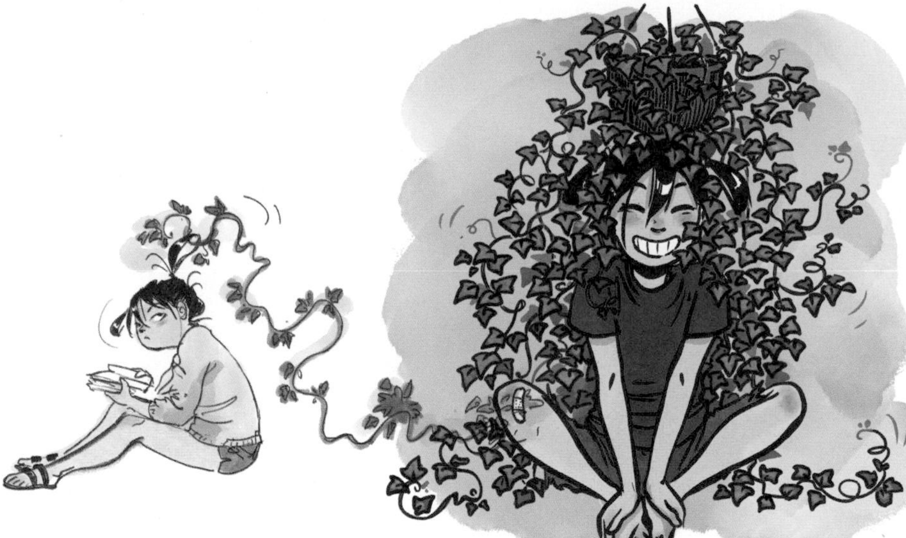

Island in the middle
of the lake.

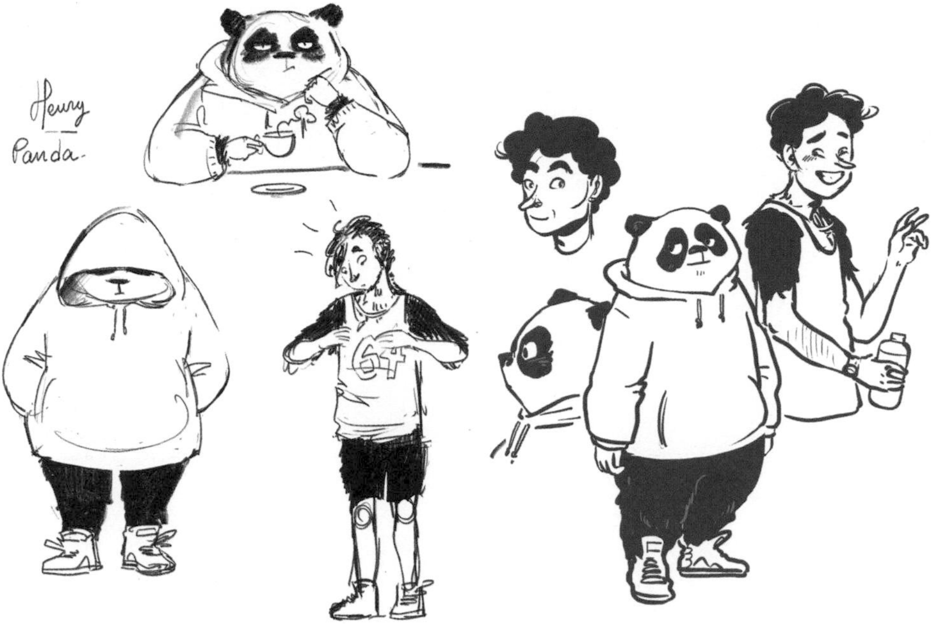

Henry
Panda
64

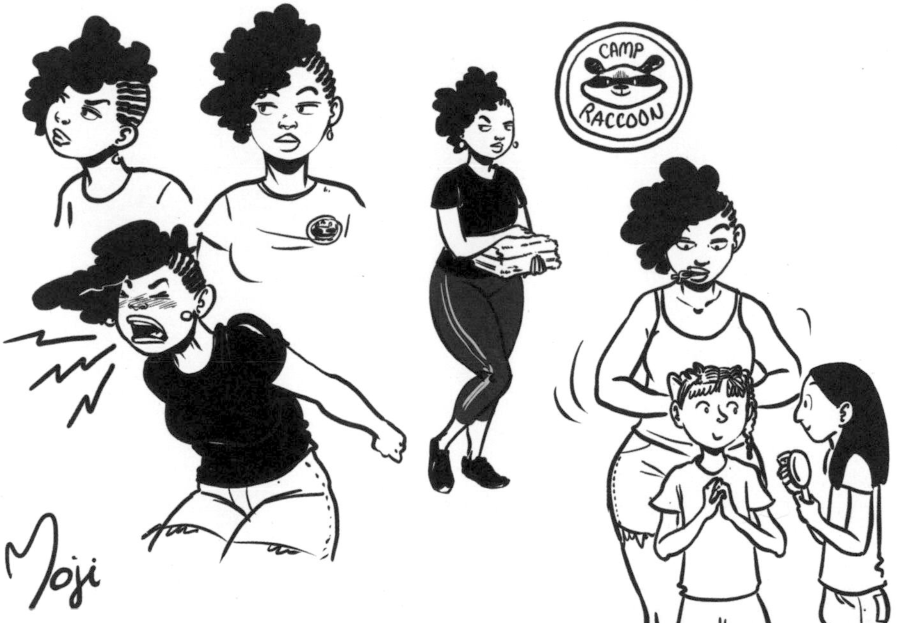

CAMP
RACCOON
Moji

Acknowledgments

Again and again, AND AGAIN, I want to thank Kelly Sonnack, my extraordinary agent. Thank you for being my first reader, for being such a good listener, fantastic person, and always standing by my side. I am so grateful to be on this adventure with you.

Shout-out to the incredible Random House team, without whom this book wouldn't exist. Whitney, Patrick, Madison, Danny, thank you for your hard work shaping today's graphic novel landscape. I am very proud that the Witches of Brooklyn are Random House books, and I can't wait to discover the next graphic novels that'll come out of your magical hats!

Extra-special thanks to my husband, Patrick Flynn, and our children, Ella, Josephine, and Arthur, for being so supportive and enthusiastic about my work.

Thank you to my family in France, who showed me so much support and sent me tons of love vibes over the ocean.

Thank you to all the readers who enjoyed the Witches of Brooklyn. Your nice words and drawings always make me feel extraordinarily lucky to do what I do, and inspire me to draw some more!

And finally, thank you to the magical booksellers and librarians who helped and supported the witches. You are the real magic. ♡

Sophie Escabasse is a french-born illustrator and comic artist. A Brooklynite at heart, she's now living in Montreal with her husband, their three children, and her old black cat.

Originally trained as a graphic designer, she worked in advertising in Paris and New York City before fully embracing illustration as her career. Her work has appeared in the Derby Daredevils series by Kit Rosewater. Hailing from a family of graphic novel lovers, Sophie has been enjoying comics since she could read. Becoming a graphic novel author has been her lifelong dream, and today she's happily juggling being a mother of three and a comic artist of a new trilogy.

It's a lot of sweat but a lot of fun!

esofii.com
🅾 esofiii

FIND YOUR VOICE
WITH ONE OF THESE EXCITING GRAPHIC NOVELS